GRADE A STUPID

A Teenage Sleuth Thriller

A. J. LAPE

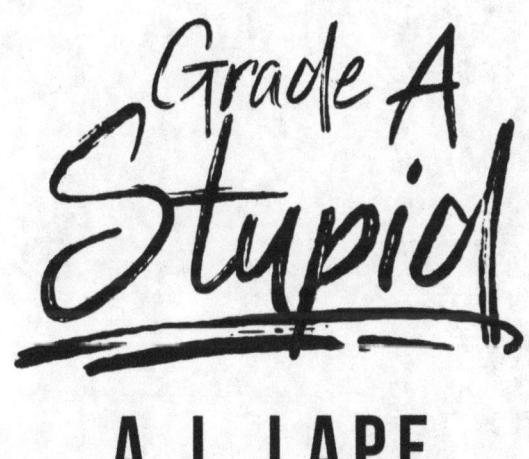

A.J. LAPE

ISBN-13: 978-0-9882641-9-9

Cover by Qamber Designs

This book is dedicated to anyone who was born with one arm behind their back or who tried to stick their square-peg mind through society's round hole. Don't ever quit...keep your head up, and don't let anyone ever tell you that you can't accomplish something.
—*Philippians 4:13*

Chapter One
BAD BOYS

There was always a boy in a girl's life that common sense and the prayers of parents told her to stay away from—fast talker, fast car, and fast hands. He was the boy her father kept a loaded shotgun by the door for and met on the front porch if he ventured onto the property...let alone the threshold. He was the tall, dark, mysteriously handsome one who had secrets. Secrets she knew weren't so honorable. He was the boy she broke all the rules over because bad boys equaled excitement, and the rebel in her liked the ride.

My name's Darcy Walker, and I had a bad boy like that in my life I was head-over-heels crushing on.

I was sitting in the cafeteria watching Liam Woods, a senior—the baddest boy in school—chat up Ivy Morrison who acted as though she'd eat him alive if cannibalism was legal. If truth be known, Liam wasn't only a bad boy. He was a *fastard*. That was a whole other level of bad the universe said was okay to dump on women. Fastards, in Darcyspeak, were boys that moved fast—they met you one time, told you they loved you, and set up a next date only for you to find out the fastard had a steady on the sly.

Right then, it looked like the school's Barbie Doll wannabe, Ivy, was dying to be added to the list of victims. They sat at a table directly across from me, about eight feet away—him finishing off a slice of pizza, her picking at a green salad that was probably only twenty calories.

I bit into a mini corndog and guzzled another drink of chocolate milk as my girlfriend, Justice Becker, flipped over the pages of her *People* magazine. She rolled her brown eyes as she took a swig of bottled water.

"This is stupid," she grumbled, her curly auburn ponytail bobbing up and down in frustration. "He's never going to go for us. First off, he's Liam-*freaking*-Woods. It's not a good sign when you have a middle name of freaking. It's just not. Secondly, we're both poor and dressed in sweats, and thirdly, we're sophomores...the invisible-fifteen. That's like the first level of Hell if I remember literature class correctly."

My God, she had a point. At least as a freshman, you could be "one of the hot, new female recruits." As a sophomore, you were just sucking up air.

"I mean, what do we really know about him anyway?" she went on. "My guess is he's one of those pretty boy serial killers that plays with baby dolls when he's home."

Everything I knew about Liam Woods was from hearsay and observation only. We'd never even halfway spoken. Just looking at him, though, my underarms needed a reapplication of deodorant.

Let's be real, I wouldn't know what to do if he noticed me anyway.

My knowledge of the XY chromosome was reduced to adolescent peach fuzz, pimples, and men's deodorant. Other than a G-rated film in health class, I possessed almost zero knowledge on how body parts worked period. Birds and the bees? Waiting on the talk. Kissed a boy? Practicing in the mirror. I practically grew up Amish without the dress and white cap.

And like Justice said, we sported white sweats pushed to our knees that had the initials VHS block-lettered in black down the left leg. That wasn't a fashion-must. We just didn't know what to do. Liam aesthetically didn't fit with either of us. Why? He wasn't just bad. He was beguilingly hot.

A part-time model, Liam had many looks. Right then, he was the preppy type, dressed in khaki shorts, a long-sleeved blue and white rugby, and Sperrys. Insanely tall at six foot four, he came complete with abs of steel and a pair of broad shoulders born from breast stroking with the swim team. Like me, Liam had a dimpled chin. Unlike me, his face was breathtaking. It was perfectly symmetrical with brown hair and eyes like rich, melted chocolate...the kind you wanted to suck through a straw.

Justice turned the page so hard she ripped the corner. "Well then, there's the, uh, other issue," she said with a snort. "You might have a chance, but I don't." Justice was biracial, and there were times she felt like she didn't fit in anywhere...I hated that. I mean, my father was from Kentucky. There was a good possibility, centuries back, our bloodline might've been a little more pure than I'd care to admit.

"Did you hear about his ex?" she asked.

If voices were lyrical, Justice was a loud bass. Still, I barely heard her. Liam threw his head back and roared out laughter. Ivy said something he obviously felt funny. I found that odd. Ivy had the brains of a toad.

"Nuh-uh," I replied.

"Went off the deep end." She whistled, blowing a bubble. "She couldn't take his cheating ways."

Liam definitely had the kind of charm that would drive you out of your mind. Trouble was, my mind was unstable enough all on its own.

While Justice flipped to the "Style" section, telling me how grossly out-of-step we were fashion-wise, I eyeballed Liam eating a grapple. I choked on my chocolate milk, watching three droplets of liquid land on the front of my white, V-neck T-shirt. A grapple was an apple that had an affair with a grape (you know, a hybrid some scientist thought was a good idea). My father called grapples "sin food"—two fruits that came together immorally when God didn't intend them to. I had a feeling he'd share the same opinion about Liam.

I was fated to be terminally single or destined to a life of wall-flowerdom. My father's edict, not mine. Whatever. It wasn't like anyone was beating a path to my door.

I lived in Cincinnati, Ohio. Cincinnati was surrounded by suburbs that made up what was dubbed the Greater Cincinnati area. My particular suburb was Valley, about twenty-five minutes north of downtown. My school was predictably called Valley High. Valley High was the biggest school in the city with the biggest wallets, biggest athletes, biggest brains, and biggest traditions. Valley kids were supposed to set the example for the Ohio Valley, the standard students shot for. It was safe to say I wasn't going to be the poster child.

My stomach picked that moment to growl.

Lunchtime was pandemonium at its best. We had thirty minutes to file through the line, pick out food, pay for it, find a seat, and choke it down. Heartburn heaven. Justice and I weren't at our normal table with the rest of our friends. We got bogged down at our lockers and grabbed two seats next to some folks who'd just exited the gym. All I could smell was body odor and a salty sweat, which wasn't sitting well with my corn dogs cooked about twenty minutes too long. Fishing the red worm out of my dirt pudding, I tilted my head back and licked the Oreo chunks, bit off its head, chewed twice, and swallowed the body whole. As I wiped my mouth on my wrist, I took a deep breath and watched Ivy flip her hair as Liam reached out to tuck it behind her ear. I sighed, and it wasn't from jealousy. It was because of who Ivy was.

Ivy Morrison was preppy and blonde, weighing about one hundred and fifteen pounds with a tiny, button-nose and rose-red lips. Ivy always dressed in white. She sported white short-shorts and a short-sleeved white designer sweater that could legitimately fit my six-year-old little sister. Everything she had was a little too kitschy for my taste, but hey, Barbie liked what Barbie liked.

For all intents and purposes, she was my arch nemesis, the antagonist in my own personal novel. She'd gossiped about me, bullied me, stole my lunch money, and peeked under bathroom stalls while I peed. My guess was it revolved around my best friend. You see, even though I had the best girlfriends in the world, my absolute best friend ever was a guy—*yay, go me*—and Ivy had had him on her radar before any of us even hit puberty. Her frustration with his lack of interest bled over onto me.

Even if she hadn't made it her mission to make my life a living hell, we were polar opposites. She was annoyingly egotistical and an unapologetic exhibitionist. I was embarrassingly self-conscious and socially insecure. Part of the problem was the appropriate things never embarrassed me. If there was a dirty joke, I laughed louder than anyone. If I was supposed to cross my legs like a lady, the message never made it to my brain. Ivy, however, knew how to be demure yet available at the same time. I watched her bat her eyelashes at Liam. If I ever attempted the feat, I'd break my eyeball.

Corralling my thoughts, I gave the room a once-over. Lunch gossip was that "something big" was going down. I'd had one eye on the crowd since I'd sat down and saw nothing but people gagging over their food.

By the time I made the circuit back to Liam, I swear, he looked me right in the eyes and mouthed, "You're beautiful."

I blinked. Then I blinked again, performing a third blink just for good measure. Jeez, was that to *me*? I looked over both shoulders and to the tile floor. Heck, I even gazed at the ceiling, wondering if an angel hovered overhead. My jaw dropped wide, and I dumbly mouthed back, "Me?"

Liam winked and added, "Yes."

Cue the goofy grin. No wonder his girlfriend fell off the deep end. He was flirting with Ivy and me at the same time.

I was an okay-looking girl, but no way in the world did I compare to Ivy. I had almost green eyes and weighed a buck-thirty, stark naked. No girl wanted to weigh a hundred and thirty pounds in a world of zeros, but not every girl came hardwired with Barbie in her genes. Barbies were cute, tiny, built for bikinis, and the perfect guy-friendly height for a female. I was five foot nine with a thirty-six inch inseam. That didn't spell swimsuit model. It screamed giraffe.

On my head was a potpourri of straw that included every shade of blonde, the majority being the dishwater kind. It fell mid-back with a bad case of bangs I was growing out from a botched job by my father. Evidently, I had a cowlick because they stood at a forty-five degree angle. I had a feeling my looks were the type that was an acquired taste. My muscles were sort of defined. My hips were relatively slim with some curves in all the appropriate places, but the operative word was "some"—long legs, partial hips, very little chest, and a whole lot of hoping it came together in the end. And to every teenage girl's chagrin, I still waited to fill out my bra and for my teeth to make it to that porcelain Mecca. I'd had braces for three and a half years, but it still looked like a wrecking ball had gone to town in my mouth. And they were to come off Friday. My orthodontist ecstatically said, "It's time." Well, eight grand and two surgeries later, in my opinion, they still were only semi-smileable.

Even though I knew Liam was a fastard, his gaze was like an anchor drawing me under. I must've said something. Shoot, I might've moaned because Justice kicked me under the table with a chuckle.

"Well, well, well," she said and laughed, her eyes darting back and forth between Liam and me. "That was one heck of a shiver-inducing stare."

No kidding. My nerve endings were twisting.

By that time, Ivy realized he wasn't giving her his full attention. She swiveled her head around so fast it was a wonder it didn't pop off. When she figured out I was the distraction, she looked at me the way vultures look at rotting corpses. I gave her a smile (kinda), but that wasn't good enough. Next thing I knew, she blurted, "Her? You've got to be kidding." Then she added an eye roll, like the thought of me with anyone was so insanely astonishing she couldn't contain her disbelief.

I swallowed...temporarily mute. I had a beef to take up with the universe if and when I ever made it to the Principal's Office in the Sky. It was my opinion people should be as revolting on the outside as they were on the inside. In simple terms, Ivy should be dog-butt ugly. I tried to imagine myself in a land far, far away, but I couldn't escape the heat of Liam's gaze. He was taken aback by her rudeness. He slowly opened his mouth—his brown eyes soft and compassionate—but then I felt a shift in the air. All at once, Liam looked like he'd stepped on a roadside bomb, and no one had to tell me who'd buried it.

Justice glanced up, grinning. "Hey, big guy," she practically purred. Closing her magazine, she started to fidget like she wished she could change out of her sweats into something more boyfriend-shopping appropriate. She gave her ponytail a quick smooth-down, kneeing me in the thigh, her brown eyes dancing.

"Hello, Justice," I heard. Then I got a velvety-smooth, "Hey, sweetheart."

Ahhh, I was right. It was my best friend. From as far back as I could remember, Dylan had a warm, rich baritone voice. It could catch you off guard if your ears weren't standing up straight, giving the okay signal to go. But honestly, I didn't know if he'd actually entered puberty, period. Dylan Taylor never had that high pitched, prepubescent tenor or bungling, gangly stage my middle school pictures immortalized. My body documented the evolutionary journey of a girl into teenage adulthood. My arms grazed my knees one entire year until my legs decided to catch up. Unfortunately, the legs kept growing.

Ivy's disdain for me magnified tenfold once Dylan showed up on the scene. Her eyes narrowed into reptile-like slits, and out of the blue, she painted on a smile like she'd just won the lottery...or someone told her nudity was okay with the dress code.

"Hi Dylan," she blurted, halfway out of her seat. Ivy spoke in a high-pitched, whiny squeak that was nothing less than sucking on helium.

Dylan returned a, "Hey." Justice kneed me again. "Not turning around?" he said chuckling.

"Nope," I practically whispered. Dylan's eyes were amber, like rich melted butter that had an affair with toffee. The last thing I needed was to fall into them. He placed his head between Justice and me, resting his hands on my shoulders. Whenever we'd been apart for a while, some cosmic force took over that neither of us could control...*we had to touch*.

I found myself briefly squeezing his large hands.

"Aw, Darc, I'm going to miss you too." It was Monday. Next week was spring break, but Dylan and his family were leaving a week early to vacation in Maui with the rest of the rich and famous. He came in for half a day to complete two tests I'm sure he'd just aced. Then he was off to swim, surf, wade through black sand, and freaking whale watch. I'd love to freaking whale watch. What was I going to do for spring break? More of the same—dream I was somewhere else.

After some small talk with Justice, Dylan rubbed my back like he tried to put out a fire. He sometimes did that when something was worrying him—like he tried to comfort himself from my mere presence. If truth be known, there was good reason to be nervous.

Bad things always seemed to happen when we were apart. And my guess was he hadn't forgotten them any more than I had.

As I popped some soggy Potato Starz into my mouth, Liam and I rubbed eyeballs again as he continued his conversation with Ivy. She was back to motor mouthing, but Liam seemed distracted. He cocked his head to one side, sort of frowning—like he debated the particulars of Dylan's and my relationship.

Well, join the club...so did I.

When Liam grinned devilishly, my heart began to hammer. Self-conscious, I quickly spun away and took another swig of chocolate milk, reminding myself that manners said I shouldn't stare. I stupidly looked up again, and his grin grew even broader. I blushed. Whenever I got nervous, bright red splotches covered my neck. It was a trait I'd had since childhood, and the melanin in my skin wasn't up for negotiations.

"Does that sound good?" Dylan asked me. Heck, I didn't know what in the world we were even talking about but said, "Uh-huh," anyway.

Dylan's voice lowered an octave. "That's my girl." Dylan had called me "his girl" since eighth grade. It insinuated we were more than best friends. I knew it. He knew it. His actions, however, did not.

Halfway looking at him, I made a kissy *mwah* sound as he said goodbye.

Dylan's grin deepened. "Yeah, when I get back, why don't we try that on for real?" Dylan inched his head over my shoulder, speaking that last sentence into my ear, circling his muscled arms around my neck in a hug. The flirt in Dylan knew no bounds. I shuddered embarrassingly as I hugged him back. I was codependent, people. No one had to shove a psychology book in my face. Come morning I would miss him, but right then, he made me look...well, *taken*.

I thought he was gone, but then I heard him yell from behind, "You know I love you, yeah?"

I wanted to crawl inside a hole and die. Dylan and I always said we loved one another. If I said it first, he responded "always." If he voiced that trio of words, then I replied in kind. It was confusing to everyone since we weren't boyfriend and girlfriend, but it merely was the extent, or should I say *depth*, of our relationship. But sometimes he spouted out those words as effortlessly as a weather report...making me fear it wasn't special.

I sheepishly turned, glancing over my shoulder, but he wasn't looking at me at all. His eyes burned like boiling butter as they bore a hole in Liam's face the size of the Grand Canyon. Hand to God, slobber practically dripped from his rabid jowls. Dylan put his fingers to his eyes in the old, silent "V" pointing them angrily in Liam's direction.

In other words, I've got eyes everywhere.

The nerve.

First thing I did (other than contain my bladder) was glance to Liam. He hadn't moved an inch, his face expressionless. Dylan's face, however, just made him a eunuch. I circled my hands around my mouth and spoke loud enough for only Dylan to hear. "You're not the boss of me, Dylan," I hissed.

What did he do? He chuckled—chuckled, for God's sake—a mixture of humor and know-no-bounds cockiness. "Just wrapping up business before I leave, Darc, and *yes*," he murmured, chuckling deeper, "I *am* your boss."

Dylan unloaded a wicked grin, knowing he'd overstepped his bounds...and not really caring.

When I yelled, "Fiend," in his direction, he winked and strutted off, his shoulders squared like he was the king of the world.

Justice closed her eyes. "The first thing that comes to mind is sweat, sheets, and wild-animal-barking-at-the-moon sort of passion." She moaned. I smacked her in the back of the head just because I knew her daddy would want me to. Justice was unde-terred. "Please tell me Dylan's in love with me," she begged. "Please, please, please. I want him, and he's just my size."

Justice was over six feet tall, a size sixteen pants with an eleven-and-a-half foot. I wasn't sure what she considered her size, but I knew he had to be the unintimidated type. She had a black belt in karate, and attracting a guy when she could kill him ten different ways was asking too much of the male ego. Come to think of it, Dylan was probably perfect for her. God knew he had the real estate to back up a threat.

"What do you think, Darcy?" she gushed. "Isn't he just dreamy?"

I heard stripper music playing. I didn't know if that was in reference to Liam or my best friend. I slumped down in my seat. Well, as far as my seat would allow but misjudged what should be a normal task. That was the moment things went horribly wrong. It wasn't going to be the setting where I told my children their parents fell in love. I tumbled backward onto the tile with a clapping smash. My head snapped back and my chin finished forward, boomeranging off my chest. I chucked my teeth together. I didn't see stars. I saw stinking meteors.

Somehow, Justice's *People* magazine wound up covering my face in a tent, and my feet were straight up in the air, practically over my head. I thought it was over, but then a barrage of Potato Starz crashed down on top of the magazine. Justice alternated between coughing, hissing, picking them off, and talking herself out of laughing. Typical. Just typical. My gaffes were usually laid out for public consumption.

After a few moments of disbelief, Justice helped me back up, picked off some dust bunnies, flicked Oreo crumbs out of my hair, and sat me aright. "I don't think anyone noticed," she lied. "Are you okay?"

I was pretty sure I'd cracked my coccyx. A hush filled the room as everyone processed what just happened. I could file that episode under *Why I'll Never Get A Date With Liam Woods*. In my brain, I knew it would be a big mistake but found myself glancing to his seat, searching him out anyway.

He and Ivy were walking out the door.

Talk about a stake in the heart.

Hand in hand, they stepped around a group of three males who argued like they were on bath salts. There was head bobbing, a little bit of chest bumping, and a whole lot of faculty not noticing. Right in front of the cafeteria entry, one had his car keys gripped tightly in his hand as though he was about to skip out or returning from somewhere. The other's jaw moved so fast it could've broken the course record at the Indy 500. It wasn't readily apparent what the dispute was about or who they were—I could only see their profiles —but getting the brunt of it was Jinx King.

No shocker there.

Jinx was around five foot seven and dark-skinned, with hair shorn so short it was merely a shadow on his head. He had a two-inch scar that ran down his right cheek, and his brown eyes were deep-set and hard—like he'd seen more than his fair share of trouble. I didn't know much about Jinx other than he'd joined school in January and always had a red bandana hanging from the back left pocket of his jeans, jeans that nearly hung at his knees. I guess if I had to sum him up, though, the first words that came to mind were "damaged goods." Something was wrong, or maybe a better word was "irreversible."

Jinx kept looking at his hands, obsessive-compulsively wiping them down his jeans as though he were removing something sticky. I was reminded of that phrase in *Macbeth*, "Out damned spot, out!"

Panicked and confused, he nervously turned and scanned the room like he was searching for a trap door. After several futile seconds, his eyes landed on mine with a disarmingly intense stare. Don't ask me why, but I felt like he was giving me—or maybe anyone—a message. I sensed frustration, despair, and a helplessness so huge it nearly choked me. I wasn't sure if that was by accident or intention—for that matter, whether they were his emotions or mine. All I knew was Jinx put the "anti" in antisocial. He went out of his way to avoid eye contact as well as relationships he felt unnecessary—premeditated in everything he did. What would someone like Jinx want with someone like me? It was a crying shame I intended to find out.

Chapter Two

ICYDK

*I*CYDK is netspeak for In Case You Didn't Know. It's a phrase that Internet chatters popularized to save keystrokes. Basically, it's the preface used before needed information is dispensed—in many cases, gossip.

Valley High is big...and when I say big, I mean campus-to-a-small-college, three-thousand-students big. So there was a lot of ICYDK going on. Right then, my cell phone blew up with: *What went down today? Did I miss anything? Was there any blood?* I typed back *nada* to seven people I barely knew, laughing to myself they'd assumed I'd have the lowdown.

My day started out with US history then anatomy, Spanish 3, geometry, lunch, English 102, drawing and painting, rounding out with human sexuality. Justice and I bugged out of lunch early...can't imagine why...and stood at our lockers getting ready for fifth period.

I wasn't sure how, but Dylan finagled it around so our locker assignments were side by side: numbers twelve and thirteen. Superstitious enough, I insisted he take number thirteen because no way in the world did I want to invite any more bad luck into my life. Apparently, that whole number thirteen is the Devil's number thing was a crock. Some of the curse bled over onto twelve. Well, you know what? Sometimes Dylan had great ideas. Other times he was an idiot.

Point of fact: couldn't he have picked a place that wasn't within earshot and eyeshot of Ivy Morrison? Unfortunately, the majority of my classes were with Ivy. Every once in a while, fortune fell on my side. Others, it kicked me in the gut.

Trying to drown out her voice, I lifted the metal handle and immediately fell in love. My locker door was covered in headshots of my friends and butt shots of professional athletes. I called their glutes a "boom boom, hoo-hah." Not many people were graced with an exceptional gluteus maximus, but I felt it important to celebrate the ones that were otherworldly.

Once I mentally wiped the drool, I determined my locker smelled like wet dog hair. Like everything else in my life, my locker was either pristine or prison bathroom-worthy. If I was happy, Messy Darcy was in the driver's seat. If I was stressed, Domestic Darcy could blow through the mess like a tornado in a mobile home park.

The smell was sewer-rank, and I was stuck somewhere between laughing and losing my lunch. Squatting down, I rummaged around under notebooks, my gym bag, a few old tests, and discovered it was a wadded up yellow footie. Like a moron, I drew it up to my nose, dry-heaved, and then snorted.

Yup, it was the footie.

While Ivy addled on, I underhanded the sock over, so it landed at her feet. When she did nothing but amp up the chatter, it stabbed like a knitting needle to the brain. I already had a knot on my head that was a beaut. Falling out of my seat at lunch sort of did that to me. Add Ivy to the mix, and it was like turning the screw.

Pulling my English book off the top shelf, I tried my best to drown out her high-pitched words.

She gave her hair a flip, anxiously looking up and down the hall. The hall was crowded, like cattle going to slaughter. Shoulders were bumping, and people either hustled to their next destination or didn't give a rat's rear end and delayed the inevitable.

I pulled an orange lip gloss out of my pocket and rolled a circle around my mouth. Not once had she voiced Dylan's name, but as expected, she paused to grin lewdly at his locker.

Eeeuw.

She halfway whispered, halfway moaned, "You know, I could have him anytime I want him. It's just not the time yet."

Only Ivy and her unbelievable sense of entitlement would have nerve enough to breathe those words. To answer her question, "No, I didn't know," that she could have Dylan anytime she wanted. Surely, that wasn't true, was it? Unfortunately, I wasn't sure Dylan would ask my opinion when he decided to take on a Mrs. Hottie.

When I didn't respond, she snorted and said, "Guess what I heard about *you*?"

All the air left my lungs...and I dropped my lip gloss.

Ivy had the corner on gossip and liked nothing more than spreading it along the grapevine. I called her Poison Ivy because she just made people feel icky. And even though I didn't want to give her the pleasure, fear rushed through my veins like a river jumping its banks in a storm. Picking up my lip gloss, I walked into the middle of oncoming traffic, bottlenecking the hallway. "Wh-what?" I stuttered.

Ivy was like a wind-up doll. Whenever she talked, it was a constant run-on sentence and never with a period or punctuation. "People are saying you've got a thing going on with Oscar Small and it's been going on for a while and they're saying he's getting tired of the games and wants it all out in the open but you know I tried to defend you but when the evidence mounts up there's only so much a person can do but I tried I really tried." Big breath.

I burst out laughing. I proudly belonged to a group of peers that had never had a boyfriend or girlfriend. Okay, maybe proudly was a strong word. It was more by default than by design. But with Oscar? At Valley, Oscar Small was a name synonymous with dipshit. It's like he had one of those red blinking signs over his head, and even if someone was a non-curser like me, the mind couldn't help but tumble into the crudeness.

I swear, right then Oscar scampered by, sort of waving, sort of acting like he had something scandalous to hide. Oscar was always working some kind of scam—so that wasn't unusual—but he definitely was a little more sketchy than normal. He glanced over his shoulder, ducked down like he dodged a bullet, and then wiped both hands down his jeans, managing a greeting. "See you tonight," he mumbled and darted off down the hall like he was outrunning the Devil. My word, it sounded like a date. Our three-worded conversation would be top of the gossip food chain by seventh period.

Oscar had been in love with me since third grade, or so he thought. Thing was, Oscar was a picker. A picker was someone that drove around at night and picked through everyone's trash. That evening was trash night on my street, and Oscar and I had struck up a friendship over the years. Hard to imagine myself "forever after" with someone who thought my rusty bicycle and old milk jugs were the best things since sliced bread. It wasn't that I wasn't flattered... he just wasn't my type. Oscar was sloppy, always in flannel, and came out of the womb looking like a man. He'd fallen into middle-aged and balding with wayward hairs coming out of his nose and ears. He wore Coke-bottled glasses, one thicker than the other. Half the time, I didn't know which to have a conversation with.

I looked at the thin lens and gave it a wave.

Meanwhile, the smug smile of Ivy was felt like a punch to the face. I flipped her off in my mind.

Ten minutes later, I sat in English class listening to Mr. Woodward remind us of a term paper due the day after spring break—which was in fifteen days. Fear was a great motivator, people, it just was. Panic filled the room like wildfire.

But then there was Jubilee Mueller. Jubilee was Black and the smartest sophomore in school. She was Justice's cousin on her father's side, and if Dylan wasn't around, I went to her when I needed a quick tutorial on what was expected (you know, when I wasn't paying attention).

As tall as Justice, she sat in the front row with her fingers threaded together smiling, bouncing her leg up and down in skinny jeans and a red cotton blouse. My guess was hers was finished and either in the editing phase or already turned in.

Continuing to discuss the term paper and carrying a stack of last week's test, Mr. Woodward stopped right in front of my desk. I swear, we either had a mild earthquake or he kicked my chair. "Check your syllabus, boys and girls," he muttered. "It's right there in black and white."

I was speechless. I couldn't recall getting a syllabus let alone remembering what it said.

My hands quivered with a cold dread as I unzipped my backpack, searching through the clutter of the last eight months. I had a habit of losing whatever it was I needed at the time—right then, it seemed to be my dignity. There were movie ticket stubs, Target receipts, a pencil drawing of a crumpled Coke can, but no syllabus anywhere. All I could think was I had plans to do nothing in the next week—nothing academic, at least—but it sounded like it could qualify as the longest, ugliest week on record.

"You, kids, need to take your lives seriously," he muttered. "These grades count."

I was aware of that. Unfortunately, I didn't know how to change it.

Mid-fifties, slim build, with black hair graying at the temples, Mr. Woodward rifled through his stack of papers, mumbling to himself. When he found what I assumed was mine, he threw it on my desk with a thwack and a deep frown he didn't even try to mask. We met eyes. "You can do better, Walker. You and I both know it. Heck, God knows it."

My word, please don't bring God into the picture.

My Liam-high took a nosedive. Right there in red ink was a D-minus. Disappointing? Yes. Shocking? Not exactly. English 102 was designed to teach argumentative and research writing. Evidently, I wasn't a good arguer, and no matter how hard I tried to act like it didn't hurt, every bad grade chipped away at my self-confidence. I blinked to keep the tears from falling.

My grades were horrible. I didn't see many As, but when I saw a B or even a C, it was an occasion to break out the best china. It wasn't easy for me to study, let alone multitask. I was distracted easily and was so hyperactive that trying to hold my attention was like wrangling a greasy pig. It wasn't for the impatient or faint of heart. What exactly did that look like? I was told to do two things... I did one. The instructions were to finish four...I did one and a half. Day of the test? I thought it was tomorrow. In most cases, it wasn't because I was lazy. It was because I merely thought of other things. And in my mind, those things were always more important.

What really threw teachers for a loop was when I aced something—something hard—something that tore apart the brains of the overachievers. That happened when we had a pop quiz on the imagery, symbolism, and metaphors in *The Pied Piper* since it was the newest production put out by the Theater Department. Our assignment was to read it over the weekend (I didn't), and I hadn't laid eyes on the story since grade school. The average grade was a sixty-nine percent. I scored one hundred and ten points, picking up the bonus.

Explanation? Evidently, I had a high intelligence quotient—the very reason I'd hit one out of the ballpark occasionally. Like all parents, mine thought I was born a genius, so at age four I had an IQ test, and the child psychologist informed my parents I scored a one-sixty. A one-sixty? I laughed in his face. By definition, the average score was one hundred. I told him he was smoking dope, and then my parents had to explain why I knew about dope in the first place. That fault lay with my Grandfather Winston.

Winston was of the opinion that ignorance was worse than having knowledge-too-soon. So when Winston unloaded all of his knowledge about illegal narcotics, I likewise unloaded all of it onto the psychologist. Needless to say, any delusions of grandeur for my bright future were replaced with a confidential letter of concern that made it to grade school before I even arrived.

*Child is precocious...needs constant stimulation...lack of guidance may lead to deviant behavio*r...blah, blah, and embarrassing blah. I only knew about the letter because I...well, because I broke into the counselor's office and read it.

That fact in itself proved the letter to be at least marginally true.

So high IQs? They didn't do any good if they didn't help a person achieve something intellectually high—well, something intellectually high that academia would be thrilled about. One thing I had going for me, though, was most girls were nouns. Darcy Walker, I liked to think, was a verb. I needed to walk the embarrassment off, and as God as my witness, I was going to bust out of the room like my butt was on fire.

First, I had to get past Mr. Woodward. He was back at his seat, flicking something orange off his brown golf shirt, but as I glanced up with half a smile, he legitimately gave me a snorting eye roll. He'd taken a seat on the Darcy Disappointment Train.

"Walker, come here," he grumbled, not even trying to whisper.

I'd rather jump in front of a moving car.

Slipping out of my seat, I attempted to paint on a smile. I wasn't sure I was successful. Once I stood next to him, I expected him to dive into a litany of phrases about hard work, determination, and character, but he was so painstakingly quiet it made my heart jump. Finally, he said, "Do you think you can bring up that grade?"

I actually crossed my fingers. My GPA was in shambles. "You know, Mister Woodward, I think this is the part where I'm supposed to find a bottle of booze and chug it," I joked.

Sometimes I laughed when things were awkward. Right then, I sounded like an insane hyena.

He wasn't amused. "Can you be serious, Walker? As in ever?" he asked. Frankly, the ability to stick my head in the sand was one of my better traits—it was a life's philosophy that had served me well. "Child, I'd like to see you succeed," he said, not sharing the same opinion. "You're one of the most creative, intelligent students I've ever had."

Oh boy, that lie ranked right up there with the Tooth Fairy.

I had moments of greatness, but nothing that seemed eternal. Since I was barely ten years old, I had an aching need to fill that constantly left me hungry. Problem was, I didn't know what to fill it with. As I saw it, my talents were limited too. One, I could burp the preamble. Two, I could put on a mean show of sock puppets. Three —and I guess that talent had some promise—I could negotiate and haggle like a gypsy. But guess what? I hadn't seen many gypsies hanging around Cincinnati lately.

I had the illogical urge to hug him before I spiraled into tears.

Digging my nails into my palms, I'd only clenched my eyes shut for a few seconds when Jinx King blurted out he didn't feel well. When I glanced his way, he was antsy, like some theater understudy anxious for the lead to crash and burn.

Mr. Woodward nodded, pointing to the door as he gave me some ideas for my paper. I attempted to listen but was fighting the sudden unexplainable need to follow Jinx and see what bad things he intended to conjure up. The crux of the matter was Jinx was a little like me. Without ever really speaking, I recognized him as the type that concocted stories to flee to another venue. I had a feeling that venue wasn't what the school would deem beneficial in Academialand. Earlier though, he'd acted like there was something I should know.

God forbid I should not catch the bone he threw.

My inner-verb started screaming. When I grabbed my stomach

with a wince, Mr. Woodward opened his planner, took a Number 2 pencil from his drawer, and reluctantly mumbled I was excused. He knew he'd lost me about three sentences earlier. I thought I heard him sigh.

Riddled with guilt, I told him, "I'll try, Mister Woodward. I swear to you, I'll try."

That could be a herculean task, but I'd try nonetheless.

From the corner of my eye, I watched Jinx immediately whip out his cell phone, frantically dialing someone as he took off down the hall. I stepped out after him, deliberating whether to ask what happened earlier, or simply follow and see what transpired.

I decided on the latter.

We were on the second floor, and the hallway was night-before-Christmas quiet. I followed Jinx as quietly as possible, past locker bays and classrooms, willing my sneakers to not squeak.

Inching closer, I hoped to catch a sliver of the conversation. "Is, um...is um—are you sure?" he asked nervously. "Really? That shouldn't have happened."

What? I thought. Once again, Jinx wiped a hand down his jeans like he tried to remove something. Looking at his hand with a frown, he stopped and peered out over the balcony, nervously listening to whoever was on the other end of the phone. He pivoted left then right, and when I feared he would turn into the restroom, he quickly exited outside through the second story, side door.

Don't do it. Don't do it. Don't do it, I said to myself. *Go ahead. Go ahead. Go ahead,* my alter ego countered.

The only way I could describe my decision-making process was that one shoulder had an angel living on it, the other a devil. Unfortunately, the little devil won out in most battles of the will.

Wearing my beloved Chuck Taylor sneakers, I put my hand on the door and scrambled down the steps like I was late for a date with God. Chuck and I had walked a million miles. My foot stopped growing in seventh grade, and I'd somehow kept my white Converse sneakers in semi-mint condition. All I did was periodically change the laces to my favorite shade of the month, and let my shoes keep on walking. Trouble was, they usually led me into trouble. Following Jinx? That might've put the *duh* in dumb.

Chapter Three
THRILL SEEKERS

Experts say they may have identified a gene for the daredevil. I believed I was first in line when God was passing out that type of idiocy. Maybe I was stupid that way because cliff diving in Hawaii or parachuting without a parachute sounded like things I'd like to try. There could be a market there—in an X Games sort of way—but my life expectancy was likely to be cut in half. A part of me didn't care. That's because in my dream of dreams, I longed to be a spy.

I always imagined myself toting a gun, protecting the innocent, constructing all sorts of aliases while I was undercover. If anything, I had an active imagination. That's probably the downfall that led to my in-class excursion. That, and I was bored.

There were roughly ten minutes before class was over, and the teacher thought I was sick anyway. I knew Justice would grab my books if I was late, so I basically had ten minutes to: one, repent and turn from my wicked ways; or two, do whatever Jinx was doing. When I pushed the door wide, wind blew in my face like a hurricane.

Where some cities barely saw two seasons, Cincinnati experienced all four. Our springs sprouted flowers even though there was an overabundance of rain. Summers were hot and dry as a desert. Autumns turned the foliage an earthy orange and yellow, and winters saw snowfall like the towns up north. Right then, we were in the rainy season. The sky had cloud cover and no mist but a wind that could knock down a sequoia.

Jinx was motoring across the parking lot, weaving around cars like he hadn't a care in the world. He met up with someone I recognized as a senior but didn't know. I did, however, always find the guy fascinating. Where Jinx looked as hard as they came, that guy's face was almost expressionless, like he was so stone-cold not one emotion ever placed a wrinkle anywhere. That in itself scored way too high on the weird meter, if you asked me. They traveled twenty more feet, dodged a blue Escort, and crossed Valley Lane, the street directly in front of the school. A bank was there along with a strip mall that held a few restaurants like Bad Frog Yogurt, Jett's Pizza, Happy Wok, and my favorite, El Rancho Grande. Next to the strip mall was Amity Health Care. Neither made a move to enter any of the establishments. They merely camped next to a dumpster behind the center, briefly looked inside, and immediately started chatting.

I put my stealth on and did my best to navigate through rows of cars unseen. I did a swift jog until I got to the eighth row, my ponytail whipping fiercely around my neck. Finally, I made it to row ten and hunkered down on the pavement beside a black Toyota Forerunner. Rummaging around in my pocket, I pulled out five jellybeans left over from God-knew-when and plopped them one by one in my mouth.

The guy with Jinx was White, a little taller, and wearing a black baseball cap with the bill turned backward. Like Jinx, his rear end was hanging out of his jeans with red and black boxer shorts peeking out over a belt cinched into his thighs. In a white T-shirt, he also sported that red bandana in his left pocket. Twin dressers, and wasn't that just odd for guys to do.

There were a few deep puddles of rain, and the wind left them babbling. I couldn't make out their words over the noise, but they talked animatedly—their hands moving almost faster than their mouths. As I inched my way closer, they both looked inside the dumpster again. Jinx then scratched his neck, No-Name Boy snarled something else, and Jinx's shoulders fell like they were carrying a two-ton weight.

In one snap, their conversation was over. They did some sort of knuckle bump, and No-Name Boy held his right hand out from his heart, showing five fingers, and then moving to one, performing the ritual twice. What the heck? I batted around some ideas of what that could mean—his fingers were cramped, he'd just left computer class, maybe he was just weird—but when Jinx repeated the gesture, it dawned on me it was some sort of signal.

You don't say...

I couldn't contain the excitement. I jumped up but cracked my head on the Forerunner's side mirror and nearly kissed the pavement. I tended to be a klutz. Irony was, I could play any sport better than a guy that was first-string. Unfortunately, there were days I had trouble crossing the floor. Apparently, the universe thought contradictions like that were funny.

When I finally came to myself, it was as if Jinx and No-Name Boy had vaporized into nothingness. Panicked, I bent down checking for feet but got nothing but a foul smell the wind carried over.

I fought a gag. The smell was so pungent it reminded me of rotting meat. Against my better judgment, I found myself crossing the street, following the odor rolling out of the brown, rusty dumpster like it was being propelled by a fan. The closer I got, however, the more I had to talk myself out of vomiting.

A small three-inch gap was between the corners on the right side, and like the idiot that I was, I still peered inside.

Oh. My. Good. God.

I had to blink a few times before it registered. There was a hand —or fingers—detached from a body, you pick. I cupped my hands around my eyes, trying to drown out my periphery to get the best look inside. All I could make out were bloody fingernails and the initials AVO tattooed on the index through ring fingers. Good God in Heaven, I could die and say I'd seen it all. Was the person alive? Dead? Sick, maimed, injured? I felt the blood leave my head and rush straight to my feet.

A smart person would contact the authorities. A dumb person would at least get a tetanus shot. An ADHD person like me would do a cartwheel and pay homage to the dumpster gods.

The internal argument started. Should I go in? Stay put? Looking down at my sneakers, the one thing I knew for sure was I didn't want Chuck to take the brunt of my decision. I quickly untied the neon green laces, and set my shoes to the side.

The dumpster was your standard ten cubic foot size from Rumpke, the sanitation company in town. It had stacks of cardboard boxes next to it and some weeds that hadn't been pulled in weeks. Stepping up onto a box, I placed both hands on the rim, hoisting myself inside in one fell swoop. I scraped my body on entry, my foot sliding over what looked like paper recyclables. My heel got nicked, and when I bounced around for better footing, I stepped in an open container of copier toner. My foot was a purpley-black. My left hand landed in something brown and smelly, and since a Mexican restaurant was nearby, I prayed it was refried beans, not the waste products of a human or animal.

The smell of vinegar permeated the air, causing my tongue to stick to the roof of my mouth. Tossing out empty rice boxes and containers that said FedEx on them, my hands brushed against something hard. Trouble was, I knew that kind of "hard." It was on something that had once been living. Taking a step back, I kicked aside a green plastic tarp and stared into the wide-eyed look of a dead man. I gulped. Then I gulped again, and I swear, I think I passed gas.

Flies buzzed his face, and my guess was maggot larvae were already breeding.

His face was covered in gray stubble, and white nose hairs peeked out of his nostrils like needles in a pincushion. He was bald with some Cro-Magnon characteristics, his forehead jutting out over his nose. The swelling on his face and limbs was so advanced that the one hand still attached to his body looked like a catcher's mitt. If the guy wasn't placed on ice soon, there was a good chance his face might explode...I think. At least, I saw that in a zombie movie once, and the sight was so horrifying it made me wish I were in protective clothing.

Stark naked from the waist up, new khakis covered his lower half. Call me an idiot, but I grabbed him by the left elbow and flipped him over. A tattoo of what looked like a demon—a red-horned body that was half man, half goat—covered his back along with gothic symbols that looked like hieroglyphics. Words below it spelled out "death" in Spanish.

I screamed, but no sound came out.

I should've stayed in class, picked a topic for my term paper, taken a short snooze, but *noooo*, I had to give myself something to be haunted about forever. Kicking a piece of cardboard from his waist, I saw it—the thing that probably killed him. Two bullet holes were in his back, and blood had drained down his torso, stuck to the waistband of his pants. My mind kept trying to wrap itself around what I was seeing. It wasn't Kool-Aid or Halloween costume synthetic stuff. It was genuine blood from someone who'd once used it to live.

But when I focused even further, in reality there was very little fluid. I would've thought his pants would be soaked. Maybe he was shot *after* he died? When the heart had stopped pumping?

My footing shifted, and to my absolute horror, his body moved awkwardly, and his neck almost rolled off his shoulders. Let me amend that, maybe his neck being broken killed him. I jumped around in a cringe, and his ankle somehow wound up on my foot.

All at once, the world started spinning backward.

I had a case of nausea that rivaled what the people on the Titanic felt when it hit the dang iceberg. Bending over, I tried to dislodge my foot, willing my corn dogs to stay put in my stomach. I swallowed down some bile, and the next thing I knew, I was yanked out of the dumpster by one shoulder and a leg. I tried to scream and beg for mercy, but "Don't disturb the body!" was the only thing that made it out of my mouth.

The blood rushed straight to my head. After a quick headshake, a look backward showed the extraction being performed by Valentine Vecchione. Valentine, AKA Vinnie, Vecchione, was a full-blooded Italian with a prominent bump on his nose next to lamb chop sideburns. Vinnie was out of place in Greek/German/Anglo-Saxon Cincinnati, but that little social minority he made up for in personality.

A senior football player, he fit the mold of the dumb jock because talking to him was like playing connect the dots and the numbers didn't match up. He was around six foot three, two hundred and seventy-five pounds, always dressed for gym with moobies. You know, man-boobs.

"Dolce!" he screamed, his brown eyes as wide as silver dollars. "What in God's name are you doing?"

The events would fall under the category of *Darcy Will Be Darcy*. His question was more a reflection of him not having a clue rather than my actions. Just my opinion.

Vinnie was sweating like he'd just coughed his way through a mile. His sticky, brown hair stuck to his forehead, his white T-shirt clinging to his gut unflatteringly. Riding up his inner thighs were shorts that looked a size too small. "Answer me, Dolce."

Vinnie had called me "Dolce" for years (pronounced dohl-chay). It meant "sweet" in Italian since we always ran into one another at Servatii's, a local bakery, getting our sugar fix.

I sighed, deciding to answer. "Looking at a dead man."

Vinnie rolled his eyes, thinking I was joking. Then he got a load of the stench and gagged two times. "What's that goddawful smell?"

"A dead man."

He wiped his nose and gave his head a brisk shake—the dead man comment still not registering. "Dylan told me to watch over you," he muttered.

"Dylan told you to watch over me," I repeated in laughter.

"Yes, Dolce. He said you have a tendency to get in trouble. Pulling you feet-first out of the smelliest dumpster I've ever run across qualifies as trouble." I had a reputation. Did I earn it? Yes, I did. If I didn't cause the catastrophe, I somehow fell into it.

Vinnie and Dylan had struck up an unlikely friendship when Dylan beat out the starting defensive end last fall on the football team. Evidently, the loser didn't take it well and took a swing at Dylan during practice. No one thought a sophomore could fight, but Dylan went medieval on him, dropped him in two punches, pillaged his pride, and ultimately dislodged a molar. Apparently, it impressed Vinnie so much he took a lowly sophomore under his wing. That sounded like a fairytale once it rolled around in my brain. Thing was, Vinnie was a "reformed" everything, loose emphasis on the quotations. His name was breathed in between every misdemeanor offense you could think of. Dylan was more or less keeping him clean since Vinnie had the pipe dream of playing college football. Yeah, well good luck with that. My guess was Vinnie couldn't make the weigh-in.

"Who's out here with you?" he barked accusingly. Basically, it was me, the dead guy, and the idiocy that followed me everywhere.

I pointed over to the stiff, pinkish gray fingers and saw Vinnie pale two shades and teeter forward. He looked at the body, then to me, and put his hand over his heart like someone would if a dead soldier from war finally made it to U.S. soil. Then I swear, he started humming "America the Beautiful."

I loved America and miraculously fought off the urge to laugh. To add to the hilarity, Vinnie drove a pink Volkswagen Bug and had somehow squeezed his moon-pie-lovin' lump of a behind into it. Why was it pink? He won it when he kept his hand on the hood all night in a contest. It even had black plastic eyelashes on the headlights, custom-made for a girl celebrating her femininity. Although bizarre, a man's car is a man's car. The moment he sang, "And crown thy good with brotherhood," he stopped with a little girl eek, like he knew his car was in danger.

A yellow Dodge Charger materialized out of nowhere.

The car plowed toward me, growling like an angry locomotive on a death mission. I had a split second of paralyzing fear, wondering if my life would end as a hood ornament, but its brakes suddenly screamed—biting and hissing—then screeched to a halt beside Vinnie's parked car.

Maybe the universe was trying to kill me.

The Charger's door was angrily punched wide, grazing the side of the Bug as one gargantuan-sized man jumped out cursing. He was wearing a black hoodie that had to be a quadruple X. I was a fan of hoodies. They could cover a multitude of bodily sins, but I must say, that man brought a whole new meaning to the term Big and Tall. The hooded figure slammed his fist on the roof of the Bug, talking about somebody's mother in a very unflattering way.

"What the..." *bleep profanity*, he cursed.

"What the..." *bleep profanity*, "to you!" Vinnie cursed back.

I cringed, actually putting my hands over my ears. Somehow, my mind bleeped out most profanity. My father rarely cursed, and I mean *rarely*, so it was on the forbidden list. And my father's forbidden list was a little longer than most folk's. He was all about "the body is a temple." Trouble was, mine thought it was a "den of sin."

Vinnie thundered over to the side that was dented, like a mad dog off his chain. Bending over, his red shorts drooped, flashing a crack so big it rivaled the Liberty Bell. "You think I can buff that out?"

I was just wondering if they made toilet paper that big.

"You," the hooded man glared, pointing a thick finger at Vinnie. "Get out of my way." *Get out of his way?* I thought. We were parked and in a parking lot. He was the one that chose to turn into it and just about mow us down.

Right then his hoodie fell, and if Darwin was still looking for his Missing Link, I was pretty sure we might've found him. Not only was he humongous, but his dark eyes were set between bushy eyebrows, his nose had been broken, and his face had a two-inch beard.

"Who are you?" he demanded of me.

I didn't know why he wanted to know, but I dumbly answered, "Darcy Walker."

It was like a jolt of recollection smacked him right in the kisser. His body gave an immediate, involuntary jerk as he moved his attention from Vinnie and onto me, mulling over every inch of my face, his eyes narrowing then relaxing, like he was reacquainting himself. Taking another step forward, he was nothing but powerful strength with emotions about to pop.

He muttered, "Good God, it can't be," to himself as he rubbed a hand over his week-old beard.

Vinnie looked at Darwin's Missing Link with a smirk, figuring Darwin was just looking for a Mrs. Darwin. "Dolce, sometimes people are just dumb." I kind of smiled, but I needed to corral Vinnie as quickly as possible. The mood he was in, he might slap the man between two slices of bread and have a sandwich.

Darwin's Missing Link jerked his head toward Vinnie. "So what's your problem, man?" he bellowed. Normally, I liked a good fight as much as the next person, but there was a dead body six feet away from us. I found conversation a waste of time.

"Right now, it's you," Vinnie said, snorting loudly. "My mind's trying to come to grips with the dead body we've found." I stomped on Vinnie's foot. I wasn't sure we wanted to release that information to the public, but Vinnie already let the cat out of the bag. The man glanced over Vinnie's shoulder and all of a sudden looked weirded out, his chest rising and falling fast when he saw the fingers hanging out the corner of the dumpster. The odor didn't faze him—maybe it's because his nose was nearly twice the normal size. Mumbling to himself, he said a few choice, profane words and ultimately looked at us like we were the culprits.

Swell.

After some bizarre posturing that basically was like two Sumo wrestlers chesting away at one another, Vinnie's temper exploded. With a teeth-baring snarl, he slammed the man chest down onto his Charger, his left arm pulled so high he was almost scratching his own neck. Darwin's Missing Link grunted loudly, and the air filled with the sound of cracking bones.

Once he sputtered out, "Okay!" Vinnie's temper came to a grinding halt. Vinnie muttered something Italian and shoved Darwin's Missing Link toward the door of his car. He piled inside and then hung out the window, wiping his nose on his sleeve. "We'll talk later," he roared.

Vinnie looked at the dented door of his Bug and out of the blue took his right foot and planted it on the driver's side of the Charger, leaving a crater the size of a soft ball. "Yeah, we'll talk later," Vinnie said, snorting in a promise.

Whatever the heck that meant in Manland.

Vrooming his engine a few times, he backed out, kicking up some stray gravel as he gave us some unflattering hand gestures. "I should've knee-capped him," Vinnie said in a gruff tone.

A breeze kicked up, stirring up the putrid dumpster smell. Considering vomiting, once again I shook it off right as my name was yelled with the force of a megaphoned howitzer. It wasn't in veneration, people. I stiffened, and when I dared to seek it out, I saw the school counselor, Laken Dempsey, storming my way like a ticked off Tasmanian devil.

It was one of those situations that proved I needed to reboot my brain. I needed to settle down, be a nice little girl, stay in class, and crochet a doily or something because the moment I stuck one foot in sin, I was the type that always got caught.

I heard, "Darcy!" Three seconds later, I heard a more formal, "Darcy Walker!"

When I gave her the trifecta of deaf, dumb, and mute, I heard it even louder. "DARCY!" she shouted.

I looked at Vinnie, he looked at me, and we both knew it was now or never. Turning around, I gave her an idiotic wave that she opted not to return.

Well, wasn't that rude.

Dressed in a tan pencil skirt and white fitted blouse, Ms. Dempsey was a bombshell by middle-aged standards. Heck, by teenage standards. She was a natural blonde, model-thin with curves that made a guy's eyes pop out of his sockets. Plus, she had a set of long legs that were practically to her armpits. Ms. Dempsey was newly single, her blink-and-you'll-miss-it marriage barely over. Vinnie grinned from ear-to-ear like he had a chance.

Vinnie was an absolute moron.

She belted out, "Whose bright idea was this to skip class?!"

There wasn't a lot of finger pointing going on. For God's sake, everyone knew it was me.

In a fit of insanity, I glued on some press-on nails the night before. They were pink, girly—everything I wasn't. I ripped off two and spit them onto the ground, back to my normal nubs. I needed some sort of stress management course. I'd just had my hands in my mouth when I'd been in a dumpster with a dead man. I spit three more times, trying to get rid of the dead body cooties.

She repeated again, "Who told you it was okay to be out here, Darcy?"

I looked in her sky-blue eyes, blinked a big smile, and like an idiot responded, "It's better to ask for forgiveness than permission, I always say."

Sometimes it was best I kept my mouth shut...it really, really was.

Ms. Dempsey massaged her forehead, releasing what looked like a massive migraine. Vinnie glanced at her expression, moaning in sympathy. He leaned up on the Bug, the car groaning from his weight. Oh, God, help us. I knew that look...he was getting his flirt on.

I no sooner gasped, "No," out of my mouth when she inhaled deeply and nearly retched all over the place.

While she was doubled-over, Vinnie rubbed small circles on her back as her gag reflex negotiated with the stench before her. "Now there-there, Ms. Dempsey. Let Vinnie take care of everything. Darcy and I weren't out here running off to get married. She's, um, untouched. I like the experienced type, and just so you know, I think your husband's a fool for dumping you."

I swear, Vinnie ate paint chips as a child.

If that was an attempt to make her feel better, it backfired. Her mouth dropped wide as she lifted one french-manicured finger mouthing, "One minute." Then she shook her head hard, either shaking off a bad memory or the thought of Vinnie as her significant other.

She ignored him, deciding to focus on me. "What's up, Darcy? What has you so curious that you'd walk right out of class?"

I opened my mouth, but nothing came out.

Vinnie roughed me up a little as he stepped in front of me. "I'll tell you what has her so curious, Ms. Dempsey. It's that smell. There's a stiff in the dumpster."

She furrowed her brows, her big blue eyes confused. "A what?"

Vinnie rolled his eyes, pointing out her vernacular with dead bodies was archaic. "A stiff."

"A dead body," I clarified.

She went statue-still, not moving, not flinching. "A dead body," she repeated tonelessly.

"Uh-huh," Vinnie started preaching. "And by the looks of things, this guy gave up the ghost awhile ago."

After Vinnie gave her the play-by-play of pulling me out of the dumpster, I pitched a thumb over my shoulder. When she still didn't move, Vinnie grabbed her arm, dragging her across the parking lot, her tan heels clickety-clacking on the pavement. Her skirt and white blouse got caught by the wind as she perched herself on top of the cardboard boxes. Vinnie had one eye trained on her thigh, the other on the dead man's hand. I cleared my throat, trying to give him the message to rein in the bad boy, but Vinnie was looking at her like she was a moon pie.

She stood there for a few seconds, gasped, coughed, and fought a vomit-filled gag.

"Yeah," Vinnie agreed with a snort, casting me a downturned

look. "Dolce didn't seem to have the same reaction as you and I did."

"Shove it where the sun don't shine," I mouthed. When he continued to frown over his shoulder, I stuck my tongue out. That coming from a male who made out with moon pies and Red Bull every night.

Once Ms. Dempsey pulled herself together, she asked the obvious. "Why would you crawl into the dumpster with a dead guy, Darcy?"

Good question. One I didn't have an answer for. "I guess I thought he might still be alive."

Vinnie's face went lax, mournful, and I swear, I saw a tear. "That was a brave thing to do, Dolce." I thought I was brave once. I had to give an impromptu speech about the fall of the Mayan Empire. All I said was "blood, war, rivalries, maybe a little too much bad luck and the shama lama, ding-dong, and voila, your tribe was dunzo." That was brave. Right then was dumb-butt insanity.

Ms. Dempsey stumbled back down into Vinnie's arms and started talking to herself—contemplating her next steps, debating whether she should go to the principal first or dial 911 and be done with it. Finally, she pulled her cell phone out of the pocket of her skirt and thumbed in the speed dial for her boss.

When she was done with both conversations, she whispered, "Who is he?"

Vinnie and I looked at one another and shrugged like nimrods. Hand to heart, neither of us had a clue. But that was Darcyville. Stuff happened in Darcyville, and I was left to either accept it or annihilate the SOBs that caused it.

Chapter Four

MURPHY'S LAW

$\mathcal{M}$y word, that was either too good to be true or too screwed up to even fathom. Had I, in fact, found a dead body? A dead body that people in school might've known about before it was even discovered? That could be the fantasy of all fantasies, or I'd taken an even deeper step into crazy.

After several *I don't know, officers, Yes, I was skipping class,* and *No, I've never seen him befores*, school was over, and Vinnie drove me home in his rattletrap.

So much for excitement. One minute you have it, and the next it's snuffed out by those in authority.

The killjoys.

My house is in Buffalo Trails Country Club off of Tylersville Road. Don't let that little CC behind our neighborhood fool you though. Ours wasn't Olympic-sized swimming pools, expensive cars, and fancy parties—that was up the street. Ours was foreclosure city and the short road to Hell.

Acquiring our name from the historic buffalo trail that ran through the area, we set out with the intentions of being a first-rate lodge, but the Club dried up before anyone could ever swing a club, period. Four holes were built, but that was when disaster struck. The original developer "buffaloed" potential homeowners, stole their deposits, and ran off to Fiji. Or so went the rumor mill. To the day, he was still listed in the post office as MIA. As a result, the remaining fourteen holes were green spaced with town homes and condominiums. But for those of us who loved to golf, we traveled those four holes on a loop, knowing we looked like morons.

Our house is at the end of the cul-de-sac on Bison Boulevard. It was your traditional red brick with black shutters and coach lights lining the drive. The design was thought out—it made sense and was appealing. It didn't matter, however, when our neighbors kept pink, plastic flamingos as lawn decorations. Their stupidity unwittingly rubbed off. Even so, homes were mostly well kept but not outlandish. No one had money enough to *be* outlandish, and even if one did, property lines were a blur. Our street was built for three homes, but when the Club went belly-up, a fourth house broke the homeowner's code and was shoved in the cul-de-sac almost sideways to close out the street.

As far as economic status went, we were a neighborhood of used minivans and affordable, four-door sedans. Where did the Walkers fit into the equation? We weren't poor, but we were barely middle class. And it wasn't that my father didn't make good money. He just insisted on having two college plans apiece for my sister and me. I tried to tell him my plan was a wasted cause, but it went over about as well as claiming I was a friendly ant at a picnic.

If the double-coverage college plans weren't enough, he had insurance policies out the wazoo. Opening his bills once, I ran across two quarterly statements for accidental death and dismemberment policies. Maybe it was a good idea to have one, but *two*? My father sat at his desk all day talking to his colleagues about the volatile world of insurance. It wasn't like his bungee cord was going to snap or a chainsaw was going to land on him. But Murphy liked to be prepared and unfortunately had some major life lessons that made him walk on eggshells, trying to plan for things he wished would happen and things he wished wouldn't have happened at all.

Our home was the standard Cincinnati two-story—front door in the middle, office to the left, dining room on the right, hardwood kitchen in rear, mirrored by a den. A mudroom connected the den to the garage. No sooner had I kicked my shoes off in the kitchen, than my father came in through the mudroom early. He'd been at some continuing education class and had taken the term "business casual" to an all-new level. He sported golfing clothes, Adidas sneakers, and a Cincinnati Reds ballcap. My father, Murphy, always wore a hat. It wasn't to hide a dirty head or balding spot. I think it was to block out the world.

With curly brown hair and Cherokee Indian lineage, Murphy wasn't short in the looks department. At six foot two, he was physically imposing with guns for arms and hands that could span a basketball. Chiseled with high cheekbones, he had a pair of deep-set brown eyes the color of gingerbread. Eyes that one minute could warm your soul—the next blow as cold as death. You see, Murphy was a bad boy—a reformed bad boy, nonetheless—but bad boys were like shelving unstable chemicals. They were fine when left alone, but shake them up and it was a whole different story.

Immediately, my palms got sweaty. *Murphy knew*, I gasped to myself. His eyes were narrowed, full of ticked-off parental privilege, and a spanking he was considering dispensing.

I needed a foxhole.

My word...maybe I needed a gun.

With no other recourse, I held my chin high and gave him a circle wave. "Hey, Murphy."

I called my father by his first name. A practice I'd observed for fifteen years. The present time probably called for something more traditional, but old habits die hard...even when they were dumb.

I slid into one of the black wooden chairs around the kitchen table, too afraid to even breathe. Murphy woke up in a bad mood and honestly had been crabby since the first burst of green punched through the ground. Why? It was diet season—his goal to lose ten pounds in the next two weeks.

Hunger could zap the sense of humor, people. It really could.

Carrying a bag of what I knew was squirrel feed (my little sister was convinced she had a pet squirrel), Murphy stalked slowly across the hardwood floor, his jaw painted into a harsh, angry line. Stopping one foot in front of me, he kicked the leg of my chair and opened his mouth.

"You ain't sittin' at my table. You smell like a polecat that took a shower in cat piss. Hit the stairs."

Murphy's Kentuckyisms always came out when he was angry. Plus, he used the dreaded P-word. I wasn't even allowed to utter that word lest I be threatened with a dunking in the nearest baptismal.

Stubbornly, I tromped over to the refrigerator, threw the door wide, and squirted some canned Reddi-wip whipped cream in my mouth. I wasn't sure why I was being confrontational—I didn't have a leg to stand on—yet, I found myself giving Murphy a dose of his own medicine. As he grumbled and opened the bag of squirrel feed, I slammed the door shut, stomped loudly across the hardwood, and even louder up the stairs.

After I took a volcanic shower—hoping to kill the dumpster breeding ground—I begrudgingly came back downstairs. In the kitchen, Murphy was getting his Kentucky on, dipping fried chicken out of a cast iron skillet onto a paper towel-covered platter. Sliding his reading glasses onto his nose, he measured out butter-milk for a quick batch of gravy.

The Walkers were simple folk when it came to mealtime. Murphy cooked Southern meals like barbecue, fried chicken, and macaroni and cheese, but six nights out of seven, it was on paper plates accompanied with red plastic cups from Costco.

My little sister tooled around town with our nanny, Claudia. Honestly, that should be against the law. Claudia was Puerto Rican and spoke Spanglish. She barely understood the road signs. And as far as being a traditional nanny? That insinuated a level of wealth when in reality Claudia might be the cheapest baby sitter on the North American continent. Nevertheless, I set the table for two and slid back into my chair, remoting on the television. Murphy angrily snatched the controller from my hand, sat his grumbling body in a seat, and shut it down with the force of a Neanderthal. He may have broken it, but I decided not to comment.

After I piled my plate full of chicken, mashed potatoes, and macaroni, I took a swig of grape Kool-Aid, waiting for him to grunt, speak, or heck, disembowel me with his fork.

I heard the Jeopardy theme in my head. Murphy could be the silent type.

After he licked some gravy from his spoon, he wiped his mouth with a napkin, praying, "Dear God in Heaven on the Great White Throne."

Not the opener I had hoped for, but I tried to capitalize on the conversation nonetheless. "So how *is* God these days?" Murphy looked at his plate, giving me nothing. "Well, how about insurance class?"

"Power down, kid," he said. Murphy always talked in terms of electronics when he felt people needed a rewiring. Unfortunately, that constituted ninety percent of our conversations.

Murphy's stare bore into mine, and I wasn't sure what he was thinking. Maybe he rued the day he became a single father or the day I was even born, but when nothing came out of his mouth, I erroneously thought we were going to leave it as one of those things best left unsaid.

I took two more bites of macaroni, thinking I was safe. But then he spat, "Okay, if you're not going to say anything, then *I* will. The Valley of the Shadow of Death called today, and I understand you happened across a dead body."

Murphy called Valley High the Valley of the Shadow of Death. Not literal death, of course, but maybe the death of innocence and a parent's ability to cope. Funny that the nickname should be taken literally.

I swallowed. "Mind blowing, isn't it."

Murphy gave me a surprised, almost painful blink. "Jesus Christ," he prayed. His eyes bugged out briefly, and he paused to breathe deep. I'm guessing he held out hope it was only rumor. "Why are you always in trouble, kid?" he eventually muttered. "Do you know how I felt when I got a call from the principal and the police?" Some air left my lungs. "Yeah," he sneered, "it was a courtesy call, I guess, because they told me they wanted to question you. Be glad I couldn't make it. I was up to my ears in flood damage, but I told them to drown you in their own version of waterboarding if they so desired."

I didn't know what to say and found silence as the best response. Murphy bit off a piece of chicken when I had a feeling he wanted it to be my head. There was some mumbling I couldn't decipher, shifting in his seat, and finally, "Good God, save me from her, from myself, and from the horned bandit that's always after me."

Murphy was Protestant...as in Southern Baptist. When Southern Baptists got rattled, they talked to God like He was sitting in the room with them—asking His opinion, begging for a sign, promising they'd do as He directed if He'd have mercy on their souls and answer the prayer on their terms.

"Let's start this conversation over, kid. Tell me why you felt the urge to go outside."

Most of the world had no creativity. They just didn't get it. I tried to summon some remorse, but frankly, I wasn't sorry. I settled on some idiotic, sheepish smile that resembled indigestion.

"Your answer?" he pushed.

I blinked and scratched my arms. Murphy had two rules: try your hardest, and tell the truth. The first was hit or miss. The second was accomplished by fluke. I was a horrible liar. Teenagers could normally fire off a lie at will. My giggle in the middle was a dead giveaway.

I had to admit sometimes I *did* tiptoe around the damning details.

I couldn't tell him about Jinx. I felt it irrelevant. Plus, he wouldn't understand. "Would you believe it was only because I could?"

Murphy gave me one of those looks that defied logic. "You can't unring a bell, kid. You're making quite the name for yourself at that school. Need I remind you that you're currently grounded?"

Oh that...

I'd done a naughty thing, like sneaking out of the house at midnight to spy on a neighbor digging holes in his backyard. First of all, the guy looked like a troll; and second of all, who did that crap anyway? I couldn't decide if his behavior was creepy, spectacular, or somewhere in between, but Murphy interrupted before I could make a firm deduction. Thing was, I broke the rules with relish. I wasn't sure what that said about the state of my conscience.

Murphy took an even larger bite of mashed potatoes. "This is nothing but Murphy's Law. Anything that *can* go wrong *will* go wrong at the *worst* possible time. No matter how hard I try, I can't undo what was bred in you."

Maybe he had a point. God knew Murphy had enough bad genes, and the name he'd given me was undeniably and unerringly symbolic. As my name suggested, I was a "dark walker." Sometimes I was flying blind and decisions weren't thought out. Other times they were minutely orchestrated but ridiculously blasphemous to the sane mind.

I wiped my mouth, neatly laying my napkin in my lap, acting overly courteous to get back in his good graces. "So I held hands with a dead man, Murphy. So what? I didn't kill him. I didn't assist anyone in killing him. I merely found him in the dumpster. I know it sounds strange, but that's what happened."

Murphy raised a brow one fraction. "Well, why don't you leave the body-finding to the body-finding people, and you just go to stupid class. Now there's a novel idea if I ever heard one."

Now I raised a brow. "So you think finding a man that was missing and hopefully giving his family some peace of mind was stupid?"

He narrowed his eyes. "I think it was stupid. Grade A stupid."

Stupid was my favorite word. It could be a noun, an adjective, or an adverb dependent upon the way it was phrased in a sentence. Murphy revered the word even more than I did. Problem was, he'd upgraded my behavior to Grade A. In the egg world that was good. In Darcy's world, it was the baddest of all bad. He'd coined that phrase when Justice and I got henna tattoos when we were bored. Mine was angel wings in the spot that every parent hated—the tramp stamp—right above the booty. Trouble was, no one explained how long it took for henna to wear off.

I placed my right hand over my heart, manufacturing a sentence that sounded legal. "I promise to the best that my abilities and faculties will allow, to cut my stupid behavior in half." I paused, adding, "So help me God."

"Well, now we're screwed," Murphy grumbled to himself. He crammed some macaroni in his mouth, and went back to looking at the ceiling. I zeroed in on Murphy's face. It was pretty much flawless except for the nose. It was slightly off-center, deviated to the right from a bar fight when he was nineteen years old. I briefly wondered where he hid the body.

"Do you want to know what I found?" I asked.

"No."

"Do you want to know what the police said?"

"No."

"Do you want to know about the severed hand?"

"No."

"Did you know I was running off to get married with Vinnie Vecchione?" Murphy's fork stopped in midair. Everyone knew Vinnie, and he wasn't always spoken of in veneration. In fact, he had the morals of an alley cat. "Okay," I said in a laugh, "that part isn't true, but I don't know what's worse, Murphy…the fact that I uncovered a shockingly brutal murder or the fact that I'm fifteen years old and wouldn't know what to do if a boy landed on top of my lips."

He put down his fork and swallowed down what I think was a regurgitated portion of his meal. No matter how hard I tried to have "that talk" with Murphy, he'd bury his head in the sand every single time.

"Let's table that part of the discussion for now," he mumbled.

"Maybe I *need* that discussion, Murphy. Maybe there are things in my life that necessitate that conversation be *now* rather than *later*."

"What things?!" he snapped.

I shrugged, honest-to-God not knowing how I maintained a straight face. "You know," I said in a wink, "the shama lama, ding-dong things."

For all those naughty words I didn't know the meaning of, in the words of Otis Day, I assigned the term shama lama, ding-dong. There was a lot of shama lama, ding-dong in my life, since I understood very little about the ways of the world.

At first, Murphy looked confused, but then he quickly deduced it was Darcyspeak for the off-color. "Kid, you have the worst potty mouth."

I had an immortal case of potty mouth, but would he rather me curse like a sailor or try to organize my thoughts in a more creative and appropriate manner?

"Of course I'm joking, Murphy. If there was anything going on in my life, it would be immaculate, and we both know God wouldn't be choosing me for the divine."

We both stopped to stare into air. I guess I'd proven my point.

"Anything else?" he finally mumbled.

"I hurt my foot." Murphy removed his readers, rubbing his eyes with his palms. I scooted my chair out and placed my foot in his lap.

He flipped it over, twisting it right then left, and when he saw barely a scratch, he gave me his suck-it-up face.

But it hurt, people, and so did my rear end. The Bug barely made it over thirty, and I was pretty sure I had a seat coil permanently stamped into my behind. Maybe that was karma because even though Murphy and I had a wonderful relationship, right then he could best be described as the burr soon to be up my a-s-s. (If I spelled it, that didn't count...right?)

I lowered my foot, crossing my fingers that I hadn't contracted some sort of flesh-eating bacteria. Trust me, it was highly possible. My body had more injuries than a prizefighter with the arthritic joints of a centenarian. At age eight, I fractured my left ulna in two places. At ten, I broke my cheekbone when I splattered face first on the monkey bars. Then I crumpled my finger in a car door at age eleven and broke my wrist freshman year when I wrecked on a dirt bike. And finally, I fractured my ankle at fifteen when I fell out of my uncle's Mercedes all-terrain vehicle and got my four-inch heel stuck in a metal grate. I wanted out...the gutter gods wanted me below.

Out of the blue, Murphy reached over to hold my hand, his large palm gripping mine tightly like it alone was his lifeline. He finished off his chicken with one hand, ending with a swig of Diet Coke.

"I love you, kid," he said.

I gave him my best shot at a smile and squeezed his hand, struck with a case of guilt that would suffocate someone that had three mouths. The smell of crispy chicken and herbs and spices filled the kitchen air. *Comfort food.* I sighed. Why was it I felt so empty and alone?

———

After I read my little sister a bedtime story, it was close to ten o'clock. I crawled into a pair of holey gray sweats and an inside-out navy T-shirt and fell into my wrought-iron bed. It was painted white with a matching down comforter surrounded by gray mist walls. As close to girly décor as I could get without pastels. I wasn't sure why I didn't like pastels. It went back to some childhood memory where

I was forced to wear a pink lacy dress. I was covered in hives for weeks.

I was a minimalist in my decorating scheme. I had one night-stand that housed a cell phone charger, telephone, and lamp. On the other side of my bed stood a chair and a floor lamp. In front of me were a painted white desk and a flatscreen television. Running around all four walls was shelving to house the books I'd stockpiled over the years.

Very neat, very organized, very perfect for the OCD-side of Darcy.

The thing of it was, most of the time my *verys* were angry at one another. That might account for the week's worth of laundry that was piled over every surface in sight. I didn't say I wasn't organized. I said I had trouble following through.

To calm my mind, I slept with a sound machine set on "white noise." Some preferred the absence of noise while they were sleeping. Not me. Noise reminded me I wasn't alone. After I clicked the machine to medium, I punched on my VIZIO, flipping through a few channels, feeling like time was a dog nipping at my heels.

In what had become a regular occurrence, I was battling my nightly bout with insomnia. I wasn't sure why I was an insomniac. At most, I probably needed some sort of medicinal help. At least, I needed some regular exercise to wear me out.

My iPhone was lying beside my bed. Murphy's idea of a cell phone was a piece of plastic that had numbers on it—the free ones our plan offered. In Teenagerland, the free ones were throwbacks to the Dinosaur Age and an insult to the forward-thinking human. Plus, the free ones didn't always accommodate a data package when the majority of my friends had all but forgotten how to dial. Murphy thought teenagers of my generation were too indulged. Maybe some were, but like my TV, I worked and saved to purchase the iPhone all on my own. Let's just say that was the first time I truly understood why it was depressing to give so much of your hard-earned cash to taxes. Every bit of headway I made, Uncle Sam took another big bite.

After a few goodnight texts to Justice and Rudi, I moved on to the television to alleviate the boredom. When I couldn't find an interesting show, I clicked it off and rolled to my side. The shades weren't closed all the way, and a small fraction of an inch blinded me with moonlight that seemed overly fierce. Too lazy to get up and shut them altogether, I stared at the stars outside—wondering what was going on in other universes—hoping my travels held a lifetime of smiles and adventures, crossing my fingers I didn't somehow mess things up. Suffice it to say that was a huge possibility. I *did* believe in destiny, but I had a preternatural knack for screwing up all things Divine.

Across the hall, Murphy snored like a buzzsaw. I had a pang of guilt. By no means was it easy being a single father, and by no means was it easy to parent me. Oftentimes, he reminded me of Atlas with the weight of the world on his shoulders. For years, he'd longed for something dear to him to return—someone to help him shoulder the burdens—but longing didn't always bring something to pass. Some things were absurdly irrevocable.

Most days, we both swung between grief and hysteria. A part of me longed to think on that fateful day—the devastating reason for the loneliness—but the horror was too great. Like Murphy's Law, sometimes things happened at the worst possible time, and it wasn't even close to fair. With that thought, the veils of my memory blasted me with thoughts that were too unbearable. I closed my eyes, willing away the grief, and called to mind the dumpster man— Dumpster Dude I'd decided to call him. Now *he* knew a heckuvalot about unfair...or he used to.

Chapter Five

MOB TIES

I awoke with a jump.

At last count, I was at three hundred and thirty-one sheep. I wasn't sure what happened to three hundred and thirty-two. Maybe the wolf ate him. Maybe he ran off with a half-sheared, hussy sheep. Either way, my head pounded from sleep deprivation, and I was pretty sure my nerves were shot to the mouth of Hades.

It took me awhile to figure out what had wakened me, but when I heard the low buzz of my iPhone, I realized someone was dumb enough to call me at two-twenty on a school night. I reached over and grabbed it from the nightstand, squinted at the screen, and saw it was ringing with an unknown caller ID.

Clicking it on, I expected to hear Dylan's soothing murmur—something flirty and inappropriate that would leave me blushing—but not the case. In fact, there was nothing but heavy breathing, and the sense that something was disturbingly off. The more I repeated, "Hello, is anyone there," the more my gut screamed it had nothing to do with a misdialed number and everything to do with the murder at school.

My mind did a little rewind...

Jinx and the unidentified guy with him had looked inside the dumpster as if they verified something. I knew they saw the body. My word, they had to have smelled it and looked out of sheer curiosity. Whether that made them guilty of the murder or not, they sure as heck acted guilty of something. Their reactions weren't typical, and to the best of my knowledge, they didn't go back inside the building and "cry foul."

Bracing myself on the mattress, I sat up and cleared my throat, realizing what I planned to do next was undeniably stupid—but it was my opinion, nothing ventured, nothing gained. Taking a deep breath, I dumbly opened my mouth.

"Why did you call, Jinx?" I tried to say calmly. "I followed you out into the hall fifth period and heard you say, and I quote, 'Is um, is um—are you sure? Really? That shouldn't have happened.' I know in my gut you were chasing that body down. Now whether you put him in the dumpster is another story. And by the way, what message were you trying to give me in the cafeteria? Pardon me for saying it, but you're not exactly Mister Congeniality, Jinx. We met eyes, so I know there was a reason."

I expected a hang up, nothing at all, or "Sorry, wrong number," but what I sure as heck didn't expect was, "You need to watch yourself, Darcy. You're already in too deep, and you don't strike me as the type that's a good swimmer. In fact, it's going to be difficult to swim when your flesh is rotting off in chunks, oozing fluid, and being eaten by scavengers. I enjoy dead bodies, Darcy. How about you?"

I cringed, goose bumps traveling from my head to my feet. I wished I'd kept my mouth shut. The caller spoke through one of those voice distortion units, the resulting sound somewhere between Darth Vader and Freddy Krueger movie scary. Even digitized, I couldn't miss the murderous intent and anticipatory inflection in every word.

It was a warning...or maybe a promise. I wasn't sure.

I willed threats to roll off my tongue—anything to make me look like a badass chick with anger management issues—but all I could manage systemically was the urge to wet my pants. What exactly had I done to warrant a threatening phone call? Yes, I'd spoken to the authorities, but even then, they sort of found me. Was someone worried I mentioned his or her name? If *so*, then *who*? The officer I spoke with requested I tell him exactly what I saw, so I told him about Jinx. But I couldn't say that I saw Jinx *touching* the body or doing *anything* with the body. If it was Jinx, however, he'd just committed an egregious error. Sure it made me nervous, but one threatening phone call wasn't going to make me heel. In fact, it told me I was onto something even if I didn't know what that something was.

As I sat in quiet defiance, next thing I knew the person disconnected, and I wondered if I should dig a hole to China or go at Jinx full-force and declare, game-ON.

———————

I barely slept the rest of the night. When my feet hit the floor, I was bone tired—my puffy eyes telling me it was the perfect day for my I-don't-care look. It consisted of a wet ponytail, little or no cosmetics, and my glasses. I was grossly nearsighted, and a lifetime of carrots, milk, cheese, and vitamin A didn't make a darn difference.

I was Darcy Walker, folks. Was I expecting a miracle?

Trying to jar my senses, I took an ice cube-flavored shower but first cranked up the music. Picking out music, in my opinion, was the most crucial decision of the day. It set the tone. I could laugh at someone's witty repartee over their breakup, scoff at an alternative mix to a classic song, or jam to a tune that only had four words but the beat left me dancing.

I chose classic hard rock—Iron Maiden's, "Run to the Hills." Evidently, I needed to get in the butt-kicking mood or drop a few seconds on my forty.

Once I was completely numb, I popped out of the shower and dressed in my standard uniform—jeans and a T-shirt. Sliding my feet into a pair of black flip-flops, I limped downstairs zombified, favoring a wart I'd picked up a week before. Flipping on the kitchen lights, the chill from the floor traveled up my jeans, giving me the shivers. I needed to find my zen—that calm, cool, and collected place where nothing else mattered.

For me, it was a coffee, Coke, and a cookie.

Anyone who was hyper could attest to the fact that coffee and other stimulants could have the opposite effect and calm, instead of stimulate. We were the lucky ones (NOT). There were many times I needed to wake up, and drinking coffee was like taking a sleeping pill. What I needed on those days was a sledgehammer.

I poured a cup, the reed of smoke rising up and tickling my nose. As I blew a soft breath into the mug, I waited for the calm to take over but got nothing. I grabbed two cookies out of the Keebler bag and stuffed one in my mouth. After the chocolate chip route, I scarfed two powdered doughnuts, raided the refrigerator, and then downed an open can of flat Coke.

Still nothing, and I was bloated and my jeans were at capacity.

Popping the button on my waistband, I forced a burp, glancing at the brass clock on the wall. Six-fifty in the morning. Bus stop time. I sighed, and then shuddered. Bus 150 was a dump. It was littered with gum wrappers, hairballs, and what smelled like urine and stale hamster food. But as Murphy grumbled on the first day of school, *The taxpayers paid for it, so be thankful*.

Whatever...I wasn't thankful.

I cleaned off the table, stacked my cup in the dishwasher, and did a few math problems while I stood at the counter. When my brain was spent, I grabbed a white hoodie, pulling my arms through, zipping it to my chin. My body was one notch above reptilian and hovered at barely alive. The temperature of the high school didn't help matters either. Some days it felt like an inferno. Others, it was an icebox. Back in the winter, someone stole the copper piping out of the air conditioning unit, and the dose of Freon versus new piping had never been regulated. Even though we were in between seasons, a Siberian air cut through us at all times.

Yelling, "Goodbye" upstairs, I fished some Go Glam! nude lip gloss out of my purse and rolled on a healthy coat of Smack Attack. The irony gave me pause. I ran through lip gloss like a car ran through motor oil. It was a crying shame my lips had never experienced any activity whatsoever with the opposite sex.

With one hand on the doorknob, I nearly jumped out of my skin when the doorbell rang. Peeking through the peephole, I felt the beginnings of a cluster headache. My word, it was too early in the morning for Jon Bradshaw. By the beady-eyed look he returned, he felt the same way.

I creaked open the door. Before I could say hi, hello, or even kiss-my-you-know-what, he forced his way onto the hardwood and blurted, "Taylor said I had to pick you up this week. I don't like it, and you don't like it, but it's the way it's got to be."

He pantomimed a gunshot to the head. *Good ole Dylan*, I thought, laughing to myself. *Micromanaging all the way from Maui.*

Jon was one of the few sophomores that had their license. Let's just say he took the whistle-stop tour through kindergarten and leave it at that. He was my height, stocky, and had average brown hair, eyes, and looks. Maybe he was good-looking—heck, maybe he was a ten on the hunk scale—but if truth be known, I wanted to punch him, and he really wanted to punch me.

I gave him a smirk that pretty much suggested he was Dylan's bootlicker. "Shut up, Walker," he groaned. "Have you ever dealt with him when he's angry?"

Every day, I thought to myself. *Every freaking day.*

...but we loved him.

High school was hard. It just was. The halls were full of people who were a friend one minute...the next they were not. Dylan was the benchmark for loyalty. He had a reputation for a razor-sharp mind with a quick-witted tongue, incredibly protective of those he loved. If someone said something derogatory about his friends, he had their back and then some. As a male, he could strengthen the backbone you had. As a female, just a little of his dominance made him dangerously addictive.

Due to his stoic nature, I nicknamed Jon, "Grumpy," the unhappiest of Snow White's dwarf friends. The youngest of the seven Bradshaw boys, unquestionably, he was the most stable. He came from a long line of high school dropouts with recreational activities best kept to themselves. Thing was, Grumpy developed a characteristic over the years of being able to negotiate and talk people out of anything. Due to that characteristic alone, he was someone I needed on my friendship roster.

Especially since I tended to be low on scruples.

Falling into more scrapes than most, I saw the need to expand the Walker bloodline with brothers that would have my back. Knowing I needed to define what qualified the initiates, in my little corner of the world it was simple: a person had to have swagger. A certain bravado with undying loyalty. What it boiled down to was my brothers and I kept secrets for one another with a commitment of 'til death do we part.

We even had an initiation ceremony and secret handshake.

When we wrecked on his dirt bike freshman year—covered in scrapes and bruises—Grumpy was the first I brotherized into my hypothetical blood clan. Presently, there were two others dumb enough to join. So in my own warped mind, I was Darcy Walker, AKA a mobster godfather. One would think number one in line to my throne would be Dylan, but he scoffed at my attempt to mobsterize my life. I didn't care. One way or another, I would mix blood with him before I officially pushed up daisies.

The weather report forecasted sunny skies with a high of seventy-nine degrees, but in Cincinnati, a person never really could tell. The only constant thing weatherwise was change. Anticipating a heat wave, Grumpy had thrown himself into a pair of black athletic shorts, an inside-out navy T-shirt, and dirty, white sneakers. Left to his own devices, he had the fashion sense of a horse. I opened my mouth to comment but reminded myself he came in a real car with real wheels—not atrocious Bus 150, being infected with God-only-knew-what.

A mahogany mirror was mounted to the wall by the door. Grumpy stole a look at himself, frowning. Pushing his wavy hair out of his eyes, he quickly pulled his shirt over his head, turning it the appropriate way. We no sooner moved for the door than my little sister came tap dancing down the stairs, two at a time...naked as a jaybird.

You could've heard a pin drop.

After a second of shock, I doubled over laughing.

Marjorie's naked phase. It was common knowledge the six-year-old had a proclivity for lounging in the clothes that God gave her. Thing was, she was naked because she wanted something. Who would've thought nudity would be such a good bargaining tool?

With almond-shaped, brown eyes, Marjorie had a heart-shaped face and a pert little nose, her ivory skin smooth and unblemished like a china doll. Her curly hair, however, was fire engine red. The color that made people think something happened during the gestational cycle or that the universe hated them.

Nicknamed M as a baby, I was frightened she'd never figure out how to write her too-long name, but she was smart. She mastered all eight letters plus reciting the Bill of Rights by the time she was two. So on top of all that cuteness was a legitimate genius. If someone had a problem, Marjorie could figure it out like an industrial engineer. If a person didn't have a problem, Marjorie was the best conversationalist in the world. Thing was, when she *did* have a problem, she came to *me*—so there must be some dumb in there somewhere.

Grumpy launched into the beginnings of an asthma attack. By that time, Murphy practically flew over the balcony, screaming for Marjorie to act like a lady. A cigar hung out the left side of his mouth, balanced between his teeth and lips. Murphy smoked cigars when he needed to relax. The first year of his single fatherhood, he alone smoked enough cigars to keep the tobacco industry and Cuba afloat.

When he landed, he saw Grumpy's face and chuckled.

"Bless him, Lord," he said. Murphy always said, "bless them," when he thought someone's life was doomed. He said, "bless their heart," when he felt someone was moronically stupid.

Marjorie busted into some bawdy, raunchy moves with her hips. The pediatrician said her behavior was just a phase, but my guess was it might lead to a lot of spandex and a stripper pole by the time she was in high school.

"Bless her heart," Murphy predictably groaned. "She's a stinking genius but can't get the little things like clothes."

Marjorie furrowed her brows, confused. "I get the little things, Daddy. I'm just hot. Besides, I'm going outside to dance naked with my squirrel."

That's all it took for Murphy to lose whatever semblance of a smile he had. It wasn't the "dance naked with a squirrel" comment. It was the "I'm hot" comment.

His face went beet-red. "Who messed with the thermostat?!"

Those were the five magic words that made me always look for an escape hatch. Murphy was a thermostat freak, and our conversation would have him pointing the finger at everyone, including even Grumpy, who didn't even live here. Grabbing Grumpy's hand, I dragged his half-paralyzed body out the door.

One thing about going to school in the dark, occasionally I'd get a glimpse of the moon. The morning moon—a brilliant orangey-red in color—hung low on the horizon, catching the reflection of the rising sun. In a few moments, the sun would say hello, so I took a moment to watch the end of one day be replaced by the beginnings of another. A long silence and an even longer sigh ensued as I realized the unbearable monotony to come. Cincinnati was a great place to raise kids. But let's face it. The 'burbs were boring—just the thought made me cringe.

Once we piled in the car, Grumpy dialed on some talk radio.

He muttered, "Did you hear about the man found in the dumpster at school yesterday?" I debated telling him I was the finder—even about the prank caller—but in all honesty, I didn't know what he'd do with the information. He could tell Dylan, or worse yet, he could tell Murphy. Even though Murphy was a scary man, the boys who visited our home all seemed to blurt out details about my life they thought he'd like to know. I decided to give him nothing but dumb and blonde. "The morning news said he was identified as Alfonso Juarez," he continued. "A mob heavy for AVO, considered the worst gang in the world. That's some scary crap, Walker, right here in Cincinnati, USA."

Overall, I didn't consider myself special or someone that fortune favored. If there was a question on a test, with a fifty-fifty chance of hitting the bull's eye, most usually the dice would roll against me. But in cases like this—things that were absolutely not my business at all—I was so lucky I'd be barred from Vegas. I didn't watch the news that morning and had planned to keep my thoughts to myself. But here I got the information anyway. I couldn't contain the smile.

Other than the information about AVO, it was a quiet drive to school. That wasn't abnormal for Grumpy. He was a psychological Fort Knox. In light of the silence, I decided to go over my plan...but I didn't have one. So I just sat there, my left leg jumping up and down like an overzealous pogo stick.

The more I thought about it, the more I realized Alfonso Juarez would be *the* topic of conversation—well, amongst the deep thinkers. Others would be talking about the latest breakups, makeups, and weekend plans. So my job for the day was to be all ears, and dang it, I was *so* talented in the ear department.

After I dumped my things in the locker, I knew the immediate place for gossip was the girls' bathroom. At least, that's what the incorrigible snoop in me figured out in middle school.

I stepped into what I called One-Last-Touch-Up-Land. If a girl failed to apply at home, all she had to do was stand in the plume of cosmetic smoke, and she was good to go. When I gazed in the mirror, I came to full awareness that was the best it was going to get. *What the Lord giveth, the Lord can take away* was my motto. I feared if I touched something, I'd perhaps look even worse.

Someone was extra desperate because the cloud of hairspray nearly suffocated me. Coughing twice, I found the offender to be Clementine Miriam Rabinowitz.

Clementine was easily one of the prettiest girls in school. She had coal-black hair, big black eyes with creamy skin, and a double zero build. But she was quiet, and when I say quiet, I mean a cricket chirped louder. Her mystique, I think, was part of the appeal. Guys knew very little about her—she was the mysterious someone to look at while she jumped up and down in her cheerleading skirt.

I sneezed.

Then I sneezed again.

When I coughed three times, my nose made the decision to exit. The moment I spun on my heels, as luck would have it, I came face-to-face with Poison Ivy. I seriously went into flight mode.

"Gotta go," I said, coughing again and raising my wrist to my mouth.

Ivy smacked some minty-gum, the aroma making me want to puke. She literally put one hand on my chest and backed me inside with that look like we were going to talk. Suddenly, I felt hotter than a matchstick. Stripping off my zipped hoodie, I coughed again as I tied it around my waist. Ivy looked aghast, like I'd committed some major fashion faux pas. I thought the rest of me looked okay. My black T-shirt had tiny white skulls on it, their tongues sticking rudely out of their mouths in an even ruder drop-dead-and-die face.

Surely, she got the message.

Wearing a little white dress and white go-go boots (no lie), Ivy had curled her hair into a mass of blonde ringlets. Normally, I'd say her hair looked great, cutting-edge, fashion forward. Right then, it reminded me of the serpents of Medusa.

Practically pushing me into Clementine, Clementine gave a

sheepish smile as Ivy vied for prime position in front of the mirror. Once she took up two spaces, she rolled on red lipstick, her blue eyes slaying me through the mirror.

"My mother talks about you sometimes," she said and puckered. "She saw you at Target and said it's a shame you don't have a positive role model because there might actually be some beauty behind all of that cotton material."

I somehow staved off the urge to punch her.

I'd met her mother once. She was Ivy on steroids, and I was pretty sure her prayers went south instead of north. Never once had I stopped to consider the way I appeared to other parents though. I wasn't sure how that made me feel. A fraction of what her mother said was true. My closet wasn't remotely like everyone else's—partly because I didn't have the dough, but mostly because I didn't know what to do. It wasn't that I wasn't open to constructive criticism... it's just that it was *her*. Ivy's comments were glib, insincere, and diabolically toxic.

She smacked her red dragon lips. "She even says she prays for you."

I stand amazed.

I held my chin high. "Tell her thanks."

Ivy gave an experimental smile in the mirror and rolled her lipstick south, replacing its silver lid. "Would you like me to give you a make-over? Maybe I can get some community service hours for it." She started at my feet, made it to my hips, actually rolled her eyes, and painted on a benevolent smile. When I didn't say anything, she looked at me like I'd grown two heads. "What *is* your beauty regimen anyway?"

File that under *None Of Your Business.*

Still, I found myself mumbling, "Soap and water."

Stop it, Darcy, my small ego begged. *You're giving her everything, and you owe her nothing.*

"Her beauty regimen doesn't involve a witch's cauldron, bats, and dead frogs like yours," Justice fumed from behind. See? This was where I hated the effect Ivy had on me. I'd lost all control of my senses. Justice literally stood a foot away with my other girlfriend, Rudi Morgan, flanked from behind. I hadn't even noticed.

My glasses fogged with embarrassment. Ivy shrugged as though

she didn't want to fight. She probably didn't. It was just status quo for her evil, little mind. She explained, "Hey, I'm merely trying to help the little charity case here nothing more."

I told her to kiss-my-you-know-what. It's a shame it never made it out of my mouth.

Dressed in yellow from head to toe, Justice looked like a banana. She snorted and said, "You don't have a self-sacrificial bone in your scrawny little body, Ivy. That means it'll be easy to snap."

Ivy gave Justice her serial killer smile. "The karate thing not going so well?" she said, smirking sarcastically.

Justice looked in the mirror, touching her right eye that was as black as coal. I knew what that meant. Justice had gone toe-to-toe with Eddie Lopez again. Eddie—real name Eduarda—was a senior female at Valley High who schooled at Justice's dojo. I'd rather pluck the nose hairs of a grizzly than to mess with Eddie. She was a demented lunatic and plain, old weird. Justice had a job at a clothing consignment store. I worked at a bookstore. Eddie? She had a part time job at Saxon Brothers' Exterminators...killing rodents all over the city.

Justice snorted once more. "I hate Eddie. She's never beaten me, but I swear, the girl tries to kill me daily." Ivy dumbly rolled her eyes. "Shouldn't you be crying or something?" Justice jabbed.

Good point, I thought. I'd read on Facebook the night before that Ivy and her longtime boyfriend, Jagger Cane, broke up. I thought a breakup was supposed to leave you throwing up in the bathroom or crying in your hands. Ivy was all easy come, easy go about it. I found it odd, however, that she'd broadcast on a social networking site that she got dumped. If I ever landed a boyfriend, the last thing I'd want to admit was he dumped me for no just cause. But that was what teenagers did. They told their life stories to their list of friends who weren't really friends. Believe me, I was in no position to judge. My criteria for cyber friends was that they were living and breathing with no known markers for future serial killers.

As Ivy continued to primp unaffected, Rudi glared on my behalf while Justice threw an imaginary dagger. Giving both girls a smile that said, "thanks," I left the room without further comment. A part of me begged to cry—to head up a *We Hate Ivy Support Group* or just succumb to the humiliation—but thankfully, the bigger part reminded me I had a job to do.

And maybe karma would one day visit her on my behalf.

My iPhone jumped around in my pocket as I merged into oncoming traffic. Changing its ringtone regularly, the newest sound was the slow drippings of Chinese water torture.

How appropriate...once I glanced at the number.

Chapter Six

DEEP SEA FISHING

*I*t was Mr. Omniscient himself.

Normally, he was my confidante. Everything we'd ever spoken stayed under lock-and-key and was repeated only in the company of the Mrs. Butterworth's bottle. But he'd want to know details if he picked up on my mood. I didn't have time for details, and well, I didn't want to cry.

Clicking the accept button, I took a deep breath, trying to sound so happy it was nauseating. "Hey, D. Shouldn't you be sleeping right now?" There was a six-hour difference. Midnight or beyond.

"I got a text from Vinnie yesterday," he murmured.

Crap. Dead air. No one breathed, and I wanted to crucify Vinnie's lard-butt body.

I juked left around a cluster of people, got jostled by two guys, and took a right at the Spirit Shop, zigzagging around some girls. "Good morning to you too," I mumbled.

He inhaled deeply, exhaling more intensely. "Exactly what happened?" he asked. "Vinnie said, 'Darcy's a bad influence.' How in the," *bleep profanity*, "can you be a bad influence on Valentine Vecchione?"

"I prefer the term iniquity engineer."

Coined that phrase on the spot.

Dylan debated laughing. There was a lengthy pause, and I could feel the faint glimmer of humor begging to live. But the urge never made it past the infancy stage because he finally seethed, "Start talking, hound dog. I'm quickly losing my patience."

He'd called me hound dog since seventh grade when I figured out Finn Lively was playing spin-the-bottle with an eighth grade girl. Wasn't hard. Finn had a permanent smile plastered on his face in pink lipstick. The brunette eighth grader wore a lot of blond hair.

"So," I started.

"Soooo," he echoed.

"Umm," I then stuttered.

"Go on, Miss Umm. I'm dying to hear your spin on things. And let me tell you," he paused darkly, "I *will hear* the spin."

I shivered even though I was perfectly warm. Dylan had a way of making me feel naked even with all my clothes on. He could strip my will and defenses bare, one painful question after the next.

The truth shall set you free, I mumbled in my head. *The truth shall set you free.*

I cleared my throat. "So how's Maui? Is it whale mating season?"

Explicit profanity followed. "What's going on, Darcy?"

Dylan only called me Darcy when he'd been pushed over the line or was trying to get my attention. In other words, when I was being stupid. Most might take that as an insult. I was used to the formality.

I heard him speak to someone softly, like he was sorry he'd wakened the person.

The hair on my neck stood on end. "Who are you talking to?"

He giggled. "Say, hello to Lailanni. We hit it off at the luau and are getting to know one another better." I think I swallowed my tongue.

"Hi," I choked out. Lailanni didn't answer. Guess she was the quiet type or didn't know English. "Isn't this a little fast?" I said, hoping it was all a joke.

Dylan gave a tired sigh. "Oh, I don't know. I was thinking of a June wedding."

"Har, Har." Okay, we both knew there was no Lailanni (I think), and if there was? Heaven help me, I would die keeping them apart.

Another even deeper sigh. "You know I have your back, yeah?"

A few beats later, I'd made my way to first period, sliding into a seat. US history was taught by Biggie Butts—no kidding—and was he a pain in mine. While Dylan mumbled something about a collar and a leash long enough to cross the Pacific, I asked a few people nearby if they'd heard about the murder. The two to my left knew nothing. The one sitting behind asked if Rudi was single, and the guy to my right was Jagger Cane—Ivy's on again-off again boyfriend.

"Hello, babe," he said with a grin. I shivered. Each time I saw Jagger, my first thought was, *Hold onto your knickers*. He had some funky mojo going on, and I didn't think it was the good kind—at least not the kind a daddy would approve of. "I saw some rumbling around over there in between classes," he said, "but I'll only give specifics if you kiss me."

I didn't make eye contact for fear of falling victim to his silver-tongued ways. I was one of those girls generally ignored by the opposite sex. I wasn't sure what was up with the week—maybe it was the new moon—but for some reason, I had been treated like a hot commodity.

Dylan murmured, "Come on, sweetheart. Talk to me."

Dylan never ceased to hope I'd fall in line like the rest of the nice, little children. Countless times I told him it was better to accept things than to keep going down the same road that led nowhere. Trouble was, I had self-destructive tendencies. And there was not a whole lot a person could do for someone hellbent on a path of self-destruction.

For the first time *ever*, I tapped the screen and hung up on him.

I drummed my fingers on the desk as Grumpy slid into the seat in front of me. I flicked him on the neck. "Does Dylan have a Lailanni in his life?"

When I told him what had happened, Grumpy squinted his eyes myopically, like he couldn't see me or maybe tried to focus on the question. "You have to be the dumbest blonde on record."

————

Right after lunch, there was a half hour period where students could grab some tutoring or head to the media center. I wolfed down some orange-colored peanut butter crackers and headed to the media center, except I picked up a stray along the way...Jagger Cane.

A little taller than me, he was dressed in dark jeans and a red polo, strutting in expensive tan loafers. And when I say strut, I mean Jagger walked on his toes in some sort of cocky fashion that was hard to describe. With spiked, brown hair and razor-sharp, black eyes, Jagger was unusually good-looking. Problem was, he was morally unmoored, adrift in a sea of bad-gone-to-worse. Long and short of it? It all boiled down to a bad attitude. He played all sports but felt his skill alone should place him as the shining star. Thing was, his star wasn't really as bright as he thought it to be, but then again, I wasn't sure he ever correctly dusted it off.

Located between the theater and lunchroom, the media center was my second choice in the gossip mill. It had two stories, only accessible by the first floor. My goal was to get to the second floor, sit and soak it in, but I needed to ditch Jagger.

He trailed a fingertip down the back of my neck. I squirmed away shivering, not even acknowledging the way he made me feel. "What are you doing this weekend, babe?" he asked. While I debated an answer, he added, "Mmm, you smell good. New perfume?"

"Yeah, it's called shark repellant. You like?"

Jagger chuckled, not in the least bit offended. "So what will it be, babe? Movie? Dinner? Both?"

Against my better judgment, I actually stopped like a fool and looked at him. No one—and I repeat *no one*—had EVER asked me out on a date. He was nice enough looking, had available funds, and could probably show a girl a good time. Trouble was, would I actually make it home in one piece? His reputation preceded him. His and Ivy's relationship was punctuated with public meltdowns and physical throwdowns so violent, one or the both of them needed to be locked up for domestic violence. Who in their right mind would walk into *that*??

Jagger's eyes smoldered like black coals. "I think you're beautiful, funny, and incredibly smart. Everything I've ever dreamt of."

Insert nervous laughter. No doubt Jagger was the lying type. Problem was, with habitual lying, the lines between reality and fantasy become blurred. My guess was he couldn't find the truth if it came up and slugged him in the happies (Darcyspeak for testicles).

Stepping into the media center, I headed straight for the stairs as my iPhone shot out some water torture. While Jagger jabbered away, I thumbed it straight to voicemail. I knew it was Dylan—where Jagger was concerned, he had a satellite large enough to contact Pluto. Dylan hated the way Jagger treated girls, and the two were in a perpetual turf war because Jagger wanted everything that Dylan had...unfortunately, it was understood I was on the list of assets.

Made me think I was microchipped.

Shoving my phone in my pocket, I tried to get in the library mode. *Be quiet*, I told myself, or at least whisper at an acceptable decibel. The media specialist ran the place like one of those Church of Scientology silent births—demanding no noise whatsoever. Why the worry? I got kicked out last week for talking in the silent reading section.

Navigating to the top of the stairs, the media specialist poofed into existence like the phantom in your worst nightmares. As soon as we met eyes, she practically screamed, "Shhh!"

God help me, but I wanted to "Shhh!" her back. She wore black reading glasses perched on the bump of her nose, wearing a mint-green polyester shirt with matching bell-bottomed pants. The woman was lost in the land of hippie.

I zipped my lips shut and headed toward a cluster of tables in the back. Wall after wall of resource books were on display that the smart kids worshiped. It came as no surprise Jubilee was standing on a stepstool, removing a four-inch leather-bound volume from the top shelf. I smiled. Then I smiled bigger. If anyone knew anything about anything, it would be Jubilee. She was in the back of the line when God handed out common sense, but her mother wasn't.

Her mother was the president of the PTA. Hang around any school long enough, and a person figured out pretty quickly that the PTA knew *everything*.

I slid into a nearby table and turned around. Jagger was missing —practically swallowed up in a black hole. Then I heard sniveling to my right and realized he'd sat down next to Ivy who appeared to be whining and studying.

Shocking on the second count.

His shoulders were tensed with both his loafers pointed in my direction, as if Ivy was something he would take care of quickly so he could get to me.

I shook my head in disbelief. "Jubilee, did you hear about the guy in the dumpster yesterday?"

Jubilee pivoted around, steadying herself on the wooden shelf. God love her, but she had pencil marks on her forehead. "Hey, Darcy," she said smiling. I asked her again. No answer. I was going to have to spoon-feed her through the whole process.

"Did you—" I said more loudly.

Someone's throat cleared. A look over my shoulder showed Jagger devilishly grinning at me.

"Her?" I heard Ivy whine aghast. "Why? She's just so...*average!*" She grabbed his wrist and held on tight. Jagger glanced down at her red manicured nails like they were handcuffs. When he attempted to pull away, she made some sort of nuh-uh sound, digging them into his skin.

Jagger dumbly and rather jerkily grinned. "Darcy's my dream girl."

Um, huh?!

If he had hope of a redeeming quality, it just got slingshot to Hades. He not only flirted with girls, but he did it in front of his girlfriend—or ex-girlfriend—whatever she was. But that was Jagger-land...nothing but me, myself, and I.

Gritting my teeth, I said too loudly, "Stop!"

Ivy's eyes flashed, giving me the quick run-down as she tried to assess if I were a worthy adversary. I didn't mind a good fight. In fact, I wanted to be a big time wrestler when I was eight. Problem was, my idea of fighting involved pulling pants down and running like the wind. Ivy looked like she'd done gigs such as that before... quite successfully, I might add. When Jagger giggled, as God as my witness, she hauled off and smacked him in the cheek.

Shocking. Simply shocking.

"Stop what?" Justice asked, falling into the seat next to me, munching on some miniature chocolate chip cookies. She took one look at Jagger rubbing his jaw, got a load of Ivy's acid face, and chuckled. "Darcy, if you were a horse, she'd have plans to make you dog food."

Couldn't have said it better myself.

Jagger and Ivy's conversation escalated into a verbal brawl not even remotely private. She said something about "lowlife cheater, scum of the earth, with an unbelievably cheap choice in replacements." In other words, Darcy was beneath him. He called her a whiny, dirty word that rhymes with witch.

When Ivy's voice rocketed—naming off every single bad thing he'd ever done to her—Justice kneed me under the table, her brown eyes itching for a fight.

"Are you going to take that from her?" she asked.

Actually, I was. A glance down at my watch verified I had about twenty minutes before next period, and Jubilee—if she even had anything—hadn't technically joined the conversation yet. Anyway, what was I going to say? *Gee, let's be friends, Ivy?*

That was where I was supposed to crawl under a table and hide, but honestly, I wanted the whole charade over. The quicker I got answers, the quicker I could leave the room and convince my ego it didn't matter. I turned to Jubilee who rubbed her hand across her forehead again, smearing the pencil lead even further. She wore khaki shorts and a white, fitted T-shirt that had three rhinestone snaps misbuttoned at the top.

"My God, Jubilee," Justice said when Jubilee and her ten-pound book collapsed with a thunk next to us. "You really ought to look in a mirror sometimes."

Jubilee cocked her head to one side, not having a clue of Justice's fashion hint. "What did you need?" she asked, ignoring Justice.

"I was wondering if you heard anything about the guy found in the dumpster yesterday. Do you know what they did with him?"

Jubilee played with one of the white beads braided into her hair. "He went to the Valley Morgue. A tow truck came and took the dumpster away after hours. One of those crime scene investigative units from Valley Police wanted it to evaluate." I kicked myself for not thinking of that sooner. My guess was they removed the body and tried to leave everything else "as-is" while they searched for clues. How in the world was I going to arrange an incognito trip to the police department?

"Anything else?" I asked.

"AP Unger's extremely upset and got into a big argument with some guys yesterday at school," Jubilee added.

"Did it have anything to do with the Dumpster Dude?"

Jubilee frowned, confused, literally with that look that said, *Why are you calling him Dumpster Dude?* I thought that was pretty self-explanatory. "I don't know," she said, "but evidently, these guys were seen loitering around the area a little while before, and he made them come back inside the school."

I blurted out, "Was one of them Jinx King?"

She narrowed her eyes as I did my best to describe Jinx, adding that he was overall bad news, a little on the secretive side, and probably a future assassin.

When Jubilee didn't recognize the name or description, we talked about the fact the victim was Alfonso Juarez, a mob heavy for AVO. Justice caught up to the conversation with eyes as big as a flying saucer. "How in the world did I miss a dead body yesterday? I thought I was in-the-know."

Justice propped her eleven-and-one-halfs on the table, back to watching Jagger and Ivy. The atmosphere around them gripped with tension, those closest in proximity caught in a torrential downpour of profanity, tears, and threats that probably weren't idle.

"Do you think they'll live to see eighteen?" Justice muttered. "I mean, I've never had a boyfriend or anything, but that's not normal, is it?"

For the sake of argument, I looked at her and said, "No." That statement immediately gave me a feeling of disquiet, as though it were a foreshadowing of doom to come. Justice technically didn't want an answer, and suddenly, I wished I wouldn't have provided one.

With time running short, I went back to Jubilee. "Could you get the names of those students?" Once again, the light went on in her brain, and I knew she debated whether that was good, bad, ugly, or somewhere in between. If anything, Jubilee was a rule follower.

Reaching out slowly as not to spook her, I gently touched her on the forearm. "It's for a good cause, Jubilee." One that remained nameless at the moment, but a good cause nonetheless. "I promise I won't cause you any problems."

Jubilee hummed when she was nervous, and it grew louder and more nasally by the moment. Locust-swarm level. I couldn't dissect the tune, but it honest to God sounded like that 1970's tune "Convoy." *Ah, to walk around in that brain*, I thought. It would either make me the true genius people thought me to be or kill me from over-stimulation.

Jubilee mumbled, "I'm not trying to nebulize things, Darcy. I just—"

Justice rolled her eyes, interrupting. "Yes, you are...whatever this nebulizing thing is. You don't have to broadcast how smart you are every five freaking seconds, Jubilee. Who even knows or uses that word?" Justice and Jubilee acted more like sisters than cousins, but seriously, call me a kindred nerd because I knew the definition for nebulize meant to be vague.

Jubilee named Juan Salas. No surprise there. Juan was an eigh-teen-karat thug who'd been in trouble since grade school. A junior, he and I had Spanish 3 together, but it wasn't like we spoke a lot. The other was Fisher Stanton. Fisher surprised me...sort of. He was on Student Council, and if he was in trouble, it was probably for his mouth. He had an over-acute capacity to get on anyone's nerves. The last two were Oscar and Frank Small. Once again, no big surprise. Frank wasn't the sharpest tool in the shed (in fact, I called him a "frank up"), but Oscar had some brains. Just last week he placed a live chipmunk in the locker of an upperclassman and used M-80 firecrackers to rouse a construction worker using a porta-potty. I committed the names to memory but grabbed a black pen and inked their initials on the inside of my hand as backup.

Right then, Mrs. Lowe strode up the stairs making a beeline for Jagger and Ivy like her life depended on it (well, probably like *their* lives depended on it). She fumed, "Stop the nonsense, or you'll both be kicked out permanently." Lord have mercy, Jagger painted on a smile that was mass seduction mixed with sincere apology and an invitation for whatever services she wanted him to render. Mrs. Lowe frowned, clearly taken aback, but a blush slowly crept its way up her neck.

Brushing back a stray wisp of graying, bobbed hair, she headed for a closet in the back. When she was out of sight, a look at Jagger and Ivy showed them making peace—hugging, touching, consoling. The type rated PG-13.

Ugh. So unbelievably freaked up.

And that was why I didn't have a boyfriend. I didn't understand the game. Ivy and Jagger had just berated one another publicly with words and phrases that in my opinion were unconscionable and unforgivable. They were tangled together like two octopuses mating. Lots of lip action, chairs squeaking. It made me want to barf.

———————

I had some names, but did they have anything to do with Alfonso Juarez? Your guess was as good as mine. What I needed to do was find out who drove that goddawful, yellow Dodge Charger. He certainly came out of nowhere. Not to mention the guy that Jinx was talking to. Who was *he*? Was I out of my mind for even caring? And by the way, could I swear to it that Jinx was the one that made that creepy, threatening call?

We had English together, and not one bloody thing happened in class. He sat ramrod straight, taking notes like a good little boy, even raising his hand to answer a question no one else touched with a ten foot pole. That in itself was so odd I came to the conclusion he was trying too hard to blend in.

It was sixth period, drawing and painting, one of my elective courses. I liked drawing—cartoons mostly—and if there was ever a class to skip, it wouldn't be the one I'd choose. Still, I needed to find out the specifics with the crime scene, and there was only one way to do that.

Leave campus.

I'd never skipped class. Sure, I'd skipped in my mind, but a part of me was afraid I was taking a step into Loserville and wouldn't find my way back out.

Shelving the thought, I hustled to my locker, carefully placed my art supplies in the bottom, and grabbed my anatomy book since there was a quiz scheduled. Before I took another breath, I stopped mid-motion and promised myself I'd study. I said it out loud three times like a brainiac's mantra. After I shoved the book in my backpack, I checked my iPhone for messages and email, sent Dylan a text that said, *I miss you, stud,* and deleted some spam. Lastly, I sent a text to my nanny, Claudia, telling her I was going to a study group with friends, and I'd be home by five o'clock. I had it all planned out.

So next? I didn't know what was next, so I just started walking.

Was I going to call a cab? Hitchhike? Crawl? Blink my way to the police department? The Valley Police Department was about twenty minutes away going west. Twenty minutes wasn't far at all, but when you didn't have a car, it was like going to the moon. My immediate plan, I guess, was to walk outside and hail down someone in a car.

And beg.

Yeah, that sounded good.

With my backpack and purse hanging from my right shoulder— and some hutzpah that bordered ridiculous—I took my right hand and zipped my jacket to my chin. My head was down, trying to appear deep in thought, but about ten feet from the front door, I bumped into (gasp!) Liam Woods. Okay, maybe bumped was a mild word. It was more like tackled. He dropped a stack of books five-high, and they scattered all over the floor with a whomping crunch.

Score one for me...

Without even looking at him, I dropped my head even lower and stammered out an embarrassed, "Ss-sorry."

Liam didn't say anything, only chuckled. I was momentarily sidetracked by his unique scent: there was no single word for it other than *muskymalemouthfulofdeliciousness.* Ignoring the desire to throw him down and roll all over him, I stooped down to pluck up his books. In the process, my own purse crashed to the floor, the contents spilling outward in a three-foot arc. I blushed like my skin was doused with battery acid. While I clearly looked like an idiot, his warm hand touched mine, silently beseeching me to calm down. One by one, he put my things back in my purse, but somewhere our eyes locked. He gave me a smoldering stare. I studied him—tall, dark, and breathtakingly dressed in stonewashed shorts and a blue and orange striped polo shirt. My brain told me to say something profound—try to impress his inner-female lover—but all I could do was nibble my lower lip and blink, "Whoa."

He threw his head back with a wolfish laugh.

That guy knew he was nothing short of tantalizing and just might have been making fun of me. I gave him half a smile, shoving his books in his arms. I thought, *This is stupid*. Down deep, I was still reeling from the conversation with Ivy and a case of the I'm-so-uglies. I didn't have a chance in heck with him, but the besotted girl in me was somehow still wishing.

"Are you okay?" he asked genuinely. For the life of me, I couldn't string a sentence together. I gathered what was left of my wounded pride and scrambled off like a spooked little mouse, tripping over my feet the whole way. "Wait!" he yelled.

I didn't.

I pushed the door wide, ran down the steps with my eyes closed, and all of a sudden felt like I'd kissed a MACK truck. I tripped backward, landing right on my arse, shaking off what could be a concussion. When my vision cleared, Vinnie materialized out of the blur. We'd sacked one another like two offensive linemen—his belly bouncing, what little chest I had deflated and concave. He wobbled, tipped back on one foot, fell down on the sidewalk, and shook the entire school. I think we were alive, but I fingered the pulse on my neck to be sure.

The cross dangling from Vinnie's neck weaved back and forth in the breeze. Once again, Vinnie was dressed in navy sweatshirt material, wearing too much bling. Honest to God, his gold crucifix was four inches long and had to weigh close to a pound. Maybe he felt like he needed a lot of Jesus.

No argument from me there.

"Are you okay, Dolce?" he said, exasperated.

My voice was as limp as the rest of my body. "I dunno."

I feared a permanent eye twitch settled in my left eye. It was nothing short of a miracle that Vinnie and I both somehow stood. "Where are you going?" he asked.

"Deep sea fishing," I muttered.

"Deep sea fishing," he repeated.

Another eye twitch. "Yeah, the thing I'm looking for is far off campus. Are you in or not?"

Vinnie gave me that look like his invitation got lost in the mail. He cocked his head to one side. "Are you going anyway?" he asked.

Probably not, but I knew I needed to answer yes if Vinnie was going to provide the wheels. Vinnie gazed hard into my eyes and even harder back toward the school and the academic rules I was pretty sure he didn't care about. He put his fingers on the handle of his Bug that was parked illegally up on the sidewalk, and squeaked the door open. Even though I told them not to, my legs reluctantly slid into the tattered, brown leather seat.

Chapter Seven

THE ELEVENTH COMMANDMENT

This was a mistake of meteoric proportions, but no one wanted to sin alone if they could help it.

We pulled into Skyline Chili for five cheese coneys—tiny chili-covered hot dogs that were heaven on a bun. We demolished them before we were even out of their parking lot and were headed toward the office of "Valley's Finest."

I was sitting on the edge of my seat, wondering if I was knee-deep in sin or all the way up to my eyeballs. It wasn't until Vinnie said, "What's wrong?" that I realized I'd been counting road signs out loud, my OCD undeniably in the driver's seat.

Vinnie deserved an explanation why I told him to drive west. I opened and closed my mouth three times, thinking I was talking, when I realized not a darn thing made it out of my mouth.

"Dolce," he said gruffly. "I don't even know where we're going."

One breath in, one breath out, and then I sighed. "We're going to the Valley Police Department. I've got to get my hands on that dumpster if I want to figure out who did what to Alfonso Juarez."

This behavior was all kinds of crazy. Speaking the address into the navigation system on my iPhone, I waited for Vinnie to pull the plug, whip into a disgusted U-turn, or open the door and boot me out. He just kept driving. His Bug coughed a few more miles, and before I knew it, we were idling in front of our destination. Trouble was, parking was like finding a needle in a haystack. Vinnie went down an alley and found a space. Unfortunately, he clipped the side of a black Camry as he attempted to parallel park, then backed up, and bumped a white Honda Civic. Cursing, he tried the whole thing again and lost three eyelashes off his right headlight. Heaven help us, we'd committed three hit and runs, and he'd blinded his Bug.

Circling the building two more times, he finally decided to park a block away.

Switching off the ignition, he scooted his body around with one arched eyebrow. "Now what?"

I spun to face him, crossing my arms over my chest. "Are you going to snitch to Dylan, or will this remain on the down-low?"

Vinnie played with the hair on his lamb chop sideburn, twisting as he replied, "I promised, Dolce."

Just what you needed—a reformed delinquent with a sense of morals. Somehow, I had to switch Vinnie's loyalty before Dylan's two-week stint in paradise was over. Vinnie proved to me he was up for a good adventure, and well, I needed someone like that on the payroll.

"Okay," I said. "Just do as Darcy says. That's like the eleventh commandment or something."

Vinnie frowned, confused. I didn't know if I should tell him it was a joke or just let it slide.

We pushed our way out of the Bug, not having a clue what came next. By the time we got to the entrance, Vinnie huffed and puffed with beads of perspiration clinging to his whiskers. Once he wiped his forehead on the back of his sleeve, he opened the door to the smell of stale coffee and microwaved lunches.

Funny thing was, we smelled that behind a bulletproof glass. The Department of Homeland Security made it mandatory a few years back that all offices were to be locked with visitors speaking to a receptionist through a bullet-resistant glass. I understood the safety concept, but by the looks of the crowd, it sounded sort of stupid. All that did was put an overabundance of crazy people in the same waiting area together.

There were two walk-up windows. One where visitors wrote their names down at the reception, and the other, I surmised, where they spoke to an officer directly. I wasn't sure if the receptionist referred visitors to that window or if that was special circumstances only. All I knew was if I didn't get what I wanted from the receptionist, the gig was over before it started.

The entire back wall was made up of safety glass, so I could see what was going on behind it even though I couldn't always make out the words. To the right of the receptionist was a door. It appeared visitors were buzzed inside once whomever the person was meeting was ready. The walls were white and the ceiling high, the room decorated with metal desks, multi-lined telephones, and silver filing cabinets along the back wall. Commendations were hung from the wall along with a large photograph of the police chief.

From what I could see behind the glass, it was fast paced. Blue uniforms were doing the cop thing while one police officer mingled amidst the dozen or so visitors in the waiting area with us. A family of four was at the window with the officer filing what sounded like a missing persons report.

We marched up to the receptionist like we were supposed to be there.

Gutsy move, stupid move—but what other choice was there?

My stomach started churning. The name badge on the receptionist's uniform said "Dixie." Dixie looked like a Dixie—southern, big flaxen hair with an inch's worth of dark roots showing down her center part. Dixie had a round face, big blue eyes painted even bluer with shadow, and a full-figure. Vinnie took one look at her Double-Ds and his jaw dropped wide. Then he started Vinnie-izing. Elbowing me out of the way, he placed one large, beefy palm on the countertop, practically molding his body against the glass.

Dixie unloaded a totally blank smile.

"Well, *hell-OOO*, beautiful," he said with a grin. Then he stopped himself, placing his meaty hand over his heart as if he apologized for overstepping his bounds. "May I *call* you *beautiful?*"

I think I threw up in my mouth.

Dixie appeared to be pulling double-duty, and by the way she smacked around her telephone, I got the feeling receptionist wasn't in her job description. After she said some words into the walkie-talkie strapped to her shoulder, she pushed a button and transferred a call.

Finally, she looked at Vinnie, half-blinking, half-smiling. "Sure," she said. "What can I do for you, uh—"

"Valentine. Valentine Juarez and this is my cousin," he said without even a flinch, "Jester."

Huh...

You know how they say the heavens will speak if you take the time to listen? I just heard a choir of heavenly angels sing a chorus. I hadn't thought a lot of things through about the caper (okay, I hadn't thought *anything* through), but the first place to start would obviously have been with a name that wasn't truly mine. Jester was as good enough as any, I suppose, and Dixie didn't seem to dispute or inquire of its origins. I had to laugh though. Vinnie was the stereotypical Italian. I was an Anglo-Saxon mixed breed just this side of freak. No way in the world could we legitimately pass for full-blooded Mexican with a last name of Juarez.

Vinnie was moments from asking for her telephone number. I could tell by the way he'd locked onto her Double-Ds. Jumping in front of him, I painted on a face of deep pain and remorse. "Hi, Dixie. We're family of Alfonso Juarez."

Dixie spaced out like those trauma victims do when they've experienced something their minds can't deal with. "Oh," she said in a small voice, covering her mouth with her hand. "I'm so sorry for your loss."

Not as sorry as I would be if I got caught.

The switchboard lit up again as Dixie answered a few and transferred callers. While she yes'd and no'd, I stole a look at a group of three complaining about their missing relative. "She's a good person," they said. "She'd never run away," and "It isn't her fault she wrote those bad checks." Blah, blah, blah, and blinded-by-love blah. The officer patiently bobbed his head up and down, writing notes in a missing person report, while looking intently at a photograph that had been produced.

About a minute later, Dixie cradled her phone and looked at us again with a blanked-out expression. "May I help you?"

Even Vinnie found that odd. He cocked his head to one side, calling her beautiful again, thinking if compliments worked once, they'd work again. Like before, she gave him another robotic, empty smile. My guess was she was overworked and underpaid.

The knot in my stomach reminded me I should be home, so I

blurted out, "We're here to see the dumpster my brother," I said, sort of coughed, "was found in. Can you take me to it?"

I cringed. Who in their right mind would ask to see a dumpster?

Dixie halfway nodded. Then the switchboard went Christmas tree again. Suddenly, the voices behind the bulletproof glass were broadcast over the speaker system in the waiting area. Dixie, I could only assume, accidentally hit an intercom button. When she turned to speak to the uniforms standing behind her, I ducked my head, digging around in my purse. I couldn't look anyone in the face, fearing they could X-ray my intentions.

"Billingsley is bringing in Kinsley," she said. "Usual charge, OVI."

There was a, "What else is new?" from the crowd.

She clicked another line. "H.R. Ratner is on line two." Peeking up, I saw one of the male uniforms go for a phone. "He wants to put a restraining order out on his wife for domestic violence," she added.

The uniform chuckled. "What'd she do?" he said.

"She stun gunned him when she found naked pictures of his girl-friend on his phone."

"That'll do it," Vinnie whispered.

When the uniform 86'd the call, he looked at the three others near him—two males, one female. "Boe, see what's up with the Ratners. Ginger, take Harlan and look for the Small brothers. Vance Unger called earlier and said they were truant again today."

Vinnie and I simultaneously moved our heads—him up, me down—trying to act nonchalant in the process. It was Oscar and Frank...had to be. That might mean something. What, I had no idea, but it was a piece of information I filed away for future use.

"The pickers?" the female uniform asked.

"Yes," he answered her. "My guess is they had a big night and are sifting through the booty." Garbage pickup on my street was on Mondays. It was reasonable to believe Oscar and Frank visited other streets on different nights.

Before the officers went out a back entrance, the one who appeared to be the highest ranking pitched Dixie a set of keys, his expression serious. "For your hands only, Dixie. I'm going to catalogue when I get back, but right now I have to take one of the calls since we're shorthanded."

Evidence Room keys??

After two more calls, I felt like I spun my wheels in the snow. When Dixie recradled the receiver, I said, "Can you—"

All at once, it sounded like a killer bee attack was underway amidst the group of people filing the missing person report. Two of the men had their hands around one another's throats, squeezing and rolling around on the tile. The officer nearest hurriedly went for his cuffs, while the one behind the glass buzzed himself out with a stun gun already drawn. I quickly deduced the man doing most of the squeezing was stuck with the late fees on the bounced checks— the husband.

It was like a car crash. I felt like I shouldn't watch, but my morbid sense of curiosity couldn't help itself. Blood poured out of one of their mouths, a handful of black hair was nearby on the floor, and somehow the cop with the cuffs had been knocked unconscious.

The visitors left standing tried to assist the other officer, but next thing I knew, two men arguing over whose-dog-pooped-where went UFC with the biggest throwing the other through the front plate glass window.

When pepper spray hit the atmosphere, Dixie jumped up from her desk like she alone was the EMT on duty.

In the process, she forgot altogether that Vinnie and I even existed.

And even better, the door she came out of was left ajar just begging to be entered. Call me the Queen of Rationalization, but I decided to take that as opportunity knocking.

While all hell was breaking loose, I dragged Vinnie inside. The ring of keys was by the telephone. I snatched it up and hurriedly continued down the narrow corridor along the right side of the building. There was an empty office to our left, a closed door to our right, and up in front at about ten feet was a room clearly marked "Evidence." An Evidence Room was where things were stored and catalogued per each specific crime. When a detective needed something, it had to be checked out with a signature.

All I could think was jackpot. It didn't get any better than that.

Except I heard a rustling in the closed office...

A look back at the nameplate on the door said "Chief of Police" in big, gold letters. My word, was he inside? I breathed deeply and began to sweat. Chief Robert T. Lynch was the last person I'd ever want to meet—well, considering which side of the law I was operating on. He played no games and was cunning and ruthless in his hunting down of hardened criminals. He even made national news for sending "Pay in Sixty Days" invoices to the Mexican government and other countries for the illegal US citizens or criminal aliens he was housing in the Valley Jail. It was a bill to cover the costs related to seizing their drugs and the man-hours used in those investigations.

Putting my ear to the door, I heard nothing. *Maybe it was the wind,* I told myself because a part of me knew instinctively he wasn't in the building. Otherwise, he would've sniffed me out and had me hogtied and shoved in the nearest cell. I pushed that thought aside along with the urge to cut and run. My actions were one of those gray areas. I didn't mind breaking rules if it was for a good cause, and if I didn't seize the moment, whatever opportunity I had would be dead in the water.

Vinnie touched me on the shoulder, looking as though he was about to barf. Thing was, so was I. He'd either passed gas or his intestines perforated and were leaking through his skin. "Things like this give me hives, Dolce. I'll just stand watch." I gave him the A-Okay to do whatever he wanted.

Leaving Vinnie behind, I padded forward a few steps and jiggled the doorknob. There were two keys. Choosing the silver one, I swallowed the lump in my throat when it slid in with no resistance. Jeez, Louise, it was like I'd stepped into one of those revolving doors. It was a duplicate scenario of the reception area up front—thankfully, with no one manning the station. Behind it was another door I could only assume was the actual Evidence Room.

Stepping around the desk, I slid the other key into the doorknob and slowly pushed the door wide. That specific area was thirty-by-thirty and utilitarian. Rectangular tables lined the walls, and shelf after shelf of numbered cardboard boxes sat atop them. Dangling from the ceiling was a light bright enough to light up New York City. Sure enough, in the middle of the room was the dumpster. It had been brought in through a back entrance that resembled a garage door.

When I got a load of the smell, I nearly fainted. It was atrocious. I seriously considered placing my head between my knees but was afraid gravity would keep pulling me down. Wasting no time, I eased up to it and saw that it had been cleared. Out to its left side were its contents, numbered and tagged with the name of the establishment they'd come from.

Cardboard boxes were labeled to private individuals, a bucket of brown ooze and rice boxes said El Rancho Grande, about twenty magazines were from Amity Health Care, yogurt cups and Jett's pizza boxes were marked accordingly, and a vinegar jug was tagged as "unidentifiable." Then there was a dead rat carcass, a set of car keys, a shirt that looked too small for the victim, a gaudy gold man's ring, a scrap of red fabric, and newspapers. Nothing seemed like incriminating information. So what could I extrapolate?

Nada.

I pulled my iPhone out and snapped a few pictures of the contents anyway, turned, and bumped the leg on one of the rectangle tables. On it was someone's lunch—half a turkey sandwich on wheat and a cup of steaming, chicken noodle soup from Panera. *Steaming*, I thought. That meant someone was on the way back soon.

No sooner was that thought formed in my delinquent brain when the garage door rose, and I stared into the face of someone who looked like he'd slept in his clothes. His black hair was messy and damp, sticking to his forehead. His wire-rimmed glasses were angled to the right, housing brown eyes that looked half asleep. His white polo was untucked with a coffee stain over his heart, and his jeans (well, I think they were jeans) were so faded that the right knee was almost white.

"Why are you in here?" Crooked Glasses barked suspiciously.

Oh the crappery I stepped into. Momentarily, I was shell-shocked, and when I parted my lips to speak, all that came out was a nervous cackle. It was one of those times conventional wisdom told me to fess up. Self-preservation, however, told me to stall.

When I stood there like an idiot, Crooked Glasses frowned, casually walking forward and placing his car keys by the soup. He slowly picked up his sandwich and carefully took a bite off one corner—like he dissected that portion—pondering whom I was (I assume) and what he was going to do about it.

That was it.

The end. Finis. Coda. Kaput.

As the color drained from my face, he finally pushed, "I'm going to need a name..." Then he narrowed his eyes, adding, "...and a reason."

I wasn't sure what protocol was in the situation. If I lied and they searched for identification, I wasn't sure what would happen if they discovered I was Darcy Walker, especially when Dixie thought I was Jester Juarez. I could say I was looking for my aunt, I guess. She was the Assistant Hamilton County Prosecutor of nearby Hamilton County (technically "former" prosecutor, but I hoped they hadn't kept up with her recent resignation). I sometimes dropped her name when I was in deep trouble. Sure, she'd have my back—well, I think she would—but there'd be heck to pay afterward.

I chose a standard line, shrugging like a dumb blonde. "I got lost on my way to the restroom." Jeez, how cheesy—especially since there was one in the waiting room. "Big case, huh?" I said, motioning to the dumpster.

His eyes burned like a laser beam on high heat. "What's your name?"

More teeth, Walker. More teeth, more teeth, more teeth.

My best bet would be to redirect his thinking. Glancing down at his hand, I noticed he wore a gold wedding band. A quick look back to his sandwich showed him in a photograph with a smiling Black son and daughter, but it was the son that nearly floored me. It looked like Jinx King. Short of picking up the photograph to know for sure, I all but passed out on the spot. Jinx was related to the case every which way I turned, and more and more, someone would have to convince me otherwise it wasn't him who called me the other night. I mean, who else even had motive? And if Crooked Glasses was his father, did he drop my name at dinner as the one that discovered the body? Would his father even have information like that?

Crooked Glasses had no sort of identification on his person, and truth of the matter, he'd probably lost it if it was considered a small detail in his day. The only way to discern for sure if he was related to Jinx was to point-blank ask him.

Extending my hand, I smiled. "Nice to meet you," I said, still not giving my name.

He shook my hand, a little harder than necessary and muttered, "King. I'm Harold King." Then he started talking to himself, running a hand through his hair, reminding himself of everything on his to-do list.

How easy that was, I thought in wonder.

And interesting...Jinx King's father??

But Harold wasn't as absentminded professor as I thought he was. Right when I decided to cut my losses and back out of the room, he snarled again, "I'm going to need your name."

It was like someone cut my tongue out.

Right then, the door blasted wide as though it had been hit with two tons' worth of explosives. Vinnie. Vinnie talking on a walkie-talkie, all business. Here was the thing about Vinnie. He might have the pre-game jitters, so to say, but was nothing but money when it counted. Somewhere along the way he'd acquired a cap that said "Guido," a tool belt dangling from his waist, a navy shirt unbuttoned acting as a jacket over his T-shirt, and a clipboard stuffed with papers. He looked like maintenance of some kind. Walking forward, he clicked off his walkie-talkie and gave Mr. King a business card.

"Guido. Guido Galucci." Vinnie didn't even sound like himself. His voice was flatter—more neutral. Before it was deep with a hint of flirtation. At that moment, it was just one-of-the-boys who sucked on a cigarette out back. Vinnie started scribbling things on his clipboard, ripping out a pink sheet of paper that was a customer copy. Mr. King scratched his head, looking back at the dumpster. While his back was turned, Vinnie gave me a tsk-tsk smirk that was nothing short of a you-owe-me.

I decided to smack him later.

Mr. King swiveled back around, throwing the card onto his desk. "I know who you are, Guido," he said on an exhale. "I haven't seen you around in a while. How's it going?"

Say what?? Cue *The Twilight Zone*, but I just went with the flow.

"The wife and kids are keeping me busy," Vinnie explained.

"Don't I know it," Mr. King said mostly to himself. "What can I do for you?"

"I'm here for my dumpster."

Mr. King lost the good humor, taking a big bite out of his sandwich. "Listen, Guido. I'm working seventy-hour weeks trying to keep my marriage alive and my son on the straight and narrow. Cut a man a break here. That dumpster's the property of Valley Township until we say otherwise."

How was Vinnie going to answer that? I knew that to be true. And furthermore, could Vinnie pull the whole thing off?

Vinnie played with his sideburns, acting as if he and Mr. King were both caught between a rock and a hard place. "Let me tell you what I'm going to do for *you*," Vinnie told him. "I'll be back in a week to see how things are progressing. What's the big hold up anyway?"

First off, Mr. King only had the dumpster for twenty-four hours. Secondly, he wasn't firing on all cylinders because I was able to successfully dodge a trip behind bars. So what made Vinnie think he'd talk? *Surprisingly*, I mused to myself, *Mr. King did*.

"There are fingerprints everywhere, Guido," he said frustrated, "and bloody fingerprints on the body according to the coroner. Whoever did this wasn't the most skilled of individuals. Unless they were trying to frame someone."

Some of those fingerprints were mine, and the police might've already identified as much. The only thing I had going for me was that my mug shot wasn't going to pop up on some government program with convictions. No way in the world would Mr. King ever be able to put Darcy Walker fingerprints with a Darcy Walker face (I hoped).

Vinnie rearranged his ballcap. "Mob hit?"

Mr. King slid into his seat and slurped some soup. "Maybe, but if it was a hitter, he's a dumb one. We're running the prints through the database but haven't had any hits yet."

"People," Vinnie said exasperated. "What's the world coming to?"

Mr. King pitched a finger over to a pile of copper on a large skid. "Third incident this week. People are stealing copper from under-construction homes and selling it on the black market. Copper's the new gold, son."

"How did you get that pile?" I asked, remembering someone stole the copper out of the air-conditioning unit at school.

Mr. King didn't like me. He went back to making eye contact with Vinnie (or Guido) but still answered my question. "It fell off the back of someone's pickup truck on I-75 in the middle of the night," he said. "Took out the tires of a semi that thankfully didn't wreck. All the driver got was half a license plate and couldn't tell if the car was black, navy, brown, or dark green."

He paused to roll his eyes.

When Guido and Harold King waxed on about the bad things in society, I took that as a perfect opportunity to excuse myself. The day was successful. I found out there were prints all over Alfonso Juarez's body, maybe mob-related, and that Harold King was Jinx's father. He also acknowledged that he had to keep his son on the straight and narrow, which was practically admitting your child had personal problems. I should know. That was said about me all the time.

Slipping out through the garage door, my sense of altruism demanded I glance over to the entrance. The beginnings of guilt were taking root since I hadn't done anything personally to stop the ruckus in the visitor's waiting area. An ambulance was loading the UFC wannabe onto a stretcher—he was moving, breathing, and cursing. I guessed that meant he was normal.

When I made it to the Bug, I slipped inside with a big, fat smile on my face. Why oh why did I enjoy getting the best of people? Hopefully, that didn't mean I was soulless, but by God, sometimes it was almost too easy to pass up.

When Vinnie crashed into the front seat, he was still wearing his Guido gear. "Who's Guido?" I said laughing.

Vinnie lifted a smirking brow. "One of the major players in Vinnietown," he answered.

He then gave me a look like, *I don't ask about your skeletons, you don't ask about mine.* Fair enough. I didn't have room to judge what went down in Vinnietown. What I'd just done made sense within the Laws of Darcy. All I knew was Vinnie could be more screwed up than me.

Chapter Eight
A FLY IN THE OINTMENT

Claudia Gonzalez was my nanny. About five foot two with inky black hair and a more than hourglass figure, she was one hundred percent Puerto Rican and a devout Catholic: Mass every morning, Holy Season Lent sacrifices, and hours of community service for the less than fortunate. Claudia was a good Catholic and did all of that to show gratitude for the supernatural Creator that saved her soul.

Claudia, however, felt God gifted her with supernatural powers of her own.

When she was thirteen years old, a tomato truck crashed in downtown Puerto Rico, and Claudia said she saw the Virgin Mary in the spray. She became a local hit, and people both young and old crossed the border and traveled to Cincinnati to get the lowdown on their lives. Sometimes Claudia got it right. Other times it appeared to be wrong...or *delayed*. Her newest mission was to provide me with an ample bosom. It was an epic FAIL, delayed in all capital letters. She and her sister concocted some Puerto Rican cream I applied to my chest by the light of the crescent moon. My cup-size hadn't increased, but I did have what I considered to be premenopausal hot flashes.

Schooled at *Sisters of the Immaculate Heart That Overran Diablo with the Wooden Spoon of St. Michael's Robe*—seriously, something got lost in translation—Claudia declared proudly that was where she honed her skills. Anyway, the long and short of it, she practiced what Murphy considered the Dark Arts. She could will away a cold with one of her jungle elixirs. She could cure the summertime flu with a mustard paste. Her next plan was to curse-away the wart on the bottom of my foot.

I assumed we'd ask for forgiveness later.

Earlier in the evening, she phoned her sister, and they came up with a plan that entailed buying a piece of pork fat from the butcher. The plan was to rub it on the wart by the light of the moon and then bury it under the stars with a flashlight.

Sounded logical, right?

Since Claudia lived down the street, as soon as the moon rose, she was knocking at the door. Dressed in a yellow and white flowered muumuu, she chanted Puerto Rican gibberish while I sat on a stool in the bathroom that separated Marjorie's room from mine. I rolled my Old Navy lavender PJs to my knee and put my right foot in her hand.

Next to me, Marjorie had her doctor's kit open, holding the pork fat ready to assist. While Claudia cleansed the area with iodine, Murphy strode in and sat down on my bed—as far away from the action as possible. Murphy was petrified of the spirit world. He swore he saw the devil rise from the ashes of a burning house and dance the hoedown with a demon during college.

My guess was it was just bad moonshine.

I knew in my gut he had something on his mind other than the quote-unquote healing service. His brows were knit together so tightly it almost looked painful. When Claudia began to rub the fat in a counter-clockwise pattern, the energy shifted in the air.

"Why did the assistant principal call me today?" Murphy said in a monotone voice.

I ground my teeth so much in the span of a few seconds I was sure I cracked my upper left molar.

Dressed in black flannel pajamas, Murphy was eating banana pudding. That could be good. That could be bad. He was a nervous eater and was blatantly blowing his diet. My gut instinct said the conversation had only one way to go—to heck in a handbag.

Picking a few imaginary hairs off my black tank top, I glanced up, giving him nothing but air and head. "Was he bored?" I asked.

Claudia stabbed me with the pork.

Murphy set his bowl on my nightstand, steam practically rolling out of his ears. "Good God, kid. Sometimes you just suck me dry." I briefly wondered where that statement originated—Murphy or AP Unger. "And don't think I haven't noticed your offenses have traveled up the gosh-danged totem pole," he finished.

Yeah, it was alarming to me too. Marjorie jumped on her high horse, pivoting toward him. She was partly dressed with pink underwear and a sweatshirt—I suppose it was a step in the right direction. "Don't swear, Daddy," she said with a frown.

Murphy ignored her. "Answer the question, Darcy, and let me remind you, you know the rules."

"Try your hardest, and tell the truth," Marjorie declared with a big smile.

I could promise you, he didn't want the truth. That would be hypertension and a year's supply worth of TUMS. When nothing came out, he fumed, "Let me jar your memory. AP Unger said, and I quote, he saw you 'fall into Valentine Vecchione's POS Bug during seventh period.'"

Ah, the POS Bug. Well, he definitely had his adjective right because Vinnie's ride was definitely a piece of shiz. AP Unger and Murphy had been in the same fraternity at the University of Kentucky—different years. So not only did they have secret handshakes and rituals, they spoke hillbilly. "Do you want to know what else he said?" he asked. Not really. I'd rather take a helicopter ride through the eye of a storm than deal with those in authority, but my choices were listen...or um, listen. "He said there's a fly in the ointment," Murphy said.

"A fly in the ointment," I repeated.

Murphy painted on a sarcastic smile. "Yes, kid, an inconvenience that detracts from the usefulness of something. Thing is, I don't know who's the fly—you, Valentine, or something else you're tangled up in."

"Vinnie is a friend of Dylan's, Murphy."

I wasn't above being a name-dropper. Murphy barely wrinkled his brow—not wanting to give away anything—but mark my words, Dylan would get a phone call or email for particulars on Vinnie's persona. Let's hope Dylan was in the lying mood or could creatively stretch the truth.

I brushed off more imaginary hairs. "What I did just sort of happened. Vinnie was merely the conduit."

Murphy mumbled to himself, "This too shall pass, this too shall pass." Murphy always threw around Bible verses when he was troubled, but he wasn't above throwing God under the bus and His hands off approach to some of Murphy's unanswered prayers either.

"Start talking," Murphy warned. I assumed he had addressed me, but honestly, it could've been an ultimatum to the Almighty.

After Claudia's final swirl, I stood up and unrolled my pants. Then I tugged a purple wool sock up to my ankle, trying to buy some time. *Tell the truth,* the little angel coaxed. *Lie, lie, lie,* the devil laughed. Finally, I decided on a mixture of the two.

I sighed out an explanation. "I didn't feel like going to class. That's the truth. I took a verbal beating from Ivy Morrison on how I was a charity case, and I didn't want to be there anymore. School sometimes isn't the sanctuary parents would like to believe as they work in their ivory towers."

Wow, sort of poetic, maybe even a little tragic.

Murphy breathed deeply, exhaling like an elephant sat on his chest. Murphy had a scar over his left eye that took out a third of his eyebrow. The cause of that injury remained nameless. All I knew was if anyone mentioned it, his stare ran icy cold. My guess was the other guy looked worse. He ran his finger over the scarred portion, then scratched his neck, and wished to heck, I was sure, that he wasn't a single father. Picking up his bowl, he ate a few more bites really slowly—so slowly, I think my hair might've grown a few millimeters in the process.

"Kid, you know you're grounded, right?"

Riiiiight...like that was doing any good. "Yes, Dad."

"Is this why you're rebelling?" he offered as an explanation. A few more moments of silence passed when he nearly floored me with his next statement. He looked me square in the eyes and said, "Then consider yourself *un*grounded."

Claudia gasped and even Marjorie stopped to scratch her head. That was where he should've tripled my punishment, but God bless him, he'd all but told me to continue on. If one were looking in the dictionary, that was the definition for "pile on the guilt." I wasn't sure if that was Murphy's angle or if he merely threw things at the wall hoping they'd stick. I wasn't even sure how I was supposed to reply. A "thanks" sounded trite and nothing at all sounded mockingly unappreciative.

Before I could make a decision, he muttered, "Regarding this thing with Ivy, you know you're beautiful, and in my book, she's just jealous."

Spoken like a biased father. "I hear you, Murphy, and I appreciate the sentiment."

Murphy grunted, giving his spoon one last lick and stood up. "Keep your nose clean, Darcy. I want to be able to defend you, but sometimes I get this feeling in my gut that I need to help convict you."

"The things I do are all rooted in the greater good."

"Whatever helps you sleep at night," he mumbled to himself. "And by the way, you're supposed to report to the counselor's office first thing. Wear your Sunday-best, and I'd advise you to not be late."

My conscience said I should do as my father said, but I feared that went against my genetic code. I couldn't help but look at Marjorie, hoping things would be different for her. Besides being a nudist, she was good—really good. I scooted away hoping my badness wasn't catching.

———

According to the eleven o'clock news, the murderer was off on round two of his dumpster fetish. Another body, this time female, was found one township over in West Chester. Thing was, it was discovered in the back of a garbage truck only seconds from the landfill. Initial reports indicated the method of death was the same, but when she'd been riding in a compacting unit, a lot of incidental damage could occur.

The news anchor said that particular garbage truck visited a dozen dumpsters, and sanitation experts—believe it or not there were people like that—deduced that by the placement of the corpse in the compactor, the body had to have been picked up at either sites four, five, or six.

Call it sucky reporting, but no one divulged what sites four, five, or six were.

It was Wednesday morning, and I woke to storms and lightning coming from the east. Most of our storms came from the west. When they came from the east, God only knew what the day would bring. I didn't consider myself a worrywart, but I did have a tendency to be superstitious.

And an insomniac...

As of midnight, I'd changed my toenail polish twice, ironed my skinny jeans, found my inner-ohm through ten minutes of yoga, and cleaned my empty fish tank.

At Christmas, I received a tank with a goldfish named George Washington. I thought caring for them would be easy. I didn't have to pet them. I didn't have to walk them. I just had to keep them alive. Evidently, that entailed some skills I didn't possess because I had an aquatic graveyard in my backyard.

Two weeks shy of four months, I'd gone from Washington to Franklin Pierce. That was fourteen presidents—one a week—Darcy Walker's bowl of death had somehow assassinated. When Jefferson died, Claudia hung a crucifix over my bed to help cleanse the room of bad juju. I hadn't given the theory a test drive, but it definitely didn't help with swarms of the insect kind.

Somewhere in the middle of the night, I got into a fight with a mosquito. There were three bites on my arm and one underneath my left eye, drooping it almost to my cheek. Things weren't going well in Darcyville, but trust me, I'd seen worse.

As I downed crispy bacon and scrambled eggs, I dialed Dylan. Six-thirty in Valley, twelve-thirty in Maui. He hadn't called, which was strange, and I wondered if Vinnie squealed and that was the freeze-out. After four rings and a trip to voicemail, I hung up and imagined that natives had taken him, he'd fallen into a volcano, or God forbid, Lailanni sunk her hooks into him, and he was helping her shave her legs.

Telling myself my fears were unwarranted, I threw back a double shot of espresso and skimmed over my anatomy notes. I think I knew it...*I think*. I fell asleep studying, and the only way I knew for sure was I inked a note on my hand that said, *Yes, idiot, you did study*.

Beside me, Murphy slid his arms into a khaki lightweight jacket, zipping it halfway. "Good luck on your test, kid."

I looked at Murphy...Murphy looked at me...and both of us smelled failure and sleepless nights. Okay, maybe that was an exaggeration. *I* smelled failure. He smelled another night of promising God he'd give him ninety percent of his earnings instead of the customary ten.

After a not so gentle reminder to visit the counselor—where I was to act contrite with the promise to stand up straight and obediently follow the rules—Murphy departed, and I closed up my book. I had a dessert of five tootsie rolls and filled my coffee mug to the brim, jogging outside to catch a ride with Grumpy. I shrugged mentally. I wasn't sure why he had been playing chauffeur, but I wasn't going to tank the good will.

Grumpy's navy pickup was just this shy of the junkyard. When I opened its rusty door, the radio was blasting a country song where the soloist screamed an anthem to hate women forever. Grumpy didn't say anything as I slid into my seat—just stared and looked as stone-faced as usual. Pulling out onto Tylersville Road, I told him what I did the day before. He was slack-jawed for a few beats and rolled his eyes, mumbling, "You're kidding."

"Nope," I said a little too proudly.

"And what do you hope to accomplish?"

I was riding that razor-thin line between stupid and dumb. I actually didn't know. Grumpy gave me a scoff that was overly loud, and all that made me do was dig my heels in deeper.

He looked a little more rough than normal. His curly hair hung in his eyes, wet from lack of an umbrella. His khaki shorts were splattered with mud. His white T-shirt was its usual gray, and his right eye appeared oddly swollen. He had a deep scar in his right eyebrow where he'd headbutted Finn. His eyebrow came out the loser. Looks like it might've been a loser again.

"What did you do?" I said, lightly laughing. "Make out with someone's fist?"

Grumpy let out a harsh sigh. I wasn't sure if he was angry or completely worn out. He finally grumbled, "Trudi Hatchett and I started a brief relationship last night. And when I say brief, I mean it lasted about two hours."

What that had to do with a semi-black eye was beyond me.

Grumpy was a failure in the relationship department. Over the years, I'd listened to bathroom conversations and even dropped notes in class to keep him informed of the goings-on of Clementine Miriam Rabinowitz, Trudi Hatchett, and sometimes even (gag) Ivy Morrison. Although I felt like none were his perfect love match, I tried to support my brothers even when things felt stupid.

He gripped the steering wheel tightly, and by the way the veins popped in his hands, I could tell whatever happened hurt all the way down to the visceral level. When I was someone's friend, his or her pain rippled down to me—that was just the way it was. I muttered an unenthusiastic, "Talk to me," and reached for his hand even though I knew that might not be a good idea.

Chapter Nine

WASTE NOT, WANT NOT.

Oh, that was a bad idea, all right. I couldn't get a word in edgewise. I could understand his angst. Apparently, Trudi told him she liked him, told him she didn't, called back with second thoughts, and ultimately gave him the "let's be friends" line that was the bane of every teenager that had a crush. It wasn't the first time she'd blindsided him. His ego took a hit on Christmas break too.

By the time we parked, I had a splitting headache. I needed a nerve pill and a mammoth dose of sugar. I hit the vending machines first thing, grabbed a Snickers bar, and collected my books for first period, heading straight for the counselor's office.

No stops, no detours, no nothings.

It was located on the first floor behind the main office. Right there in prime viewing to watch the people that had problems. *Whatever*, I told myself. Just get in, get out, and get it done. I waved to a few people as my two-dollar Target flip-flops puttered across the tile, pulling some Cherry Bomb lip balm out of my purse, trying to multitask. When I finished, I finger-combed my hair, trying to undo what the humidity had already destroyed.

About ten feet from the office, Vinnie muscled his way through the crowd and grabbed me by the elbow, yanking me to his side. Vinnie was Vinnie—duplicate outfit as the day before: cotton T and shorts, only in white. Frankly, his clothes defied the laws of physics because they were a size too small for his body. "What's going on between you and Bradshaw?" he barked acidly.

Somebody shoot me.

When he told Dylan he was looking out for me, he was *really* looking out for me. I sighed, getting the distinct feeling he wanted the explanation for himself more than for Dylan. Then I sighed more deeply, wondering why I was obliging. "Nothing. He's a brother. I don't date brothers. That's incest."

Lord have mercy, I was convinced there wasn't anything I wouldn't say.

Vinnie looked as if I was trying to explain the world's mysteries in a five-second sound bite. He didn't push for particulars. I didn't offer. No way in the world was I going to try and explain my brain to Vinnie when I barely understood it myself.

Almost to the office, I glanced outside and saw the big, white van for Saxon Brothers' Exterminators. It had a three-foot rat on the side along with a picture of a dead roach and other oversized critters. It was fondly called the ratmobile. The ratmobile needed to be driven to the crematorium for cars. Once someone washed it, all the paint was going to rub off.

Eddie Lopez, Justice's arch nemesis, had parked her over-six-feet-tall, probably two hundred-plus pound body at the passenger door talking to someone. They'd just finished kicking the tires and were conversing like they were on the job. Guess the school had a rat problem.

Vinnie glanced at my mosquito-bitten cheek, frowning. "Dolce, buy some Clearasil."

I didn't even dignify him with the story. The last thing on my mind was another piece of advice when I was pretty sure I was about to be ripped a new, um, conscience. Two steps into the clear, lo and behold, I heard that sound...that sound that made me wish I would've dressed a little nicer.

It was Liam Woods' voice, purring my name.

I didn't know what to do...keep walking or worship at his feet.

When the sadist in me turned, the first thing I thought was... Oh. My. Good. God. This was what Eve felt when Satan offered her the apple.

Between his V'd shoulders and long, muscular legs, Liam was put together like a rippled bodybuilder. In jeans and a blue polo, he sauntered toward me, his knockout teeth grinning one of those heart-stopping grins. The kind that made my mind hiccup and my body go limp. After my brain got with the program, I think I grinned back.

What could I say? He was cute.

Vinnie could ruin any moment. He territorially draped his arm over my shoulder, acting as though I were a cheese-dripping slice of pizza. "What's up, Woods?" he asked him.

Blatantly ignoring Vinnie, Liam's piercing browns held me captive when all at once he dipped his head and sniffed right underneath the curve of my chin.

I moaned...I hoped inaudibly.

"Wow, you smell great," he murmured.

What could only be interpreted as a growl left Vinnie's lips.

Liam wasn't a fool. He knew Vinnie's rotund shape was only dwarfed by how strong and mean he could be when crossed. He held up both hands in a back-off motion.

"Valentine," he murmured laughing. "I actually might be in love here, and if it's not love, it's the most intense infatuation I've ever experienced. Go out with me, Darcy, or are you already going out with Taylor?"

Honestly, if Dylan and I ever went out, there were possible apocalyptic implications. To answer the question, though, Murphy had never really nailed down a day when I was allowed to date. Was it the day I turned sixteen? Six weeks after? It frankly was a nonissue since no one had been beating down my door. Maybe I was boring, or maybe the small amount of hormones I'd discovered were reserved for certain people—ahem, Liam Woods—or maybe I was asexual or a late bloomer. Either way, I'd eventually venture into the dating scene, but then again, maybe not.

Still...

Somehow, I coaxed my tongue into answering. "I've never gone out." (Hint, hint.) "I'm not allowed."

Liam furrowed his brows. "Would you if you were allowed?"

Cough. Stare. Sniff. Wriggle uncomfortably. Stare some more. Try to be subtle. Give up and stare with my mouth wide open. In that moment, I thought of everything unholy. It was a shame the message my mind sent me—that he was a dangerous, intimidating specimen of a male who threatened my virginity and sense of decency—never made it to my lips. Liam was so good-looking I literally watched my hand reach up and touch his flawlessly sculpted chest, leisurely exploring its muscled planes, and then moving onto the strong curve of his jaw. In what only took one heartbeat, he snagged my hand in his and pulled it to his lips.

I had a fertile imagination, which went beyond ridiculous. Had I just *touched him*? Liam seemed to have read my mind. He grinned and said, "Yes, you did, if I need to clear that up for you."

I shivered with the knowledge.

I was an idiot, and right then, he knew it.

Vinnie laughed, and his belly jumped up and down. He pulled me tightly to his side, like we were really close—or worse, an item no one was talking about yet.

"Ah, Liam, you're a fool. Dolce's not interested in you."

"I think my hand just said otherwise," I mumbled to myself.

Liam gave him one of those we'll-see looks he was so famous for. You see, Liam was a fastard at the end of the day, and I hadn't run across one girl that had successfully unfastardized him.

Liam flirted, "We'll have lunch together. Sit with me?" Uh, come again? "Please?"

I honest to God whispered, "I'm not worthy."

Vinnie laughed...the punk.

Thankfully, Liam didn't hear me. He threw off a scent that smelled like first-time kiss, and surprisingly, I was a little more than willing. We stood there looking at one another until an unscheduled gasp fell from my lips. No, it wasn't mine...it was Vinnie's. Vinnie sucked in some air and started tapping his white sneaker on the tile. My guess was it would be up Liam's rear if things didn't change.

One would think I'd give Liam my undivided attention. In my opinion, he was the equivalent of Halley's comet—rare and gone in a moment—but Jinx King walked by, and my attention span was suddenly wrecked. Jinx talked to that guy he had been speaking to when I saw him at the dumpster. Both had hostile looks on their faces, like they were doing society a favor by even being at school. And both were sporting red bandanas hanging out of the left pocket of their beat-up jeans. New trend? No trend at all? Insert another guy. Brown hair, average looks, sort of sheepish looking and tiny. In fact, he had the physique of a toothpick.

I pitched my head in their direction. "Who's that guy with Jinx King?" I said to whoever would answer.

"The type that would leave a horse's head in your bed," Vinnie said with a snort, referring to mob games. "Justin Starsong."

"The guy following like a puppy dog is Adam Neeley," Liam added with a frown.

I glanced up at Liam as he said something else, but all I could see were lips moving. I knew Adam Neeley from somewhere. It escaped me at the moment, but I'd eventually ah-hah with the answer. While Liam said something like "I'll see you at lunch," I realized I was late for a date myself.

I peeled Vinnie's arm from my shoulder and double-timed it to the school office. Number one on the Mind-Scrub Squad, AP Unger, was on his way out as I was going in. I waved like we were long, lost friends. He lowered his eyes with a boom, looking at me like I had some deep-seated issues. It wasn't like that was an all-points bulletin, people. It pretty much was common knowledge.

"Love you too!" I yelled.

AP Unger mumbled to himself as he punched his arms into the sleeves of a navy blazer that had tan patches on its elbows. As I made it past the office receptionist, I realized Vinnie was once again right on my heels.

Dressed in a gray sheath dress, her hair pulled back in a smooth ponytail, Ms. Dempsey was seated at her desk, balancing her checkbook among a pile of unopened mail. She peeked up with a smile, motioning for me to sit in one of the black fabric chairs in front of her. Vinnie's breathing grew heavier, and I knew it wasn't from walking too fast. Vinnie was certifiably crushing on a woman ten-plus years older than him, and he legitimately thought he had a chance.

"Good morning, Laken," he murmured more deeply than normal.

She looked up with one eye and politely corrected, "Ms. Dempsey."

Vinnie ran his hand through his hair and looked at her with

sincerity. "You're absolutely right, but if you ever want me to call you Laken, you know where to find me."

My foot rose up and stomped his sneaker all on its own—I didn't even have to tell it to. Thing was, I knocked her desk, and the jelly doughnut balancing on its edge slow-mo'd in the air. I jumped up to catch it, and while one would think that'd be an easy enough task, unfortunately my body and brain didn't always work in tandem. My toe nipped Vinnie's shoe, and I swan-dived across him, landing hard on my knees and hard enough on my chin to produce a rug burn...ugh.

If that wasn't bad enough, when I finally got back up, I clipped Ms. Dempsey's hand causing her to drop the doughnut she'd caught earlier. It did a double back flip and landed with a splat. Vinnie snatched it up with a, "Whoopsies," quicker than a snapping turtle snagged a frog, loading it into his mouth like a shovel digging dirt. "Waste not, want not, I always say," he said, smacking his lips.

I giggled, throwing a hand over my loudmouthed laugh. Ms. Dempsey's face never changed. She closed her checkbook, pushing away from the desk. "Vinnie, why are you here?"

No one helped me up. As I dusted myself off and slid back into a seat, I turned with a sarcastic smile, not even once considering throwing him a lifeline. Vinnie plopped his hefty body into the seat next to me all serious. Crossing his hairy legs, he patted me on the knee. "Dolce's the shy type, and she's terrified of those in authority. I'm here to offer moral support."

I choked on my own spit, wondering if I was in danger of being dropped dead by Heaven. Such hypocrisy. That was the problem. I *wasn't* afraid.

Ms. Dempsey closed her eyes, sighing like she didn't have time to deal with the likes of Vinnie. When she batted them open, she said to me, "I heard about your little field trip yesterday."

Before I could talk myself out of it, I spat out, "Well, Vinnie shouldn't get all self-righteous because he was field-tripping it with me."

In retrospect, I probably should've sat there and not admitted to anything. Instead, I threw the fat boy under the bus with me.

Vinnie licked his fingertips and touched my hand softly. "See what I'm talking about, Laken? Dolce gets nervous when authority figures place demands on her."

I could tell she debated reprimanding him again for the Laken comment, but she let it go. "Staying in school is placing a demand on her?" she asked him while she looked at me.

"Sometimes," I mumbled.

Jeez, I just wanted things over. While Ms. Dempsey mentally flipped through the pages of her counseling book, the door to her office blasted wide with Oscar Small walking inside—no, it was more like running.

Oscar acted as if something was about to explode. His hand gripped his chest, and his eyes were golf-balled to twice their normal size—like the pressure inside his brain wasn't balancing with the air around him. Oscar, I'd lay money, didn't even see Vinnie and me. He just kept gripping his plaid shirt like it was the end of a rope that was fraying.

Ms. Dempsey's blue eyes widened with fright. She quickly stood up, steadying herself on her desk as she hurriedly told Vinnie and me she'd get with us later.

It was absolutely none of my business, but I whispered, "Oscar, are you okay?" His head moved toward my voice, but I might as well have been a vapor in the wind.

Growing more frantic, Ms. Dempsey again excused us, but when we stepped out into the hallway, neither Vinnie nor I were interested in leaving. Without saying a word, we both remembered Valley Police were looking for Oscar and Frank the day before. Could their visit be some sort of follow up?

When she closed her door, we snuck into the empty office next to hers and stuck our ears up to the wall, listening. The walls were as thin as ladies' lingerie. Ms. Dempsey, who bordered being the nicest person in the world, spat out harshly, "Oscar, you have to tell me what's going on! I can't help if you don't open up!"

Sometimes a whisper spoke louder than a platoon of loud-mouths. Oscar spoke so low I knew it was out-of-this-world bad.

After a few more minutes of unsuccessful eavesdropping, Ms. Dempsey finally screamed, "What?!" It was like she'd heard something that scared her to death or at least made her want to quit her job.

A little louder, Oscar took a trip down memory lane, telling her exactly what he did on Monday. He said he went out to his car between classes and saw a group of guys around the Amity Health Care dumpster. They acted guilty of something, which incited the curiosity in him. At first, he thought there must be something worth picking that he and Frank might've missed, but the guys ran scared when he ventured over. That's when he saw Alfonso Juarez in the same condition as I found him.

Ms. Dempsey went stone-cold. She wasn't saying a single word, or maybe she was praying. We heard Oscar stutter, "Y-*yyou* believe me, right?"

Oscar's voice said he was scared out of his ever-lovin' mind.

Once again, we got nothing but dead air. With Oscar, there was always more than met the eye. I wasn't sure he had a good home life, and he and Frank struck me as doomed to be eternally over-looked. No way in the world was he going to be overlooked going forward. Whether Ms. Dempsey believed him or not...*I did.*

Right then, Oscar said the words my gut had been waiting for. "M-Ms. Dempsey," he stammered, "I didn't know the other three, but one of them was Jinx..."

I was right, I whispered in my mind. For God's sake, I was right. I relaxed my head back on my shoulders, drawing in a deep breath of victory as I closed my eyes. But then Vinnie grabbed me by the arm, twisting it with an abnormal amount of force. "Dolce, some-body's coming. I feel it in my gut."

You know what? I did too. A window was to our rear, and when I looked outside, I saw two black Valley Police Department cars, and my heart fell all the way to my feet. *Oh, God, help Oscar*, was all I could think. I said it over and over until I heard a deep voice asking for Oscar Small.

Vinnie cracked the door open, and we saw two of the uniforms from the day before—one male and one female—knock on Ms. Dempsey's door as Principal Grim Ward, the man we knew ran the place but never saw, escorted them down the hallway toward us. Vinnie held his index finger up to his mouth *shooshing* me—he didn't need to tell me twice.

Principal Ward, dressed in a black suit and tie, knocked on Ms. Dempsey's door with a loud authority. He was a large man, head and shoulders above most, and his brown eyes were hard, like he wasn't going to enjoy what he was about to do, but he'd successfully pushed any residual emotion down. "Ms. Dempsey," he said formally, "do you have Oscar Small?"

There was a brief lull, but she finally answered, "Yes, sir, I do."

That's all it took for Valley's finest to blast open the door. It was like a television show—the male twisted the door open, while the female had her hand on her revolver ready to use whatever force necessary. "Oscar Small," the first one said, "you're under arrest for the murder of Alfonso Juarez."

I was dumbstruck.

The radio said Juarez was AVO. What kind of hypothetical beef would Oscar Small have with someone from AVO? All I knew was since he and Frank were absent the day before, it didn't look good in their defense.

Oscar immediately cried, "No! No! It wasn't me!"

Ms. Dempsey immediately dissolved into tears, telling Oscar everything would be all right, and for God's sake to keep his mouth shut. "What are your grounds for arrest?" she desperately asked.

Uniform number one (the male) said, "We have witnesses that place Oscar at the scene of the crime, and there's evidence of his bloody fingerprints all over the body and dumpster. You were absent from school yesterday, son. Is there anything you want to tell us?"

"Say nothing!" Ms. Dempsey begged.

Except Oscar repeated absolutely everything like a mocking bird. What he didn't know, though, was that in defending himself, he placed himself at the scene. The scene of a crime that he fled. The seasoned police officer was a pro at pulling things like that off —getting people to give up the goods before a lawyer stepped onto the scene. That way it was placed in an incident report and subsequently handed over to the prosecutor's office.

Oscar's eyes were like a wild animal as his hands were cuffed behind his back. "I didn't do it. I swear!" he said. "I was just in the wrong place at the wrong time. All I wanted to do was see if there was something in there worth picking!"

"Save it for the judge, kid," the female uniform said while cuffing him. "Three individuals said they saw you with a weapon."

I released a breath I didn't even know I was holding. Vinnie had a death grip on my hand, but I somehow wriggled away. Oscar hadn't been sufficiently Mirandized, and his blabbermouth was part of the problem. I heard the beginnings of his Miranda Rights.

But Oscar's mouth kept running...

"Just shut up!" I yelled to Oscar, shoving the door wide. Everyone gave me that where'd-you-come-from face, but I didn't care. I looked Oscar in the eyes and saw the panic—the paralyzing fear that his particular lifestyle was going to hang him—even though I knew in my gut he was innocent. Could Oscar weather the storm of scrutiny? Everything the policeman said about eyewitnesses punched holes in his argument about being in the wrong place at the wrong time. He'd just admitted publicly he saw the body and ran. Even if he *was* in the wrong place at the wrong time—which I believed—he didn't do the decent thing like contact the authorities.

My mind did the mental rewind where I ran into him before English class—when Ivy made fun of our hypothetical relationship. He was nervous and sketchy. Oscar was a lot of things, but he wasn't a murderer. And you know what? I didn't think he'd even know how to shoot someone if the instructions were tattooed to his hand. Plus, I think if he did it, he wouldn't be able to shut up about it. An example? Oscar ate dirt as a kid and got a case of worms. He wasn't embarrassed. He told the class all about it and brought a dead one to school in a glass jar. Hands down, he won Show-and-Tell that week, but what just happened trumped Show-and-Tell, and he acted as if he wanted to put a noose to his neck.

But who could've seen Oscar? Oscar was there before me, but so was Jinx King. Could it have *been* Jinx King? *No,* I thought. Jinx left class after I saw Oscar, but was he going back for a second trip? Whoever he was talking to on his cell phone was just as mixed up in things as he was. In fact, it sounded as if they were giving him instructions. In my heart, I knew Jinx was up to something. Trouble was, I had no concrete proof of what the something was.

I couldn't help it, but the tears fell as Oscar's shoulders dropped in defeat. I buried my head in my hands not even trying to mask the overwhelming display of grief racking my body. Was Oscar going to get a good public defender? It would be a toss up. Many were brilliant with spotless conviction records. Still a few were half-wits who couldn't hack it in the larger firms.

As Oscar practically tripped out the door, a group of people large enough to crack the fire code had gathered in the hallway, looking inside the office's glass enclosure that provided no privacy whatsoever. Some students had their hands over their mouths. Others were crying. My eyes fell into the middle of the crowd to a wide-eyed Eddie Lopez and hard-as-nails Jinx King. While Eddie pulled her hoodie down over her face and looked away, Jinx's face was hard, in a disturbing display of a lack of compassion. The scar running down his cheek made my mind work overtime, wondering how he'd gotten it. I looked him square in the eyes and mouthed, "I'm coming after you."

Jinx narrowed his brown eyes, shifting his weight from foot to foot, reminding me of a boxer in the corner anxious for the bell to ring. A few heartbeats went by where we told one another our intentions—mine to take him down, his to give me a dirt nap. If we weren't enemies before, I guess we became enemies then.

I slid down the wall, my hands shaking so bad I sat on them.

Hamlet: Why then 'tis none to you; for there is nothing either good or bad, but thinking makes it so. To me it is a prison.

—Hamlet Act II, scene 2

Chapter Ten

HUMBLE PIE

Humble Pie: the fee you pay to your ego. Here's a helping, whose good or evil but human pride: it is so far from aught that is of a person.

—*Unknown, Just Desserts*

*J*ust when you think you can't eat another piece of humble pie, the universe will serve you up another slice.

I got a C on my test, a pimple on my chin, and was listening to Ivy berate, degrade, and stomp all over what pride I had left.

She said, "I'm sorry, Darcy, does Oscar's arrest break up any long-term plans of yours I hear prison relationships are hard to maintain but that's what happens when you date guys that are questionable you should know that didn't your dad tell you?"

"Run-on sentence," I mumbled. Unfortunately, she never heard me.

"I just care," she continued, "and want the best for someone who's not had the privileges that I was born with that's what good people do and I'm striving to be a better person."

What the…?

I hoped I was around when Ivy hit rock bottom. I really did. I should have been mortified, but a part of me was so used to her barbs they'd begun to roll right off my back. I didn't know if that was good for my self-esteem or not.

It was Thursday, and I waited at my locker for Vinnie. So far, I'd successfully hidden our relationship from Murphy—who still assumed I rode home in the muck of Bus 150. I was pushing my luck, but that was the least of my worries.

Placing my textbook on the top shelf, I alphabetized and realigned its spine while devising ways to run into Liam Woods. I realized at bedtime I'd told him I'd meet him for lunch. The first sort-of date I'd ever had, and I'd stood someone up. Can we say, *Relationship missile?* I heard through the grapevine he had been looking for me everywhere. Right then, however, he was MIA every place I turned.

Why the blow-off? At lunchtime, I parked myself in Ms. Dempsey's office as she called Valley Police about Oscar (I'm not sure why she allowed me to eavesdrop, but I didn't ask). When she got nowhere, she contacted Valley Juvenile Detention Center, or jail for minors. Once again, nothing. Call it presumptuous on my part, but I suggested she phone the social worker assigned to his case. After two calls to Division of Youth Services, we got a young woman who really needed a refresher course on confidentiality. She regurgitated everything she knew about the case—even that they were trying to tie Oscar to the murder of the female macerated in the garbage truck. After we finished, Ms. Dempsey cried like her world was ending.

As I patted her hand, my resolve strengthened. I was going to free Oscar. I was just trying to figure out how.

Ivy and I'd just left human sexuality. Subject of the day: hormones. Rolling on some clear lip gloss, I gave her the once-over. She didn't need the class. In fact, if she were a car, her engine was in danger of overheating. Example? When she bent over to rummage in her locker, her white micro-mini rode sky high, flashing the world her hot pink panties. I gasped. Ivy got sent home regularly for pushing the dress code boundaries. One would think her parents would mind, but I think that was SOP in the Morrison household— Ivy did what Ivy did, and they rubberstamped it or turned the other cheek. I mean, who wore a short skirt to school anyway? Unless you *wanted* to show your business, as Murphy said.

Maybe that was my problem.

Maybe I didn't know how to play the game or what constituted "business."

I thought I looked nice enough. I was sporting new capris with a brown leather belt, my Chucks, and a skintight orange T-shirt with a white number ten on the front. I had gone for the subliminal effect, ranking myself a ten. Okay, maybe not subliminal. It was in your face...so shoot me.

My iPhone buzzed with a text from Vinnie. It said, *Running late... stay put and out of trouble.* What Vinnie was doing was hitting on his girlfriend du jour. I groaned.

Ivy turned on her high-heeled sandals with a smirk. "Who's that?" she asked.

I returned an equally nasty smirk. I wasn't giving her anything.

Perturbed, she flipped her hair, shoving one textbook and a spiral pad into her oversized Louis Vuitton tote. "Has he finally confessed?" she asked.

Back to talking about Oscar. Apparently, she forgot she was working on being a better person. "He didn't do it," I said confidently.

"Spoken like a loyal girlfriend."

If she was dead, I swear it, I'd spit on her grave. Before I could tell her to shove her attitude up her you-know-what, Finn Lively, brother number two, came up beside me and uncharacteristically jabbed, "Shut up, Ivy."

And shut up, shuttin' up, I added in my mind.

Ivy didn't care. She was the exact species of mean-girl to not be offended.

Finn had just finished baseball practice—his seventh period class. Baseball, for God's sake. Made me want to join the team. Looking a little helter-skelter, it wasn't from sweating in the outfield.

"Bonjour, mademoiselle," he murmured.

"Bonjour," I answered back in French. He gave me that face that said he was stupid but he knew he'd do it again. Finn had girlfriends —lots of girlfriends—but his relationships were short-lived and amicably dissolved. My guess was his latest "amicably dissolved" turned stalker and was certifiably all kinds of scary.

I could see why girls went loco. Finn wasn't handsome. Finn was beautiful. Taller than me, he was a blue-eyed Scandinavian blond with a Malibu tan. His chin length, tousled hair was as light as sunshine, his eyelashes as dark as night. Finn's player ways was to unload a different accent a day on the females, and it worked. Sometimes a little too well.

He pulled my Rubik's cube off the top shelf (which he could solve in nine seconds) and then slumped down the wall, hiding behind me.

I stood in front of his white baseball pants, trying my best to... well, hide him.

"Hiding you comes with a price," I said.

"Name it."

Finn was the resident geek-slash-genius. *What* I needed him for wasn't the problem. He could pull off anything. It was more like the *when*.

"I don't know yet, but soon...no questions asked."

"Oui," he mumbled. Guess that meant he was game.

It was well past two-thirty. The hall was thinning out, and Ivy was motor mouthing how she and Jagger were back together...better than ever.

"Sounds like a match made in Heaven," I said with a sigh.

"Or the other place," Finn added in a mumble.

Ivy was so entitled the social cues the rest of us picked up on, she didn't. She had no clue we'd slammed the particulars of her dysfunction-driven love life. She flipped her hair, stalked across the hall, and clutched me by the hand. My God, my first thought was I needed to wash it.

Ivy sneered, "I hear there's free counseling in prison for those in relationships just a thought."

My jaw dropped. I actually heard it crack.

Even though Oscar and I were nothing, I hated shrinks. I did a two-year stint in counseling where my brain was scraped, scrubbed, and reprogrammed by one of the best psychiatrists in the Heartland. Kids didn't want to talk, but she threw so many popsicles at me, I regurgitated out most of my demons. Trouble was, they all found their way back in.

After Ivy left, I stood there for a second, wondering why I was so spineless where she was concerned...a question for my Magic 8 Ball.

By that point, it was only Finn, me, and a few brainiacs trying to stuff all their books in their backpacks "just because." Pulling him off the floor, I marched us toward the parking lot. I was done waiting for Vinnie. If he didn't show? Well, I'd find Finn and me a ride elsewhere.

The air was a little humid from raining the day before, but the sky was a perkier shade of blue, the clouds in shapes that looked like fat sheep. A warm breeze was blowing, and black birds were lined up on the Amity Health Care Building, eagle-eyeing the parking lot. Instant heebie-jeebies. It's like they were staring, wondering where the food in the dumpster went. I shivered off the image and thought of Oscar.

All day, I wondered how juvie life was treating him. He'd had a five o'clock shadow since seventh grade, and I hoped that made him look tough. I didn't consider myself a mindless bleeding heart—I liked for bad people to pay—but it ripped my heart out the way an innocent had his life judged like he'd had.

I'd asked around, and no one knew a lot about Jinx. He was new, and oftentimes students like that were transient. I'd had friends over the years whose parents were doing a two-year stint in the area, and many were standoffish. I think they wondered, *Why bother?* Like making true friendships was a waste of time. *But Jinx did have some friends*, I reminded myself. Some friends that (chances were) hated me as much as he did. Who did I think I was anyway? Wonder-freaking-Woman? *I'm coming after you*, I'd said. I mean, really. Just to be sure, I did a quick circle spin and looked at my clothing, wondering if I was falling out of a blue and red bathing suit, holding a golden rope.

Nope, just me.

Me and my not-so-memorable boobs.

If I were to be honest, my Wonder Woman-wannabe-thing was a wake-up call. I shouldn't threaten someone until I had something substantial to back it up. It hadn't come back to bite me yet (Jinx was suspiciously absent), but I had a feeling it would.

As in everything, I longed for Dylan's take on the situation. We spoke the night before, but that idea to get his take on things was just that...an idea that never made it out of its genesis. So that left Vinnie. I told Vinnie what I knew about Jinx, and that's when I saw a brief glimmer of his brains. Vinnie pulled on one of his lamb chop sideburns and said, "I noticed him in the crowd, Dolce. He acted like he had a vested interest. Why would he even care unless he was glad it wasn't him?"

Maybe the both of us marshaled together could unearth the specifics, but as God as my witness, that would literally be a miracle. When Vinnie wasn't trying to make out with the nearest female, he was eating half his weight in food. What I had to work with was that brief interlude in between...which meant I was screwed.

Then there was the issue of Frank, Oscar's twin. He was nowhere to be found—not to mention, I still needed to uncover what sites four, five, and six were on the sanitation run. A feeling took root in my gut that those were the works of the same killer. Could Jinx be that killer? What could Alfonso Juarez and a female in a neighboring township have in common?

Logically, nothing. Gutwise, everything. It was Valley, for God's sake. Nothing bad ever happened in ritzy suburbia, but there was a first time for everything.

Once outside, I located Vinnie's large belly hanging over the door of a white Hyundai Sonata, chatting with some bleached-blonde bimbo. Well, bugger me. She had a serious case of the hold-me-backs going on. I wasn't sure what it was with Vinnie. For a man close to one hundred pounds overweight, he had something that shot off a scent to mate for the willing female. I stopped to scratch my head. A look back at Finn showed him doing the exact thing.

"I don't get it, ma chérie," he muttered. My POV exactly.

Putting my fingers in my mouth, I whistled. "Vinnie! Our baby and I are ready to go home!"

I rubbed my stomach for emphasis as the Italian male paled as white as an Eskimo. The blonde in the Hyundai said a few choice words and squealed her car into reverse, kicking up gravel, probably stripping her transmission.

Mature...

Vinnie went nuclear, giving me a look like he wanted my tongue cut out permanently. He hoofed it toward me, his barrel chest bouncing, thighs swish-swooshing together, madder than a hornet that had its nest torn down. He was a heart attack waiting to happen. I said a prayer his arteries were unclogged.

———

I disconnected, wondering if the prank caller was Darth Vader. All I got was heavy breathing, garbled sounds, and standing hairs on the back of my neck—Freakoutville. Pinching the space between my eyes, I debated if I should place caller block on the number. If I did, I wouldn't have to worry about those conversations. If I didn't, I could pray that the person would slip-up and provide something incriminating.

Call me genius or call me stupid, I decided to leave things status quo.

Settling into the car with Claudia—she was chauffeuring me to work—I took a few moments to steady my breath, pause and look at the sun. It was setting into a deep red blanket, exceptionally pretty up against the midnight blue the rest of the sky had faded into. A welcome change considering the Tundra we'd all just survived.

It had been a particularly rough winter. Snowfalls were higher than average with temperatures dipping into the single digits. Cincinnatians were chomping at the bit for a new season, but some of us had to keep doing the same old thing that most of the time gave us a heaping helping of the doldrums...go to work.

Since age thirteen, I'd worked every Thursday night and weekend at Belinski's Bookstore, or The Double-B as customers called it. Let's just say I'd rather gouge a stick through my eardrum.

Located in a red brick strip mall about a mile from my home, most of the time I floundered through my shift. A glance inside looked like a bad case of déjà vu—no traffic whatsoever. That wasn't surprising. We carried a sparse amount of bestsellers, but the people that frequented The Double-B came due to its close proximity, or maybe, like me, they enjoyed the entertainment value. Mr. Belinski cursed like an entire construction crew, and his communiqués were so creative I didn't know whether to be repulsed or impressed. They always included the word pork. *What the pork? Ah, pork it. Pork the porkin' world,* he'd say.

Whatever. I shrugged to myself. It was a paycheck.

Kissing Claudia on the cheek, I filed out of the car and forced myself to go inside.

Dropping my things behind the checkout counter, I looked for

Mr. B's bowling ball body. A hefty three hundred pounds, his standard clothing was bib overalls with a sport coat one size too small that was littered with dandruff. Bright pink cheeks dotted his face with no discernible cheekbones and cloudy blue-gray eyes. His head housed a thatch of blond hair that made a ring around his scalp. Thing was, he was either balding or he'd grown out of what hair nature intended.

Picking a few balls of lint from my yoga pants, I repositioned my Belinski's shirt and shook my head at the idiocy. On a quest to be hip and relevant, Mr. B made us wear black T-shirts that said "Belinski's is the Bomb" in red lettering. The "O" on the bomb was a picture of a smoking grenade with a burning fuse of fire. Far from the truth. It was more like a Molotov cocktail made up of overpriced books, leftover food, and backroom booze—his.

I squatted down to retie my silver and black Nikes. When I stood up, Mr. B hovered overtop me smelling like lager and a stale fart...Limburger.

God. Help. Us. All. Tonight was going to be a doozy.

He took a big bite, pointing to his shirt he was finally able to snap up to his chin. "I lost weight, Walker. My neck is now skinny."

I gave him a lying thumbs up. He had three necks, maybe a fourth. I'd have to peek under his chin to know for sure but decided to leave it as one of those phenomenon not meant to be understood. Another phenomenon? Why I hadn't quit. It was the same for any teenager—I needed the money.

If the evening had a highlight, it was some much needed girl-time. I worked with three other females: one senior citizen, Coralue; Rudi, a fellow junior with only thirty percent hearing; and Chichi, the resident psychic/palm reader/necromancer of dead pets. I didn't have firsthand experience of Chichi's pet raising, but it was something I filed away since I had a tendency to kill things.

While Mr. B practically bulldozed a new customer, I grabbed the trashcan, wondering why Maintenance hadn't been cleaning the place. On the floor were animal droppings of some kind, candy wrappers, and the dust on the countertop rivaled the Gobi Desert. It was the same batch from Sunday because I'd taken my index finger and written Darcy and Liam inside a big heart.

Ah, Liam, I thought. *I don't have time to think of you now.*

Grabbing the broom, I attempted to sweep up the animal poo, but it was stuck to the carpet. Wrapping some masking tape around my hand, I crouched down and taped them to my palm, unwound the thing, and tossed the remains in the trash. That went beyond the call of duty, but I'd look at them all night if I didn't do something. I wiped off the counter with a rag, threw the candy wrappers away, and ambled to the break room to grab a snack.

Mr. B was a narcissist, evident by his decorating scheme. On the ceiling was a replica of Michelangelo's work at the Sistine Chapel—beautiful if you were an art lover, nauseating since he'd made himself the star figure. His face was on Adam, a cherub, and—the most sacrilegious-to-the-human-eye—a well-developed, studly-looking King David.

No one could write that stuff—maybe if the person was drunk with one heck of an imagination—otherwise it couldn't be done.

The break room was equally eccentric. It had a lime imitation leather couch, a white plastic table with metal chairs, and a rusty washer and dryer. There also was a vending machine that could feed a football stadium. Opening the refrigerator, I found a wilted Cobb salad, soggy fries, and a pizza box that a lift of the lid showed nothing but crumbs...and more animal droppings.

I shivered. Even I had standards.

After I washed my hands, I grabbed some quarters and made a plate of carbohydrates—i.e., a candy bar, bag of chips, Ho Hos, and Goobers. Then I went searching for Rudi.

She was behind the customer service desk in the middle of the store.

Framed in wire-rimmed glasses, Rudi had big brown eyes and a bobbed haircut that fell right at the point of her genuine smile. She was teeny-tiny with the physical attributes of someone who should be riddled with date after date, but she was deaf and dirt poor...and too good.

Rudi could speak in that underwater-muffled sort of way but only did so at work. The attention at school embarrassed her. She went a few semesters at a school for the deaf but wanted to mainstream her life and came to Valley. Valley provided her with a signer.

Problem was, half the time he never showed. As a result, she sat in the front row and read lips, or I was the signer's replacement.

Sorry state of affairs, folks, when I was supposed to help someone succeed.

We unpacked and shelved some novels, and then we got separated as I helped a customer find a book, change her mind on a book, only to leave the store and come back and purchase a bookmark.

The evening was devoid of excitement until Rudi found me once again at the vending machine. I'd eaten through one entire row and had moved on to the second. She grabbed me by the wrist, twisting it anxiously.

"Hey—" I said shocked.

Do something, Darcy, she signed frantically.

"About?"

Cocking her head to the side, she looked at me like I must be deafer than her. That's what sugar did, people. It either geeked you up or dulled the senses. I slipped my seventy-five cents back in my change purse, giving her my full attention.

"It's Mr. B," she actually said out loud.

Well, surprise, surprise, surprise. Mr. B was one temper tantrum and profane sentence away from winning "Worst Boss of the Year." By de facto, it had somehow become my job to defuse him. But defusing a three-hundred-pound man—who liked to argue as much as eat—was like trying to keep a hungry boll weevil from a field full of cotton.

"He's mad at Frank," she said.

"Frank Small?" I eeked, my emotions somewhere a mixture of aghast and jubilation. If I had any hope of helping Oscar, Frank was my best bet at getting him out of jail.

I eased over to the shelf that held the *Popular Mechanics* magazine and watched Mr. B rake Frank over the coals for reading but not buying. Frank attempted to speak, but Mr. B had his don't-talk-to-me face on, his customer service freaked up beyond all recognition. Plus, I was pretty sure he might've been tipsy on lager.

Frank was...Frank. Where Oscar was prematurely balding, Frank had so much hair he'd make Paul Bunyan jealous. It ran straight down his neck and covered his back in the shape of South America. Adding to the weird, his deodorant never worked, and the rings under his arms rivaled those of Saturn. He also had a mouth of reptilian teeth but could boast the fact his protective headgear occasionally broadcast 700 WLW talk radio, live. Frank was as weird as weird could get with the emotional makeup of a grade schooler. No wisdom, no long term plans, and no skills to leave him safe unattended.

Like I negotiated with landmines, I touched Mr. B on the shoulder. When he spun around with a frothy mouth, I shucked off the eeeuws, dug deep, and gave him a lot of teeth.

"What, Walker?" he thundered.

"I was getting ready to ring Frank up," I told him.

His anger recoiled a bit, but when he straightened the magazines, Frank felt compelled to help and "franked up" the entire display. He swiped his hand across the top shelf, causing the *Vogues* to tip sideways, and the *Vanity Fairs* to tumble to the floor. I quickly bent down to gather them as Mr. B turned on his heels and hauled his lard butt to the back of the store.

After a few blinks, Frank blurted out, "He was arraigned already."

My breathing slammed to a halt.

I knew Oscar's arraignment was coming, but hearing it made it all the more real. Arraignment was when the accused stood before a judge and heard the official charges against him or her. Most usually, the accused pled not guilty. If the accused couldn't afford an attorney, the state would appoint one called a public defender.

"What were the charges?" I wheezed out.

"Murder One."

The room started spinning. Murder One, or aggravated murder, was premeditated with the intent to kill. In a nutshell, that meant the killer had to have "laid in wait" to murder a certain individual. An individual someone most usually had a beef with. Oscar was smarter than Frank, but he wasn't a coldblooded killer who could plot out anything more than whose garbage to pick or some off-the-wall practical joke. Where and how in the world would small-time picker, Oscar Small, run into Alfonso Juarez on a day-to-day basis anyway? Let alone make plans to kill him? That didn't make sense because Alfonso Juarez was an AVO member.

Still, I had to ask. "Did Oscar do it?"

Without hesitation, Frank emphatically shook his head with a, "No." Frank didn't strike me as an A-list actor, and furthermore, I wasn't sure he had the mental acuity to reason things out. His conversations were usually one noun and one verb only. Plus, people that lied tended to avoid eye contact and offer up too many details and qualifiers. All he gave me was a negative answer with a cold, hard stare, daring me to say otherwise.

Leading him to a table in the center of the store, we both fell into a seat. Frank played with the hem of his gray T-shirt and rubbed his hands up and down the thighs of his holey jeans. He was nervous, and nervousness of that kind usually meant one thing: he was about to bust out with something that was choking him, or he was going to blow the joint altogether.

I jumpstarted the questioning. "What do you know about Jinx King? Oscar told Ms. Dempsey Jinx was involved somehow." Frank stared at his feet as though he was telling them to run. "You can trust me," I said softly.

Frank lifted his brown eyes. "We sometimes run into Jinx at night. He's not a good person."

"What do you mean?"

"He's not nice."

"Can you give me an example?" I asked, except Frank just stared. I decided on another avenue. "Do you know what sites four, five, and six are on the sanitation run in West Chester?"

"I live in Valley," was Frank's answer. Well, duh, but I thought a picker might know.

"Would Oscar know?"

He gave me a shrug. Frank either avoided the question or his brain opted to do something else. Right then, he recited what sounded like a grocery list. Finally, he whispered, "Who do you think lied on him?"

My guess was it was Jinx and the others. Thing was, they must be guilty of something pretty substantial because why even care? What I needed to do was shove a yearbook in Oscar's face and hope for an ah-hah moment where he could finger them. The longer we stared into a silent oblivion, the more I was convinced I was doing the right thing. "I promise I'll figure something out, Frank. I swear it, I will."

"You swear it, you will," he repeated weakly.

His eyes glittered with unshed tears. Heaven help me, Frank looked at me like I was his lifeline. If it were up to me, Jinx would be sporting an orange jumpsuit and ankle bracelet by week's end.

Chapter Eleven

PINKY SWEAR

" ow much longer do you want to live, Darcy?"
Oh, to a ripe old age, I guess? I wasn't sure how I
wanted to play my mystery caller. If I even wanted to play the
person at all.

Darth Vader was back, even scarier and eerier than the other
times. It was half past the witching hour Friday morning, and my
iPhone had been doing 360s on the nightstand for several minutes.
Once I figured out what it was, I didn't take the time to check the
caller ID. I basically wanted to shut the person up ASAP. When I
groaned out, "You've got to be kidding me," the digitized voice of
Satan himself literally shaved twenty years off my life.

I popped out of bed so fast I was battling motion sickness.

"I'd always heard you were crazy with an undeniably big mouth,"
Darth Vader said. "I had no idea the rumors were correct."

I almost said, "Look who's talking, moron," but didn't. I opted
not to speak, hoping it would irritate the person into giving me
something more.

"You're not so talky tonight. What's up?" Still nothing on my
end. "Are you even there?"

Afraid the person would hang up, I decided to answer, keeping
my voice as neutral and unemotional as possible. "Call me old-fashioned, but I've always preferred knowing who I'm talking to."

I got a hair-raising, "Hmmm."

"Obviously, you think I've done something to threaten you. Why don't you tell me what that is?"

"What is it you *think* you've done?" Darth Vader said. *The Good Lord only knows*, I thought, but I wasn't an idiot. Whoever it was wanted me to confess everything I'd engaged in recently, so he could figure out how much information I actually had. Guess what? Wasn't going to happen.

I did find it interesting that someone found me threatening. I wasn't used to that sort of attention. "Oh, I'm just doing the normal things," I said, "but to answer your question, I intend to outlive *you*. There's no other way for me to take the phone call other than a threat, but that's okay. I operate on high alert most of the time anyway." It had to be Jinx. Had to be. Jinx was who I told, *I'm coming after you*. Strange that I was being direct when he was masking himself as one of the worst theatrical villains of all time.

"You're wearing a white sleepshirt. Your hair is in a messy ponytail, and you went to bed eating a chocolate Popsicle, talking to someone on the phone. I'm all over you and all around you, Darcy, so I'd watch the smart lip."

It felt like I'd been shot right between the eyes. Stumbling to my window, I gave my blinds a quick, hard jerk closed. I'd left them up so I could watch the moon. Big mistake since it appeared someone else had been watching me. Maybe I should've processed the ramifications of the conversation before I started it—such as, I've grown an ulcer, I'll never sleep again, or worse yet, I might die before I kiss someone—but that wouldn't have made me a verb.

I gave him a complementary nervous laugh just to make him think he'd scared me.

"You're scared."

"No, I'm tired. But tell me something, *Jinx*," I emphasized, "why did you want to kill the woman in the dumpster? Her name's not been released yet, but when it is, I promise I'm going to find out the connection and nail you to the wall."

When he said nothing more, I grew frustrated. It was late, people, and if he didn't want to play, then I wasn't going to beat my head against the wall. "Listen, a-hole—"

Next thing I knew, I heard a dial tone.

Dylan had been the buzzer on my alarm clock for years. In fact, he SKYPED me goodnight and texted me good-morning. Five o'clock wasn't good-morning time. Five o'clock was I'm-going-to-strangle-you-if-I-get-my-hands-on-you time.

Groping around for my glasses, I slid them onto my nose and sleepily drew my phone to my eyes:

SERIOUSLY, U R GOING 2 HURT MY FEELNGS IF U DONT ANSWER MY CALLS...GRRRR

Jeez, all CAPS. I hated it when he got shouty. When I inspected my phone more closely, I saw the reason for his bad attitudeness... three missed SKYPE invitations around eleven o'clock in the evening. I actually fell asleep all by myself, a rarity on its own. It was a shame Darth Vader interrupted before I fell into REM.

I texted back, *Sorry, you pompous, overbearing, megalomaniac of a best friend,* but my hand never had the chance to hit the send key. All of a sudden, I got nailed with water torture. I jumped. I jumped so high I could've cleared a freaking pole vault bar.

When I punched accept, he cut me off before I could even speak. "I'm not used to having to track you down, Darc."

"I'm in bed, D. How's that hard to track me down?" He went silent, a tiny bit of annoyance in the air. "Hello?" I said and laughed.

"I'm glaring at you, for the moment."

I let him glare while I patted my thumping heart. "Shouldn't you be getting ready for bed?"

He sighed amidst a sleepily sounding voice. "I just woke from sleeping five hours. I've pretty much given up acclimating to the new time zone. So how's Darcyville?"

Dylan was the person who coined the phrase Darcyville. My guess was he wasn't going to like the recap of the exciting parts.

I opted for a safe opener. "Did I tell you Ivy said I was a charity case, and that she and her mom talk about how pitiful I am? She claims they even pray for me. I didn't know they were the religious type." I didn't want to take the time to debate Ivy's particular relationship with God, but that incident in itself happened on Tuesday. I wasn't sure why it had started to bother me, but it had. Maybe I should deal with things when they happen instead of shoving them down into my subconscious. Sometimes when they resurfaced, they weren't always so friendly.

Dylan's voice suddenly went clinical. "And what did you say to *her*?"

"Nothing," I mumbled. "Well, nothing that really mattered, I guess."

He sighed in a rich, deep tone. "Ah, sweetheart, you know she's been jealous since grade school. You're flawless and the most beautiful thing I've ever seen, but I'd prefer it if you'd defend yourself." Dylan had the best friend gig down to a science. He knew when I was going to laugh. He knew when I was about to cry, and he knew the precise time to say I looked beautiful when I looked like a rat's behind. So I was tall and blonde. So what? That didn't mean a hill of beans if there wasn't anything substantial between the ankles and neck.

When I didn't say anything, he murmured softly, "Are you okay?"

"I dunno," I mumbled. I was so un-okay that I didn't even have a definition for okay anymore. Darth Vader was after me, and my insecurity had reared its ugly head. I had a feeling neither would go away without extreme effort.

"What else is bothering you?"

As much as I'd like to, I couldn't bring myself to talk about my cyber stalker. I did, however, give him a rewind of the last forty-six hours, sparing no gory detail. Telling him I skipped school (again) and met Jinx King's father...how Vinnie had an alias of Guido Galucci...how I was summoned to the Mind-Scrub Squad for deprogramming...how Vinnie crashed the counseling session (left out Liam Woods)...how a woman was macerated in a garbage truck...and —disaster of all disasters—how Oscar took a public flogging and arrest for the murder of Alfonso Juarez.

All of that tumbled out of my mouth before I could stop it, and once it was out, I wanted to shove it back in. Dylan yelled at me. Well, what resembled yelling. It was more like the earth moving, yet it wasn't termed a quake. That didn't happen often. Honestly, I couldn't remember it happening ever. Tiptoeing downstairs, I put him on speakerphone and laid my cell down on the countertop by the stainless steel fridge. I had the munchies. Not a good way to start the day and probably ensured I would pile on five pounds simply because it was out of the ordinary.

First, I started with a container of orange Jell-O. I then ate my way through a bag of blue corn chips, swallowed down some guacamole, and licked the creamy center out of one row of Oreo Double Stuf cookies. When my stomach still growled, I spread cream cheese on a cinnamon raisin bagel, decided I didn't like the looks of the raisins, and sucked off the white goop. Still famished, I cracked open a jar of black olives, slurping my way through one third.

By that time, it was five-thirty in the morning, and Dylan was still going strong. Officially, I was sick. Unofficially, my munchies weren't going away until I found something to curb my mind's appetite. In other words, a lead in the Alfonso Juarez case.

Next thing I knew, Dylan growled he was hanging up, that he wanted to "see my face," and was resorting to SKYPE. Not a good idea. I was bloated like a bowling pin with a major case of wardrobe malfunction. My old white sleepshirt was not only inside-out, its hem was completely gone, and guacamole stained the neckline.

When I accepted his call, I exhaled deeply. He was as beautiful as ever, and funny how one look at his gorgeous mug made everything right in the world. "Hey," I said softly.

Dylan closed his sleepily hooded eyes, murmuring, "Hey," back. "I don't like to argue with you, Darc. So let's ditch the arguing thing."

Sometimes it was difficult to look at Dylan. Even if I was fudging on the truth, he could undress my soul with his eyes. I tiptoed back upstairs, listening to Murphy snore and Marjorie talk in her sleep. Walking into my room, I slid once more under the covers. "*I* wasn't arguing. *You* were arguing," I clarified.

Dylan did an exaggerated eye roll. He was shirtless, jet-black hair in disarray, lying in black sheets with one well-muscled arm propped behind his head as a pillow. *He was eye candy*, I thought, and I was trying to decide whether to bite or suck on it for a while.

Note to self: debate whether that was an inappropriate thought later.

"It takes two to tango, sweetheart, but maybe I just don't like the subject matter."

"Would you prefer me to lie to you from here on out?"

Dylan actually stopped to ponder, contemplating that ignorance-is-bliss thing. "You've never lied to me, and it would crush me if you did. Pinky swear you're going to leave this thing alone."

Dylan's and my pinkies had been participating in profanity since age eight. We swore to one another over a split candy bar and intertwined pinkies that we would "always tell the truth, nothing but the truth, so help us God, God willing that the creek don't rise." We didn't know what it meant about the creek rising, but Murphy said it so much it sounded like gospel. After all of these years, we'd held to that oath. As in anything, it worked in his favor more than mine. I couldn't lie if my parents were deranged psychopaths inbred with compulsive liars.

"Darcy?" he pushed. Oh, God, what he didn't know wouldn't hurt him, right?

I sidestepped the pinky swear. "He didn't do it, D. You know it, and I know it."

"Let it play itself out, sweetheart."

Now *I* was yelling. "Let it play itself out?! What good is it going to do Oscar if it plays itself out?"

Dylan set his jaw. He was upset—PO'd or about to cry. Whatever it was, he was trying to calm or console himself. He had two characteristics that showed his feelings. If something warmed him or moved him to painful tears, he'd touch his heart like he was comforting it. If he was frustrated or needed to compose himself, he'd rake his hand through his hair or rearrange his hat.

He reached over to his nightstand and punched a red ballcap onto his head, shifted it around, and flipped the bill backward. "Now *you're* yelling, and *I* don't like it," he murmured. "This isn't a good way to start the day, Darcy. It just isn't." Well, who started it? And furthermore, why did I feel like apologizing?

He was stubborn, and every time that characteristic surfaced, I found myself acting like a golden retriever. As lovable as he was, if he thought he was right—or wanted his way—he'd dig in his heels, and I'd wind up heeling at his size twelves like a well-behaved dog. But I wasn't going to heel on that one. Short of a lobotomy, my OCD ways wouldn't allow it.

I did a complete-180. "My braces are Endsville today."

He sort of laughed, repositioning the sheets. "Nice shift in dialogue."

"We weren't getting anywhere."

Dylan nailed me to the wall with a good hard stare. I gulped. I swear it...gulped. "I have another week here," he said, "and I won't be around to untangle another Darcy-related mishap."

"An exercise in futility," I added.

He blew out a big breath of air, rubbing his forehead like he rubbed away the thoughts of me in a dumpster. "Let's switch subjects. Exactly why was Ivy picking on you?"

I snorted because the answer was obvious. "Oh, jeez, maybe because she's evil?"

Once again, the clinical voice. "How's Jagger?"

I quickly changed the subject again. "How are the sea turtles, D? Are they really as big as textbooks say they are?"

Dylan grumbled a low, warning sound—impatient and demanding. "Let me guess, Jagger has been hitting on you, and Ivy didn't like it. A major dirtbag move when he has a girlfriend. Am I right, Darcy?" Sheesh, it felt stupid to admit that, and it didn't go unnoticed he kept calling me Darcy.

"He hits on everybody," I said, exhaling in defeat.

"Maybe, but with you he means it. That makes me extremely nervous. Is Valentine still in the picture?"

Vinnie was convinced I'd broken up what could've been the love of his life—or at least for the next fifteen minutes or so. Call me a genius, but I'd say he was mad. "Vinnie's mad at me," I told him, "so I can't answer that question for the near future."

Dylan looked like he needed CPR. "My God, what in the world did you do?"

"Nothing."

"Nothing," he repeated. "If it were nothing, then he wouldn't be mad."

"Quit attacking me, D."

"I'm not attacking you. I'm merely exploring the inconsistencies in your story."

Smart mouth, I thought. "If you keep exploring my inconsistencies, then I'm going to hang up." I paused for effect, holding my chin up stubbornly. "Goodbye," I spat.

Even though he was sitting, I think his knees buckled. "Hey," he murmured quickly, "we're only talking. Don't run away when things get tense."

"I'm not running away. I'm merely opting to not continue this line of questioning."

My goodness, my voice didn't even sound like my own. Dylan bit his lip, stopping himself from saying whatever it was he was considering. After a few beats, he murmured, "I understand, and if you need this part of the conversation to be over, then consider us copacetic."

Dylan's fatal flaw? He always gave me what I wanted. I had him right where I wanted...a little bit of guilt with the beginnings of an apology I didn't deserve. Let's hope Heaven took into account good intentions because right then I felt kind of yucky. "I love you," I said in a big grin.

His smile branched from ear to ear. "Always, sweetheart," he murmured out in a whisper, "and I miss you."

I swear, Dylan's voice was so seductive it would make any girl walk right out of her clothes.

After some mundane chitchat about baseball season, we unplugged the conversation around six forty-five in the morning—right when I was going to leave for school. He even stayed online talking to Murphy when I showered. What he feared I would do, I didn't know, but the boy needed another hobby than keeping tabs on me.

When I jogged outside to load into Grumpy's death cab, the first thing out of his mouth—other than a grunt—was "Walker, what's going on with you? Taylor's on a warpath, and when he's on a warpath he makes..." long pause, "well, the world as we know it stands still."

My eyes had to have bugged out of my head. "You talked to him this morning?"

"About five seconds ago. Not so happy and chipper as usual, I might add." He then mumbled to himself, "Certifiably institution bound, if you ask me. The guy's such an enabler."

The day was grueling, and I was as rigid as a ten-day-old corpse. Contrary to my physical state, my mind felt like it was running on amphetamines. It turned over and over, not able to put Oscar in a box I felt comfortable with. Killer? Victim of circumstance? All I knew was people like Oscar tried and failed and then prayed for the emotional fortitude to try again the next day—all the while watching those that had it easier lap them on the track of life. I attempted a period of self-reflection, wondering if I was simply rooting for the underdog, but it was still my opinion Oscar couldn't and wouldn't hurt a fly.

I padded into the orthodontist's office, hoping it would be my last go-around with braces. It hadn't been a pain-free process, mentally or physically. Teeth were twisted, missing, and there was a one-hour surgery to coax an incisor out of hiding.

As I grabbed a seat next to another girl, my iPhone rang. It was Justice. "Hey," she said. "I've got a pair of size twenty-seven True Religion jeans that look mint-worthy for twenty-nine dollars and ninety-nine cents. Do you want them? I think I was a twenty-seven in fourth grade."

I bought a Lucky patchwork purse at T.J. Maxx—Murphy paid half. I paid half. Fumbling around in it, I opened my wallet realizing all I had was three dollars and seventy-four cents. "Can you keep them until I get paid tomorrow?"

"No problemo. I've also got a really pretty shirt the color of a sunset."

Justice suffered from red-green color deficiency, and in light of her color-blindness, she had a tendency to dress like fruit. Monochromatic all the time—well, what she thought was monochromatic. There was a good chance the shirt could range from nuclear waste to puke green.

"Just the jeans," I said and killed the call.

My phone rang again...Murphy. A heavy throat cleared, and the receptionist gave me a rule-breaker face, pitching her chin to the sign clearly marked "No Phone Zone."

When she resumed filing her too-long coral nails, I mouthed an embarrassed, "Sorry," and stepped outside. Vinnie had forgiven me and was still sitting in the Bug, finishing a BK Whopper before he hit the road. Our relationship wasn't on the down-low anymore. In fact, Claudia saw him dropping me off a few days earlier, ratted me out, but Murphy mumbled, "It's fine," when he was fully aware of Vinnie's reputation. There was a story there, but I was smart enough to leave it alone.

"What's wrong?" Murphy said in a gruff voice.

"I'm outside. Evidently, Doctor Baxter hates cell phones."

Murphy jumped on his high horse, citing his monthly payment down to the last "red American cent," arguing Dr. Baxter's a minion of Hell on insurance claims.

"It's okay," I told him.

"Whatever," he said snorting, and I could see his eye roll. "I'm running late. Just hang tight until I can get there."

Dropping my phone back in my bag, I absentmindedly ran my tongue over the braces one last time. I tasted popcorn...from the night before, for God's sake. Evidently, I did a lousy job brushing that morning. Inside the doctor's office was a small vanity where patients could brush before their appointment. I had an emergency travel kit in my purse, so I ripped out a three-inch brush and squirted some Crest on it. I no sooner got it in my mouth than I spun around and ran right smack into Jagger Cane, exiting the neighboring eye doctor in the same strip mall at Voice of America Plaza.

"Hey, beautiful," he said, laughing as our faces all but kissed one another. I couldn't help it, but I blushed. Jagger was switching up his standard babe greeting. Apparently, he was feeling the word beautiful.

We did that awkward thing where we both turned left, then right, finally deciding on somewhere in between and bonked our heads. My toothbrush lodged in the back of my throat, and when I coughed out, "Can't breathe," Jagger's eyes went wide, and he immediately began to pound on my back. On the third pound, it popped out onto the mulch by the door, toothpaste side down in a bed of begonias.

I stared, wondering how crap like that happened to me.

I figured I had two choices. I could leave it and act like it wasn't mine, or I could pick it up and brush my teeth anyway. Without a second's thought, I whisked it up and shoved it in my mouth—dirt and all.

"I love it that you're so weird," he said under his breath.

I spit some froth into the mulch, realizing I'd reached an all-time level of stupid. I literally was brushing my teeth outdoors with the son of Satan.

"I'm no' weird," I said, spitting again. "My teeth juth ha' pupcorn in thim."

After a few more strokes, I removed the brush and smiled widely. "Do I have dirt in my teeth?"

Jagger giggled, shaking his head no. I shoved everything back in my bag, trying to maneuver around him when he grabbed me by the forearm. "Hey, I heard Oscar's up for Murder One. That's awful."

Peeking back inside the glass door, the girl in front of me was still reading a magazine. "Yeah," I said.

We stood there while "yeah" hung in the air, me nervously nibbling my lip, him throwing off pheromones so pungent they'd begun to choke me. Suddenly, I remembered his indecent proposal from earlier. He said he saw something but would only tell me if I'd kiss him. I stared at his pinky-red lips, the same color as his shirt, and didn't want my first kiss to be because I'd sold out.

I think.

The fact that I'd even considered it would haunt me in infamy. I counted to five, trying to get my bearings. "You told me you saw something, Jagger," I said.

Jagger paused, wearing a big grin that shouted X-rated. "I did, but do you remember my condition?" I frowned, remembering that it made me feel skeevy. "Come on, beautiful, kiss me," he said. "I promise I'll respect you in the morning."

He didn't respect me any more than an atheist respected a prayer wafer.

I rolled my eyes. "I've got to go, Jagger. Just tell me what you saw."

Again, the off-color grin. "Listen, beautiful, I've got to scram too, but if you want to know, take a look who's walking into Target."

Okay, I was wearing contacts, but even they didn't give me vision perfect enough to see two hundred yards away. I squinted anyway while he laughed.

"Juan Salas. He's got the answers you need."

I did a few mental cartwheels, smiled until my face hurt, and then lay prostrate on the ground in a thankful prayer. All in my head, people, but that's what I would've done if there were room. "How about Jinx King?" I asked.

He gave me a headshake. "I didn't see him, but I know they're friends." I could place them both at the scene: Jinx at the dumpster via Oscar, and Juan in the parking lot via Jagger. Plus, I knew AP Unger was arguing with Juan. I'd already deduced Justin Starsong was the male arguing at the dumpster with Jinx, so that only left Fisher Stanton, according to Jubilee Mueller. I was getting somewhere, but I just didn't know where yet.

"Thanks, Jagger. Our secret?"

This is Jagger Cane, the little angel gasped. *I know, I know,* I explained, *but I need him, and I'm not above exploiting his bad boy ways to get what I want.*

Jagger gave me a wink, sidling even closer. Heat rose up my neck, ending at my cheeks. I didn't want to feel anything—he was Jagger, for God's sake. That would be like lying down with a hissing copperhead.

"Hey, my parents are having a party tonight," he said. "Want to come?"

I loved to dance, but I hated parties with the blah, blah, blah conversations people had about the blah, blah, blah guests once they left the room.

"I'm nervous in large groups," I halfway lied.

In the snap of the fingers, Jagger's eyes went soft, even hungrier, and dare I say, *loving?* When he reached for my face, Vinnie was suddenly at my feet madder than a crocodile that had her eggs destroyed. He shoved a beefy finger into Jagger's chest. "You touch her again, and I'm going to rip your spine out and clean my toilet with it." Jagger—dumbly, I might add—took a step toward Vinnie, taunting him with a smile just this side of evil.

Before I could intervene, I heard my name called through the door. Call me a conflict avoider, but I left their conversation to chance.

A few minutes later, I sat in a pink reclining seat, my orthodontist standing overtop me as I stared at the fluffy, white clouds painted onto the baby blue ceiling.

"Let's see what we've done," he said, rubbing his hands together like a mad scientist. That could go one of two ways. They could come off and be the same. They could come off and be worse. Before I knew it, a pile of scrap metal was in a bowl and a mirror had been enthusiastically shoved in front of my face. "Smile," he beamed.

I wasn't sure what I did. I half smiled, half eeked, half prayed. By that time, Murphy was in the room with his video camera, smelling like a tobacco plant, humming "The Dentist" from *Little Shop of Horrors*.

"Open up, kid, before I pry your mouth wide with my bare hands," he grumbled chuckling.

Slowly opening my mouth, I caught a glimpse of twenty-eight teeth that were relatively straight, sort of white, no traces of vampiric canines anywhere. They appeared strong and healthy perched up next to bright, pink gums—the way God intended before bad genetics twisted them up in the womb. I gasped. Murphy nearly dropped his camera.

Insert drumroll...my teeth didn't fall out of my head.

Chapter Twelve

BARE NECESSITIES

I left Dylan a message, prank phone called Liam, and then wound up vomiting "my bad" all over Jagger Cane. What precipitated that temporary moment of insanity? I wanted someone who understood me. Imagine my relief when I realized calling Jagger was all just a dream.

Why was I depressed? Other than the fact that a genuine psychopath was after me, I'd just had my braces removed. I should be ecstatic...I wasn't. On some level, I thought the skies would open up with potential boyfriends recognizing my true beauty beneath three-plus years of metal. Didn't happen. I still was on the slow boat to nowhere.

Whenever I had days like that, I ate lots of sugar and danced to the *Jungle Book* soundtrack. My favorite tune was "Bare Necessities." Right then, it played on a loop in the background while I refused to get out of bed. It wasn't making me feel better. It was making me hate bears.

A deep-fried Oreo was stuck to the roof of my mouth. While I debated to let it dissolve or throw myself down in a modified Heimlich maneuver, my iPhone rang. Imagine my surprise when the caller ID said Valley Juvenile Detention Center.

Baloo belted out a low note, but nothing was lower than my gut that dropped to the lowest level of somebody-help-me.

Oscar.

Oscar Small.

Arrested-and-up-for-Murder-One, Oscar Small.

Why—how—whoa—and let me ask why again was Oscar calling *me*??

On the fourth ring, my hand figured out how to push the accept button. "Oscar?" I whispered.

"I've only got thirty seconds, but listen...Frank said you could help me. You need to get a PAY-TEL account on your phone."

"A what?" I asked.

"Call 1-800-PAYTELL, and use your credit card. Without that account, I can't speak with you."

I coughed out the frog in my throat. "I don't have a credit card."

Silence while he talked to someone. "That's okay. Go to Walmart and get a MoneyGram. Then set up the account."

"Oscar, I—"

"*Please*," he begged, his voice cracking. "I don't have a lot of people in my corner." *Why not your parents?* I wanted to ask, but why bring up something that was obviously better left unsaid?

Before I could talk myself out of it, I exhaled and said, "I'll do it. Just keep your mouth shut, your head forward, and..."

Our call was terminated before I could finish the most impor-tant part of my prison-life advice. Which was? Above all, don't stare. Eye contact just a little too long could get a prisoner involved in a fight—or worse. It was kind of scary that I knew how to exist amongst criminals—a byproduct of one too many prison docu-mentaries.

If finding the murderer was a hobby before, it officially became my unofficial pastime. The faith Oscar had in me meant I'd have to deliver. I wasn't quite at DEFCON 1, but Oscar claiming that he didn't have a lot of people in his corner was like throwing a match-stick on an oiled-up pile of wood. He needed me—and maybe I needed to be needed.

While I drummed my fingers on my bedside table, I contem-plated the bombshell he'd just dropped. Immediately, I knew what to do...trade one bombshell for another.

I dialed my aunt.

Tabitha Arthur—A.K.A., Red Arthur—was the Assistant Hamilton County Prosecutor of nearby Hamilton County. Er, the "former" Assistant to be specific, fallout due to a fight six months earlier. Red's (barely the ink is dry) ex-husband *was* and *had been* the Hamilton County Prosecutor for well over a decade. Thing was, they'd been divorced four times, and on divorce number four, she hooked up with a private investigative firm in town and took down bad guys feeding information to the authorities she thought they should know.

My mother's twin, she had flaming red hair like Marjorie—hence the nickname Red. Everyone said I inherited her looks. We had the same dimpled chin, loudmouthed laugh, and unfortunately an identical thirty-six inch inseam. That pretty much was where the comparison ended. She had the sweet, innocent face of an angel (okay, fallen angel was more like it) but a body that said nothing but sin. My guess was my body said yard sale.

Problem was, her know-it-all mind wouldn't be easy to fool. Truth be known, I had no starting point, but sometimes the scariest place was the easiest to start—just so a person could get it out of the way.

When I asked Red if she had any information, she said word on the street was things didn't look good for Oscar. No shiz, Sherlock. Evidently, Oscar had scored a relatively good public defender, but what Oscar needed was a miracle.

She said, "Baby, they're bringing the feds in because of who Alfonso Juarez is...or *was*, I should say. He was a hitter in AVO, but word underground is the story got out he was in town and a rival gang off'd him. The only gang organized enough to do that is River City Smugglers."

From what I could remember about sociology, people had certain needs. There was the obvious, like food, water, and shelter, but there was also the psychological need to belong. But what made certain individuals want to belong to gangs? Did they not fit into normal society? Could they *not* for some reason? Did they long for camaraderie so badly they didn't care if it came with illegal activities and ultimately a price of some kind? I knew what it felt like to be wired differently, but picking out a group to belong to that was immoral, unethical, and illegal—just because I was lonely —sounded like the appetizer to jail time. Did they not realize how much easier life would be if they only conformed? My thoughts almost made me laugh. Look at me. I wasn't conforming by a long shot.

I snorted sarcastically. "I can promise you Oscar wasn't in a gang," I said. "So does the prosecutor think someone hired a local picker to do just that? That's dumb. Why would a local picker, someone with the reputation of going through trash, hide his kill in a big trashcan?"

Red sort of laughed, sort of sighed. "Reese Sanders could have a meteor land on her Botox'd face for all I care, but she's not stupid. She must feel she has some credible intel or she wouldn't be lifting a finger."

Reese Sanders was the Mack County Prosecutor, servicing Valley and the surrounding townships in the county. If Ivy was my arch nemesis, Reese was Red's. More for reasons along the personal than professional. Reese wanted Red's ex-husband in the biblical way, if you know what I mean, and she didn't care that anyone knew it. Least of all Red. But Red's and my Uncle Rookie's relationship was all shades of the rainbow. Somehow, they'd managed to maintain a close and loving friendship after four divorces, and that always confused me. If people could still be close and loving, why didn't they just stay married?

"If you were to guess, what would be some credible intel?" I pushed.

Cue the crickets chirping. "And you're curious *why*?" she asked.

First of all because I was me, and second of all because I had to figure out what kind of connection Oscar had to Juarez, not to mention the female in the garbage truck. "Can't a girl be concerned about her friend?" I lied, feigning hurt feelings.

Red mumbled something to herself. "To answer your question, Reese must have what she feels is concrete proof Oscar was connected to both victims. There must be motive, and when there's motive, most usually there's a relationship."

I tried another lie on for size. "I heard from his brother they've connected Oscar to the female found in the garbage truck a few days ago."

More crickets chirping. In fact, Red was so silent I feared she would clam up altogether. "Sounds like someone in Reese's organization has a big mouth."

"Did you hear that?"

"Maybe," she said cryptically.

"Do you know what the relationship was?" I asked. When Oscar phoned again, I suppose I could get specifics then, but frankly that meant I'd have to tell him that someone he might have had a relationship with was dead. I didn't want to be the bearer of that kind of news. Been there, done that. Didn't want to do it again.

Red uncharacteristically let the cat out of the bag. "The poor girl in the garbage truck, her name was Annie Hughes. She was nineteen years old and lived in a trailer park off Tylersville. It's sad, baby. She'd been gone for a few days, but when the report was filed, it was pieced together that Annie was the body parts in the garbage truck. Dear God," she prayed, "I sometimes hate the line of work I'm in."

I gulped. Could that have been the missing person report that caused the fight at Valley Police Department on Tuesday? The timing made sense, and if they found something on Annie's body—er, what was left of it—that pointed to Oscar, no wonder the cops immediately took him into custody on Wednesday.

"Will they try Oscar as an adult?" I asked. Oscar was sixteen—not your standard eighteen-year-old adult—but considering the severity of the crime, sometimes the prosecutor could pull things like that off.

"I heard she wants to," Red said. "You understand this stays between you and me, right?"

My aunt practically raised me the last few years, but our relationship was sometimes more like peers. What she told me would be a legal no-no if she were still a practicing attorney, but since she'd been doing the private detective thing, details sometimes slipped out in everyday conversations. If anything, I knew how to keep my lips sealed, and that was coming from a person that liked to talk.

"I've already forgotten what we were talking about," I assured her.

"Good girl. I gotta go. Easter's right around the corner, and I'm getting my hair dyed blonde before I go to work." Ah, I knew that was coming. She changed her natural red hue after every divorce simply as an up-yours to her red-loving ex-husband. I didn't want them divorced: I just didn't.

It was Monday morning, and the last thing I expected was a wake-up call at six o'clock from Oscar...but suffice it to say, I had direction. Spring break officially started at the end of seventh period, and if it were up to me, I would be busy from daylight 'til dark. One might ask, why did spring break start on a Tuesday instead of the standard Monday? It was because Old Man Winter made us the butt end of a cruel joke. Back in December, we missed nine days straight—best nine days of my life, or so I thought—but there was always a payday. Instead of going until mid-June, the Board of Education elected to shave one day off of spring break and get rid of some teacher workdays.

Since the temperature was supposed to reach seventy-two degrees, I pulled on my True Religion jeans I bought from Justice. I paired it with a black T-shirt that said "WHY ME?" and then added blush, mascara, and some rose lipstick in the shade of Secrets Suck. Lastly, I stepped into some silver flip-flops and was reminded that I still had a wart. Flipping my foot over, I realized the wart was larger and crustier than before. So the wart ceremony was a crock.

Popping a Hebrew National hot dog into the George Foreman Grill, I waited eight minutes for my breakfast to be just the way I liked it: slightly charred and oozing fat.

I loved hot dogs, and although my favorite cuisine was Mexican, the hot dog was hands down, my favorite meal ever. If I had to dissect my penchant for the processed, on some level it could be that they were the underdog. Even the all-meat one I was having for breakfast was a mutt in the meat family.

Finding a bun, I dropped the dog inside, slathered it with mustard, and drizzled it with some shredded cheese. I then poured myself a cup of coffee in my favorite coffee cup. Grabbing my things, I jogged outside to meet Grumpy. By the time his truck backfired twice, my breakfast was nothing but crumbs, and I'd reapplied my lipstick.

"How was your weekend?" he asked first thing as we pulled out onto the road.

"Uneventful. I endured sixteen hours of slow, inactive torture at The Double-B. Frankly, I would've invited physical torture since it would be something more than watching the paint peel."

The boy actually smiled. His lips curved upward and everything. "Sounds great."

I lifted an inquisitive brow and swallowed down some coffee. Shoot, it was cold, which was pretty much close to syrup of ipecac. "Why are you being so friendly?" I asked him.

His normal rolled-out-of-bed self, Grumpy reached over to lightly caress my hand. Bizarre behavior. So bizarre there had to be reason. "Taylor said I need to talk to you so you can get all the rebellion out of your system," he muttered. "He thinks if you talk about things, you won't be so inclined to participate in them."

I laughed loudly. "Idiot," I said.

"My thoughts exactly."

I could picture Dylan lounging back with his long legs propped on a table, hands behind his head—checking on his favorite pastime. One would think he'd want the two-week reprieve, but here he was pawning me off on his cronies and then making them tattle.

After I showed Grumpy my new and improved mouth, I messed around with my hair, readjusting my black headband, all of a sudden self-conscious. "What happened to your hair?" Grumpy said snickering.

One of Murphy's coworkers told him the key to cutting bangs around a cowlick was to snip and then texturize. At my prodding, Murphy gave my bangs another go, but that woman was either an idiot or God enjoyed making fun of me. My bangs were so thin they looked like they'd been singed in a light socket.

After Grumpy snorted in laughter, I could tell he mentally slugged himself because he took a deep breath, back to being a supportive friend. "Dylan would say you're still the most beautiful thing he's ever seen," he muttered.

"Dylan's blind," I mumbled, and let's face it, he had better hair than me. His parameter of what constituted beauty was probably dumbed down in my case anyway.

I took another sip of cold coffee and held my travel mug between my knees. Grumpy's car was so old, cup holders weren't invented when it came out of the factory. Pulling a Crest White Strip out of my purse, I glued it to my teeth. "Wha' arth you gitting from thith lil' arrang-ment, Grumpy?" I slurred.

Grumpy grinned, not saying another word.

———————

I'd been sitting for two hours, and no one had discovered I'd skipped US history and anatomy. I could look at that one of two ways: I wasn't memorable or both my teachers were morons. Oh well, rules schmules. What good was it to have them if you couldn't break them sometimes?

I found a place upstairs in the media center, tucked away in a corner, sitting at one of those brown wooden desks that had walls partitioning it for privacy. I pulled out my iPad, the product of six months of hard labor at The Double-B. Then I drew my feet up under my body in case Mrs. Lowe decided to take roll call.

The longer I sat there, the more agitated I became. What was going down with Oscar? And had I stumbled upon the information to make a difference, or had I stumbled upon it because I was Darcy being Darcy? Whatever the truth, the walls were crashing in, and it was hard to breathe. I was *thisclose* to quitting, but I didn't want to fall before I got to the finish line.

Firing up Safari, Apple's browsing software, first thing I did was type AVO into Google. With a couple of clicks, I was looking at the history of AVO. AVO started in Central America when a group of children in war-torn times were being hidden in a convent for safety. When the children grew restless, missing their parents, the priest would always say, "Amor Vincit Omnia" or "Love Conquers All!" It instilled hope in the children they would see their loved ones again...at least for a while. When political rivals discovered the children, the priest and nuns were slaughtered in their presence to send a message. Somehow, a few of them made it out alive and were smuggled to America by sympathizers. They stuck together in a portion of Texas, but when they ultimately were sent to an orphanage in Corpus Christi, it seemed they lost their hope for happy endings. Their organization was formed, and their battle cry became the same "Amor Vincit Omnia" —or their future gang symbol of AVO.

AVO was considered the worst gang in world history. Its members were ruthless, developed specialties, and were known to have blind allegiance to whoever the "padre" was to their specific faction. Their known felonies were murder, rape, home invasion robberies, drug trafficking, and anything else they saw a profit in. One only got out by death or turning evidence to federal officials. If it was discovered a member was a nark, AVO performed its standard amputation of the tongue. In other words, someone held the nark down while it was cut out.

With a click on images, I was looking at the tattoos on Alfonso Juarez's back. Juarez had a demon that ran across his shoulder blades with the word "death" spelled in Spanish. According to a nearby blog, members usually tattooed their backs with their specialty. That demon, accompanied with the word "death," meant Juarez was a hitter. In the world of AVO, it meant he not only defended himself, but those too weak to do so themselves. Also, in the world of AVO, hitters were the ones tapped to punish those that began to look like weaklings. My word, it was like they had their own Internal Affairs Division, and Alfonso was the head.

The Gothic symbols on his back supposedly meant, "Me, Us, and Them." Some gang members tattooed their fingers with a MUT along with the standard AVO. The AVO was indeed on Juarez's dismembered hand, and my guess was that was the first clue law enforcement had that the gang was in suburban, let's-play-soccer-and-sleep-with-our-windows-open Cincinnati.

Sitting back and rubbing my eyes, I recalled that Red said authorities believed a local gang assassinated Alfonso. I didn't push Red for particulars, but like she said, the only gang big enough to even care or have nerve enough to take on AVO was River City Smugglers. I knew from past experiences and a brief secondary search that River City Smugglers didn't dismember, and their hits were mob-like—a double-tap in the head, in the heart. Also, they would've spray-painted RCS all over the place because they liked to take credit. They would want AVO to know—or more aptly put, the people around them—that they were settling the score. Alfonso, in my opinion, looked like a sloppy job.

The day started subpar, but when I was just about to term it a red-letter day, someone whacked the side of my cubicle twice with a ruler. I jumped, squealed like a pig, and looked into the beady, little eyes of AP Unger.

Oh, jeez, talk about a buzzkill.

"And here she is," he growled into his cell phone. "All studious and practically singing the school's fight song."

I chewed on my lip for a minute. "This isn't appropriate, right?" I asked. When he rolled his eyes, I said, "Did you hear that?"

He gave me his what-are-you-talking-about face, appraising all four walls. "Hear what?" he snapped.

"It's villain music playing in the background," I explained laughing. I hummed out a few bars of "You're a Mean one, Mr. Grinch."

I swear, he looked at me like if there was a cliff around, he'd push me over. File that under *Should've Known Better* because AP Unger had somehow sniffed me out. At first, I wasn't afraid. I could talk my way out of it—I think—but by the snarky gotcha look on his face, I knew he'd come with backup. He placed his phone on speaker, shoving it right into my face, and before the person even identified himself, I knew who it was by the ticked-off grunt through the receiver.

"Darcy Walker," the voice seethed, "we're going to have a conversation as soon as your feet hit the threshold of my home. You'll do as AP Unger says. You'll scrub the stinkin' floor. You'll put your hand in the toilet and wipe it clean. You'll do the hillbilly hoedown in the middle of the gosh-danged cafeteria if he sees fit. Do you hear me?"

Murphy...my worst nightmare. I clicked off my iPad, shoving it in its case, half afraid AP Unger would apprehend it and never give it back. "Maybe if you knew what I was doing, you would agree with me, Murphy," I tried to explain. "You wouldn't be so quick—"

"To judge?" he interrupted, laughing sarcastically. "You just judged yourself, kid. I don't want to hypothesize about why you *say* or *do* the things you do. That's going to give me a headache, freakin'-every, freakin'-single, freakin'-time. You better get your wallet open too. You owe the Stupid Jar some money." Where some had a swear jar, Murphy had a glass Mason jar on the countertop that Marjorie and I would drop fifty cents in every time we did something stupid. When it was filled to the top, we'd unload the booty to a charity of our choice. Almost made me hate charity.

I gulped down the boulder in my throat. "How much?" I said.

"That's undetermined at the moment, and because you didn't

learn your lesson the first time you skipped class, we're going to do some payments retroactively. And by the way, I don't appreciate the way you're exploiting the relationship between Vance and me. That's low, kid, really low."

I knew what would come next. Murphy would issue his standard parental disclaimer. "AP Unger, this message is to you. The Walkers do not endorse nor are they associated with her behavior. Any circumstances real or fictitious are totally coincidental and do not represent the opinions residing within my four walls. Thank you, Jesus, and God Bless America."

"Ah, a parental disclaimer," AP Unger muttered, trying not to laugh. I swear, he looked at the cell phone in his hand, and for a moment, I think he might've been struck with the revelation as to where the brains and creativity I possessed came from.

Murphy grunted, and I heard something break on the other end of the line. "I prefer a public service announcement," he grumbled. "It's my gift to society to steer clear."

Slam. Disconnect. Go smoke a cigar in the parking garage.

I'd been taught to dot every "I" and cross every "T," but that seemed a little too predictable. And predictability was one short step away from boring. I opened my mouth, but Murphy somehow closed it even from miles away.

The silence was deafening, but a sudden minute screech was louder than the lack of words. Right then, a tiny, gray-furred creature scampered across my flip-flop and idled at AP Unger's feet. If that wasn't enough, two babies toddled behind it. If a man could scream like a girl, I think I'd just witnessed the spectacle. I burst out laughing as AP Unger all but put on a bra and took up the war for equal rights and estrogen. He danced around as the mouse family squeaked some more and scampered off toward the baseboards.

"I hope you have Saxon Brothers' Exterminators on speed dial," I said in a giggle.

He rolled his eyes and left me sitting.

Chapter Thirteen

CARPE DIEM

arpe Diem was the Latin term for "Seize the Day." It was the call to live in the moment and not put all your energies into tomorrow. So I was kicked out of the media center...so what. Where that might deter someone with a lesser fortitude, it wasn't going to deter me. I was Darcy Walker, by God, and when I wanted something, I wanted something.

Third period, Spanish 3, was one of those classes that made people sweat. My one advanced class, it most often was taken by upperclassmen. Growing up with Claudia, I'd become somewhat of a pro, and although her native tongue was a tad different, I could speak the language fluently and read and translate. Mr. Rafferty was the teacher—a fossil was more like it—and near retirement. The thing with teachers near retirement, they were like trying to teach old dogs new tricks. Mr. Rafferty had his ways of doing things and wasn't going to change no matter what.

Typical example? In all his years of teaching, he'd never taken the time to learn students' names. He called them by their seat number, so all year long I was—you guessed it—number thirteen or número trece.

Life really despised me.

As I slid into my seat and opened my book, he stalked me like a lion did its prey. His bald head was dipped low, his glasses falling off the bridge of his crooked nose, his hairy hands clenching the piece of chalk he probably wanted to stab me with. While I wished I could've dissolved away into the ether, he jarred the windows bellowing, "Número trece, llegas tarde."

He informed me I was late. Well, no kidding. To get some brownie points, I responded in Spanish. "Lo siento."

Mr. Rafferty snorted an echo. "Lo siento."

"Si," I repeated. "Lo siento."

"Suck up," I heard someone say four seats up. "Can't you just say you're sorry in English?"

Unfreaking real.

The voice of negativity sprang from Eddie Lopez, Justice's arch nemesis, and in my opinion just this side of sociopath. Of Mexican descent, Eddie didn't need the class, but one credit short from graduation, she was allowed. Totally wrong in my book, but no one cared to ask my opinion.

Eddie shot a dark look over her shoulder that nearly rattled my bones. Her black hair and eyes were honestly as faded as the cranberry-colored hoodie she always wore—like something internal had sucked up all the brightness in her body. Eddie wasn't in danger of unseating VHS's prom queen favorite. Maybe if they were having a prom in Hell, but not at VHS.

I gave Eddie my version of a smile and then met the blue eyes of Finn Lively, in seat número uno. He sat by the door in most classrooms because he couldn't wait to get out. He must've heard Eddie's barb because if looks could kill, she'd be wearing a toe tag. Eddie was an equal opportunity bully, occasionally beating up and ragging on the boys. She hadn't been treated with the implied respect society gave females since junior high.

A few seats back in seat número cinco was...drumroll please—Juan Salas. Like Jinx, Juan had been absent since they'd dragged off Oscar to juvie. I heard a nasty cold virus was going around, and by the way he wiped his nose on his white hoodie, he might've been a casualty. I took the time to appraise Juan. He had nice clothes, light brown hair, medium height and build, and all honors classes that totally didn't fit his stereotype of the well-known hoodlum. Academically, he was some sort of electronics genius and the reigning science fair champion.

I couldn't have scripted things better. Seat five was across the aisle, one seat up. Remembering Jagger said Juan had the answers, when Mr. Rafferty stopped to answer the phone on his desk, I figured no better time than the present.

"Psst," I whispered. "Juan."

Juan spun around, his brown eyes all allergy-puffy and frankly... mean. Good thing to know some things never changed. "Yeah?" he said suspiciously.

I decided to play the ditz card, twirling the end of my hair. "Did you hear about Oscar Small? Aren't you two good friends?" As far as I knew, he and Oscar weren't even acquainted, but I needed an icebreaker even if it was a dumb one.

"I heard, but no, we're not friends."

I made my eyes wide and gossipy. "Do you think he did it?"

"And why would you care *what* I think?" he retorted coldly.

Firstly, I wanted to say, *Shut your blowhole*. Secondly, I was beginning to remember why we never talked. And thirdly, when I went fishing, I'd throw my pole in anywhere.

Juan's voice was tight and hardly friendly. I wasn't a confrontational person but somehow found a what-the-heck face...adding on some unspoken profanity.

Juan backtracked on the bad attitude. "Listen, I think it's a real shame," he said, "but Oscar always seems to be in the wrong place at the wrong time. All I know is, he's a kook."

"Takes one to know one," I mumbled. Somebody needed to put me down...before any irreparable damage occurred.

Juan gave me that death stare like he wanted me six feet under. "I tell you what," he offered, "give me your number, and if I hear anything, you'll be the first to know. But here's the thing...that information isn't going to be free."

Most days I considered myself a fairly smart person. I took a vitamin, choked down some veggies, and drank thirty-two ounces of fluid, albeit mostly sweetened and caffeinated. But in matters of self-preservation, I could be the biggest idiot that was ever a twinkle in some daddy's eye. Cutting a deal with Juan Salas? He'd sooner kill me in my sleep.

"So do we have a deal?" he asked.

I swallowed hard, wondering how in God's Name he started steering the conversation when I'd started it. Still, I found myself exchanging digits, nodding a "Sure," and wondering what sort of future consequences that might bring.

———

Somewhere in the back of my mind, that still, small voice told me I might've gotten in too deep. It wasn't unlike the deal I'd made with Finn, but I knew what I would ask of Finn (although currently unclear) wouldn't involve selling his or my soul. Why would Juan—who'd never really spoken to me before—be so ready to cut a deal? Did Jinx perhaps tell him of my unquestionably stupid threat? If they were connected, reason would say that'd be the first thing he'd do. Before that voice grew any louder, I ran into Fisher Stanton at the water fountain on the way to geometry.

My mind did the mental rewind of my conversation with Jubilee. She said Juan, Fisher, and the Small brothers were the ones AP Unger had run-ins with the day Alfonso Juarez was found dead. I'd spoken with Juan, and I'd spoken with Frank. All that left was Fisher, who was practically standing inside my body.

Fisher was wearing red Bermuda shorts with little blue whales on them, a white oxford rolled to his elbows, with a pale pink sweater draped and tied around his neck. Brown loafers. He looked like a dork—his inner Hampton lover totally out of place in the Midwest.

He ran a hand through his sandy, blond hair—his baby blues getting his flirt on.

"What's up, Darcy?" Jeez, I felt like I needed a bath. Fisher was one of those males that for lack of a better phrase, was an octoman—all hands and arms. First was the hair, then the back, next the waist, followed by whatever else he could get by with.

I sneezed—his Polo cologne bordering Skunkville. "Hi, Fisher," I said, pulling my notebook to my chest, twisting away. "I was just thinking."

"I try *not* to think," he flirted. "I've found it best if you just *do*."

Thank God, I couldn't track that dialogue because it would probably leave me decking him. "Anyway," I diverted, "I've been worried about Oscar Small, and I know if there's anything to be known, you're the man."

When in doubt, flattery works.

Fisher gave me that step-into-my-office look, his office a corner right outside the school's theater that was basically a darkened foyer. First thing I thought was, *Trapped and nowhere to go.*

I reluctantly shuffled down the right side of the double-door entry, following the red carpet until it dead-ended into the wall.

Fisher stopped and whispered, "I saw him with Jinx King."

My heart started pounding. "Jinx? When?"

"Right before fifth period. Jinx was crossing the road coming back to school, so he'd been on that side of the street. Strange, huh?"

Yes, strange, and even stranger Jinx went to English class, feigned sickness, and went back outside where I found him talking to Justin Starsong.

"Oh, well," Fisher said, his brief stint with sympathy gone, "he was a nice guy. Weird but nice."

"*Is*, Fisher," I said and frowned. "He's not dead."

"Oh, that's right. Just the wrong verb tense." But that wrong verb tense meant everything. It was the difference between seeing a future or trying to outrun the past. No one understood the pain of talking about people in the past tense more than me. The wound was so fresh I didn't even have to fake a mourning face.

I shoved the emotion down. "Anyone else?"

Fisher slowly blinked with a naughty smile, and it struck me of that saying, *Come and get it.* Oh. God. Help. Me. I *sooooo* did not want anything Fisher had to offer.

When he lapsed into some sort of testosterone heavy trance— eyes hovering at the neckline of my shirt—I literally grabbed him by the elbow and shook him. "Spit it out, Fisher."

He shook his head hard. "I swear, I looked into your eyes and got lost in the sea of green." I almost gagged. He wasn't looking at my eyes. "Okay," he said and laughed. "It was that tall guy." Gee, how profound. Fisher put his hand above his head, mimicking someone around six foot two or so. "I think he's an athlete."

"What sport?"

"Does it really matter?" he said silkily. "I think we're making some sort of cosmic connection."

"It's probably just indigestion, and yes, it matters."

Once again, he gave me that wide-eyed, glazed over googoo crap. "I'm spazzing out again." Then he put his hand over his heart, like he was delivering a soliloquy.

Doubt thou the stars are fire;
Doubt that the sun doth move;
Doubt truth to be a liar;
But never doubt I love.

"Hamlet, Act Two, scene two," I said. Beat the heck out of me how I remembered that, but I'd bet my life I was right.

Fisher grabbed me around the waist, dipping me to the ground. "I love you."

Jeez, Louise. I gave him a totally saccharine smile. "Did you tell anyone what you saw?"

"Funny you ask because my parents told me I should call the prosecutor's office."

"I would agree that's a good idea."

"How about a kiss?" he said grinning.

Talking to Fisher left me exasperated and frankly unvirginal feeling. "How about not?"

Fisher stood me aright, suddenly perturbed. "You're no fun. My parents and I already called the prosecutor and told AP Unger. End of story."

We exchanged numbers, and he promised to call *if* and *when* he remembered anything else. But even with the information, did that mean I could cross Fisher off the list altogether? Why would Fisher want to kill a hitter for AVO? For that matter, why would Oscar, Jinx, or Juan? The longer I thought about it, the more I realized I still was running on suspicion.

After an unusually boring bout with geometry, I met my normal gang for lunch. I bought an order of beef nachos, chocolate milk, and two cookies just to make sure I got my day's supply worth of carbohydrates.

When I sat down, all I heard was gossip, more gossip, and you guessed it...gossip.

Our table was NCIP—No Crap In Particular.

Right when I scooped some nachos in my mouth, Rudi pinched

me on the arm while Justice elbowed me in the ribs. Standing overtop me, breathing down my neck was—shock of all shockers—Liam Woods. No one had to broadcast his name—I could smell the fastard on him. Fastards had a distinct smell. It oozed sugary sweet with a hint of dark, peppery undertones. Two competing tastes that left my nose overstimulated, begging for boring.

Instantly, I lost all body control. One moment I was shivering—the next, sweating like I stood on the face of the sun. Heart hammering, I grimaced backward. Oh, Lordy, Liam looked super smoochy. His hair was a mass of brown curls, and his Coldplay T-shirt and dark, relaxed fit jeans looked...? Well, my mind couldn't find the words. At least any that weren't utter filth.

"This seat taken?" he murmured, pointing to the one on my left.

You know me...I just sat there like a moron.

Grumpy grumbled, "It actually—"

"Isn't!" Justice yelled over top him.

Liam slid into the empty space, carrying a tray of two slices of pizza with a salad drowned in ranch dressing and lots of cheese. "I've been trying to contact you," he murmured. Then he stopped unexpectedly—focusing on my mouth—like lightning jolted him. "Somebody pinch me. You got your braces off."

I heard a noise and feared I was panting. My word, it wasn't me. It was Justice. She grabbed Rudi's napkin and dabbed her forehead.

"What do you need, Woods?" Grumpy said, exhaling loudly.

"I'd like to ask Darcy a question—"

"Oh, yeah?" he interrupted.

Liam frowned, one dark brow arched inquiringly. I couldn't tell if he was angry, or if the conversation was one he wasn't used to having. He almost acted nervous. "Exactly what are the terms between you and Dylan Taylor? Your relationship's the biggest are-they-or-aren't-they game Valley's ever seen."

"Really?" I said surprised.

"Really. Rumor has it he's crazy with jealousy over you."

Jeez, not the sort of opening dialogue I wanted from someone I might (okay, *did*) have a crush on. That was the second time he'd asked me about my best friend. *Note to the wise: don't talk about another male or female when you're trying to impress someone else.* He just lost a point with me.

Dylan tangled up my insides regularly. The only answer that made sense was, "He's my best friend," and I hoped that was explanation enough.

Liam popped the top on his milk, drawing it to his lips for a slow drink. I didn't think any of us did anything—the girls at least. We just watched his mouth, wishing we could change places with the carton. "Listen," he finally said, "I'm going to cut to the chase. Your best friend doesn't intimidate me. In fact, he's sort of made you more attractive."

Grumpy chuckled, stabbing a pear with his fork. "I'm not so sure that's a compliment, Walker."

I wasn't either. Theirs was more than a healthy rivalry. Both were named Athlete of the Year in their respective sports, but the story about Dylan only being a sophomore received top billing all over the tri-state. My guess was Liam's ego didn't take too kindly to the slight. Like Dylan, he wasn't only on the cocky side. He possessed a short fuse. Notoriety said he welcomed the occasional scuffle when crossed. He wasn't the type to start it, but he did enjoy finishing it. Oh, well, the good ones usually did have a vice.

"Bradshaw," Liam said, laughing suggestively, "I have nothing but praise where Darcy's concerned. Taylor has girlfriends anyway, right?"

Did I hear him right? "What—are—you—talking—about?" I asked. I cocked my head to one side, directing the question to Grumpy who all of a sudden buried his head in his plate. He gave me no reassuring words, no sympathetic glances, nothing but gee-look-at-these-great-nachos-on-my-tray. What in the heck did *that* mean? Dylan and I told one another everything...within reason, of course. What I presently was doing was in my own private life and didn't affect him. Maybe that was a drastic, one-sided spin of the truth, but I couldn't rationalize it otherwise.

When I didn't say anything, Liam grinned and said, "Are you in an arranged marriage or something? Isn't that so seventeenth century?"

Thing was, Dylan didn't want me with anyone. He didn't want me (I think), but he didn't want anyone else to have me either. As much as I was all tunnel vision with Liam, the thought of a marriage with Dylan stopped me cold. He'd be stubborn, opinionated, and out-and-out old fashioned, wanting the little wife safely tucked away at home. You know, sort of like he was now. But then there'd be *the love*...the kind that just might leave me dead if I wasn't strong enough to take it.

I swallowed, suddenly overwhelmed, wondering if I'd like to try it on for just one day. The thought of his big strong arms wrapped around me, those dimples, and the feel of his hard body next to mine was definitely appealing. Holy crap, I almost hyperventilated. One day wouldn't hurt anyone, would it?

Nah, too messy. "So?" he pushed again.

Liam was fishing for information on Dylan, and he wasn't going to get it from me. That was the one rule we insisted upon. Everything between my best friend and me stayed under lock and key— until death do we part, blah, blah, and everlasting blah.

I gnawed on my pinky nail, blurting out, "Take me home after school?"

Who in the world was piloting my mouth? Maybe I'd learned the fine art of manipulation, or maybe it was nice for someone to want to spend some quality time with me. Or maybe...maybe I wanted to get back at Dylan if he had some deep, dark secrets I didn't know about. At any rate, I was pushing the envelope here, people. A week earlier I was riding the bus. Then it was Vinnie behind Murphy's back. Since Murphy was surprisingly aboard the Vinnie train, I added a fastard to the mix. Murphy would die. Let me amend that. I'd die if Murphy ever found out. Right when I almost retracted the statement, Liam's smile quirked up toward his dimples. "My pleasure," he said.

I mentally put my tongue back in my mouth.

Grumpy dug the heel of his sneaker into my flip-flopped foot, spearing me with a pain so sharp I mouthed, *I hate you*. His eyes were fixed and dilated, reminding me of a corpse that died in its fright. Sheesh, he genuinely acted frightened for me. Was there something about Liam my friends had never told me? That wasn't a look where he just didn't want his friend dating. It had something else more diabolical at its core.

Chapter Fourteen

THE NAKED TRUTH

was so hyper I had a bad case of the God-help-me-before-I-jump-off-a-cliff or something. I'd checked my watch at least a dozen times and watched the hands tick closer and closer to two thirty-nine o'clock...the end of the day. When the bell rang, I jumped out of my seat and hightailed it to my locker, hoping I didn't chicken out with Liam, hoping even more he didn't stand me up.

Shoving my English and geometry books in my backpack, I threw my Lucky bag over my shoulder and started pacing up and down the tile. One couldn't miss the relief on the majority of faces —make that 99.999 percent of people present. I was that other miniscule percent that was troubled, feeling like I had a short amount of time to make a difference in the fishbowl called Oscar's life. If I didn't? Let's just say he'd better get used to not seeing a lot of sunshine on a regular basis.

The moment I gave up and headed for Vinnie, Liam came sauntering toward me. I got goose pimples—the hair on the back of my neck standing straight up. Liam had that primo supremo, knock-your-socks-off thing going on. When he painted on one of those heart-stopping grins, my chest thudded, and my courage shriveled up and died. He was smooth, relaxed, and everything I wasn't. I was supposed to appear genuinely interested, but I honest to God didn't know how to flirt or give guys the appropriate signals. I lowered my lashes demurely and morphed into Little Miss Needy, mentally smacking myself because it felt too unnatural.

I barely got a smiling, "Hey," out of my mouth when Ivy—dressed as a dang snow bunny—came out of left field and practically threw her body on top of Liam's. Huh, maybe she and Jagger broke up again, or maybe her behavior was one of the reasons she and Jagger were constantly fighting. Liam's muscled arms stiffened as he kept eye contact with me and peeled her arms from his waist.

"Hi, Ivy," he murmured as she began to pout. "I was just leaving. Actually, I'm taking Darcy home."

If you opened an encyclopedia to villainess, Ivy's mug shot would be listed below. She shot a mental dagger straight to my heart, adding a hair flip. "You're kidding," she guffawed.

Tired of Ivy's slams, the tough girl in me decided to walk forward and (gasp!) take Liam by the hand. All I could think was, *I hate you, Ivy*, and *now I hate bunnies*.

I was sort of on autopilot when we sat down in his black Ford Explorer.

Ivy embarrassed me, and once again I did nothing. One day soon, Ivy's face would have an introduction to my fist. I just hoped it came sooner rather than later. Part of the problem was she wasn't used to seeing me with good-looking guys—other than Dylan, of course. Frankly, the attention was so bizarre it made me wonder if something weird was in the water.

When Liam soothed, "Ignore her, Darcy. She's nothing but trouble," I took a long, hard look at him as he patted himself down searching for his keys. Liam didn't just sit in a chair. He owned it and the space around him. Long and lean legs clouded my vision until I spied the curly, brown chest hair peeking from the top of his T-shirt. I'd never seen male chest hair up close. Murphy was smooth and chiseled as a statue—when he wasn't overweight—and the marvel left me wondering what it felt like. I swallowed, realizing I needed an intervention or was on a one-way ticket to Badgirlville.

As I buckled myself in, Liam merged into traffic, driving past Vinnie who was doing a one-handed lean up against the Bug, gazing at some redhead like she was the Christmas ham. Slumping down in my seat, I tried to hide. I didn't want Vinnie angry. In fact, he told me last period he'd purchased a MoneyGram (I'd requested him to), and I needed him a happy employee of the Darcy Walker Misfit Society. The moment I constructed a text of my whereabouts—you know, a lie—he suddenly belted my name, going gutter with profanity when he saw Liam behind the wheel. He started running. Well, what I think was running. All I knew was it was a whole lot of body shaking in slow-mo.

Shove down the guilt, Darcy, I told myself. *Just shove, shove away.*

When we left the parking lot, my iPhone immediately rang, and when Vinnie's mug popped up I tapped decline, sending it straight to voicemail. I pointed to the radio and said to Liam, "May I?"

Liam grinned and winked. "Have at it," he said.

I settled on Q102, a local pop Top 40 station in town, shoving Vinnie down in that compartment of my brain that covered the things I'd think about later. When Liam hummed along to a love song, I drank in the beauty of the day. The sky was cerulean blue, and the smell of budding flowers lingered in the air. I should have been thinking about spring break. Instead, my mind was flooded with what I needed to accomplish. First and foremost, I had to speak with Frank (because it was trash night), and secondly, there was the subject of Liam—my personal life.

Thing was, I didn't know what to do with him.

I started out with the obvious, telling him where I lived. After he punched my address into his GPS, my mind couldn't muster up any small talk. All I had on the brain was Oscar, Liam, kissing, more Oscar, throw some Liam in there again...and Alfonso Juarez.

I tried to appeal to his inner car-lover. "Nice ride," I somehow said.

Evidently, that was a sore subject. "My father's," he said not masking a snort. "I won't get a car until I can buy one." Obviously, there was some tension with daddy. Wonder why? "Darcy," he said when I started rocking back and forth, reverting to toddler behavior, "you can put your things in the back if you want."

Ugh, how embarrassing. My hands were clutching my belongings as if they were an armored shield. Pitching them into the back, I noticed a pile of his books: AP English, AP math, and honors science. For the love of everything holy...I couldn't stop smiling.

Liam was smart. Juan was smart. Both seniors, my guess was they had classes together, or maybe they had in the past. If my motive for asking Liam to drive me home was quasi-personal before, right then it was nothing but business. When we paused at a red light, I dove right in, forgoing any icebreaking communication. Pivoting my body across the leather seat, I said, "Liam, do you know Oscar Small? I have this theory—"

He held up one finger in a hold-that-thought gesture as he fished his ringing cell phone out of his pants pocket. When he saw the number, he sucked in a big breath of air with a grimace. He barely breathed, "Hello," when the caller cut him off with a rehearsed conversation. He sat in silence, and after a few beats of *That's not true*, *You know me better than thats*, and *Sorrys*, he held the phone out from his ear as a string of profanity filled the air. He grimaced when the caller started crying, accompanied by a disconnect so loud it might've burst his eardrum.

When the light switched to green, he glanced at his dead phone and solemnly looked over the dash.

I got a distinct feeling it was into the future.

I realized I sounded like a shrink, but I said softly, "Is there something you'd like to talk about?"

I nearly laughed. Just the thought of a shrink almost put me in a straitjacket.

His jaw clenched but just as quickly went lax with emotion. I watched every move he made, every expression, seeing if he would give me a glimpse into the part of his life that was leaving him torn. On the surface, he was outgoing. Beneath, he was unusually guarded. Perhaps as guarded as me, and two guarded people dating probably wasn't the best foundation for a lasting union. Still, a part of me wanted to kiss him. Okay, major understatement. It wasn't part of me, it was *all* of me, but I'd be an absolute fool if I didn't realize he was talking to his ex (jeez, she'd better be an ex) on the phone. Regardless, the thought of us alone, on a dark, stormy night, sent shivers down my spine. In an instant, I was fidgety and claustrophobic.

I feared he read my mind because he threw his head back in a fastard laugh. "I need a coffee," he said. "Would you like some coffee?" A man after my own heart. I had a coffee every day after school. If I didn't, it was a slow descent into madness.

Scoring major brownie points, Liam pulled into United Dairy

Farmers, my favorite gas station/coffee shop. He exited the car first and ran around to open my side. When we made it to the entrance, once again he got his gentleman on, holding the door wide, and taking me by the hand to the coffee machine. As tempting as it was to let things play out like two-people-getting-to-know-one-another-better, I needed to strike fast.

He pulled a large Styrofoam cup from the dispenser. "The works?"

I took that as meaning heavy on the cream and sugar. "Yes," I said nodding. As he filled mine up and worked on his, I started again. "Liam, do you—"

Yep, you guessed it. Right then, my iPhone cranked loudly. Talk about rotten timing. Pulling it out of my back pocket, it came as no surprise it was Dylan. If anyone could screw up my plans, I could always count on his impeccable cut-ins. Even though I was with Liam, I hit accept, gushing out a codependent, "Heeey."

"Darc, are you with Vinnie?" he said worriedly. Dylan acted like I was his pet and Vinnie was dog-sitting. Cute but sometimes annoying.

Liam held his cell out in front of us, molded his cheek to mine, and then clicked a picture. When he showed me the shot, his café au lait eyes were bright, his smile arrestingly gorgeous. I, however, looked guiltier than sin with coffee froth in the corner of my lying mouth.

When he strutted off toward the potato chips, I couldn't help but admire the view. I smacked my forehead, trying to reconnect with my morals. "Darcy?" Dylan said again.

"I'm at UDF," I hoped was answer enough.

A sound of relief. "Listen, I had a bad dream about you, and I prayed for you all day. Is everything okay?" Instant guilt trip. Dylan was one of the few that were on a first-name basis with God. My tombstone was going to read, *Death by Salivation.*

I made some explanation like, "S'all good. Just your typical day in Darcyville."

Turning right to grab a Hostess apple pie, one aisle over I saw... drumroll please...Jinx King. Well, huh, I was momentarily struck with the stupid stick.

Once my brain caught up with my eyes, I had to admit I didn't know how or why such things were transpiring—I was lucking into the information. Jinx was speaking to the guy Vinnie identified as Justin Starsong. Both had a red bandana in their back pockets and were wearing black baseball caps. Creeping forward, I sandwiched myself between the personal products aisle and magazine rack and then picked up a tabloid, flipping through the pages. Across the board, the headlines were your standard stuff with stories like, *Big Foot Spotted in Appalachian Coal Mine* or *UFO Touches Down at Fort Worth Wedding Reception*, etcetera. All the while, Dylan told me about his day's plan of taking a helicopter ride around the island.

"I miss your face," he murmured.

I somehow managed a "Me too," as Justin took a step closer, punching an angry finger in Jinx's chest. Stealing a look around for Liam, I found him in front of the ice cream case, motioning me over with an enthusiastic finger.

Mouthing, "Be there in a sec," I listened harder.

Jinx said persistently, "I didn't say anything."

"Then why did the cops stop by my house?" Justin snarled.

"I don't know, but not one bit of information came from me."

"I'd better not find out you're lying, Jinx, or you know what will happen."

Jinx acted like someone threw him in shark-infested waters. "I'll talk to my dad and see what I can find out," he promised. "But it might not be a lot. He's really mum on this one."

"You do that," Justin said in a threatening voice, "and it'd better be good news. Tomorrow night, Jinx. Be there. You have some explaining to do."

I gave Dylan a laugh as he chuckled about something that happened that morning. Thankfully, he kept talking and didn't mind I wasn't adding anything of value to the conversation. Right then, Justin whispered too low for me to hear. Whatever he said, Jinx stiffened, shifting foot to foot, his posture giving away he felt threatened. Knowing I chanced getting caught, I leaned further over the rack, but my elbow clipped the top row, and the whole thing rained down like a hailstorm. As I jumped to catch things, I knocked the shelf of panty liners behind me to the floor. When I pivoted around, I tripped over a pile of Big Foot and slipped again. Just when I thought it couldn't get any worse, I somehow soared sideways over the magazine display, my coffee and iPhone flying through the air like a mortar round.

Times like these, I understood the throes of impulsivity. It came with a price. But that was the thing with verbs—verbs acted—verbs didn't just watch. Jinx and I clonked elbows, but when I tried to corral my coffee midair, it landed right at his feet—the lid popping up, my coffee oozing toward him in a rising flood. Twisting abnormally, I jacked up my back and landed face first with a thud. As I rubbed my chin, coffee dripped down my nose, and for a moment, I had an out-of-body experience. I tried to convince myself I was watching someone other than me, but when a backwash of Colombia's finest came up my throat, I knew I could raise my hand as the moron.

Clothed in head-to-toe embarrassment, I glanced up mumbling, "Sorry."

Both gaped in unfathomable disbelief...guess I wouldn't have had a conversation starter either. By the time Jinx opened his mouth, Liam straddled my body, pulling me to my feet.

"What the eff did you two do to her?" he bellowed.

Nice to know chivalry wasn't dead, but things like that were usually my fault.

"N-n-nothing," Jinx stammered, surprisingly afraid of Liam. Liam threw a hard, menacing stare while both fumbled with magazines—then scattered like roaches do when someone hits the lights.

You know, it didn't get more embarrassing than that, so if Liam and I worried about that awkward-first-date stage, we sailed right past it into not-embarrassed-anymore familiarity. When everything was reshelved, he found my cell phone burrowed underneath a package of panty liners.

I couldn't help it, but I started giggling.

"You are quite the individual," he murmured, giggling back.

The jury was out on whatever that was.

Liam paid for two coffees—they didn't charge for the spilled one —and skipped the ice cream and Hostess pie. When we piled into his car, he turned over the ignition but only went a few feet when he put his sneaker on the brakes. "Stay away from them, Darcy. Justin especially," he said.

If I was going to play the innuendo game, I would play it as direct as possible—well, as directly as possible without giving myself away. "Are you speaking from personal experience?"

"Yes, and no," he said, shrugging and pulling into traffic. "I have a class with Justin, and I don't like the way he treats people."

Could I connect Juan the same way? "Is Juan Salas in that class?"

Liam got the funniest look on his face as he took a deliberately slow sip of coffee. "Just stay away," he said, surprisingly bossy.

Suddenly, I felt mulish, wanting to goad him even more. "Just because *you* don't like them doesn't mean that *I* won't."

Liam slowed the car, giving me a noncommittal shrug that diplomatically said nothing but insinuated absolutely everything. "I think they're bad news, that's all."

Wow, not a good conversationalist. "Not many bad things happen at Valley, Liam. Are they in a gang or something?" I asked. A muscle ticced in his jaw. I'd hit a nerve. "Do you mean as in a *gang-gang*?" I clarified. Still, he said nothing. I put my finger in the shape of a gun followed by a switchblade movement across my neck. He didn't find it funny. That would explain the matching bandana and the hand signals. But the whole idea sounded so asinine I wondered if we both were operating on fantasized and overstimulated minds. Valley wasn't a gang school. It was a nice mixture of athletes, brainiacs, musicians, and indies making their way in other avenues. Sure, we had the occasional fight, but frankly, they were so rare that when they happened, we talked about them for days. The types of things I feared that group was guilty of was totally out of character demographically, yet I feared they'd wormed their way into the school's society anyway.

"There must be something else that leads you to this opinion," I said.

He blew out some air, his voice as sharp as a stiletto. "I saw them and some others at Oxford a few weeks back."

I took pause. Why in the world would they be in Oxford? The only notable thing up there was Miami University, and even though he was evidently smart, Juan didn't strike me as the sightseeing type. My guess was he tested well, and what grades he received were from inadvertently absorbing things in class like me. Jinx? I didn't know much about his grades. But Justin? God only knew. Justin had a chip on his shoulder the size of a two-by-four.

Liam interpreted my lack of words as a request for more information. "I was at the college up there," he clipped out, instantly embarrassed. Ah, I got the feeling that's where the ex-girlfriend resided. "It's a college town, Darcy, and a lot of new construction. When I made small talk and simply asked what they were doing, they flipped a switch and got confrontational. The conversation ended with guys doing the things guys do when they don't like each other."

That could range from nonverbal behavior, to verbal exchange, to a fist in your face, or elsewhere. Time was running short. Maybe it was rash, but I decided on the direct approach. "I'm friends with Oscar Small, and I don't believe he had anything to do with killing Alfonso Juarez. In fact, the naked truth is I'm the person who found the body and reported it to the authorities."

Liam's mouth practically dragged across his chest in shock. He closed it, opened it again, and then whistled. "You're joking," he said, and I shook my head no. "What did you see?" he pushed.

Do I? Or Don't I? I blew out some air, not having a clue what would come out of my mouth. "Honestly?" I finally said. "I saw Jinx and Justin there too."

And I guess I was using you for information, I didn't add.

By the disappointed look in his eyes, he'd already figured that out. We had one of those moments where he tried to look into my soul, and I tried to look into his. I think we both wound up confused. It hit me in that instant that I might never find a guy that understood or celebrated me for who I was...and what would that be? That remained to be seen, but it certainly wasn't the prototype of the girl you brought home to mom.

Liam was the first to break the silence. "Let me get this straight. You feel Jinx and Justin are far from innocent, and you're planning to do something about it."

Listen, anyone who's worth anything would be curious if they'd discovered a dead body in a dumpster. Granted, I took curiosity to a whole new level, but when Oscar entered the picture, the curiosity became an insatiable drive.

When I said nothing, he simply asked, "Why?"

It took awhile to gather my emotions to answer the question in the spirit in which it deserved. I suppose it was because I believed we were born with the ability to choose—which was a very black and white concept. However, in my meager fifteen years, I'd come to see that the world was full of gray—society itself muddied up the primary colors. Were some things meant to be? Probably. All I knew was Providence sometimes dictated that you felt pain.

In regards to Oscar, it was like the universe said his demise was okay to happen. That didn't mean it delighted in his pain. It was simply that the pain was permitted to enter his life. Well, I was banking on the fact it was okay for me to undo it. And if it wasn't? Then that might mean he'd be having a roommate at the county jail.

"I just care," was all I said.

After a left and a right we pulled into Buffalo Trails Country Club. Suddenly, I was at a loss for words. I didn't know what to do about Oscar. I didn't know what was normal when in the car with the opposite sex. Heck, I didn't know anything. I made a mental note to hit up Ask.com and Wikipedia but had a feeling there wouldn't be any takers.

I didn't even have the chance to complete the thought because the garage door activated, and up it went with a savage and bloodthirsty Murphy positioned like a human battering ram.

———

Like Liam, Murphy was (or had been) a fastard. How did the universe pay back those reformed fathers for their wanton, selfish, and unfeeling behavior? It gave them daughters. But the universe wasn't totally without mercy. It balanced out that judgment by giving them the special ability to sniff out other bad boys like a dog could sniff out a bone. They saw it in their stride, the hidden messages in their everyday talk, the way a guy held a girl's hand or even *avoided* her hand. Reformed fathers saw all those little innuendos, both verbal and nonverbal, and shot out a warning scent to take a hike or prepare for a physical reminder that it was wisest to stay away.

Liam swallowed so loudly it practically bounced off the sidewalk and echoed up into the air. Talk about a red flag. If he couldn't handle Murphy, no way in the world would there ever be a relationship, real or fictitious.

Taking a deep breath, he slowly opened his door. I followed suit, trying to be supportive, wondering why Murphy was home three hours early. I almost asked, but the white heat rolling off him knocked me back to a respectable distance. Murphy didn't have introductions on his mind. All he needed was a torture rack because it was obvious he wanted to rip Liam from limb-to-limb.

"Liam Woods," Liam murmured, extending his hand to Murphy. "You must be Darcy's father. She's such a great girl. I've been dying to meet her parents."

See, he hadn't done his homework, had he. Number one, Murphy was a single father. Number two, if he knew Murphy, he'd pee his pants.

At first Murphy stayed put, leaning against his silver Camry. After a pause where one could hear a feather drop, I swear, Murphy circled him like prey and started sniffing. Sniffing, for God's sake. A breath caught in Liam's throat, but point for him, he never wavered or shrank away. When Murphy finished, he turned to me and belted out a string of expletives, the only one repeatable was of the h-e-double toothpicks variety.

I ducked. Liam ducked even lower.

I didn't know whether to faint, cry, hold Liam's hand, or tell Murphy he was being rude. I was so confused between the four alternatives I did the usual and nervously giggled. Liam honestly didn't appear fazed, which made me think he had some major cojones or was out-and-out stupid. Murphy glanced to the sky and mumbled, "Help me, God," and then boomed, "Five minutes, Darcy. You've got five minutes before I'm up for murder."

Jeez, Murphy behind closed doors with no supervision. Made me wonder if his pistol was loaded.

As I moved toward Liam, I expected some visage of repulsion—something other than the full-faced grin plastered on that perfect face. "Single father, eh?" he said.

I didn't respond, fearing he'd ask for details. "I have no complaints," I said shrugging.

Liam closed the gap between us, brushing his fingers against mine, his lids growing heavy with emotion. He was going to kiss me. Did I look okay? Was my coffee breath offensive? As I worried about a million different things, I had the abrupt realization my first kiss shouldn't be like that. It should come after some magnanimous occasion where the guy went all-out to impress me. My hair should be pretty, my lips nice and moist. It should be—perfect. *Beggars can't be choosers*, I heard my inner-idiot scold. The moment his lips parted and slanted toward mine, his cell phone cranked, immediately killing the moment.

Ergh, figures. The universe hated me.

Jumping, he checked his watch, sighed, and promised, "I'll call you."

Famous last words, I thought. Suddenly self-conscious, I shoved my hands in my pockets, wondering what kind of absurd tricks my mind was playing on me anyway. Murphy would never agree to any sort of relationship, and his bad boy radar was definitely in working gear. But how bad was bad? The truth of the matter was Liam scared me...and I didn't scare easily. Maybe that was half the thrill.

Chapter Fifteen

POWWOWS

*R*eality came up and bit me in the butt. It was Easter time, the season of miracles, and I needed a miracle like a ditzy bimbo needed a special on two-for-one hair color. All I knew was Murphy said if I didn't believe in miracles, then I wouldn't recognize them when they happened.

But Jesus on a cookie? Even that was a stretch by my sense of humor's standards.

Slumming in my red, snowman-clad flannel pajamas (I didn't want Christmas to end, people. I just didn't), I was standing in the middle of the kitchen watching Claudia and her local priest. Evidently, as she had a snack that morning, she pulled a chocolate chip cookie out of the Keebler bag that looked like Jesus. *Seriously?* I guess it could happen, but I didn't expect a man of the cloth and a camera crew to be filming live.

Wearing black priest clothes and a white collar (and so giddy it was disconcerting), he snapped on surgical gloves, holding the cookie to the light like he inspected a one-of-a-kind diamond.

I popped open the refrigerator, pulling out a can of Coke, eyeing the crumbs in the Keebler bag. No one had to tell me they were off-limits, but my body needed a sugar fix like its next heartbeat depended on it. When I took an overly loud swig, Claudia made a hissy sound in my direction, motioning that I go upstairs and change. Guess what? Wasn't going to happen. I took another sip, making a very dramatic, broad-sweeping motion with my arms. "What's all this?" I asked, referring to the setup.

The living room was squared-off with portable floor lighting, the wattage alone capable of powering the state of Rhode Island. It must have been a slow news day to put that kind of equipment power on a human-interest story.

Claudia's explanation was simple. "He's returned, niña," she said ecstatically, referring to the Christ child. Then she and bald Father-What's-His-Name had a stolen moment where they acted privy to Heaven's secrets, and we were just the little people.

I looked them both square in the eye. "I thought Jesus was supposed to return in the eastern sky, Claudia." I smirked, referring to my limited knowledge of prophecy.

"No, niña, just to visit. Look," she said, pointing to the cookie. On a gold charger plate on the countertop was the lone cookie in question. I must say, the distribution of the chips did resemble a dying Jesus on the cross. At least in all of the pictures I'd seen. A clump made up his hair, two flecks were eyes, and it was distributed on a portion of dough that purposely looked bleached-out for his body. It was too uncanny to dismiss without a thought, but to call a priest? And a camera crew? A little farfetched if you asked me.

Claudia immediately dispensed the niceties, introducing Father Phillip. Father Phillip had that look in his eye like he wondered if I was a Believer or bound for Hell. I had that look in my eye like I wondered if he were legit. After we both gave up on the not-so-subtle discrimination, he introduced everyone.

Odd that he knew their names, but hey, maybe he was the friendly type.

"This is Richie," he said, pointing to the cameraman. "Jack," he motioned to the one with the furry microphone, "and Rainn Webster." Richie and Jack were fresh out of college. Both had medium blond hair and builds, baby faces, and looked completely worn out. Rainn was a pretty boy with perfect brown hair, a blemish-free face, and big, brown, intelligent eyes. Rainn acted like Cincinnati was his feeder market to the big time.

I rolled my eyes in my mind. The guy was in love with himself.

Apparently, he was the roving reporter because he was clad in a white dress shirt and green tie, his bottom half in khaki shorts and three figure sneakers.

I gave them a cheesy smile as my six-year-old sister waltzed into the room wearing black patent leather shoes, white tights, a pink ruffled dress, and cockeyed bow on the top of her head. I stifled a laugh. She thought it was her big break.

"Sit, M," I told her, patting the space next to me.

As soon as her tail hit the counter, she grabbed my hand and began with a, "*Well*..." Oh, sweet God. I wasn't much of a praying person, but I felt the need to drop to my knees. Whenever the girl began a conversation with "well," it was a thirty-minute recap of what was probably a thirty-second exchange.

I nodded appropriately and even offered a couple of "oohs" and "wows."

Once she finished, we listened to Claudia and Father Phillip wax on about the wonders of God's miracles and how it took faith and belief for them to happen. Rainn couldn't hide his skepticism. Say what you will, but I'd always felt the person needing the miracle would be the best judge, but far be it from me or the Keebler elf to protest otherwise.

After ten minutes, Rainn made a whirly signal over his head to wrap up. He then fished his cell phone out of his pocket, checking a text. "Come on, guys," he beamed excitedly. "Some man showed up in a dumpster, and it looks similar to the Juarez and Hughes cases."

Wait...*WHAT?!*

I jumped off the counter. My word, that right there was a miracle for Darcyville. "Was he dead?" I butted in.

Rainn looked at me like I was part nuisance, part kindred spirit for even entertaining the thought. A smile lit up his face as he expelled a laugh that grated to my core. Maybe that's what crazy people sounded like. "Gee, I hope so," he said. "The 'burbs kill me. There's nothing up here except a frigging Jesus cookie."

All I knew was he'd just insulted Jesus. I was going to shower as soon as he left.

Vinnie brought over a MoneyGram for two hundred dollars—it emptied my savings. We were pseudo friends again, but I wasn't exactly back in his good graces. While he frothed at the mouth at how horrible of a person I was, I stood there and took it like a woman. I deserved a medal for making it through that conversation without stabbing him...or myself. I then called 1-800-PAYTELL and set up an account.

When Marjorie was fast asleep, Murphy and I had a family meeting. He called them powwows. Last one we had was when we changed from crunchy peanut butter to smooth. The agenda right then, however, involved who I was allowed in the car with...long and short of it? A demon was preferred over Liam Woods.

Murphy left my room, stupidly assuming I was in total agreement. "I'm beat, kid. My tank's on E."

I faked a yawn, sufficiently waited until he snored like a rhinoplasty-gone-bad, and pulled on my white robe, stepping barefoot into the cool, night air. Like clockwork, Oscar and Frank picked through our garbage around midnight. I needed to get word to Oscar that my phone line was open, and the best way to do that was via Frank.

Clutching my robe to my chest, I stared up at the moon through a break in the clouds. The crescent shape was filling in nicely, almost to a full circle. Even though it was partly illuminated, I could see the rocky ruins and craters made by the onslaught of atmospheric elements. It reminded me of life and the way our insides were permanently affected by the forces around it. The "man on the moon"—the face one could make out during a full phase—was the only face we ever saw. It was never changing, but what was on that other side? What personality was it hiding?

If your past defined you, it was no wonder Frank and Oscar were looked upon as potential problems. Oscar's latest escapade had criminal-in-training all over it, but he didn't have any of the telltale signs of psychotic behavior. I couldn't speak to bedwetting, but he wasn't an animal torturer, nor did he blow up...

Shi-i-i—I almost cursed out loud.

Oscar *did* like to blow things up. He once brought fireworks to school and took out a porta-potty. Then there was the incident where he stuffed a chipmunk in a locker. He didn't kill it, but he sure as heck scared it. I hyperventilated so fast and hard it hurt my esophagus. *Maybe I'm defending someone that shouldn't be defended*, I thought. I quickly talked myself out of the idea. We were talking about Oscar. Oscar was good—weird, but good.

To take my mind off the confusion, I gave the nightly news top billing in my brain. Another victim had been found in downtown Cincinnati in a place called Over-the-Rhine. Over-the-Rhine was no place a person visited just to visit, unless he or she came strapped with explosives, wearing a flak vest and wanting to have dinner with the local gangs. It was bad decision after bad decision gone awry. Lately, however, there'd been a local effort to revitalize the area, and some nice restaurants and housing were built. It hadn't totally lost its bad reputation though. Things like that took time.

The man, according to a less-than-detail-oriented Rainn Webster, was shot twice and had a broken neck. Although he never mentioned a severed hand, the method of death was eerily similar, but was it similar enough to take some heat off Oscar? If law enforcement even remotely felt they were the works of the same person, then shouldn't they be looking for another killer? One couldn't pin another murder on someone who was currently incarcerated. I could only hope the death of victim number three placed a morsel of doubt in the back of Reese Sanders' mind.

Right on cue, Frank crept up the street in his old, gray Chevy pickup truck. White smoke poured out of the tailpipe, and the engine purred so loudly it sounded like it belonged on an airplane. The tailgate was already down—the bed full of scrap metal, a rusty refrigerator, tires, a strand of Christmas lights, and a naked female mannequin. God only knew the story that accompanied that one.

Frank stopped at the oversized mailbox at the end of our driveway. We had nothing of value—just four black trash bags. When I gave him half a smile and wave, he screeched his car into park, creaking his door wide to stand in front of me. I found that odd. We could've spoken through the window, but it's almost like he was running away from perhaps what got Oscar in trouble in the first place.

"I saw him," he mumbled.

The "him" in question was Oscar. After a few silent seconds, Frank told me what he did during the day—what he and Oscar would've done if they were together—and I realized he just needed to connect with someone. Frank was the needy one in the relationship, and my guess was, he was totally lost without Oscar telling him which foot to put in front of the other.

"Is he okay?" I asked.

Frank kicked his dirty, white sneaker at some imaginary pebbles in front of him. "He's scared, but Oscar can be scary too."

I wasn't sure what that meant—only that he'd found a way to coexist without getting killed in the process.

A few hours earlier, a storm front had rolled in. A large cloud was overhead, and a burst of rain sprung from its core, deluging us as if we stood underneath a waterfall.

"Great," I mumbled.

Frank just stood there, not even trying to shield himself. It might have been a mistake (since trees drew lightning), but I pulled us underneath the big maple in our front yard. Its skeletal remains were sprouting leaves but not enough to keep the pounding rain from drenching us. "You have to think, Frank," I screamed over the torrent. "Why would someone think Oscar was easy to frame?"

God love him, Frank had an airhead quality I thought was only reserved for females. All he could do was shrug and lick the water that ran down his nose.

"What do you do every night?" I asked. "You have to have crossed paths with someone."

He grabbed my gaze as though he'd suddenly remembered something. "We only pick on Mondays and Tuesdays, but sometimes we travel to new construction sites. Once we saw..."

Frank sucked in a breath like if he didn't get one he'd pass out. He was legitimately scared, and Frank was—well, sometimes I think he was too dumb to be scared. "Who?" I asked. When he wouldn't answer, I said, "Okay, where?"

Frank pitched his head north. "A few miles up the road."

"And what do you *do* at the construction sites?"

Frank's hands were shaking, and it wasn't from the chill. "It's not always legal," he confessed, embarrassed.

Well, duh. Not for one minute did I think it would be.

I grabbed his hands. "I'm not here to rat you out. That's your business. I'm just trying to help Oscar...because I can," I added cockily.

Frank vigorously nodded his head up and down, believing every word, but the fact he put his faith in me so readily put me ill at ease. It dawned on me that he had no one. I didn't know anything about his parents, but not once had he mentioned how they were handling things and what their plans were—if they even had any—of getting Oscar out unscathed.

"Get in," he said, nodding to his truck. "I'll show you what they do."

———

Frank waited while I grabbed some jeans, laced up my Chuck Taylors, and shoved my head through a black hoodie. All the while I had that little angel on my shoulder telling me someone needed to medicate me, lock me up, and throw away the key. There was no method to my madness. I usually let my urges take the verb in me places. Trouble was, there were people all over the world with impulse control issues that were on Death Row and in padded cells.

Trying to stave off sleepiness, I shoved a stainless steel travel mug underneath Murphy's Keurig. I punched the button, and within minutes made two piping hot cups of Black Tiger—one for me, one for Frank. You gotta love science.

The entire time I wondered what I should take on an excursion like that. Rat poison? Arsenic? Antifreeze? When I sat down in the truck, the best I could come up with was to tell Frank to lock the doors.

We left BTCC and after a few turns were on Valley Road. It ran north to south with potholes big enough to swallow a semi. Frank didn't seem to mind if his tire fell into one, so I just held onto the dash and crossed my fingers I didn't lose a tooth in the process.

As the storm picked up, we rocked like we were on a roller-coaster, tree pollen hitting the windows, the weather not lenient in its assault whatsoever. One of the wipers hung like a broken bird wing, so there was a segment of windshield that didn't get cleared. Frank hunched over the wheel, peering through that small, smeary space and humming to himself like a crazy person.

Right about then, I realized how stupid my plan was...especially if the storm woke Murphy. Before I could tell Frank to put the skids on the stakeout, we hydroplaned and went airborne over a hill. My stomach bottomed out as we came down so hard the load shifted in the rear.

Frank looked over sideways as he corrected the tires. "You okay?"

Most of my stomach was still in my mouth. I really wasn't sure.

Ten minutes later, he cut the lights and slowly pulled into a new development in the city of Monroe. Several houses were being built at the same time, but no electricity was on in either of the homes that looked finished. My guess was they weren't occupied yet.

We parked the car behind a portable white trailer that said HQ on its door. I quickly filled Frank in on what I thought happened the day Alfonso Juarez was discovered—that someone killed him before Oscar found him (probably the night before), but when they saw Oscar, the person or persons got the bright idea to frame him. Frank frowned, undeniably confused. I explained if I could get certain evidence (unfortunately, the specifics were vague), then we could hopefully set Oscar free. When Frank's frown grew even deeper, I realized that was too many caveats in a brain that couldn't harbor the complex.

I then asked if he knew of a relationship Oscar had with Annie Hughes. Frank had no clue, so strikeout on that point too. That meant Oscar was hiding something—something he kept personal even from his own brother. I hadn't verified a relationship with Oscar, but there *had* to be one—especially if the social worker was correct, and they were trying to pin a double murder on him.

Pulling my hood over my head, I creaked open the door and stepped into a sloshing mixture of mud and sawdust. Frank came to my side, the cold rain hitting our heads so hard it felt like wayward golf balls. We quietly hurried to a parked backhoe and crouched down, peering between a large wheel and the space right underneath the engine. At first, it was hard to make out details, but once my eyes adjusted, I could see bodies. Standing in front of the headlights of a dark SUV were whom I recognized as Jinx King, Juan Salas, and Adam Neeley. They seemed oblivious to the thrashing rain, Juan intent on drilling Jinx, whose body language was defensive

—like someone taking a verbal beating. I almost felt sorry for him, but before I could take the emotion further, a dark sedan pulled up and another individual entered the scene wearing a trench coat with a hood. That person's back was toward us, and he stood taller than the others and broad shouldered. Each of them gave the person the hand signal, yet the hooded figure didn't return it. Could that have been Justin Starsong? And if so, why ditch the signal? Especially when Justin had been the one that insisted Jinx attend the meeting anyway?

Even though the meeting was odd, I didn't see anything out of the ordinary. So Jinx was the butt-end of an argument...so what?

I got antsy. "Frank, I don't see—"

"Be patient," he whispered. "Watch the hooded one."

Mr. Hood walked toward the trunk of the sedan and removed a bundle of what looked like pipes. Even if it wasn't Justin, I recognized that gait. It was a no-nonsense walk of determination and confidence. "Who is that?" I asked.

Frank was silent for a spell. "I don't know, but once you cross evil like that, you recognize it when you feel it again." Come to think of it, I was catching the same vibe. I'd only seen Justin standing at the dumpster and a few other times I could count on one hand. Could that be him? God knew he felt evil enough. I didn't have time to go through my mental white pages because the sky cracked, and a beam of lightning caught the pipe's reflection.

It was reddish-brown. What the heck? "Copper?" I gasped.

Frank nodded. "They steal it and sell it. Oscar and I ran into them at Traders' World where they were trying to unload it." You could've knocked me over with a feather. Traders' World was a well-known outdoor flea market off I-75, only a few miles north of the school. Vendors sold things like antiques, clothing, bicycles, crafts, etcetera. It was so large a person could take an entire day to discover its contents, but I'd never heard of anything illegal going down there. In fact, it was a pretty reputable landmark, but there must be a black market connection the Smalls had discovered.

"Does the buyer have his own booth?" I asked.

Frank vehemently shook his head. "No, Traders' World has no part of it. There's a guy up there that acts like he's with Traders'

World, but he takes you over to his van where he sort of feels out your intentions."

So had Oscar cut into their copper profits? And if so, was cutting into the profits reason enough to frame him for murder? That meant they would have to "happen" upon a body and get the bright idea to get Oscar out of the picture so they could make more money. Weird? Too weird? *But copper theft was big*, I remembered. At least three busts a week, according to Jinx King's father.

"Who's your contact up there?" I asked Frank.

Frank wiped water from his eyes. "His name's Buggy. He used to sell garden tools, but when Traders' World got wind of his illegal activities, he was banned forever. Before he was caught, we'd lay our copper under a tarp by his truck. We ran into Juan doing the same thing."

As I struggled to make sense of it, a car slowly crept up behind them, lights off, engine barely making a sound. I wouldn't have noticed, but moonlight bounced off the chrome of the front bumper. Thing was, it was a yellow Dodge Charger. *No waaaaaay*, I whispered to myself. *Just who all was invited to this little party anyway??*

The only Charger I'd encountered was the day I found Alfonso Juarez, and I thought that was by chance. Were they friends? Acquaintances? Competitors of some kind? The way he was lying low, it was obvious he wanted to remain as incognito as me.

As God as my witness, right then the rain let up. Just stopped on a dime. Like it was a message from Heaven for me to get out while the gettin' was good. Pulling my iPhone out of my jeans, I activated the video camera. Stupid since it was dark, but I decided to pan the crowd anyway. Zooming in on Juan's mouth, I tried to capture his words. He kept barking at Jinx who acted like a kicked dog, periodically saying something I assumed was to defend himself. That went on for a while, but then Mr. Hood went bonkers, getting in each person's face, releasing his inner-snake.

Juan immediately corralled the chaos and railed something at the group. One-by-one, they stopped—like a chorus of trained Chihuahuas—all attention immediately falling on Adam Neeley. In the course of a few words, scrawny little Adam Neeley was suddenly Public Enemy Number One.

Omigosh. It dawned on me who Adam was.

It was easy to lose track of someone in a mega school. Adam fell into that category that life made invisible. He was the kid always picked last on the playground. He was the kid that if he *did* make an organized athletic team, his uniform was a size too large. He was the one people played with in preschool, but when they went on to bigger and better things, they forgot about him. Adam was the definition of eternally overlooked, so why was he hanging with people I felt were in no way fair?

A few words passed between Juan and Jinx. Then both their attentions riveted on Adam. If the calm before a storm meant something tornadic was coming, then the feeling in the air was so quiet, nothing short of mass destruction was next. Juan took one purposeful step toward Adam, both his hands clenched like he held something valuable he didn't want to drop. Adam shifted left then right, his eyes glued on Juan's face that was contorted with an emotion I'd never seen before. Taking a frantic step backward, next thing I knew, he was penned-in like he was a piece of meat, and they were a hungry pack of dogs. Juan launched forward with an uppercut so fierce his head shot back. Adam went down on his knees, splashing in the mud, catching himself on the ground with all ten fingers splayed wide in a puddle. One leg at a time, he shakily righted himself, but a look of fear landscaped his face. It wasn't fear that he was being attacked. It was fear of what he knew was to come. Understanding came faster than a speeding bullet...I knew what that was. Adam was being "jumped in" to their particular gang, ergo getting the tar beat out of him as initiation.

It was organized chaos. Jinx came at his jaw in a right-footed kick while Juan wailed away on his lower ribs. Adam coughed and sputtered and then glanced upward, but there was no chance to say, *No thank you, I've changed my mind.* Right then, Mr. Hood joined the group, and the three swung and punched like they were ridding society of its deadliest vermin.

Tears slid down my cheeks. I wanted to help. I wanted to end his pain and send them to jail. When I looked at Frank, however, in no way whatsoever was he behooved to intervene. He stood transfixed, almost as if he'd seen it before and wasn't shocked at the level of violence.

Curling into a fetal position, Adam took a blow to the lower back and then erupted into little girl tears. I couldn't help it, but I cried harder. I needed to go home. I was nauseous, and I wanted to put the whole thing behind me. When Adam took Mr. Hood's heel to the head, inadvertently he moved by instinct—just enough for Juan to land a punch to his jaw that left him lights-out.

I screamed at the top of my lungs, but Frank shoved his hand over my mouth. It was too late. I'd given us up, and the three standing practically lay rubber barreling toward us. The Charger revved its engine and blinked its lights, trying to get the attention off Frank and me and onto it.

Frank and I gasped at the same time and then took off like we were running with the bulls in Pamplona, waiting for them to spear us from behind. I didn't want to die. I figured I'd meet someone who didn't mind settling, and we'd have two point five kids and fight over the unpaid bills every month. Amidst voices and a cyclone of profanity, I realized this could be the last thing I ever did.

We jumped over wood framing and drywall scraps, dodging puddles swollen with an unapologetic rain. Stepping in one a foot deep, I lost my sneaker in a quicksand of mud. I felt as naked as the day I was born. Chuck Taylor had been with me since seventh grade. My first instinct was to dig him out and then run even faster. Instead, my mind cursed, @#$%^&* as I made mental plans to come back for him at daybreak...that was, if I saw the light of day again.

Chapter Sixteen

TOO CLOSE FOR COMFORT

*H*ands. Down. Best. Night. Ev-uh. Except I lost Chuck. Moment of silence, people. He was first on the to-do list—well, actually second—because I needed to have a conversation with Jagger Cane. Like Liam insinuated (darn him for not being more direct), I was under the impression it was a gang meeting. Jinx delivered something, perhaps only information, but whatever it was, his status with Juan was on shaky ground.

The punk-arse mother-truckers sure as heck embraced teamwork when it came to Adam Neeley though.

My soul clenched with the memory. When Frank and I peeled out of there, Adam was still lights-out, facedown in the mud. Surely, they took him home, right? Just to make sure, we made an anonymous call to Valley Police from a burner phone Frank snagged during a picking escapade. We told them we'd witnessed a vicious beating and wanted to make sure the victim was still breathing.

Short...to the point...and hopefully enough to get some manpower on the scene.

I picked up my iPhone, realizing calling Jagger was stepping into sin, expecting my body to stay pure—but he identified Juan Salas as the man with answers. If I was going to play the game, I had to follow up on every tip—no matter how uncomfortable the circumstances or the ramifications that might come to pass.

"Babe," he groaned in greeting. *It's a little early* was left unsaid.

Ah, crap. I'd never even considered the time, and unless the world stopped spinning, it was six twenty-three on Tuesday morning.

"Sorry," I mumbled.

"No apology necessary." I lay there for a few seconds wondering what to do next. Dive right in? Make small talk? Apologize again and claim I misdialed? *How about hang up, Darcy, and do what normal teenagers do on spring break? Oh, I don't know,* my conscience snorted, *like maybe sleep in?* No wonder I couldn't get a date. I was crossing the normal boundaries that made me too much of a freak to join the dating pool.

Jagger broke the awkward silence. "Babe, this is where you're supposed to tell me why you called."

"Oh," I said embarrassed. "I've got a question for you."

Jagger laughed, the cameo of a rogue. "Well, I've got something for you too, but it involves our lips getting better acquainted."

I imagined myself hosing down with Clorox. Even though he couldn't see me, I pulled the blankets all the way up to my chin. "L-llisten, I didn't call to flirt," I stuttered. "I just have—"

"A question," he repeated groggily.

"Yeah, it's about Oscar. You said Juan Salas had answers, but Juan isn't exactly the friendly type. At least with me."

I could almost hear Jagger's pulse rise through the phone. "Did he hurt you?" he snarled.

My mouth paused wide open. Jagger never struck me as the gallant type. "No," I quickly answered, feeling like I might've started something.

"Then tell me exactly what he did, what he said, and how he said it."

I held my iPhone out from my face, squinting at the number. Yup, it was Jagger, so why did it feel like he had channeled Dylan's voice and emotions?

I explained, "When I asked if he knew anything, he got really testy."

"Babe, you're going to have to give me a little more than testy."

I rolled my eyes. "I couldn't find an appropriate opener, so I told him I knew they were good friends and then asked if he'd heard of Oscar's predicament."

"And how did he answer?"

"Not very friendly. He said he'd heard that they *weren't* friends, but Oscar was always in the wrong place at the wrong time."

"That doesn't sound so bad, babe."

"Well, when he called Oscar a kook, I might've blurted out, 'it takes one to know one.'"

Jagger breathed in, breathed out, and then said to himself he didn't know how Taylor did it. "Will you take my word for it he's not someone you want mad?"

Who did he think I was? When I called someone at six twenty-three on the first day of spring break that technically didn't make me someone who rolled over and played dead. I simply answered, "No." Once again, a breath in and out. "Jagger?"

"I'm still here," he muttered sarcastically. "I'm just trying to figure out how to formulate a response that will cause the least repercussions."

I duplicated his tone, throwing it right back at him. "I won't tell anyone what you've told me, Jagger. I might be a lot of things, but a blabbermouth isn't one of them. So if you're worried about repercussions, then don't."

Wow, I was actually impressed with that line of sarcasm.

"I'm not worried about me," he murmured. "I'm worried about what you'll do with the information once I give it to you."

I guess he should be, but that wasn't really my concern at the moment. "I'm going to think on it," I hoped was answer enough.

Jagger groaned like someone was pulling his wisdom teeth. Finally, he conceded to the pressure. "This is what I've got, babe. It's not rumor or conjecture. It's what I know to be fact. Juan Salas isn't only a thug—his particular brain borders the sociopathic. I believe he and Jinx King and a few others—that the cocky in me thinks are so unimportant I don't know their names—are involved..."

"In a gang?" I interrupted.

Jagger laughed loudly. "I was going to say they're robbing construction sites. Gang? That might be your overactive imagination Italianizing this whole thing."

I stuck my tongue out at him. Made me feel better, and furthermore, it made me feel uncomfortably weird he was reminding me of

172

Dylan. For years, I'd considered him Dylan's arch nemesis. Ergo, he was hands-off in the relationship and friendship departments. If he actually had some redeeming qualities, I was going to have to throw out my *Evil Jagger Cane File* and reconstruct a new one.

"And you know this *how?*" I asked.

"You don't want to know," he said evasively.

Actually, I did, but I let it slide. "What's it got to do with Alfonso Juarez?" I asked.

"I have to admit I've given the thing some thought."

Jagger thinking...*wow.*

"And here I thought you were just a pretty face," I stupidly said out loud.

Somebody help me. He moaned seductively. I fought a sigh. I didn't want to lead him on, but before I could talk myself out of it, I said something dumb like, "Thanks for the moan."

Jagger busted out laughing again. "If I had to answer, Darcy," he said, "my guess is Juarez was involved in some way too."

I couldn't dispute the logic, but that meant I'd have to get close to AVO. Yeesh, even *I* wasn't that stupid...I think.

"Do you think Juan might know what that involvement is?"

"Perhaps."

"Well, at least we've got an arrangement where he's going to call if he, quote-unquote, 'remembers anything.'"

I heard dirty words I'd never heard before. I steeled my resolve, preparing myself for a thrashing like I'd never experienced. I wasn't used to this Jagger. Heck, I wasn't used to *any* sort of Jagger, and a part of me was worried I might like to keep him around. "Why don't you define this arrangement, Darcy?" he demanded. "God help me, you're on the speed train to self-destruction."

He was channeling Dylan again. "It's no big deal," I told him. "He just said he'd call if he remembered anything. Have you ever noticed him do—"

"That hand signal?" he completed.

"Yeah, it's five fingers then one, repeated twice."

"I've noticed, but I don't understand the meaning of the digit twelve."

Huh, I never thought of it being the number twelve, but maybe

Jagger was onto something. Jagger used words like devious, cutthroat, premeditated, and five-star manipulator liberally when describing Juan. He knew little about Jinx, however, but I had an early morning epiphany of someone who could fill in the blanks.

———

It was six fifty-two in the morning. By rough guestimate, I'd clocked less than six hours of sleep, but after a stiff cup of coffee, I convinced my neurons it didn't matter. Remembering I videotaped the event, I couldn't tell you how depressed I was when all I got on replay was blah, blah, blah words, Frank's big fat head, and nothing but blur.

Not wanting to ruin my euphoric mood, I tapped in the speed dial for brother number two. One thing about teenagers and cell phones: ours were always by our beds, charging with the power on. We never knew when we were going to get the invitation of our lives or the gossip smorgasbord of all smorgasbords.

"Bonjour, bella," Finn answered in a French accent.

"Bonjourno. Do you remember when I hid you from whatever-her-name-is that I said it came with a price?" Scary those were the same words Juan used.

"Oui," he said sleepily.

"I'm cashing in, big boy. Can you get a juvie record on Jinx King?"

Finn could hack into anything and was the perfect blend of deviant, cool-headedness, and looking-the-other way. As long as I didn't ask many questions, he was my ticket to the land of the all-knowing.

"Bella, bella," he said testily. "Can Valentine Vecchione sniff out a moon pie?"

I disconnected with a laugh. I must've nodded off into a narcoleptic stupor because next thing I knew, I was talking to Liam. I didn't know if I called *him*, he called *me*, or something supernatural happened and simultaneously placed the phones in both our hands. Finishing up a morning swim at Lifetime Fitness, he asked me to go to the library and then catch a movie—incredibly stupid move on his part since Murphy wanted to roast him and eat his entrails. What's more, he thought I was the library-type. Whatever. If he wanted me to be the library-type, then by God, I was the library-type. Thing was, Liam said we needed to discuss something serious and mentioned the word confidential three times. I told him I'd call back just as Murphy strode into my room at seven o'clock, on the dot. If anything, Murphy was a creature of habit. He left every morning, come heck or high water, at seven o'clock.

When I asked permission, he rolled his eyes, snorted, and then demanded I change my cell phone number that afternoon. Call me a genius, but my interpretation was he vetoed the experience. Meant I'd have to do things...*on the QT*.

Murphy sat on the corner of my bed, rolling his light blue oxford shirt to his elbows. "Give me the 411, kid."

Suuuuuuure.

Sitting up, I gave him lie number one: "I'm going to the mall with Justice and then to Target," which was lie number two. "Then I'm going to the library with Rudi," which constituted lie number three because I planned to go with Liam. "How 'bout you?"

Murphy's eyes squinted up like two raisins. When my father was happy, his eyes were devoid of slits. For that matter, when he was mad they pretty much looked the same. "I'm buying a lottery ticket," he said with a big smile.

Murphy's adult way of gambling. I laughed to myself.

Murphy was a bookie in his younger years. Evidently, he was so convincing, he could talk people into betting on how long it took an ant to cross the road or the Loch Ness to show its face. Obviously, he'd mellowed, but God only knew what atrocities went down in the man's brain.

After we discussed the science behind his number choices, he reminded me I needed to buckle down and gather information for my term paper. No kidding...not to mention I needed a topic. The moment he opened his wallet to give me a twenty-dollar bill, Claudia stormed into the room, her face practically spitting flames and channeling Beelzebub. Why the possessed look? In her right hand was my mud-encrusted, sopping wet sneaker.

The missing Chuck.

Returned by God only knew whom.

Time stretched to infinity, and my brain short-circuited. I

opened my mouth to speak, and for a moment, I feared I'd stroked out.

"My shoe," I somehow gasped, throwing my hand over my heart. "*Wh*-where...*d*-did you *g*-get it?"

I was a stuttering fool.

"It in mailbox!" she screamed. That was too close for comfort. Whoever returned it knew it was mine. That meant they knew I had been spying on them. That also meant they were in the driver's seat—not me.

I needed to confess or dig a deep hole and hide. But how in the world could I word a confession that covered my rapidly multiplying offenses? I mean, it made sense to me...but to the average mind?

"Where you be, niña?" she spat out accusingly. "These clean yesterdays. This morning dirties. You goes out at night, si?"

Claudia's English was good, but she hadn't quite mastered the verb tenses. I opted to give them the silent treatment. After a few beats of me swallowing, understanding dawned on them quickly.

"There by the grace of God, go I," Murphy grumbled, standing up to pace around. My guess was God's grace might not cover my current sins, but I was hoping Heaven graded on the curve.

"Sorry, Murphy," I apologized.

His face turned murderous. "What exactly were you doing?!"

None of your business. Thank you very much.

When he crossed his arms and dug in his heels, I sighed out an answer. "I went outside to talk to Frank Small."

Murphy knew Frank was a picker because Frank and Oscar had backed over our landscaping several times. That didn't endear them to the population, but once Murphy got a load of their lifestyle, he backtracked on his hypothetical wish to behead them. "You couldn't have *called* Frank?" he asked infuriated.

I gave him half a shrug. "I didn't have his number, and I just feel sorry for him."

Murphy snorted, narrowing his eyes. "I tell you what, kid. People need to feel sorry for *you*."

Every survival instinct I had kicked into high gear. God love her, Claudia must've felt it because her black eyes went frantic. She belted out, "*I* wearing shoe!"

That was classic Claudia. Squeal, and then get upset when

Murphy got angry. Thing was, she always inserted her own brand of lying when it was too late. She should've taken ownership four sentences ago.

Murphy snorted louder. "I don't know what upsets me more. The fact that my daughter plays nighttime ninja, or the woman I hired is willing to lie for her." He settled his eyes on me as Claudia started speaking rapid Spanish. "It was practically Noah's flood last night. A sinkhole could've swallowed you up, and you'd be down there with the gosh-danged dinosaurs!"

I tried not to laugh, but when a squeal whistled out, Claudia jumped on the bed and slammed her hands over my lips. The woman needed a new support bra. One was higher than the other, and lefty fell out of her orange muumuu and bonked me in the chin.

Murphy continued to pace, oblivious to anything else. "I see it in my business all day long. There are people that are one-time stupid and people that are two-times stupid. Kid, you might be three-times stupid, and that's just an extra value-add the good Lord gifted me with." He stopped to take a breath saying the word "stupid" three more times. "You're grounded. You can't drive, you can't go out on dates, and you've lost your iPhone, iPod, iHome, and whatever other contraption the Apple people make."

I threw my hand over my chest, gasping, "No more fruit?"

Murphy's eyes were dark and unyielding. He bent down into my face, purposely crowding me with his big, angry body. "You're off fruit altogether."

My laughter burnt out. That was one of Murphy's classic overcorrections. His discipline rivaled that of the Romans. All that was missing was the blood and gore.

"For how long?" I said with a wince. "You're going to throw off my vitamin C intake."

He didn't find the pun funny. "Until I say you can have fruit again."

Yeesh, that was a *real* problem. I closed my eyes, ferociously kneading my temples. I couldn't drive nor did I have a boyfriend, but take my phone and he might as well have cut off my right hand. How in the world was I going to have my morning wake-up call, talk to my friends, and entertain myself? Not to mention, finish everything I'd started??

Realizing my thoughts were growing scattered, I blurted, "But what about the library?"

Murphy stopped in his tracks. "Funny you act so concerned right now, kid. All you've been doing is diving in dumpsters, skipping school, and traipsing around at all hours of the night. That behavior isn't going to get you anywhere, and it certainly isn't going to get you a passing grade. So to answer your question, it's the library only. But I tell you, Darcy, I've got spies everywhere. You'd better do right by me, or I'm going to make you pay. Speaking of paying," he said and sarcastically grinned, "that'll be twenty dollars to the Stupid Jar."

The MoneyGram broke me. The only twenty dollars in my possession was the one he gave me five minutes ago.

Murphy turned on his heels, his light-hearted mood from earlier all but snuffed out. I looked at Claudia, tears instantly pooling in my eyes.

"I sorry, niña," she apologized. Claudia stroked my hand, offering a forced smile. What she needed to offer was a barf bag. I currently wanted to hurl.

———

Sometimes people committed egregious acts because they had no fear of reprisal. That wasn't true with me—Murphy could scare the crap out of anyone. My problem was I had no self-control. Regardless, even I didn't feel it wise to go to the library with Rudi when I hoped to meet Liam. If Murphy found out, there would be hell to pay. So what did I do? I ghosted on Liam and didn't phone him back at all. Still curled up in bed, I dropped my gaze onto the photograph of Dylan and me by my bedside table. In desperate times, I'd phone him for backup. Right then, I couldn't chance it. If he had but a mere inkling of my actions, he'd release his inner-caveman, and things would undeniably be worse.

I did my own DIY (do it yourself) pep talk, knowing it would take some major creative thinking to outthink Murphy. Unfortunately, I revved the engine on my imagination and got nowhere. Immediately, defeat leeched onto me, and I had the urge to sob like a baby. Murphy was right. I'd been engaging in stupid behavior and dwelling on things that certainly wouldn't help my academic nor intellectual futures. Instead, they'd probably wind up shortening my life.

Right as my confidence flatlined, the house phone rang, and the caller ID flashed Valley Juvenile Detention Center.

My eyes were glued to the dial, my ears transfixed.

If the universe wanted me to be a good girl, then why did it keep throwing temptation into my lap?

"Oscar?" I answered quietly, sniffling back tears.

He didn't answer with a yes. Instead, he exhaled a, "Thank you."

Talk about adding fuel to the dying embers of my resolve. "Are you okay?" I asked.

Oscar, normally-jovial-and-good-for-a-joke Oscar, expelled some humorless laugh. *He'd changed.* I shivered. I didn't know what he'd encountered, but he'd already changed. We had your basic small talk about what he'd had for breakfast and how he'd been sleeping, but the conversation bumped and careened along like a dying car. Oscar was too content on hearing my voice when frankly I was worried about the charge-per-minute for the phone call. How long would it take to blow through two hundred dollars?

What did I have to cover anyway? First was, what do they have on you? What did you see Jinx do? What do you know about AVO and the copper industry? My God, did you know Annie Hughes? And even worse, have you heard about her death?

I said, "Oscar, we don't have much time. Let's start with the basics. What did you find out in Discovery?"

Discovery took place after the accused was arraigned. It was when the prosecution revealed what they had on the suspect, so the defense could prepare. In that phase, the defense attorney would send the prosecutor a list of questions that he or she would answer along with any documentation they might have. Once those were in hand, the defense would sit down with the defendant and discuss the specific charges and figure out how best to defend the person.

Oscar sounded embarrassed but nonetheless told me they had his fingerprints, a ballcap that contained a strand of his hair, DNA on the hand (because he'd scraped his knuckles and then bled onto the hand as he dumbly picked it up—only in the world of a picker), and of course, the eyewitness accounts of him being in the vicinity.

The public defender never gave names, but a pretrial hearing was set for a week later. That was when a list of witnesses would be given out, and Oscar would discuss his plea. My guess was the prosecution would try and protect their identities, especially if they were minors. But what if those minors were the ones who framed him?

On a different note, was the defense following up on what could be the works of a serial killer? Did Oscar's attorney think the three deaths were mere coincidence? And hello, what about motive? Thing was, if it were the works of a serial killer, the FBI would take over and push everyone to the sidelines. My aunt said as much, so were the feds already in town?

"Tell me about Jinx King," I said. "Frank told me about the copper business. Do you think Jinx could have anything to do with this?"

I told him Juan was seen on the premises and that I'd personally seen Jinx and Justin on the day Alfonso Juarez was found, and I suspected they were the culprits. I then added that I'd witnessed Justin threaten Jinx at UDF. Unfortunately, Oscar could only provide a positive identification on Jinx. He didn't recognize the names of the other three.

"Jinx has everything to do with this," he sighed out in answer. "I'm not clean, Darcy. Frank and I needed money, and it's just what I do. Jinx and I fought over the same construction sites. I was better at getting a jump on things than he was."

"So this was basically over competition?"

I heard the shrug in his voice. "I don't know. He hates me, I hate him, I saw that body, and that's all I know."

Everything I needed to cover was swimming around in my brain, dying to surface for answers. I opened my mouth two times, but Oscar cut me off.

"How's school going?" he asked. "I never thought I'd miss something like school, but I do. I miss lunch, I miss my friends, and I miss being free." My first instinct was to hold his proverbial hand through the emotions, but time was a luxury I didn't have. Plus, his voice was nothing more than an emotional black hole. If I took one step inside, I wasn't ever going to find my way back out. I recognized that sound. It was honed into me at an early age, and only something traumatic did that to a person. And here I was going to add something else just as traumatic to the mix.

I had to bring up Annie, and hearing his voice descend deeper into despair wasn't going to make it easier. For some unknown reason, he was keeping their relationship under wraps—even from his brother. Before I could formulate something sensitive and well thought-out, my overly stupid mouth blurted, "Oscar, do you know Annie Hughes?"

Nothing. More nothing. Then that nothing moment grew into such a loud, uncomfortable agony, it was obvious he was hiding the association for good reason.

"Um, yeah," he said quietly. "I loved her."

Cue the stomach cramps. Could things get any worse? Bile rose up my throat when I realized I had to tell him she wasn't breathing anymore. How in the world would I do that? His life was already screwed up beyond all recognition. Then I realized he said the word love in the past tense. Could he mean in-the-grave past tense?

"Oscar, I—"

There was a bittersweet breath. "I know she's dead, and no, I didn't kill her. And no, there was nothing between us. It was just me occasionally talking to a married woman who had a horrible home life."

Unrequited love was horrific—no objection from me there. I told him softly, "I heard Alfonso Juarez was thought to have died sometime Sunday, found Monday. Annie died Monday, discovered Tuesday. Did you happen to see her on Monday?"

Please say no, I thought. *Please, please, please.*

"I talked to her, yes," he answered. "She was planning to leave her husband and go to Michigan. I gave her all the money I had on me...and yes, I know I'm a suspect."

Death nail in his coffin—I heard it in my head. *Excuse me while I cry a moment,* I almost said. Soft whimpers filled the dead space when I realized he was crying. I wasn't equipped for this, but I was all he had. "I'll fix it," I said soberly. "I promise."

I was a liar. A big, fat liar whose soul would rot in Hell if I blew his only chance.

Scattered voices filled the phone as someone informed Oscar his time was up. After a simple "Goodbye," I stared at my dead phone and willed answers into my head that didn't come. We were cut off before I could ask about the third body, and that third body could be the key to everything. I crossed myself even though I wasn't Catholic and said, "Help me, Jesus," even though I never really prayed. It was barely eight o'clock, and I already felt like I'd scaled Mount Everest.

Chapter Seventeen

WINNERS AND LOSERS

I blew into my hand. My breath smelled like one of those poop-throwing monkeys...complements of four cups of coffee, half a chocolate cake, and two pickle spears. All of that bodily harm took place because I promised Oscar the moon and had an argument with my father. I had better odds of delivering the moon than defusing Murphy. That would take an Act of Congress.

I dropped my pajamas and stepped into the shower, shifting the spray from hot to volcanic, enjoying the pound of rivulets down my back. As I lathered up with some body wash, hot steam coiled around me like a snake, nothing visible but the sin that festered in my brain.

Once I was sufficiently pruned, I dried off and pulled on some inside-out white sweats, wearing my favorite tie-dyed T-shirt. In black letters, it said, "I'm not crazy. My split personality is." Finishing the ensemble with my I-don't-care look, I sat in the middle of the closet wondering how I would salvage my day. My brain needed to slow so I could think. With the portable house phone in my lap (since mine was impounded), I put in the earbuds of Marjorie's iPod, leaving it on shuffle at the highest setting. What relaxed some people—peace and quiet—often was the opposite for me. I needed loud, random noise, and lots of it. Thing was, her iPod was full of Disney tunes. Nothing against Disney, but there was only so much "Whistle While You Work" a sane person could take.

As I arranged and rearranged my shoes on their shelf, the house phone started vibrating. A look at the number showed Mr. Do-The-Right-Thing himself.

Aw, for the love...

I read somewhere if two people passed DNA, they were cosmically connected forever. If you were particularly intuitive, you could feel the other's presence and emotions as if they were your own. Mothers had known that since the beginning of time. It was that maternal instinct they felt when their young were threatened or merely thinking of them.

Dylan and I hadn't swapped DNA, but as a rule, he could be totally engrossed in a task, and if he felt I needed him, he'd drop whatever he was doing and make me his first priority. Trouble was, he sometimes felt it miles away.

It was no surprise he was dialing. There was a really good chance I wouldn't live to see sixteen.

I didn't know Juan or Jinx that well, but when one of them stuck my shoe in the mailbox, obviously they were throwing me a challenge. Was I scared? Sadly, no. For me, it came down to winning and losing. Winners rose to the level of their competition. Losers descended to the level of their own incompetence. I'd rather chew glass than lose a challenge to the likes of them and banked on the fact they were incompetent screwups that lived in reactive mode.

Why the confidence? I was crossing my fingers that "good" won out for once. Whether they pulled the trigger or not, they knew something and weren't helping Oscar. I'd always felt when people laid down at night they needed to like themselves. No way in the world were these guys on the road to self-actualization. Was I? Doubtful, but I was closer than they were.

Tapping the talk button, I barely got, "Heeeey," out of my mouth when he cut me off, his voice crashing like rolling thunder.

"Pinky swear you're not involved in anything, that you're bored out of your mind, and you're doing everything that normal teenagers do." Add some heavy breathing.

Normal teenagers either did as their parents requested or rebelled and snuck out to places, partying until sunrise. Then there was me. I wasn't sure a category had been defined for me yet.

I coughed. "Could you define normal?"

Explicit profanity that probably made God plug his ears followed. Dylan went ape poopoo, and when his breathing became labored, I developed a guilt so heavy it nearly toppled me over. He was the only one I gave my thoughts to, uncensored—but on Frank and me? That was like plugging a dam with a piece of gum. An explosion was imminent.

When he revved up the cursing, I buckled, telling him where we went, what I saw, down to the least of details like Frank and I drank Black Tiger coffee specifically. The issue with my shoe was on the tip of my tongue, but that's where it stayed. No matter how hard I tried to spit it out, it anchored and wouldn't budge. I didn't know what Dylan would do with that information once he returned. He barely wrapped his head around Adam Neeley. Would he confront each of them? In some form or another, yes. Would that screw up my yet-unplanned next steps? Most definitely.

After some silence where all I could hear was my heart beating, Dylan lowered his voice with a growling, "Stop." Immediately, I got a set of angry chills. I didn't like Dylan's one-word commands. I really didn't, but when he added a soft begging, "*Please,*" I stumbled around with a promise we both knew was a waste of breath.

The boy loved me. Yes, it was friend love, but he loved me none-theless, and it was nice to know someone actually cared if I had air in my lungs. And I admit, the concern was kind of hot when that guy was the stud of all studs.

It was ten o'clock in Valley, four o'clock in the morning, island time. "Shouldn't you be sleeping?" I asked, trying to change the subject.

Dylan was fighting a yawn but somehow managed another stiff lecture. "I happened to be up when I got an email from Murphy, and it worried me, Darcy. Now I realize he gave me the condensed version that's barely truth at all. What if down deep Frank's an axe murderer or something? He could've thrown you in the back of his truck, and we'd never see you again."

"There wasn't room," I dumbly said. "A naked mannequin was already taking my spot."

My best friend gasped and expelled a breath like someone had just stabbed him. "Oh, God," he prayed. "This is beyond twisted. Can't you see that?"

Dylan and Murphy occasionally ganged up on me. Most usually —okay, *always*—I could count on Dylan being on my side. He'd agree with Murphy but somehow transfer my meted-out punishment into a guilt trip only. By the tone of his voice, he'd slug me if I were a guy.

"You're not going to stop, are you?" he murmured desperately.

I gave him an honest answer. "Would you believe me if I said I'd try?"

Dylan's voice wouldn't go dormant, and he'd gone from best-friend-concerned to full-blown predator. Here was where I checked out altogether. Pushing off the floor, I stood in the middle of my room and looked around. Dirty clothes hung from my desk, a pair of socks dangled from the lamp, and a week's worth of paper plates had begun to reek in the waste can. In the next twenty minutes, I mobilized like a happy rent-a-maid. I stuffed a trash bag to capacity, my underwear drawer was color-coded, dust bunnies were set loose in the backyard, and my fish food (for the fish I'd yet to kill) was grouped into large and small flakes.

Dylan hadn't remotely run out of gas, and my latest escapade was only the tip of the iceberg where his temper was concerned. His pride was still smarting from our dropped call a few days earlier when Liam took me home from school. That was a particularly unpleasant conversation. Apparently, my phone switched itself off when it sailed over UDF's magazine rack, and Dylan automatically assumed I had no desire to talk to him. To make matters worse, Liam uploaded the picture he took of us to his social media accounts right there for mankind to see. It didn't take long for Dylan to put two-and-two together. Fastard move on Liam's part and sort of mean. I didn't like anyone being mean to my best friend, no matter if I did have a crush on the guy.

Question was, why were Dylan and Liam friends on the social networking site if they clearly weren't friendly with one another in person? Dylan's answer was slightly on the Mafioso side: *I keep my friends close...my enemies even closer.*

Well, guess what I was going to do with Jinx King and Company? The answer was a five-lettered word: ditto.

Walking over to my desk, I pulled out my spinny black chair and plopped down. Quickly firing up my laptop, after a brief search, I discovered that Juan, Jinx, Justin, and Adam all had Facebook accounts. With a few trusty strokes, I sent each an invitation to be on Darcy Walker's list of friends. Reclining back in the chair, I propped my feet on the desk and clasped my fingers behind my head with a big, stupid smile.

The way I saw it, I was back in the lead.

Dylan finally stopped for a breath. "Listen, Darc, I'm not trying to be a jerk. You're there. I'm here. I miss you, and I've got this nagging worry that I can't shake. So you agree with me then?" he murmured. My word, I hadn't the foggiest idea what avenue he'd turned or what I'd agreed to.

I gave him a codependent, "Sure," certain I'd just lied.

———

Semi-arguing with Dylan made me feel hypoglycemic, completely without energy and out of balance. I ate four cookies and felt better...crisis averted. In my heart, I knew he meant well, but my urges were beyond my control. The best thing I could do for myself —and my loved ones—was to plan my next move and work within some sort of safeguard.

You know, make out a will or power of attorney or something.

Other than the library (which Justice's mother said she would take us to), my plans were nixed for the day—or the way I liked to look at it, delayed. That didn't mean I couldn't plan ahead. Plus, I was hoping for a miracle on Murphy's part. A miracle where he'd come home and backpedal on the discipline. A girl could dream, right?

After I ran a load of dishes through the dishwasher, I colored kangaroos with Marjorie, pulled my geometry book out of my backpack, and sat down at the kitchen table. For once, I wasn't going to wait until the last minute to finish an assignment. I wanted to be unencumbered for the rest of the week when I was going full-throttle with Oscar Small.

Flipping through the book, I thought about my relationship with numbers. Sometimes we got along. Others, we'd rather slap one another into unconsciousness. I wasn't sure why, but my brain's complexities were just that...complexities. I jacked up a test two weeks once on your basic stuff. Normally, I did well in math, good enough for an A or high B, but on that particular test I was four points from failing. I spazzed out. No excuse other than I spazzed out and didn't even finish in time. Mr. Gordon gave a retest for people in the same boat, but even if I got everything correct, the most I could get out of my effort was a seventy percent. Made sense, I guess, but I found it hard to get geeked up for a C.

I sailed through eight problems when the portable phone broke my concentration with "Home on the Range." I thought that ringtone was funny when I set it, but it had become categorically annoying. Scribbling down an answer, I saw the caller ID listed Finn Lively, so I hit the speakerphone.

"Bonjourno," I greeted, remembering he was walking in the land of France.

"Bonjourno, bella. I called your cell with no answer."

"It was impounded."

"Ah, sorry. Seems ole Jinxie boy hasn't led a charmed life."

"How so?"

"First off, he's not Jinx King. He's Gavin Hilliard."

Huh...you don't say.

I picked up my jaw and then laid down my pencil, giving him my full attention. "Adopted?" I asked.

"Yeah," he said. "Your typical story. Biological parents were both users with OVIs, reckless endangerment, and other crimes out the yin-yang. As a result, Jinx was made a ward of the state at age nine and thereby was in and out of the foster system for the next few years until the King's took him at age eleven. Evidently, he was with them for only a short time before they started the proceedings to adopt."

That would take some time to digest, but what I was most concerned with were his own particular offenses. I told Finn, "I got the feeling from Jinx's father that Jinx may have inherited the knack for falling into trouble from his parents. Does he have a file in juvie other than being a ward of the state?"

Finn laughed—a mix between sarcasm and disbelief. "Oh, bella. Jinxie has been one naughty, little boy. Petty theft, grand larceny of a school bus, public intoxication, public nuisance, robbery, felonious assault, filing false reports, desecrating a grave..."

Finn and I both stopped, allowing that last offense to jell in our brains. That statement in itself was all I needed as corroboration. What kind of person messed with corpses? Plus, that voice in the back of my mind reminded me that Darth Vader claimed he liked dead bodies.

After Finn cleared his throat, and I massaged away the goose bumps on my arms, he finished with, "Most of that stopped when the King's stepped into the picture. Jinx was brought in as an 'unruly' a few times new into their relationship, but other than that, it looks like he's stayed clean."

Or dear old Dad was keeping his record clean.

———————

Claudia's sister, Ana Rosalina, and her son, Choncho, made the trek to Cincinnati to verify the validity of the Jesus cookie. Who would've thought the Walkers would spawn some sort of religious pilgrimage? As they say, reality's stranger than fiction.

The seven of us sat around the kitchen table finishing up chicken pollo, Claudia's traditional Eastertime dish that put pounds on a person simply by smelling it.

I popped the button on my jeans and then wiped my mouth, complimenting her with an, "Oooh, delicioso."

Ana Rosalina gave her a tight smile—not even an appreciative burp.

Ana Rosalina was the competitive type, even in cooking, and more specifically in the afterlife. If Claudia got Jesus on a cookie, then by goodness, Ana Rosalina wanted a piece of the action too. Thing was, she was like the Black Death. She got inside a car...it crashed. She broke a mirror...it was fourteen years bad luck instead of seven. Black cats ran in the other direction and good luck horseshoes tumbled and crawled back to their horses. Hard to say whether she deserved a visit from the Divine—especially when she'd been compared to Satan.

While she examined the cookie like a dog would a bone, I stole a look at Choncho. He was dressed as usual—gray sweat pants and a matching shirt on an eight-year-old body at least twenty-five pounds overweight. The kid had no neck, and frankly, I had to look hard for his eyes. When I gave him a smile, he stood up from his chair and tossed his white plate up against the wall. It crashed, split in two, and tumbled like a rockslide to the floor. Murphy's jaw dropped, and Choncho's behavior could only be explained—like most things—with a really good, profane metaphor. Surprisingly, Murphy kept his metaphor to himself.

Murphy angrily pointed to the mess—demanding a cleanup—but Choncho jumped on his imaginary horse and galloped into the living room, spanking his own behind. Dude was jacked in the head.

Murphy turned to Claudia, saying with some force, "They're gone tomorrow. Bad stuff happens when your sister's on my property."

Bad wasn't the half of it. It was weird beyond weird beyond weird.

Claudia had a one-bedroom townhome down the street. When Ana Rosalina was in Valley, she and Choncho stayed in our guest bedroom. It sounded like a good idea at first until they brought the drama of a Mexican soap opera with them...literally. Ana Rosalina was an on-hiatus soap star made famous for killing her cheating husband with a pickaxe.

Hmm, made you wonder, didn't it.

Claudia grabbed a dishrag, falling to her knees to clean up the mess. "She's got good hoo-doo now," she protested nervously. "She jest want to see the koookie."

Murphy flicked some rice off his light blue Ralph Lauren button-down, pushing back his chair with an angry screech. "Hoo-doo, boo-boo, ca-ca, juju," he mocked. "I don't give a darn. Ana Rosalina's staying on the porch. Choncho, bless his heart, needs to be scared straight and his scalp checked for 666."

Well, there you have it, folks. Murphy thought Choncho was moronically stupid and possessed the devil's mark. I scratched my head, wondering if I agreed.

Earlier, I'd changed into a navy, long-sleeved T-shirt and a new pair of dark-wash, hip-hugger jeans that rode a little too low for public decorum. Cheesy rice was somehow squished down into the waistband—close to my butt cheeks. I flicked it out as best I could and wiped up the last of the chicken, tossing the paper towel into the stainless steel waste can. Needing dessert, I tiptoed to the top shelf of the pantry, reaching behind the Cap'n Crunch box for my secret stash of cookies. There were none. The only cookie on the premises was on the countertop.

Home to Jesus Christ.

Off-limits.

Right then was where I knew I had bad in me because I reached for it and actually had to smack one hand with the other. After I paced the counter a few times, I decided to eat a Fudgsicle and save what little bit was left of my soul.

For the next twenty minutes, I folded laundry and talked Choncho out of pulling the wings off a moth that hovered in the kitchen chandelier. Choncho wasn't Einstein, but stuff like that should be obvious. When he was shoving his pudgy feet in Marjorie's tap shoes, I spied Marjorie's squirrel scampering outdoors, searching for acorns on the patio. I grabbed the portable phone, a handful of mixed nuts, and traipsed over to the back door, stepping outside into the night.

It was gloaming, the period from sunset to nightfall. The sky was a dusky blue, and the night air was fiercely cool on my bare feet. Pitching some nuts in the squirrel's direction, I gazed up to the stars, fixating on one so visibly clear I could almost reach out and touch it with my hand.

Adam Neeley was on my mind. Was he alive? Dead? Grossly injured or brain damaged? Dialing 411, I took a chance he was the only Neeley in Valley and requested the phone number for his father. While the operator surprisingly relayed the digits, for a split second, I pondered if my actions were a mistake. The Neeley phone, if it had caller ID, would denote Murphy Walker once I dialed. But what would it hurt? If Adam had spoken with the others since his beat down, then they'd probably informed him I witnessed the whole thing. The way I saw it, I might as well gather what information I could.

Punching in the digits, someone answered with a sleepy, "Hullo," on the third ring.

"May I speak to Adam?" I said.

"Asleep," was the man's answer.

"But he's breathing?" I asked. I squeezed my eyes tight, wishing I could retract that statement.

The man grumbled something to himself. "I haven't checked, but I assume so." There was no offer to wake him, and I wasn't sure it was wise to ask. The longer it took me to respond, the more the energy mounted through the phone. "Is there a message you'd like me to give him?" he finally asked.

Jeez, I didn't know what to do. The man was growing paranoid, and if he was even remotely in Murphy's league, the moment Adam woke, he'd ask him who Murphy Walker was. I decided on the truth. "Um, yeah," I said. "Tell him Darcy called and that he's making a mistake." There was a pause that neither of us chose to fill. Seconds from disconnecting, he recycled my phrase, repeating it back verbatim. "That's right," I told him again. "He's making a mistake."

I hung up and immediately went numb. I could've been skinned alive, and I wouldn't have felt it.

I was getting in too deep but reminded myself everything was for Oscar. We hadn't covered the specifics of when he'd call again, and I honestly didn't know the rules on prison communications. Regardless, I needed to see him, but how was I going to score a sit-down session? Shielding my body from the cold, I crossed my arms over my chest and bounced up and down, trying to birth some creativity. Figures, it would fail me. The instant I made a move to go back inside, headlights lit up the back of the house, blinding my eyes. It was like someone was purposely leaving them on...either to scare me or let's face it, take a shot.

Normal people would be scared stiff or maybe dive for the bushes. Instead, I took three brazenly, stupid steps forward when a glint of yellow lit up my vision. *A yellow Dodge Charger*, I gasped. Whoever the jerkaholic was, he revved his engine twice, flicked the lights, and circled around the cul-de-sac, leaving Bison Boulevard. Our street was off the beaten path. It wasn't like people pulled in accidentally because they'd taken a wrong turn.

Had the driver sought me out to just...*what? Spy on me?*

An uneasy feeling crept up my spine, and I shuddered at the thought, wondering if perhaps this person was the one who placed my sneaker in the mailbox. If so, then why? Why and for what motive? When I saw that car last, I had been convinced the driver

GRADE A STUPID

was trying to give me a head start away from the gangland beating. Now, I wasn't so sure. Maybe they were trying to rat me out instead.

Before I could panic or find a way into the witness protection program, the house's foundation shook, Murphy's normally boisterous voice sounding like a startled elephant charging in the jungle.

"I won! I won!" he bellowed.

Curling my hands into makeshift binoculars, I smooshed my face into the glass door, peering inside. Murphy was swinging Marjorie around by the waist as she held the white receipt for his Powerball Pick Three numbers scrunched tightly in her hand.

Oh. My. Word. He. Won.

How much, I didn't know, but I was somehow going to work it to my advantage.

Chapter Eighteen

UNEXPECTED WINDFALL

*I*f you were a high jumper, the goal was to raise the bar each attempt. If you were talented, the legs did what you asked of them. They stretched to scale the height the brain told you was impossible. I liked to keep the bar low. That way I saw more success.

Problem was, my idea of low would trip an Olympic athlete in a full sprint, with no head wind, and nothing in his path. I didn't shy away from things the logical person would say were stupid. Probably why I was wearing a black pencil skirt, fitted blouse, a smooth and polished ponytail, and heels that made me well over six feet tall. I wanted to look like a law clerk.

My guess was I looked like an idiot.

An idiot with a plan, I should probably amend.

I was off to see Oscar. How was that possible when I was grounded for running around with a questionable guy my father barely knew? It all came down to Murphy's windfall in the lottery and a little bit of creative thinking. I told Murphy if God blessed him, then he needed to bless me by *un*grounding me and gifting me with my Apple products. That's what good people did. It was a simple approach—actually asinine—and he shockingly agreed with an overzealous, I'm-freaking-rich smile. That wasn't Murphy Walker though—I debated taking a blood sample—but I wasn't going to spit in the face of his benevolence.

I topped my outfit off with my studious, black cat-eyed glasses and stared in the mirror. "Are you in or not, Vinnie?" I asked impatiently, appraising my smile. Squirting some toothpaste on my brush, I quickly swept it over my teeth, trying to remove my breakfast of Mexican wedding cookies and microwave popcorn.

Vinnie grunted. "Dolce, you hurt my feelings taking off with that Liam character. I don't know if I'm in or not." Our conversation was déjà-vu all over again, a rewind of me asking him to go to the Valley Police Department. Who would've thought Vinnie was the sensitive type or the type to hold a grudge? The longer we spoke, the more I realized the subject of Liam was far from over. All the same, I couldn't help but wonder what Liam wanted to talk about that was confidential.

He wasn't going to be one of those guys that used me as a sounding board about his ex, was he? I could be desperate, but not *that* desperate. Still, he requested I call him back. Granted, Murphy vetoed my going anywhere with him—I was too embarrassed to unload that little morsel—but not following through made me look uninterested and frankly rude.

I sighed, spitting some froth in the sink, concentrating on the teeth in the back. The no-braces thing was making me a hyper-brusher. What I was looking at was the final product, and even though they were straight, I didn't know if I was truly happy. Grabbing a Crest White Strip packet, I swished some water through my mouth, dried my teeth with a towel, and affixed the bleaching strips to the top and bottom rows. "Claudia jus' made some Mex-can weddin' kookies," I slurred out.

Vinnie actually moaned. "How should I dress?" he asked.

"Like a law-yur."

———

Twenty-five minutes later, Vinnie was standing in the foyer of my home. His hair was gelled back like someone from New York's or Jersey's mob, with a gold nugget pinky ring on his left finger. He was dressed in a navy suit and tie, spit-shined black shoes (he needed a size wider, but who was being picky), a briefcase in his hand...toting a bouquet of multi-colored tulips. Did he actually think we were getting married because of the wedding cookies?

I already had a bad case of heartburn, and that sent me into an acid reflux coughing fit. Vinnie pounded on my back. "It's Secretary's Day, Dolce," he grunted chuckling. "These flowers are going to come in handy. If I teach you anything, know your audience."

Vinnie was sliding by through school with no immediate plans for the future if he didn't get an athletic scholarship. Pity was the first thought that came to mind. He had potential, but I feared he would blow whatever opportunity came his way anyway. Thing was, I *knew* my audience. I'd gotten my law clerk on and was somehow going to score a meet-and-greet with Oscar.

Did I know how? No. Would I figure it out once I got there? Yes.

_____

Oscar was incarcerated at the Valley Juvenile Detention Center, or JDC. It was a few blocks over from the police department and was the holding facility for juveniles (under eighteen) who'd been charged with an unruly or delinquency offense. Once incarcerated, its residents were separated by age, sex, and the nature of their crime. Oscar's was Murder One or aggravated murder as we called it in Ohio. My guess was he was hanging out with the baddest-of-the-bad, hopefully not in a pit in the ground. If convicted, the JDC wouldn't be his final resting place, for lack of a better phrase. The JDC was a temporary housing facility until an inmate's fate was determined. For Oscar, since they were trying him as an adult—because it was a capital offense with a weapon involved—he would be going to the "big house."

When we pulled into the parking lot, I thought on the various stories behind those four walls. Some were guilty, some were innocent, and some were probably guilty-by-association. Whatever the situation, I was sure when they all got up on that one fateful morning, the last thing they thought was, *Gee, I'd really like to go to jail today*. But society had rules—break the rules, and offenders were either given another chance or deemed it was their day to pay.

Some had no sense of principle, so crime came easy for them.

They stole, cheated, murdered, and bent the rules to serve their own hedonistic purposes. Others, I think, did crazy things when they fell into the depths of despair. They felt trapped with no way out, and actions that would mortify someone in a stable environment were eclipsed by "if you can't beat 'em, join 'em."

I understood the depths of despair. No, I hadn't broken countless laws, but I'd gone to places so dark, the only way I found my way out was by following the voices. Those sorts of things left an irremovable mark—something that woke a person in the night with terrors, gasping for breath with lungs that had collapsed in fear. All those places I'd been were about the same on the Richter scale of pain—*except my mother*.

Viciously shaking my head, I buried that memory, doing a mental checklist of things I'd need. Clutched in my hand was one of Murphy's old black briefcases that included a yellow legal pad, two black ink pens, my yearbook, and iPad. I didn't know what I was going to do with any of it, but the lawyers I'd been around always came armed with paper and electronics.

Luckily, the day was sunny with a forecasted high of sixty-nine degrees. Pop-up showers were likely, but I hoped it was one of those days the weather forecasters got it wrong. That happened a lot here, people. We're told one thing, and it wasn't even close to what transpired. To show my optimism, I told the monsoon season to kiss-my-unstable-bum and wasn't even going to carry an umbrella.

Squeaking wide the door on the Bug, I stepped out onto the sidewalk. Rolling my neck around, I jumped up and down a few times as though I was getting ready to be put in a game—geeking myself up. Then I swallowed deeply, squared my shoulders, and walked side-by-side with Vinnie toward the front door.

The JDC was a big, red brick building with two American flags flying in the front. I paused while Vinnie said something about "America the Beautiful" and then continued inside. The ambience was, in short, stunted. Even if a person didn't know prisoners were housed there, one could feel the defeat in the air. I imagined row after row of inmates pacing inside their cells or trekking to the cafeteria—realizing I took for granted the simple joy of sunshine, freedom to move, or a meal of my choosing.

Vinnie shoved me toward the front desk. I had a moment of

panic. If I couldn't get past the receptionist, I had no backup plan. As I raised my chin and semi-confidently walked forward (okay, I was scared as ca-ca), I recalled Frank's words. Oscar was assigned to Public Defender Odell Whitmeyer under Judge Ronald Van Winkle. Van Winkle was a hard-nosed blankety-blank, according to reputation. My guess was his public defenders had to stay on their toes.

That probably meant Whitmeyer had already done his homework. That also meant he could be so on-the-ball he constantly thought of things he'd like to ask his client. At least, that was the angle I was going for.

With a round face and black hair a little late on a dye job, the receptionist (Mona by her nametag) had single mom written all over her. Single mom and recently broken up with somebody, to be specific. Her mascara was raccooning under both eyes as she dabbed a nose that was Rudolph-red. I fought a smile. That was luck—luck kissing me right on the mouth. Slumping over her desk, surrounded by pictures I assumed were her children, she sobbed, "Oh, Tony," and then blew her nose so loudly it sounded like a foghorn. Giving her a few moments to collect herself, she gave one last honking blow and attempted a smile.

I crossed my fingers I didn't look like a teenager. "Your name?" she said, sniffling to me.

An idiot, I thought. *On too many levels to count.*

My voice took the Midnight Train to Georgia because suddenly I couldn't find it. Vinnie must've felt my panic because he magically appeared at my side. "Corleone," he said deeply, extending the tulips. "Carlo Corleone. And may we take this time to say Happy Secretary's Day, Mona. Without you, I'm sure this place would fall apart." I was in no place to judge, but *Corleone?* Couldn't he have picked a surname that didn't come from *The Godfather??*

Just like Guido Galucci, Vinnie pulled out a crisp, white business card and laid it on her desk. She half-heartedly looked, not taking her eyes off the tulips.

Mona sniffled and gushed. "Thank you," she said. As with every other female, Vinnie had one of those moments where he rushed them with testosterone. He would never be my type in a million years, but it wasn't like I didn't appreciate the spectacle or find it entertaining. Vinnie was as big as a barn, but he had something because he brought out the barn-lover in everyone.

Mona started blushing.

She had a glass bowl full of hard candy on her desk. Once Vinnie was convinced he'd cast his spell, he plunged his beefy fingers inside and plopped a few in his mouth. Pulling his cell phone out of his jacket, he said, "Take over, Greta. Odell is expecting me in forty-five minutes, so let the pretty lady know what we need."

He gave me a sheet of paper and then turned and left.

Greta? Well, Greta didn't know what lying called for, but I had a feeling the credentials fit me perfectly.

Mona stretched across the desk in her high-waisted Mom jeans and popped the button. I acted like I didn't notice when she anxiously refastened it. "What do you need?" she asked me.

I put on my thespian smile. "Hi, Mona. I'm a law clerk with Odell Whitmeyer, and we're here to talk to our client, Oscar Small."

A look of recognition crossed Mona's face. "It's Wednesday," she said confused. "Visiting hours are only in the evening."

I nearly fainted. I stupidly assumed we could walk in whenever we wanted, but when I looked down at my hand, the sheet of paper Vinnie brought was a confirmation of a "Special Visitation" for an authorized visitor. Somehow he'd thought of everything.

I slid it over to Mona with a confident smile. After she briefly appraised it, she said, "Follow me." Standing up, she strode toward what I assumed were inmate rooms.

I stared, stupefied.

Once I came to myself, I fought the urge to look over my shoulder to see if I was being set up for entrapment or something. That was too easy—too easy and grossly against the law. As Vinnie and I followed, I immediately was hit with a case of nerves so severe I almost toppled over. My knees hit a few times, but I talked myself out of running for the car. A look to Vinnie showed a big grin of satisfaction, where he knew he'd done his part.

Thing was, it was then all up to me.

After a guard patted us down, we were led to a ten-by-ten foot room that had a one-way viewing glass. For us, it looked like a big window, but I surmised it was the place where authorities talked amongst themselves, considering their next move. We barely sat down when a prison guard led Oscar in, his hands and feet in shackles. I swallowed some grief. Oscar had always appeared older than everyone else, but the pain on his face wasn't age—it was of someone who had grown up too soon. His beard hadn't been shaved, his glasses were taped together at the bridge (like they'd been broken), and worse than anything, he looked gaunt. My guess was he wasn't eating.

I jumped out of my seat before he could say anything. "Hello, Oscar. I'm Greta. I work for Odell Whitmeyer. We have a few more questions for you."

Oscar's right eye was swollen black and blue. Before I could ask what happened, Vinnie wrote a note on my legal pad and gave a look so ferocious to the prison guard it nearly floored him. "Make sure that doesn't happen again," Vinnie snarled, jerking his head to Oscar's eye. "You're supposed to be protecting him. I'll be placing that in my report to the judge along with your name."

There was a moment where I wanted to know how Valentine Vecchione knew the ins-and-outs of prison protocol because the guard didn't refute that was even typical procedure. He gave an austere nod and then crossed his hands behind his back, staring at the clock on the wall.

Pulling out a chair for him, Oscar slid into it—his shackles clanging—afraid to even speak. "Oscar," I said softly, trying my best to give him a nonverbal signal to play along, "Mister Whitmeyer has some additional questions about the day you saw Alfonso Juarez. Specifically what you saw in the school parking lot and your relationship with those individuals before that day."

Oscar looked straight ahead—no doubt considering future ramifications.

We were sitting at a silver, stainless steel rectangular table. Two chairs were on each side, one on each end. Scooting one of the end chairs directly to his side, I touched his shoulder, whispering, "I'm here to help."

He gave a quick chin jerk to the camera mounted in the upper right corner of the room, the camera taping our exchange—the camera that would inevitably bust us if I couldn't figure out how to block its view. Vinnie was okay, his back was to it, but my profile was as exposed as a naked baby's bottom.

Propping my elbow on the table, I covered my right cheek with my hand, pivoting to where I was almost sitting with my back to the lens like Vinnie. Vinnie slid the brief case across the table. I unclicked its latch and pulled out last year's yearbook. Oscar told Ms. Dempsey there were four people at the dumpster that day. The only one he could identify definitively was Jinx King. I knew myself that Jinx was there with Justin Starsong, so that's two, but could I put the others at the scene—more specifically around the dumpster?

Going through the index, I presented photographs of Adam Neeley and Juan Salas.

Oscar whispered, "Yes," to the photograph of Adam, and an even more vehement, "Yes," as I produced the picture of Juan. In less than five short minutes, I'd placed all four males at the scene—males I knew were involved in the copper business like Oscar. Boys I'd bet my life were the eyewitness accounts of Oscar at the dumpster.

"Oscar, you need to tell me what you know about the copper business in town. Frank told me a little, and I saw some things myself, but I get a feeling there's more to it than two guys competing with one another. It's organized, isn't it?"

Oscar gave a nod. "Jinx is in a gang called Northside."

"Northside," I repeated.

"Yes, Northside."

I thought of the numbers six and twelve that were in that hand signal and wondered if, in fact, they were the Northside 12. "Could they be Northside 12?"

"I don't know."

"Who leads Northside?" I asked. "Jinx?"

He shook his head no. "Not the type."

"Could it be any of the other three?"

Oscar furrowed his brow, wheels turning in his head. "Adam, no. Juan, maybe. Justin, most definitely." Who *was* this Justin? Even Liam would give me very little information about him. Made me think he was one of those bad guys that were so bad, you didn't even want his name to pass over your lips.

I thought back to the two instances where I saw Juan and Justin in action unbeknownst to them. In UDF, Justin undoubtedly portrayed himself higher up the hierarchical structure than Jinx. He was giving Jinx commands, telling him he had some explaining to do. At the construction site, Juan was doing all the talking when I would've expected Justin—if, in fact, he were Mr. Hood—to be the person jawing the most. Instead, Mr. Hood-slash-maybe-Justin wouldn't even return the hand signal, which almost appeared as him breaking ties.

Whatever the case, I had incontrovertible proof that placed four other individuals at the scene of the crime. Granted it was Oscar's word, but I personally could corroborate Jinx and Justin.

"Oscar, did you describe these males to Odell Whitmeyer?"

"Sort of. All I could tell him was they dressed alike with that red bandana. He spent a lot of time on that."

"Had you ever seen Alfonso Juarez before that day?"

Oscar vehemently shook his head in the negative. "No," he said, "but I know he's AVO. Mister Whitmeyer told me as much. Did you know AVO was already here?"

I scratched the back of my neck, feeling like I was about to crawl right out of my skin. I figured as much. I mean, why would Alfonso Juarez even be in town?

"Did you tell him about the copper?" I asked.

Oscar breathed a deep breath that caused him to wince. Made me think he had a cracked rib. "I did, and I told him about Jinx and Northside. He wrote some notes down, but I think he was frustrated."

My guess was he was frustrated because he couldn't tie anyone else to Juarez in some fashion or another. I knew how to do it. Tie Alfonso Juarez to copper and then you could explain the connection to Jinx King. Once again, that part of my brain that had no sense of danger informed me I had to introduce myself to AVO. Once that was birthed in my mind, I realized that conceivably could be the last thought I ever had. AVO didn't play around.

Shifting in my seat, I told Oscar that another man was found in a dumpster, killed almost identically in the fashion of Alfonso Juarez. The victim hadn't been identified yet. Was it plausible to believe the vic was another AVO member marked for assassination? If so, then why kill him? And if it *were* an AVO member, wouldn't he have a criminal record, tattoos, or fingerprints to identify him as such?

"Were you told of this man, Oscar?"

Another negative answer. Frowning, I cocked my head to one side, knowing if Oscar's lawyer was worth his salt, he had that man's death on his radar already.

"I know AVO's recruiting," Oscar said, suddenly whispering, "and they're recruiting people that don't even look like gang members. That might be why his name wasn't released. If this other man found in a dumpster is new to the gang, then he might not have earned any ink yet."

"Ink?"

"Tattoos."

"He'd be like a fraternity pledge?"

My father was in a fraternity, and before a guy was initiated as a full-fledged member, he went through a probationary period where he was called a pledge.

"Yes," Oscar whispered lower, "but initiation into AVO isn't through your normal crime. It's by killing someone."

My body didn't know what to do. Should I faint, laugh, or crawl in a hole and hide? I thought about hyperventilating, but when I remembered I was masquerading as a law clerk, I somehow managed a breath. Killing someone would make sense. AVO was considered the deadliest gang of all time, so they're not going to take your run-of-the-mill criminals. They'd want members that proved wholeheart-edly they were loyal, wanted to belong, and would do anything to make that happen. I tapped my stiletto against the gray tile, trying to think of what to do next. Did Northside have something AVO wanted? Did AVO have something Northside wanted?

There was one last thing I needed to discuss...Annie Hughes. Oscar knew he was considered a suspect in her murder. I wasn't sure how to broach that subject again, especially when the mention of her name brought him to tears last time.

I briefly closed my eyes and then opened them, trying to distance myself. "I've been thinking, Oscar. Why is it you're a suspect in Annie's murder? What evidence do they have?"

Oscar looked like I'd just slapped him, his robot persona of earlier suddenly on high alert. "I was the last one to see her apparently," he muttered, clearing his throat. "I met her in a parking lot at Tire Town and drove off while she was still sitting in her car. My face is on a security camera somewhere."

I rubbed my temples like I tried to claw my brains out. That meant her husband must've had a legitimate alibi. If he'd been preliminarily cleared, then who in the world did Annie tick off enough to kill her?

I exhaled. "Anything else?"

Oscar looked at the cuffs on his wrists. "They think I'm in a gang and said they'd give me a deal if I'd provide names of other gang members—the big players. I don't know anyone in AVO." *So he wasn't going to get a deal*, I thought...*unless I could come up with the names for him.*

I wasn't sure exactly what was the catalyst. Maybe it was because I brought up Annie again, or maybe Oscar realized the depths of his desperation if I were taking things upon myself. Whatever the origins, he burst into tears and grabbed at the lapels on my suit. Nearly pulling me to the floor, I only stayed seated when I latched onto the leg of the chair for support. I couldn't help it, but tears showed before I could stop them. When he blubbered, "Help me, Darcy," I fell short of smacking him before he gave up my identity altogether. It didn't take long for the guard to pull him off of me and lead his blithering body back to his cell.

Glancing over to Vinnie, I was hoping for some guidance—some miracle broadcast—but got nothing. The entire time I'd assumed he'd been taking notes, but honest to God, his note pad was doodled pictures of moon pies and women with big boobs. He reached across the table and grabbed my hand tightly. "Dolce," he muttered wide-eyed. "You're in over your head."

No kidding, and I was drowning.

Chapter Nineteen

DELUSION 101

Once out of the building, Vinnie gave me a what-are-we-doing look. I didn't know, and it was a little unnerving we already had one foot in it. (*I'm sorry, two feet and a whole lot of crap for brains.*)

My legs suddenly felt like Jell-O, and I barely made it to the park bench without crumpling into a heap on the sidewalk. That sometimes happened with me. I was good in a clutch, could talk my way out of anything, but the anxiety of the what-could-have-been came afterward. I literally spread my legs wide and put my head between my knees, begging Mother Earth to help me breathe.

"Shhh, Dolce," Vinnie soothed, patting me on the back.

"He's..." I sniffed. "H-he's..." I tried again.

I was embarrassing myself. I was crying buckets of tears like my heart had been ripped out of my chest in a love-affair-gone-wrong. Not to mention the sidewalk had started to spin. "I need..."

"Shhh," Vinnie murmured again. Somehow I spit out I needed all three autopsy reports to tie the bodies together. I needed to prove the person who killed Alfonso and Annie was the one who murdered the man downtown—he was the key. If I could do that, then maybe it would be reasonable enough doubt to have the charges dropped against Oscar. Why? The timeline wouldn't fit. Oscar was already incarcerated.

I think Vinnie got it, but sometimes I just didn't know.

Vinnie crossed his legs, ripping a seam on his pants. "It's going to work out, Dolce. We're going to walk right into the coroner's office, lie, they're going to believe it, and we'll have all the answers we need."

Sounded simple enough, but sometimes Vinnie had a naïve take on the world. Things would be far from simple. First off, it wasn't Valley—where I successfully masqueraded as a law clerk. Downtown would be a totally different story. I looked too much like my aunt who'd recently dyed her hair blonde. If I drove downtown to find information, the Hamilton County Coroner would wonder why the Assistant Hamilton County Prosecutor (er, former Assistant) was worried about an autopsy report on an unknown with no known suspect as the perpetrator. Attorneys didn't get involved until the police brought the case to them, ironclad. That would definitely be getting the cart before the horse.

Vinnie must've read my mind because he whipped out his cell phone, googled the number for the Valley Township Coroner, and within minutes was speaking to someone I hoped was a decision maker.

"Hello," Vinnie said professionally. "This is Detective Russo with the Cincinnati Police Department. I need the autopsy reports for Alfonso Juarez and Annie Hughes. I'm down here at the station, and we, uh, might have a little situation on our hands." Some talking on their end. "We didn't want the press to get ahold of this," Vinnie continued, "but now that they have, we've got to move quickly to see if we can tie these cases together. We're getting squeezed by Odell Whitmeyer, and I can't say I blame him. I guess he's got a kid that's being accused of knocking off someone and then storing him in a dumpster. Yeesh, what's this world coming to?" More talking. "I can believe that," Vinnie added. "Sure, I'll hang on."

Major dead air with Vinnie giving me a shrug. We just stood there—him, pulling a Red Bull out of thin air...me, not knowing *what* to think. I laughed in a shaky voice, expecting them to say there was a lengthy request form to fill out that took two weeks to process—and a fingerprint just for good measure. After a few nail-biting moments, I heard someone come back on the line uttering a simple, "Okay."

Vinnie didn't appear a bit surprised. In fact, he said, "Here's my badge number." How Vinnie had someone's badge number, I didn't know, but when his identity wasn't questioned, Vinnie told the person we'd send over a runner to pick it up ASAP.

Who would've thought getting the Coroner's report for the third body found in Over-the-Rhine would be just as simple? I pulled myself together, stepped into my big-girl voice and within minutes had an envelope waiting at the front desk. Times like these, I got the impression it was okay to do the things I did. I was sure there was some codicil in there—and maybe I'd contemplate that later—but right then, I took those two successes as a sign to motor on.

After a minor celebratory dance, I speculatively looked at Vinnie who'd long since checked out. The thing with Vinnie? He could get things, but he didn't know what to do with them once he had them. He was back to eating moon pies, flirting with nearby women.

_____

It was Thursday evening, my normal shift at Belinski's Bookstore.

All day, I felt myself falling into a despair so deep I didn't know how to claw my way out of it. I came to the realization my boundaries between right and wrong were seriously skewed. God only knew what I'd be convicted of if anyone discovered I'd messed with government resources, but try being a teenager on a mission. A teenager, likewise, on a short rope.

Oh, well.

There were only a few days left of spring break, and that in itself added to the despair. What would happen when I went back to school? A phone call to Frank said he expected the trial to happen within the next few months. That wasn't a good sign. That meant the prosecutor felt she was so odds-on, a conviction was all but reality.

If all else failed, I could take what information I had to the authorities, but what did I really have? I was excruciatingly aware that all I possessed regarding the copper thievery was Frank and Oscar's word—and personally seeing Jinx, Juan, Adam, and Mr. Hood on the premises of a construction site. That wasn't physical proof of anything. And, most importantly, it didn't connect them to Alfonso Juarez. Plus, I knew the way law enforcement would see things: being a crook didn't make you a murderer. I made a pledge to myself that if I had nothing else in one week, I'd take what I had to the prosecutor personally.

Let the chips fall where they may.

Other than working on my term paper, I'd been a bum all day, lying around in my pajamas reading the coroner's reports repeatedly —the coroner's reports Vinnie's cousin picked up disguised as a faux runner. A runner in a law firm filed, served, and picked up documents. Good to know people who know people, I guess.

Regarding Alfonso Juarez, the cause of death was not the two gunshot wounds. It was the breaking of the neck. The gunshot wounds were that little extra value add. Sort of like the toy in a Happy Meal. The hand was dismembered several minutes after the fact as I suspected. The heart had stopped pumping, ergo the reason for very little blood around the severed limb and his clothing. All I could think was the murderer must've stood there and stared at the body for a while. That thought made me shiver with fear. It hadn't been a normal murder-for-hire. It was recreational enjoyment.

Here's the interesting thing. I'd already assumed Juarez's body was transferred from the actual murder site, and to prove my point, the report confirmed his body had particulates—or unnatural substances—on it (sawdust, drywall, and animal hair) reminiscent of a construction site or warehouse. Yay for Darcy. The buzzword there was construction site. Yes, Oscar robbed construction sites, but so did Jinx King. Toxicology/drug reports were pending, but traces of various chemicals were also found on the skin.

Regarding the third body, the report detailed exactly as Rainn Webster reported. Cause of death was a broken neck. The two shots to the back didn't do it. The male was an eighteen to thirty-five-year-old unidentified white man. He had no particulates on the skin similar to Juarez—insinuating he may have been killed in the alley in which the dumpster resided—but likewise, a full report wasn't due for weeks.

Annie Hughes, body number two, was a conundrum. She was like piecing together a ripped-up paper doll, then hoping she could talk and tell you what went on. Her limbs were torn apart by the compactor, and two bullet holes were found in the back. Once again, a broken neck. Here's the thing—she had DNA underneath her fingernails. One could dispute a lot of things in criminal trials—DNA you couldn't. Other than DNA—and I didn't know whose it was—there was nothing that pointed to Oscar on her or in the back of the garbage truck compactor. Could they solely be going on the security tape alone? That made no sense—unless there was something captured on tape that was incriminating.

I never asked Oscar if they argued. That didn't pop into my mind at all, but what if they had? What I did find out, however, were what sites four, five, and six were on the sanitation run. How did I do that? One phone call to the *Valley Gazette*, and I got a reporter that liked to talk. And guess what? The sites were on my stomping ground. Even though in a different town, all three sites were close to The Double-B. And site five? Site five was where Oscar was caught on videotape—Tire Town.

Thank the dumpster gods.

My mind went back to the fact that my aunt said word on the street was a rival gang off'd Alfonso Juarez. If that part was true, that would insinuate Oscar was in that gang. Oscar, point blank, wasn't. As the minutes stretched on, the more I was convinced something went wrong with the hypothetical "hit" on Juarez. If the rumor mill was correct, why would his hand also be dismembered? Sure, another gang could have some raving psychopath as a hitter— who basically enjoyed the process—but I had a feeling they would've shipped Juarez's body back to AVO with a big red bow on it. That brought me back to the murderer residing within the worlds of Jinx, Juan, Justin, and Adam.

After a few bites of spaghetti, I showered and dressed in my I-don't-care look. I cared, people, but it was Delusion 101. Pretend something wasn't there long enough, and maybe I could forget it.

Tugging on my Belinski's shirt and black yoga pants, I stepped into my Chuck Taylor's that I'd gotten clean, complements of half a bottle of Spray and Wash.

The weather was back to Cincinnati-weird. It was almost six o'clock when Claudia dropped me off, and a fog had settled in as thick as pea soup. As Murphy often said, *Mother Nature's a fickle wench, confused, not knowing her arse from a hole in the ground.*

Sort of like me.

When I arrived at the store, it was devoid of customers but still its usual emotional pandemonium. I dropped my purse behind the counter and crossed my arms over my chest, watching Mr. Belinski —in his overalls—freakish as usual.

"I'm gonna jump!" he screamed. Oh, boy, cue the stupid. I rolled my eyes as Rudi ran from the rear, her petite feet puttering faster than the eye could see as she launched into disaster mode.

At least once a month, Mr. B would stand on a chair and feign injuring himself from what he thought was a life-altering jump. What was the worst he could do? Twist an ankle? Blow out a shoe? It was a twenty-inch drop at best. Thing was, he sometimes took his idiocy outdoors. If it wasn't his hypothetical quote-unquote jumping from a chair, it was his sitting in the middle of the parking lot in his version of a political sit-in. His wasn't for reasons of politics. It was to guilt people into buying a book from his store. Without a doubt, the man needed counseling more than anyone I'd ever met—me included.

Beads of sweat dripped from his bushy brow as he inched his three hundred-plus pound body to the edge of the chair, tipping it back and forth. Rudi frantically signed for me to do something, her brown bob swaying with emotion. What was I supposed to do? Talk him down? The process honestly made me feel stupid. Still, I found myself inching closer and closer—palms up in a mean-no-harm pose —as if he was truly standing on the ledge of a skyscraper.

The things I do for a paycheck.

Talking in a whisper, I tried to calm him. "Come down, Mister Belinski," I eased. "You know you don't want things to end this way."

A laugh slithered up my throat, but I somehow coughed it out. "Can't do it," he mumbled.

Turning back toward the counter, I picked up the manila folder leaning up against the cash register containing restaurant menus and coupons. You lured a mouse with cheese, a crook with money, Mr. Belinski with takeout—free take-out.

"What'll it be? Pizza? Subs? Chinese? Barbecue?" I asked.

I'd already eaten—granted, not a lot—but thankfully my metabolism so far had cooperated with my in-between-meals snacking. In the back of my mind, though, I had to wonder if one day I'd wake up the happy hippo. I ordered the Big Four pizza from LaRosa's, which contained every edible meat known to man, and after twenty minutes, the place smelled like an XL meat-heaven. Somehow the order got transcribed wrong, and we were delivered five extra pizzas loaded with various toppings. Thank God they didn't make me pay the difference.

Two pizzas later, Mr. Belinski had lost some of the crazy. He was a simple man, sort of like a baby: you feed him then put him to bed. At least, that was the plan, but as soon as he stepped one foot onto the green carpet—yes, he ate standing on the chair—he forgot to put down the landing gear. He bowling-balled across the floor, took out a potted fern, teetered forward, somehow landing flat on his behind. Pulling himself up on one knee, his pants split—fanning us with dirty boxers—at the same time he broke wind. Hand to God, I couldn't reproduce that sequence if I tried. Like a fool, I tried to assist, but hit a pizza slick, scissoring my legs into the splits.

He blamed me for his faux pas—of course he would. Somehow, Rudi and I stood him aright and shoved him toward the break room, covering him with a blanket once he passed-out on the couch.

Close to seven o'clock, we sat down in the middle of the store at the pine table. The smell of pizza permeated the air, so I sent a group text to my address book:

4 leftover pizzas at BB. 1st come, 1st serve...D

I want a boyfriend, Rudi signed when I finished.

I sighed and signed back, "I know."

For a brief time the past summer, Rudi had a boyfriend. Unfortunately, it was Jon Bradshaw. She might as well have been talking to a dead dog. The biggest obstacle wasn't the language barrier. The biggest obstacle was Grumpy masochistically wanted girls that didn't want him. Rudi looked unusually sad for a relationship that was doomed from the start. That was the life of the teenage girl though—we just wanted somebody. I barely completed the thought when Vinnie—flanked by Grumpy and Trudi Hatchett—barreled through the door, yelling, "Where's the pizza?"

Talk about rubbing your face in it...

Rudi warily eyed Grumpy, probably wondering if he'd found his true love match...and well, wondering why she wasn't good enough. Vinnie's face lit up with an instant sympathetic recognition the minute Rudi flushed and primped her hair. I gave Grumpy my patented you're-an-idiot look. Unfortunately, he was so into Trudi it sailed right over his head.

In top-to-bottom gray cotton sweats, Vinnie gave us half a wave as he tried to sign, "Hello." His fingers must've twisted because as God as my witness, he fingered out "Hooters."

I bit the side of my cheek to keep from laughing. Embarrassed, Rudi blushed and zipped her black hoodie up to her chin. After a few more failed attempts at communication, they both went to the break room to fetch the pizzas and left me with Grumpy and Trudi.

I'd rather swallow a grenade...

Grumpy turned into a totally different person when he had his girl-vision on. Normally, he was all male, opinionated, and hard-to-approach, but Trudi had him dressed exactly like her in matching Valley High T-shirts. His attraction to her, my guess, was one of desperation and loneliness and maybe a case of opposites attract. Trudi was designer everything. Grumpy was bargain basement closeout. Apparently, that brief relationship they had was back on. They were hand in hand, making googoo eyes, and for a boy who was always brooding, it was definitely an upgrade in behavior. But with Trudi? Trudi reminded me of a wild boar.

Problem was, she felt she was more beautiful than she really was. Her nose jutted out over her chin, her eyes were set too close together, and her hips were slightly wider than her shoulders. Plus, she had man-hands. But looks were a funny thing. When you had enough dough, you could camouflage what Nature didn't give you with top-of-the-line accessories. Trudi's father was an executive at Procter & Gamble. She probably bathed in one hundred dollar bills.

She pursed her thin, red lips together in a tight smile. "Hi, I'm Trudi. T-R-U-D-I." Trudi spelled her name with an "I." Last year was "Y," and before that was an "EE." Guess she was trying to find herself. Thing was, every time I saw her, she introduced herself. She either had early onset dementia or honestly considered me so unmemorable she forgot.

Not that I cared...

After I begrudgingly reintroduced myself, I looked Grumpy square in his dumb-butt eyes and smacked him in the back of the head. "Wha-why?" he griped.

"That's for being a face-rubber," I said on Rudi's behalf, my lips curled up in an accompanying snort.

Grumpy rubbed his head, grumbling, "You need a personality transplant." I did, however, see a light bulb moment of guilt. He honestly hadn't even considered Rudi or her feelings...*men*.

As everyone polished off the remaining pizzas, I hoisted myself up on the counter, remoting on the TV hanging from the ceiling. After an hour of *Cupcake Wars*, Grumpy finally acknowledged me when Trudi went to the restroom. I was glad for the Trudi-reprieve. I'd just about barfed as she fed him, in between massaging his biceps and fluffing his late-on-a-cut hair.

"How are you today, Walker?" he cooed—cooed, for God's sake. "Things good in your life?" I cocked my head to the side, thinking so hard it hurt. The boy had either found his soulmate and was riding the happy train or was channeling Dylan in his everyday conversations.

I hopped down and stood next to Vinnie who leaned up against the counter eating—you guessed it—a moon pie. "Hunky-dory," I told him. "Did you just talk to Dylan?" He gave me a shrug. "What exactly are you getting from this arrangement, Grumpy? You're too nice, and nice doesn't fit your normally barbaric brogue."

"I'd like to know that too," Vinnie muttered. "I'm basically working for free, and let me tell you, it *is* work."

I elbowed him in his blubber gut. One day I was going to shove that moon pie down his throat and choke him. I swear it.

While I wished I'd poisoned the pizza, the silver bell rang at the front door as a gust of cool breeze brought in Jagger Cane and Ivy Morrison. Oh, God, just when I thought the PDA couldn't get any worse. I couldn't tell where she began, and he ended.

Yucky.

"H*ellooo*...anybody home?" Jagger said underneath Ivy's lips. She had his head between her hands literally in a mouth-to-mouth rescue fashion. I rolled my eyes and imagined myself in nun school. Watching those two together made me almost swear off the opposite sex altogether. It was too sticky, nauseating, and frankly, unclean. While she still attacked his face, he mumbled out the word, "Pizza," as Vinnie pointed to the last of the crumbs.

Jagger—dressed in his crimson-usualness (made me think he liked blood)—peered out from behind Ivy's fake, white fur. It was springtime, for Pete's sake. We weren't living in the Arctic Circle.

My glasses were smudgy, so I cleaned them on the edge of my T-shirt. Jagger met my eyes as I slid them back onto my nose, his douchebaggery begging to be unleashed.

"I'm in love with a librarian," he flirted, dropping Ivy's arms and taking a step toward me. Wow, how sleazy.

Ivy flipped her snow-white blonde hair in a swirl, her blue eyes firing like hot laser beams. "Shouldn't you be at visiting hours or something?" she snapped at me. "Oscar doesn't have many days left before, you know…"

She waved her right hand in a sarcastic bye-bye motion. You'd think she'd yell at Jagger for flirting with someone in front of her. Maybe she didn't care, or maybe she felt he was doing me a favor. Either way, I was tired of her shortsighted, blatantly harsh, and unsympathetic comments.

The room grew quiet. All that could be heard was the faint hum of Mr. B snoring and the crinkle of Vinnie's empty moon pie wrapper he'd started to lick. When he finished, he pitched it over the counter toward the trashcan. "What are you going to do about that, Dolce?" he whispered.

I mentally pulled the sharpest arrow out of my quiver and shot it straight through her heart. When her smile unfortunately widened, "You look like the Abominable Snowman" came out of my mouth. It wasn't the best comeback in the world, but evidently, Vinnie liked it because he smacked me in the rear. I braced myself for Ivy's head to spin or shoot off poisonous darts, but in a rare moment of humanity, she only gave me a glare and flipped her hair, storming out into the cool, night air. No Ivyness…no nothing. Jagger chuckled and made a kissy *mwah* sound in my direction, then turned on his heels and strutted after her.

Standing next to me, Rudi signed, *They're so dysfunctional*.

"Yeah," I knocked out in a fist.

"I wish I had someone dysfunctional." Vinnie groaned.

I surprised myself when I said out loud, "Me too."

The three of us stood there for a few breaths, wondering why none of us had a significant other. I suppose all of us had one valid reason or another, but I had a feeling both would find their true love long before I did. When the reality became uncomfortable, Vinnie broke the silence. "Want to go to a movie?"

Grumpy and Trudi had that we'd-rather-be-alone thing going on, but when Rudi quickly signed *Yes*, I told her to have fun and that I'd close the place.

While she hurried to get her things, I grabbed Vinnie's chin with one hand, squeezing hard. "She's a good girl, Vinnie. You'd better be on your best behavior."

Vinnie was Vinnie. In Vinnietown, her saying yes was tantamount to let's-get-married-and-procreate. He opened his mouth to say something but settled on a bigger smile.

Fastard...I'd better not find out he was a fastard.

"We're out of here," Grumpy said, turning to me. "Two hours of teenage angst is too much to handle." Whatever. I didn't want to spend time with him anyway.

It was half-past eight when everyone left. I logged onto my Facebook account and saw that Juan Salas, Jinx King, and Justin Starsong all had accepted my invitations to be friends. Everyone except Adam Neeley, but in my humble opinion, he just took up space in the equation anyway. As I cleaned up the mess, I texted Dylan, talked to Murphy who was running late, laid Mr. Belinski on his side in case sleep apnea choked him, and closed out the register. By then, it was minutes until nine o'clock.

My phone rang. Expecting it to be Dylan I answered with, "I miss you, stud. My life sucks, and I really, really miss you."

There was panting, rustling, and what sounded like a low growl. It didn't take a rocket scientist to figure out it wasn't Dylan. After a few more seconds of staring blankly into the air, I was greeted with a digitized, "You've ruined my life."

Criminy. It was one thing to encounter Darth Vader in the comfort of my own home. When I was alone at work on a dark night, it was invariably another. Chills rippled down my spine, and it took everything in me to keep from yielding to gravity and splintering to the ground.

One might wonder why I didn't disconnect when my body clearly wanted me to, but it was like the common sense bled right out of my brain. Stupefied, I did what I do best...I played the dumb blonde card. "I ruined your life? How so?"

"Everything was okay until you started sniffing around."

Ah, the call was definitely regarding Oscar, wasn't it? Perhaps even the fact I saw Adam Neeley get the crap kicked out of him. Could it be Adam? I *had* left him a message.

I said, "Last I checked Oscar Small's the one with the ruined life, whoever-you-are."

I wasn't sure what was said next. It was almost like the person was having a conversation with himself on what he should do...and how to do it. Even though the voice didn't sound human, the menace was undeniable. It wasn't teenage melodrama. It was blood-curdling, kill-you-in-your-sleep type of insanity. The caller wasn't even close to playing with a full deck.

Pulling a white Valley hoodie over my head, I turned the placard on the door to "Closed" but made the mistake of peering outside. Staring back at me—meaner than a drool-dripping tiger at feeding time—was Jinx King.

"And folks who put me in a passion may find me pipe after another fashion."

—*The Pied Piper*

Chapter Twenty

NEWTON'S LAWS OF MOTION

 $\mathcal{I}$ was up to my eyeballs, in stark, raving mad. I squeezed my eyes shut, hoping when I opened them he'd be gone. He wasn't. I thought dimly in the back of my mind it wasn't a good idea to provoke someone like him. In fact, it was inordinately stupid, but it appeared it was a little too late for regrets. Had Jinx been speaking with me and then decided for the more personal approach?

My breathing kicked up a notch as my pulse pounded in my veins. When I came to myself, my fingers nervously fumbled for the lock, but Jinx muscled his way inside—the little silver bell jingle-belling on overdrive from too quick an entry. Startled, I stumbled back a few feet, catching myself on the counter with my right hand, wondering what his plans were. My question was answered all too soon when the deadbolt clicked like a bullet meant for my head.

His hands jumped out faster than I could stop them and clamped down onto my shoulders. When he dug his fingertips in deeper, I gasped when my clavicles strained against my skin. What was he going to do? Shake me to death? Gazing at his face, I couldn't tell. His eyes were obsidian-black. It was like falling into a bottomless well, and unless I felt comfortable in dark waters, I'd better be clawing for the surface.

My resolve and bravery unraveled by the seconds. I could scream and get backup from Mr. B, or I could try (stupidly, I might add) to switch things around to where I was back in the driver's seat. Against my better judgment—and the sense of survival I didn't seem to have—I decided to spur things along. I straightened my spine, looked him square in the face, and smiled. "Hello, Gavin," I said.

He looked at me like I'd grown a new head.

Heck, maybe I had, or I'd reached a whole new level of stupid. "*Wh*-what?" he stuttered.

"I said *hello*, Gavin," I replied more slowly for emphasis.

I heard the evil *bwahaha* in my brain. In my experience, things were either bad or worse. Right then might qualify as catastrophic. All of a sudden, Jinx was a merciless predator, moving blindingly and frighteningly fast. He latched hard onto my wrists, and as no surprise, he muttered a threat. "I'd suggest you look for an epitaph for your tombstone if you keep walking down this road."

I think I peed my pants. When exactly are you too young for incontinence? If I were smart, I'd bust-a-uey and head straight for the door, but somehow I managed a tight smile and kept standing.

"What's your motive, Darcy?" he barked. His breath fanned my ear, but I willed myself not to shake.

"I have no motive," I answered. Okay, maybe I had motive...so there. I let that statement hang in the air, knowing my lack of words would make him angrier and angrier. I had two theories on how to deal with psychopaths: make them angry so I could find a chink in their armor OR calm them down so I could talk them out of the unspeakable. I'd decided on the first theory probably a little too quickly. "Why are you here, Jinx?" I finally asked.

His eyes flashed furiously. "You sent out a text about free pizza, remember?"

Dumb, Darcy, dumb. "You're not in my address book," I said. "That means Juan must've told you."

He gave me one of those smiles that crazy people have. The smile that said there isn't a soul inside because they'd lost it amongst all of the bad they'd ever done. My thoughts toward a human being like Jinx were unspeakable. I wished bad on him, and I'd never wished bad on anyone. Okay, maybe Ivy Morrison, but she was so soulless I didn't think it counted.

As hard as it was, I held my chin high. I tried my best to give him my bored voice, as though he had no effect on me whatsoever. "You know one thing I just figured out, Jinx?" I said. "You're an errand boy. The real mastermind wouldn't come for me personally. He'd send someone else, but I guess that still leaves you on the list of murderers. And we *are* talking about murder, right? This isn't only about copper." No admission, no denial, just more of those crazy eyes. "So how *is* the copper business, Jinx? Did your father bring his business home and you got the bright idea to get in on the action?"

His eyes narrowed. "What do you know about my father?"

"I know he's in forensics with the Valley Police Department. So if you think you're smarter than me, I'm two steps ahead of you. My guess is Alfonso Juarez wasn't. Did he cut into Northside's profits somehow?"

He snorted. "AVO was already here, and they didn't like to share."

Bingo, I yelled in my brain. I'd just filled up my whole, darn card.

I would call that motive in the good old-fashioned American way of getting rid of your competition. For a brief moment, I saw Jinx psychologically pull that statement back into his mouth. He'd just given up something he wished he hadn't. If Alfonso was already in the business, though, then that meant he—or someone in AVO— was stealing copper before Northside. Red said word on the street was a rival gang murdered him—could the police have meant Northside? Northside was new—to my knowledge—and the only gang she'd ever mentioned was River City Smugglers. Only way to know for sure was to rule out River City, and the only way to do that was to get on the inside.

Oh, jeez, things kept getting more and more twisted.

I didn't like to be pushed, but I didn't realize how stupid I clearly was until the next statement left my lips. "You just established motive, Jinx. I accept that gift on Oscar's behalf."

Jinx was undeterred. "Consider this your last warning, Darcy. What comes next might not be reversible."

"Like the blood on your hands?" I countered. Jinx's jaw tightened. The image of him rubbing his hands up and down his pants the day of the murder flew into my mind. Jinx literally had blood on him then. No one could convince me otherwise.

"I have no blood on my hands," he said not very convincingly.

I snorted sarcastically. "Oh, you have a lot of blood, and I'm positive I can add Annie Hughes to the mix." His eyes flew wide but quickly narrowed. "That's right," I said smirking. "I know all about Annie too. I'm not sure why Annie's life was shortened, but maybe you're the type that doesn't need a reason. Maybe you're the type that's just evil. Did you kill the man downtown too?"

No answer.

After some threats that left my blood cold, Jinx dropped my wrists and literally shoved me down into a chair. I watched his chest rise and fall with emotion, his eyes darken with intent, and when his mouth opened, I innately knew he was considering something heinous that would permanently alter my life. I never got the opportunity to beg, "Please, or at least make it quick," because next thing I knew, he suddenly turned and bolted out of the building in an emotionally unpredictable squall.

I sat there for a few stunned seconds, convincing my arms and legs they actually had a job. After I fumbled to lock the front door, I ran to the bathroom, bolted myself inside, and slumped down the wall in a heap, feeling violated. I wasn't your normal teenager. I should have been pining away for boys that weren't good for me—Liam didn't count. That was only a part-time pine. I should have been going to the movies with Vinnie and Rudi and signing about hooters all night. I shouldn't have been tearing myself up inside because of threats I'd basically asked for myself.

I didn't remember getting into the car with Murphy, and I didn't remember the ride home, but I'd never forget what came next.

Newton's Third Law of Motion says, *For every action there is an equal and opposite reaction*. What did I expect to happen? An invitation to their next birthday party? A fruitcake for Christmas? No, I wasn't so naïve to think we'd all be holding hands, singing campfire songs. I knew exactly what I was doing shooting that cannon across the bow, calling Jinx by his real name. What I didn't know was the return cannon would be one dead squirrel—skinned and gutted—on my front porch...along with the number "12" written in blood. My God, it was Marjorie's squirrel—had to be.

A smart person would phone the authorities. A dumb person would back pedal on the threats. An idiot would snap a picture and post it on her Facebook page along with the caption: *I got the message, so bring it on.*

I would be impressed if it wasn't so alarmingly bizarre. Blood and gut droplets haloed its upper body, and its tongue hung out its mouth from what looked like a quick, hard blow to the head. Question was, how did someone get close enough to a squirrel to hit it? It was the most intriguing spectacle I'd seen since Dumpster Dude. The lesson? Never underestimate the power of fear—it compelled people to do some really crazy things.

As Murphy cleaned it up, blaming the neighborhood boys—or worse yet, Choncho, who was still on the premises—I found a chocolate chip cookie to eat and went to my bathroom to get ready for bed...in Darcyville, four hours early.

Peering into the mirror one last time, I shuddered as the wind whistled outside. I was jumpy. It wasn't every day I got a dead rodent on my front porch addressed to me personally. And it wasn't every day I had to explain to my little sister that someone murdered her pet squirrel. My guess was we were going to lie to her. Maybe I should have allowed myself the luxury of a little bit of fear.

All of a sudden, it felt very lonely in the hole I'd just dug for myself.

———————

It was bright and early Friday morning, and I'd slept with the lights on. I hadn't done that since I was nine years old, but it made me feel like I had one leg up on the boogeyman. If I ever figured out who was *vadering* me (oh yeah, the bugger was back), I'd place them number one on my personal *Fry Him With A Blow Torch List.*

He'd vadered all night. As a result, my lashes were glued together, and it took the force of a crowbar to pry them open. The outcome, I suppose, of only four hours of uninterrupted sleep.

I must've had my finger on the speed dial for Dylan a dozen times. I had confession on my mind. Problem was, I couldn't get past the "Guess what I just did?" part of the conversation. The only thing productive I accomplished was my term paper was finished (yay, me), but it was completed in between sobbing over my interim grades.

Posted a few days back, I only mustered enough courage to look before I went to bed. I got a C, B+, A, C-, C, C+, and an A+. Murphy wondered why my only A+ was in human sexuality. It worried him. Frankly, it worried me more. I would've had an A in drawing and painting, but I forgot to hand in an assignment. Try having a ninety-five percent and then averaging in a big, fat zero. It nuked my grade. I planned to try and work out some extra credit and beg. I didn't know what to do other than to beg on bended knee.

When I cried myself to sleep, my dreams were all over the place. The parts I could remember were rated-NC-17 for violence followed by a double feature with Liam Woods that was XXX. At three o'clock, Darth Vader woke me in a hiccupping sweat, so I changed my clothes, hoping that would return me to my good girl dignity. I saw the crucifix shimmer above my head and figured that was futile.

It was some major suckage.

Before I could find my inner-self-help guru—that little voice that told me things were going to be fine—I jumped when my iPhone sang with the voices of four-year-olds. That's right. During an insomniac event, I got tired of China and changed my ringtone to a choral arrangement of "This Little Light of Mine." The actions of an unstable individual—I realized that—but I needed Heaven on my side. I really did.

Punching it on with my thumb, Justice belted out, "Stupid Eddie broke my nose."

Eddie, Eddie, Eddie, I thought. *I need to resurrect my inner-Eddie.*

Pulling the white comforter up to my chin, I winced at the sound of the weather. Heavy rain was plip-plopping on the windows, sounding like marbles on a tile floor. I didn't have many plans for the day, but what I did have involved sunshine and activity. Well, maybe it included Liam too. I hadn't heard from him since Tuesday, and I had to say, that hurt my feelings. To be truthful, I was supposed to call *him*, but I couldn't get my fingers to do-the-walking. What then sounded like hail might've torpedoed everything.

I muttered, "Sorry, J," as I remoted on the TV. "Eddie's a doofus and a half."

"She's a..." *bleep profanity*, Justice corrected. "I hate that..." *bleep.*

"She's like this big sea of angry instability coming at you all the time."

I had to agree. My dealings with Eddie were on an as-needed-basis-only in Spanish. Not many people creeped me out—gangs included—but Eddie was just this side of a Halloween ghoul.

"Well, did you at least hurt her back?" I asked.

Justice told me she and Eddie were sparring in their dojo downtown. Justice took her out legitimately with some sort of knee-drop move, but when the match was supposedly over, Eddie went with a sidekick to the back of Justice's head. Luckily, Justice turned in time, or she'd be food for worms. Thing was, it blacked her eye and cracked the bridge of her nose.

Oh, yeah," she said, laughing darkly. "Eddie's not going to feel good for some time. I dragged her to the ground by that stupid hoodie she's always wearing, and then yanked it off, and dug my fingers in her scalp. I literally left her crying in the bathroom trying to cover up the patch of hair I pulled out. Sometimes, you've just got to fight like a girl."

I high-fived her through the phone. "So what else is going on?"

"Um," she paused, "I had a dream."

Justice's I-had-a-dream recaps left me feeling a cross between skanky 'ho and frustrated virgin.

I giggled. "Starring?"

"Uh, your best friend...Mister Hottie."

That was a visual I could do without. Of course it was Dylan. He was an in-your-face stud, his visage burned onto the backs of every girl's eyelids that'd ever encountered him.

"So what happened in this dream?" I mumbled.

"I couldn't say. Nothing but blur and fuzzy on recall."

Whoo, it'd better be. Otherwise, I would have a serious eval on my relationship with her. "Good," I blurted. "I mean, *oh*," I said, quickly trying to act as disappointed as her.

Justice laughed so loudly I wanted to deck her. "I'm going to venture a guess that makes you happy, Darc, but what are you going to do when a Mrs. Hottie comes to town?" Dylan's girlfriend? Everyone need not apply. There was no room for a Mrs. Hottie as long as I was still breathing. "No, offense, Darc," she continued, "but sometimes I think he likes you, and you're too dumb to know."

I felt the beginnings of a life-sized headache. Dylan was certainly an enigma. One minute he treated me like one of the boys, the next a rare piece of art. Something you didn't touch but looked at admiringly and bragged about.

"Dylan's Dylan," I said, laughing in explanation. "Bossy, entitled, and insisting on things his way."

"Are you immune to that?" she guffawed. "I'm pretty sure I'd do whatever he told me to. How do you do it? How do you hang around him and not fall all over him?"

First of all, I usually did fall all over him. Secondly, I got to hug him whenever I wanted. To answer the question, I wasn't sure I understood wanting something I'd always had.

"You're making me feel insecure," I mumbled.

"Hey, it was just a dream, and I'd never take what's yours anyway. But you need to put a stake in the ground and claim him. You need to, Darc, before it's too late." We made plans to catch the new action movie *Vengeance with a Smile* during the weekend and disconnected.

I refused to think about Dylan.

My mind was too submerged in details, deluged with thoughts regarding my conversation with Jinx. What would happen if I did *nothing*? What would happen if I did *anything*? No matter how I tried to paint on a happy smile, I felt despair looming, sucking me down into that bottomless pit with no way out. After I wallowed in self-pity, I did my thing in the bathroom and changed into some clean clothes.

I liked my outfit. I pulled on a gray long-sleeved, stretch-cotton T-shirt, paired it with some painted on dark jeans, and threw a baby-blue knit scarf around my neck and wrapped it twice. Fur-lined brown flip-flops bottomed out the ensemble. It didn't make me feel better. It made me realize I was dressed up with no place to go.

By the time I made it downstairs, it was a little past eight o'clock. Murphy was late for work, pacing the floor like an expectant father. He went to bed in a bad mood in what I'd come to recognize over the years as an IRMS episode or insurance-related mood swing. A hurricane tore through the South a few days back and took out the top two stories of a financial institution he underwrote off the coast of North Carolina. It was a craptastic loss—his words, not mine.

Claudia was frantically running back and forth beside him, trying to keep in step with his stride, her black orthopedic shoes squishing like she'd stepped inside a bucket of soapy water.

No sooner did I expel the phrase, "What's wrong?" than I heard the dreaded words: Jesus cookie.

He might as well have gored me with a pitchfork.

My eyes darted over to the kitchen countertop—not there. I then scanned the floor...the table...even the vaulted ceiling...when I spied the empty gold plate on the stove.

A cold chill settled in my chest as my mind quickly did a rewind of the earlier events: read coroner's reports, ate spaghetti, took a shower, went to work, talked Mr. B off chair, ordered pizza, got extra pizzas delivered, texted friends with leftovers, watched the Food Network, watched Trudi grope Grumpy, watched Ivy devour Jagger, watched Vinnie leave with Rudi, texted Dylan, talked to Murphy, got a visit from Jinx, might've peed my pants, found dead squirrel, grabbed a cookie...

I heard the record player screech in my mind...

I'd grabbed a cookie off a plate on the oven and gobbled it in three bites.

Oh, God. Oh, God, forgive me...I ate Baby Jesus.

Did that mean I was holy?

I barely choked out, "Sorry," when I was struck with the surreal idiocy of the entire situation. Not only was Claudia speaking of her "poor bambino cookie," but Choncho was waving the dead squirrel carcass he must've dug out of the trash in the air. I debated laughing, but when I saw Murphy puffing a cigar like a smokestack, I considered stealing it and taking a draw.

You couldn't write this stuff, but it was status quo in the Walker household. We were a sitcom.

Ana Rosalina was like a bull seeing red. Her pink muumuu flowing, she came at me claws bared, like I was nothing short of Mary Magdalene stealing something holy from the good people. Claudia shoved me behind her back chanting, "Niña! Niña! Niña! Pull her away from Diablo, Mister Murphys!" I burst into laughter. If there was any doubt before, we knew where Claudia felt was my final destination.

...Hellfire and Damnationville.

Murphy's hillbilly was on steroids. "Git out of my house!" he yelled to all of them. "Now, git!"

Claudia lifted a heavily beaded crucifix from her neck, waving it erratically around in a figure eight. Jesus went flying high then low, but when he swiveled around and knocked the cigar onto the floor, I knew the poop was about to hit the proverbial fan.

"Die already!" Murphy roared, stomping it out. "For God's sake die, or go back to Spanishland!" They started arguing, or maybe they were trying to out pray one another. I couldn't tell. Sometimes they had a showdown of who could make it to the Throne quicker, Hillbilly and Spanish dialect neck and neck.

Ana Rosalina pulled a small, glass vile of holy water out of her bra, untwisted the gold cap, and flung it in the air around us. When nothing happened, she let out a loud huff, then gave up, and doused it in my face. Thank God, I didn't go up in smoke, but I couldn't help but wonder if I'd have one of those unconcealable scars like vampires got in the movies.

As I giggled and wiped my eyes, I stepped backward into Murphy, was caught off balance, then ran headlong into the wall, cracking my cheek, leaving me with a shiner that was going to be black and blue.

"Sweet Lord," I heard Murphy pray, taking my face in his hands.

That's what I was thinking. Sometimes I wondered what God thought of us.

As I stood there waterlogged, Ana Rosalina looked at me like I was evil incarnate. Funny coming from her whose son was playing with a dead squirrel. Murphy threw up his hands, barreling off to work, saying he'd call every hour to make sure Marjorie and I were still alive. I shrugged it off. I had bigger things on my mind than some holy water and a dead squirrel. It was becoming more and more clear I had bitten off more than I could chew.

Chapter Twenty-One

SIX DEGREES OF SEPARATION

I had every intention in the world of falling into a rom-com coma on the Hallmark channel but instead attempted a prayer out loud. "I'll brush every night. I'll eat my veggies. And I won't ever, ever think about the shama lama, ding-dong." Okay, the shama lama, ding-dong part was overkill, so I scrapped the prayer altogether.

Murphy moved toward the stairs, half awake, half asleep, half his chocolate ice cream dribbled down the front of his ratty white sweatshirt. Guess the diet wasn't going so well.

"Who were you talking to, kid?"

"The man upstairs."

He raised a brow as he licked his spoon. "Well, be on your best behavior because we're going to his house on Sunday. God knows the Walkers need to make a good impression." Murphy dragged us to church twice a year. Christmas and Easter. We weren't front row people. We were in the balcony, last row. It reminded me of those little gargoyles on the tops of buildings. Just there to scare everybody.

It was bedtime, and that's why I'd decided to pray. I was in over my head, plus the day was so unbelievably draining I needed *something*. Trouble was, once I opened my mouth, everything that came out felt sacrilegious. I didn't know a lot about a relationship with the Most High, but I *did* know I shouldn't confess sins—and promise better behavior—if I intended on living the same life again the next day.

At least, that was what seemed fair.

My moral compass, unfortunately, was absent in my life. I'd missed Dylan's calls all day. When Claudia "took to the bed"—a Kentucky phrase for taking a nap when your life sucks (translation, I ate her cookie)—Marjorie and I went to the mall with Finn, Justice, and Rudi. I must've hit a dead zone. On the way home, I noticed I had five missed calls and two ignored invitations to SKYPE. Frustrating on every level conceivable, but I was somehow stuck in the ether black hole. When I checked my voicemails, predictably he wanted to know why a dead squirrel was on my Facebook wall. Gee, if the roles were reversed, guess I'd be asking too.

My nightly SKYPE, consequently, was with Grumpy. Guess who just broke up with whom? Can we say, T-R-U-D-I?? The other day they'd gotten along like a house on fire. My guess was it finally burned down. The pattern was obvious. Last time they were a couple was Christmas break—spring break was days from ending. Made me think she didn't want to be seen with him. I hoped Grumpy never put two-and-two together—I didn't know what it would do to his psyche. I tried not to say, "I told you so" and surprisingly was successful.

When I told him about the dead squirrel, Justice's broken nose, and the shiner of all shiners, I found myself whimpering, "I ate Jesus, Grumpy. All of this happened because I ate Jesus."

"You ate the cookie?" he said with a chuckle.

It was just me alone in the den, huddled on the couch underneath a faux fur, chocolate-colored blanket we'd bought at Costco. In Murphy's words, *It's ginormous, but it's going to take something ginormous to cover your sinful body.*

Maybe he had a point.

I took the time to sift through my motives. I loved cookies, but honest to God, I didn't mean to eat Jesus. "I didn't mean to," I said, "but to leave a cookie untouched is like heresy or something. But why did he show up on a cookie? If I wouldn't have eaten Jesus, maybe Marjorie's squirrel wouldn't have been murdered."

"That dead squirrel happened *before* you ate Jesus, Walker. Do you think you were punished beforehand?"

229

Good question—one that was beyond my paygrade. "No," I finally decided on, "but I feel like I destroyed my religious karma or something."

I was PMSing, and what little filter I had was completely gone. Plus, a part of me—granted, a small part—had finally registered how wildly troubling and heartbreaking everything had been lately. Especially with the realization that Oscar could be hiding something (by the way, why hadn't he called?) and how I cheated the Grim Reaper where Jinx was concerned. Needless to say, I was frazzled. That wasn't like me. Normally, I didn't see the peripheral when I was tunneling on a specific target, but you try all of that on for size and see how sane you were.

Grumpy replied in his usually impassive voice. "Walker, Jesus wasn't on a cookie."

"That priest thought he was on a cookie."

"That priest wanted to get on television." My friends were equally divided on the Jesus cookie, feeling it was either fact or farce. Grumpy, however, felt it so ridiculous I wondered if he were an atheist down deep or a disenchanted Christian. "What's this about the squirrel being murdered?" he asked.

Divert, Darcy. Divert, divert, divert. He'd tell Dylan and God only knew what would transpire then. I blew my nose into a tissue, tossing it onto the carpet. "Oh, I don't know," I said sniffling. "Things die, Grumpy. It was the squirrel's time, I guess."

When he pushed for particulars, before I knew it—once again—I confessed my actions. Okay, I left out all of the juicy, life-threatening stuff, but he got the gist of it. Surprisingly, he was nonjudgmental with a smidgeon of curiosity. Made me think we needed to form some sort of working relationship, or I needed to quit accepting his calls.

"You understand the brotherhood rules say this is confidential, comprende?" I said. He grunted. I took that as a yes. "So you see," I told him, "Jinx leads me to believe Alfonso had some secrets of his own. Red said a rival gang off'd him, but the only way to know for sure if I can finger Northside is to talk to someone within River City Smugglers. Get their spin on things because my guess is they have a mighty big spinner."

I don't know what I expected from Grumpy, but it certainly

wasn't what came out of his mouth. "Would you believe my brother knows one of the guys in River City Smugglers?"

My smile grew as wide as the Amazon River. "You don't say," I said.

"Say," he replied.

"Does he know him *well*?"

"Very."

"Interesting," I muttered.

Grumpy's voice turned self-righteous as though I were accusing *him* of something. "I'm not my brothers, Walker. Make no mistake about that."

"I wasn't implying that, Grumpy, but I'm going to need this guy's number."

His voice suddenly bottomed out. "Sounds sort of ominous." I could tell by his voice the full brunt of the situation finally hit him. Not only had he probably pieced together the parts I'd omitted but was well aware of my potential to do even crazier things. "Slam on the brakes, Walker. You're not qualified to get involved, and God knows me making a phone call feels more underhanded than what you've already done."

Clearly a matter of opinion...of a perpetual rule follower, no less. I hung up and dismissed his concern, not wanting a roadblock from anyone.

Six Degrees of Separation was the concept that all of us were six steps away from an introduction to anyone else on Earth. It's that friend of a friend of a friend thing taken literally. When Grumpy called back fifteen minutes later, I became a firm believer.

He grunted, "I don't know how in the world I got shanghaied into helping, but the head honcho's dead, Walker. River City's wiped out. AVO took them over and a few of the remaining RC boys were jumped in. The other little guys in town wouldn't mess with an organization like AVO."

"You believe him?" I asked.

"I do."

I would have kissed him if he was within striking distance. It was probably a massive mistake (of eternal repercussions), but the cell phone number Grumpy provided, I dialed as soon as we hung up...after I hit *67, that is. I needed to block my caller ID as long as possible, especially if the guy was as psycho as Jinx King.

―――――

"This is Jester."

The background was somberly calm—maybe creepily was a better description. I wasn't sure what I hoped to accomplish, but it dawned on me I should've had a list of questions beforehand. Grumpy twisted his brother's arm into calling as a buffer, but at the end of the day, it was only me—and was the guy willing to talk? But what had I learned to take into the foray? Never underestimate my enemy, and always watch my back. Plus, as Vinnie said, *Know your audience.* I'd watched him approach people twice with success, and he'd never had a more complex thought than where his next moon pie was coming from. Knowing my audience was to be nothing but business, and I had a feeling if I spooked him, he would hang up—or worse yet, put a bullet in my chest simply because he could.

"Hello, Jester," was all he said. The man's voice was deep, and dare I say, sort of sexual.

Business, Darcy. Business, business, business. "I understand you're a friend of Markus Bradshaw," I greeted.

"If Markus says we're friends, then we're friends."

I took a deep breath. "May I ask your name?"

"Depends on what you want to do with it."

Jeez. "Nothing," I assured him. "I'd just like to know who I'm talking to."

"I suppose I could say the same for you...*Jester*," he said sarcastically, "but the correct verbiage in your sentence is whom, not who. Whom is a prepositional object. It's not the subject."

Huh. Just what I needed—a smarty-pants. "Okay, if we're going to debate my locution,"—yeah, I actually knew some big words— "then why don't you at least tell me what you call yourself?"

I heard him chuckle when I returned a cannon. "I'm Jaws," he murmured.

"As in Great White?"

"Let's just say I don't always need to use a gun." I think my heart stopped. It flip-flopped and fell straight to the floor. Surely he didn't bite people to death, did he?

I cleared my throat, shivering off a case of the willies. "How old are you?"

"How old are *you*?" he countered.

I added a few years. "Eighteen."

"Then I'm eighteen too."

Wow, the guy was good. Who would've thought I'd run into someone who was better at my game than me? I decided to shoot straight. That could be the only chance of getting the truth out of him.

"Okay, I'm not eighteen," I confessed. "I'm fifteen, and I'm calling you about Alfonso Juarez and a gang called Northside. Northside 12...maybe? I added the twelve, and if there's *not* a twelve, then I don't have a clue what their hand signal means."

I heard a door shut and a long, exhausted sigh. Walking to the countertop, I pulled a stale glazed doughnut out of a Servatii's box, took one bite, and crawled back onto the couch. It was almost midnight. Murphy and Marjorie were asleep, so it was just me...and my sin.

"What do you want to know?" he murmured.

"First, let me ask about you, if I may. I promise to never break your confidence, and I ask the same of you."

"Fair enough."

"When did AVO take over River City Smugglers?"

"Two years ago they assassinated our leader when he was getting out of his ride downtown. Bloody mess but an effective message. Next thing I knew, everyone with any power was getting knocked off until they busted up a meeting of ours with an ultimatum."

"Join or die?" I asked.

"In so many words."

"You didn't join?"

"I'd rather be castrated and sing like a girl for the rest of my life. Fortunately, I made my way out the back and was spared by a court date that didn't go my way. I'm on house arrest."

"For what offense?" slipped out of my mouth before I could talk myself out of it.

"I need to keep my jaws shut, Jester. That's all I'm going to say."

I shook off another visit of the willies. "Was Alfonso at that meeting?"

"Alfonso delivered the message," he said.

"Why would someone want to kill him? I've already figured out AVO was in the copper business." I think I figured that out. Jinx didn't confirm nor deny, but I had a feeling Jaws could and would do both.

No word from him for a time. That was okay by me. I needed to figure out my next line of questioning. I licked my fingers and went back to the box for a deep-fried doughnut, crawling back underneath the blanket again. I waited for an epiphany from Heaven but didn't get a doggone thing.

"Jester," he finally said, "you're a scary person to only be fifteen. But yes, AVO had the copper business wrapped up."

"Did it interfere with River City's business?"

"We didn't do copper," was all he'd divulge.

"You didn't answer about Alfonso...why kill him?"

"I hear Alfonso developed a big mouth."

"A snitch?" *Hooollllly Mooollllly*. Did his own gang kill him? If that was true, punishment in AVO for being a snitch was removing the tongue. No questions asked. Alfonso and the man downtown both had their tongues intact, according to autopsy reports. And honestly, the manner in which they were killed wasn't AVO's modus operandi either. AVO was a little more creative. They liked the stiletto, they liked to blow people up, and well, they tortured and dismembered via machete (gulp). AVO didn't kill Juarez. I knew it in my bones. But could someone from River City Smugglers—someone with an axe to grind—have tried to frame AVO?

I decided to ask. "Jaws, do you think someone from River City could've killed Juarez? Someone that made it 'out the back' like you?"

He breathed in and out a few times, no doubt wondering why he was talking to someone he'd never met before. "No. River City Smugglers were notoriously known as the 2-taps: one shot to the head, the other in the heart. If someone within our organization hoped to frame AVO using bullets, then that person was an idiot. You don't frame AVO by using a gun. AVO likes the more personal approach that knives give you."

"Would AVO have cut off the hand of a snitch?"

"Depends on who the hitter was. Perhaps. Don't try to make a hit by AVO always be all neat and tidy...ergo, done in the same way. They're ruthless."

I decided to not press for further details, fearful I'd faint. "Do you know personally of this Northside group?"

"I've heard of them, but they're really unorganized."

"How?"

"There's a lot of in-fighting amongst the members, and they're not only in your neck of the woods. Some are downtown, and they absolutely hate AVO."

"They're not scared of AVO?" I asked.

"They should be."

If I would ever get anywhere, I needed names. "Can you come up with the names of the major players in Northside at Valley High?" I asked him.

"Maybe."

"What about AVO?" No answer.

———

"It's one o'clock in the morning, Dolce. What's wrong?" I'd moved from the couch to the floor to the bed, and believe it or not, just flowcharted all of the information onto six squares of toilet tissue. My mind could handle copious amounts of information, but an ADHD brain had its limits to organization.

"I spoke to a guy named Jaws about Alfonso Juarez," I answered in a yawn.

You would've thought I'd called Jesus, Mary, and Joseph every dirty word in the book. Vinnie went ballistic, the only recognizable words being four-lettered ones.

"You spoke to Jaws?" he finally gasped.

Better question was, how did someone from Valley even know Jaws, who hailed from downtown on house arrest?

"I did," I answered, "and it's not the time for you to judge. You knew I was going to follow up on this, and I did."

"I thought you'd get bored with it or something. You have a

tendency to be ADHD." I wanted to hit him. If he were in my presence, I swear I'd haul off and smack him in the face.

"Whatever," I said, rolling my eyes, "I guess you don't want to know what I found out." Vinnie was as nosy—or nosier—than me. Of course, he'd want to know.

"Spill it, Dolce. You woke me up, so at least make it worth it."

I told him everything Jaws had said and actually nailed down how he even knew Jaws in the first place. "Jaws and a friend of my cousin's did a little bit of business in the past," he explained. "The Smugglers specialize in artillery. All kinds. He was in the market for a firearm, and Jaws provided him with the unmarked kind. I thought it was strange. My cousin's only seventeen, but not everyone leads the pure life I do."

Somehow, I didn't judge that narrative on a pure life. I mean, look at what I was doing. My brain had packed its bag and hit the road years ago. Regardless of Vinnie's rose-colored glasses where his own life was concerned, why would a seventeen-year-old boy need a firearm? The list of things I needed could be found at a drugstore or Target.

"Dolce, I've never asked why you're doing this, but I'm going to now...*why?*"

My word, the last thing I needed was a guilt trip. "You're taking this deal you made with Dylan a little overboard, doncha think?"

He grunted. "This is Valentine Vecchione speaking. Not Dylan Taylor. Normal girls don't do this. You should be reading *People* magazine, painting your nails the newest shade, talking to boyfriends on the phone. Something that remotely includes some estrogen."

I exhaled a tired breath. "I have no boyfriend to talk to, Vinnie. The Liam boat sailed days ago."

Vinnie spoke very carefully, as though it were a conversation he'd rehearsed, and right then was the day to perform. "And why do you think the Liam boat sailed days ago?"

"I told him I was going to call him back but didn't...for various sundry reasons."

Vinnie burst out laughing, coughing and snorting like I was the biggest idiot in the universe. "Dolce, if a guy likes you, that would've in no way been a deterrent."

Wow. Thanks for not sugarcoating it, I thought. "I'm just not what guys want, V, and this is the way I've found to entertain myself. Plus, he said he wanted to talk to me about something confidential. What would something like that be?"

Vinnie inhaled and exhaled, his voice coming out hard. "Who knows, but regarding this thing with Jaws, you're traveling a slippery slope. I suggest you stop."

Time and again, I reminded myself of the rules of society. Be a good citizen. Pay your taxes. If you're not a part of the solution, don't be a part of the problem. Well, I intended on being a part of the solution, and no Vinnie-lecture was going to castrate my plans. Though he hadn't realized it, I'd accomplished a lot. In the course of a few hours, things were falling into place. AVO took over River City Smugglers. Northside 12 hated AVO, and Northside 12 was extremely unorganized. And the biggie of all biggies—Jaws alluded to the fact that Alfonso Juarez had developed a big mouth. The only thing that could mean in gangland was Fonsie-boy was a snitch.

God rest his soul, the punishment Alfonso Juarez endured had been horrendous. As I rolled over and switched off the light, I wondered what the punishment would be for those that just interfered.

Chapter Twenty-Two

WALKIE-TALKIE

"No," he said apologetically. "I still don't have the name. I've been so wrapped up with this production I sort of forgot. I promise next time I see him, I'm literally going to walk right up and ask his name."

Fisher Stanton was an idiot. Maybe he could remember line after line in Valley's theater productions, but why in the world couldn't he remember the name of the individual he saw the day Alfonso Juarez was discovered?

"What part are you playing anyway, Fisher?" I asked out of curiosity.

He gave me an evil laugh. "The Pied Piper. What's a drama without a villain?"

I shut down the convo, figuring I'd never hear from him again and hoping his play bombed.

Even though Jaws gave me tons of information, like the conversation with Fisher, the rest of my weekend was a blazing disappointment. First thing I did was check out sites four, five, and six just to get a feel for them. Site four was Valley Post Office. Site five was Tire Town (where Oscar was videoed), and site six was The Cupcake Shop and Whole Foods. What was their connection? More specifically, what was the connection between Tire Town, Valley High School, and the area downtown—those were the specific sites the bodies were found.

Anything? Nothing at all?

I wasn't sure what I thought would happen when Claudia drove past them—maybe I hoped an angel would appear—but it certainly wasn't *nothing*. All we did was waste gasoline.

The resulting frustration led me to lose myself in a little bit of entertainment. On Saturday night, Justice, Rudi, and I snuck Marjorie into her first PG-13 movie. Ahem, wrong move (I know), but we covered her eyes and ears during the improper language, adult situations, and gunfights. Unfortunately, that was the entire movie. To cover my guilt, I OD'd on two buckets of buttered popcorn and three XL Cokes, and I still was on carb-overload.

Looking at my cell phone in hand, regardless of everything else, I couldn't seem to muster the courage to contact the person I really wanted to contact. *Liam Woods*. I sighed to myself. *Liam Woods, Liam Woods, Liam Woods*. It only made matters worse when he was presently sitting across from me at lunch, purposely avoiding eye contact, chatting up Ivy Morrison—and slap-me-in-the-face-with-her-beauty—Brynn Hathaway.

I didn't hate Brynn, but I didn't like her either. She looked amiable enough. Her smile was sort of genuine, but for some reason she was friends with Ivy. Trouble was, Ivy had one foot in demon. If I'd learned anything from Murphy, demons could corrupt. Even ones that looked like angels. It didn't help matters that Brynn was in love with my best friend.

Yeah, that really stuck in my craw.

Speaking of Dylan, his flight was delayed because of tsunami-like rain on the West Coast. He was supposed to be at school first period but hadn't materialized yet, and the codependent in me was impatiently waiting for him.

I needed a hug...and some quality time.

I'd futzed up again—royally. Apparently, I was to get my term paper topic preapproved. Someone with the same topic had already turned his in and mine was considered null and void. When I burst into tears—snot flying with my body racked in an embarrassing display of emotion—instead of giving me a zero, Mr. Woodward granted me what I considered another stay of execution. I had until Monday. I had to work a miracle.

Preoccupied, I shoveled a bite of broccoli and cauliflower into my mouth and then spit the offense into my napkin once I realized what I'd done. I understood the argument for vegetables, but my guess was the USDA hadn't taken a big bite of anything served in a cafeteria.

"Horrible, right?" Justice said, putting the lid back on her pink nail polish. I fought a gag, moved onto my overly greasy cheese-burger, and willed my tastebuds to not be offended.

Rudi was on my left, happily eating her sack lunch of a peanut butter sandwich and Fritos. She poured some Fritos onto my tray as Jon and Finn sat down, eating a slice of pizza before their rear ends even hit the chair. It was a somber affair realizing spring break was over, but I kept telling myself that meant one step closer to summertime. As I licked the salt off a corn chip, I must've been staring into no-man's-land because next thing I knew, everyone was yelling for me to answer my phone.

"This Little Light of Mine" screeched in a pitch so high we all were left with a mind-bending cringe. I winced, punching it on, as Dylan's gut-wrenching mug popped up on the screen.

"How's my girl?" he murmured before I uttered a word.

I almost burst into tears, wishing I could crawl inside the phone. Dylan and I had a complicated relationship—best friends weren't supposed to act that way—especially those who were strictly platonic. Still, I could never get enough of him. Hugs weren't deep enough and goodbyes weren't long enough. If there was any doubt before, it was pretty obvious how I felt about him. I cry-hiccupped twice, snorted once, and when Grumpy groaned, "Good God," I somehow sniffed out, "Missing you."

I heard a commanding, "Turn around."

My heart sped up, and I felt the omnipotent presence of Dylan behind me. I only knew for sure when Justice grabbed my hand, growling, "Dee-lish."

Hanging a right, I peered at him through my shaggy bangs. First thing I thought was, *Swooneth my butteth off*. The sight of him nearly undid me. He sported his favorite worn-out jeans, black leather flip-flops, and a painted on black T that hugged his muscles so provoca-tively it was probably against the law in Thailand.

My eyes squinted, refocusing. "Did you forget what I looked like?" he said, chuckling deeply.

Never...

He was like a black panther—pretty to look at, but something told me only the trained were safe enough to touch it. Dylan threw off a certain vibe. Ninety-nine-point-nine percent of the time, he was sophisticated, gentlemanly, compassionate, and inviting. The other point one percent, it left me wondering if he needed a cage. A lot of times when girls had guys as their best friends, they weren't dealing with a male who could be an incendiary device. They were dealing with a guy who didn't know how to—or better yet, couldn't —hang with the other guys. Not Dylan. He was totally an alpha, and unfortunately too delectable for his own good.

At only fifteen, he was an impressive six foot two, two hundred and twenty pounds of mouthwatering real estate. His muscles were strong and defined, hinting at an unusual strength. While everyone has heard of six-pack abdominal muscles, after swimming with him a few weeks ago, I had firsthand knowledge some were gifted with a full case. Then there was the hair—jet-black, totally touchable, that he wore parted and sophisticated or bed-head messy. Everything that spelled he had options.

With a sigh, I fell into his amber eyes. He blinked them long and slowly, raking me over from head to black toenail, giving me time to think about my answer. When my mouth just dropped wide, he added a laugh—his little girl laugh. That was another idiosyncrasy peculiar to him. He had a rich, baritone voice, but when he was happy, he sounded exactly like a little girl.

In his hand was a box of chocolate-covered, Hawaiian macadamia nuts. My mouth started watering. I literally ripped them out of his grasp, popped the top off the white box, and pitched three in my mouth, sighing.

"You're welcome," he murmured, giggling loudly.

My word. How good. So good, I lost myself in the ecstasy and sprawled backward out of my chair, bounced twice, my legs pointing up to the freaking North Pole. My back cracked in three places, and I bit my tongue.

Wow, déjàvu all over again...right there in front of God and everybody.

While I lay there amongst the muck of uneaten lunches, Dylan swallowed a giggle behind his perfectly white teeth. Squatting down on his heels, he gazed at me as if I were a tiny animal hiding behind a glass at the zoo. "Come here, sweetheart, and let me love on you."

Dylan was a lover and a hugger. If I was upset, he'd tuck me under his arm or pull me onto his lap, whispering words of encouragement that made me think I was capable of anything. Right then, however, I wanted to ram his teeth down his throat.

When he helped me back to my seat, there was a glint of humor he was still stuffing down. It was obvious the effect he had on me, and even more obvious, he enjoyed causing the effect.

I wasn't sure what I did. Maybe I stuck out my tongue. Maybe I was picking burger out of my teeth. Whatever it was, Dylan grabbed his heart like he negotiated with a coronary. "Omigosh," he murmured, "run your tongue over your teeth one more time."

I mimicked a spit in his direction. "Guess what I'm thinking, D?"

A slow smile curved on his lips, making his dimples implode. "What?"

"I'm seeing you on a tall building, and I'm pushing you off."

He threw his head back in a throaty laugh, giving me a lot of teeth. "Ah, sweetheart, only if you land on top of me." Murphy thought Dylan was perfect. Be that as it may, Murphy didn't know about the flirty banter. If he ever suspicioned a single, suggestive word, Dylan would be tongueless, sucking his meals through a straw.

He reached out, caressing my dimpled chin with his thumb. Then as God and everyone else in the cafeteria as my witness, the boy kissed me so low on the cheek it might've been on my mouth.

Dazedly, I heard an explosion and lusty outburst of laughter. I'd been gripping my chocolate milk so hard, it had exploded like a geyser in my hand.

Dylan's smile turned smug. "Yeah, you feel it..." Abruptly he stopped, placed both hands on the table behind me, straddling my body with his arms. He bent into my personal space, dragging a long breath against my neck.

Coming up inches from my mouth, he hissed, "Where've you been, and who was it with? You smell completely different."

I rolled my eyes. Sometimes he had no manners. I smelled underneath both arms, and realized it could be my sin.

Dylan not so gingerly yanked me up by the elbow. "Walk with

me," he ordered angrily. When we pivoted toward the door (Dylan pivoted, I was dragged along), he got a bellow across the room from Coach Wallace, frantically motioning for him to join him in front of the salad bar. Dylan growled, feeling the tug-of-war. He wasn't through with me, but not respecting those in authority's wishes was like desecrating hallowed ground. He had too much Boy Scout in him. Lifting my chin with his finger, he demanded, "Stay put, Darcy. We're going to have a little talk."

There was no room for negotiation in his stubborn jaw. When I heard more laughs and whispers, I reluctantly turned to see all eyes on us, realizing we'd become the afternoon dinner theater.

Dylan's frustration was palpable. He grunted a loud disapproval, and for any that so much as snickered, he wrote their names down in his *I Hold Grudges File* in his brain. Don't get me wrong, Dylan was more angel than anything else, but he never forgot a slight and would remember those faces until his heart beat no more. Me, I was an absolute moron. I probably gave people too many chances.

When Coach Wallace yelled even louder, Dylan gave him a begrudging nod then reached into his back pocket, pulling out a ratty, red bandana, laying it on the table before me. "What's with the bandana?" he asked. I was frozen solid. I couldn't move, breathe, swallow, or do anything but fear drool was dripping from my paralyzed mouth. "Darc?" he said laughing.

I yanked my T-shirt out from my neck, suddenly choking. "I, uh...where did you, um, get...that...*th*-thing?"

"It was tied to your locker door."

I needed prayer. I needed someone with a direct line to God, like yesterday. Yes, I went to church on Easter Sunday, but I wasn't sure that did any good when I darkened the doors only twice a year. Shakily taking it from Dylan's hands, I watched him saunter over to Coach Wallace, only to turn around and mouth, "Stay put," with a bossy frown.

I sat there in helpless fascination, wondering why I had no backbone. My legs weren't working anyway. Next thing I knew, Brynn Hathaway and Trudi Hatchett stood beside me with smiles as fake as the meat stuck between my teeth.

I glanced up, suddenly wishing I'd curled my hair. Brynn was so glamorous it was almost bewitching. She had a heart-shaped face with bright blue eyes and trademark chocolate brown waves. Throw in the fact that she was captain of the cheerleading squad, and it was almost too much to bear. Brynn was the It Girl. Everyone else (especially me) was the sh*t girl...do the rhyming yourself.

Barely bigger than Marjorie, she weighed around ninety pounds soaking wet and less than a zero size. In fact, the white jeans and black sweater she wore were probably found in the kid's section.

Instead of looking me in the eyes—which basic politeness called for—they both gave my clothing the once-over. That wasn't a good sign. My guess was that meant I was out of sync with the rest of the world. Wearing dark, skinny jeans and flip-flops, I'd topped off the ensemble with a blue T-shirt that had two fingers proudly in the peace sign.

Funny, since I felt like I was at war.

Taking the napkin Rudi offered, I wiped my hands and swallowed down some chocolate milk, delaying a response just for the heck of it. "How's Jon these days, T-R-U-D-I?" I smirked when I was good and ready.

Justice laughed out a "Ba dum-tss," mimicking the roll of a drum-cymbal sequence delivered after a punch line. Believe it or not, Grumpy chuckled. Rude behavior wasn't the norm for me, but Trudi brought out the rude.

Trudi started to fidget with a gold bangle, glancing from me to Grumpy, willing him to defend what little bit of honor she had left. When he sat there stoically, Brynn finally found her voice. "We were waiting to speak with Dylan," she cooed overly sweet. *Oh, is that so?* I thought. Trouble was, if Ivy had a crush, Brynn was flat-out *in love*. My jealousy swam to the surface.

Can we say, *Awkward tension?*

None of us were good with awkward tension, I suppose, since our eyes darted back and forth, wondering who had cojones enough to cut it. Finally, Finn spoke in a Scottish dialect, answering all those questions we knew Brynn was really asking. Like, *Do I have a chance? Is he taken? What's it going to take to get Darcy out of his life?*

"Doona git in a fankle, lasses," he brogued, "but the Laird pledged his fealty to the bonny lass years ago. She'll come first, and the Laird usually gets what the Laird wants."

The Laird, I scoffed to myself. That meant he was a landowner. My word, was I the land?

Grumpy grunted, shaking his head. "Ain't that the truth. Whenever Walker's in the vicinity, Taylors one step from needing the zoo."

Brynn didn't like the sound of that, sticking her lip out in a pout. Brynn was one of those people normally conscious of her appearance. The type that went to finishing school even though she was from the Midwest and not even close to debutante society. With Dylan—or maybe I should say sans-Dylan—she didn't even try to mask her resentment.

She said through gritted teeth, "I need to talk to him." She added a silent, "Or else."

Suit yourself. I shrugged.

Brynn and Trudi stood there at a wooden attention, only distracted when a faculty member asked Brynn about a paper she was writing.

Justice whispered, "Hear the scoop on Brynn-baby?"

Yeah, try that one on for size, folks. Brynn's nickname amongst the boys was Brynn-baby. Brynn-baby from Hathawaywood. I added the Hathawaywood—like Hollywood where all the beautiful people hailed from.

Grumpy and Finn leaned forward so fast they shook the whole table. "No," they replied in unison.

Justice's eyes sparkled. "Collin sideswiped her and dumped her quicker than a load of bricks. I heard she didn't take it well. Er, she was a witch—with a *b*."

Brynn dated (or *had* dated) the Student Council President, Collin Lockhart. I didn't have any dealings with Collin but knew he was notorious for being a fast-talking, silver-tongued pretty boy. The type headed for Wall Street capable of screwing the IRS code to the craptastic of levels.

I finished off my burger, stole a look back to Dylan, and nearly died on the spot when Liam maneuvered his rock-hard body in between Brynn and me.

Once again, another pout from Brynn.

"Hey," he murmured. "Best friend back in town?" I gave him a smile. I didn't know what to do. If I was shooting a jump shot, let's just say I got nothing but air.

Grumpy took another bite of pizza, answering for me. "Yes, and word to the wise. He's jet-lagged and not in a good mood."

Liam ran his hand through his thick brown hair. "*I'm* in a good mood," he flirted. "So good I'd like to take you out on a date this weekend."

I think the world stood still. Liam's voice was like velvet, melodic in nature. If he wasn't such a fastard, I'd agree on the spot. My face grew hot from a head-to-toe blush. Liam reached out, stroking my cheek with the backs of his knuckles. "You're blushing."

I gave him a whole lot of no-comment.

"Well, she's a fool," Grumpy grunted. His eyes slid out over my shoulder, his voice unexpectedly belting out a belly laugh. "And so are you. Taylor's giving you the evil eye, man. My guess is you aren't long for this world."

Liam dropped his hand—not intimidated—just irritated for the intrusion. He smoothed down the hem on his untucked, preppy pink polo that grazed a pair of jeans with a hole in the right knee.

"So what do you say, Darcy?"

Absolutely nothing...

Dylan was suddenly at my side, nuking whatever chance of a sweet reunion my romance-lover mind had dreamt up in those thirty seconds. If you can say "instant entertainment," it's like we were in a Roman Colosseum watching gladiators duel to the death. Liam seemed to be aware of the crowd. Dylan couldn't have cared less about the crowd. Dylan grunted...Liam grunted back. Liam leaned in toward me...Dylan bumped him in the chest. Liam angrily breathed in and out...Dylan sucked it out of his mouth and metaphorically spit it back in his face. Then Dylan absentmindedly played with a strand of my hair while he hummed (hummed, for God's sake). No wonder everyone thought we had something going on. Trouble was, neither one of us could define the "something."

Thankfully, Liam's phone rang, and when he pulled it out of his back pocket, I saw that the prefix was for Oxford, OH. The place I was certain the ex-girlfriend was...well, riding the cuckoo express. He declined the call with a blinking frown.

"How's the girlfriend, Woods?" Dylan said smugly.

Liam ignored that statement and slammed the brakes on the posturing when he saw the bandana clutched tightly in my hand. "Our conversation," he said flatly. "We never had it."

"I, uh..."

When I didn't respond, he TKO'd me with his eyes. "Later, Darcy," he snarled. "I'll call you later." Then he abruptly turned and marched out of the cafeteria, not looking back one time. I couldn't help it, but I watched his rear end move around in his jeans. My word, I was a sick individual.

Dylan yanked me up by the elbow, and I felt my shoulder go in-and-out in what might've been a minor dislocation. He wanted to talk...I didn't. But Brynn—who I almost forgot stood next to us—was hellbent on talking even if it made her look desperate.

She latched onto Dylan's wrist. "Hi, Dylan," she said with a wistful sigh. He gave her a tight smile. Brynn looked all dreamy-eyed. Honestly, she appeared a little vapid, but I was sure that was mere wishful thinking. She was in the gifted classes with a goody-goody reputation. No way in the world could I compete with that.

Case in point? I held hands with a dead man two weeks earlier and was holding a red bandana that meant something...something I was sure Liam might know the answer to. "D, there's something I need to take care of," I said on an exhale.

Dylan bellowed so loudly it would've wakened the dead. "Walkie-talkie," he growled.

Aw, crap. I hated Dylan's walkie-talkies. They consisted of him talking and me walking around, trying to get away from him. When we were six years old, Murphy bought us walkie-talkies, and in my opinion, they were an electronic miracle that ranked right up there with the toaster. We tromped through the woods, hid inside the house, climbed atop roofs, and acted like we were super spies. The teenage version, however, was reminiscent of drinking strychnine. Dylan would fish my arm through his, clamp it tight with the other, and I'd listen to every chastising word in a bobble-headed agreement.

Before I knew it, we were standing at our lockers, my rear end backed up against the cold, gray metal—cornered with no place to go. "What's going on, Darcy?" his voice boomed.

I kept it simple. "Liam asked me out, and I was thinking about going."

Dylan's jaw dropped, and he acted like I'd committed some unpardonable sin. "You do not ever speak to him again," he said lowly. I nodded like a fool. "You do not date anyone *ever* without asking my approval." I moved my head up and down. "In fact, you do not go out on a date, period," he murmured. It was almost like time stopped turning. As he calmly breathed, waiting for my acquiescence, I coughed, gagged three times, and my nose ran like someone cranked its spigot on full blast.

Only he could provide such a systemic response from my body. I considered spitting in his face but was afraid he'd return the gesture.

Dylan then lectured me on overall appropriate behavior, what some boys were really after, and what I concluded was proper teeth brushing, and the mating ritual of the peacock. Ten minutes later, he expelled his last breath in discipline. For what, he didn't know. He was just relying on his gut. All I was thinking was, *I need a new best friend.*

Chapter Twenty-Three

INSURANCE POLICIES

*D*ylan always found that metaphorical sock to shove in my mouth...and I was dumb enough to eat it. Finally, I got a word in edgewise. And when I say edgewise, I mean edge-to-the-freaking-wise. "You don't like him," I muttered.

Dylan had his locker door flung wide, slamming books in and out, clings and clangs ricocheting, as he was clearly unusually perturbed. Since our lockers were connected, my Spanish book fell to the floor from the aftershocks. I quickly picked it up, alphabetized, and replaced it on the top shelf.

"No, I merely understand who he is," he muttered.

"Which is?"

"The type that takes advantage of girls. They never call again, and they make girls cry and best friends consider homicide."

Dylan did, at times, have a flair for the dramatic. Unfortunately, his logic was universal fastard law, and I couldn't dispute it. Still, I wanted to fight him. "You don't have to use the pronouns *he* or *they*, D. We both know you're talking about Liam Woods."

Another book fell from my shelf. Completely frustrated, that one he picked up, sliding it back in place—alphabetized and all. "I try to depersonalize him as much as I can."

"Depersonalize?" I said with a snort. "It's not like some torrid love affair, Dylan. I just like him. That's all."

"I swear, you exist merely to keep me humble."

I wasn't sure what I heard next—frankly, it sounded like a wounded animal.

I stopped for a minute and took a look at him, pounding away inside his locker. Had he grown? Or was the anger merely making him appear larger? The tension in his thighs was straining to explode, the power in his biceps begging to pound someone into the ground.

I lightly touched his lower back, afraid of what I'd unleash if I didn't tread lightly. "I need to talk to you, D." When he didn't respond right away, I added a whispering, "I need my best friend."

Dylan slowly and methodically closed the door to his locker, his English book gripped tightly in his left hand. His jaw clicked a few times while he negotiated with his emotions, probably telling his tongue to stay put and let me do the talking.

He gave me a tight and exhausted, "Okay."

I took a deep breath, wondering how in the world things were going to play out. I was interested in Liam Woods. For various reasons. I didn't know if it was clearly of the male-female variety or the Darcy's-really-nosy variety. "Before you say no," I said softly, "*should* I go out with him? I've never gone out with anyone, and maybe I need to jump right in with both feet."

Dylan visibly swallowed, blindsided. Tucking a stray wisp of hair behind my ear, he acted like he was trying to fix something that might not be as perfect as he'd like it to be. His eyes softened. "I believe if you have to think about whether you like someone, it's not a good sign that it's going to be something everlasting."

Well, what in the heck did that mean? I was a simple person, people. Was he deliberately trying to confuse me? I clarified, "So I should only go out if I believe it's everlasting?" Dylan deliberated like he was trying to figure out how to rephrase...or dumb it down. Let's face it, it was *me*.

Dumb was what I did best.

He grew more serious, raking his hand through his hair. "You should only go out if you can't help but be around the person. There should be a pull. The person should be someone you think about all the time," he murmured slowly. "You long to hear their voice. You ache to hold their hand," he said even quieter. "You just want," he stopped with a whispering shrug, "to be with them."

"I should know," I rephrased.

"Yes, sweetheart," he said, nodding with a wink. "You should know." Dylan always winked as a way to tell me things would be okay, but the subject was raw, too raw...for both of us.

I grabbed his right hand, drawing it to my lips, not caring that anyone around could see the depth of our connection. "Dylan, the last thing I ever want to do is hurt your feelings."

I might as well have dropped the A-bomb.

He cleared his throat, eyes wide, visibly surprised and upset. Anger, sadness, and frustration tensed in the muscles in his body. For the life of me, it felt like its origins were of something other than disdain for one of Valley's notorious fastards.

Another day, I told myself. *A question for another day*.

His eyes searched mine frantically. "Take me out of the equation, Darc. Even if you weren't afraid of my feelings, never go out with someone who uses you and his current girlfriend as an insurance policy."

I understood insurance. My father's an underwriter. Trouble was, Murphy said you could never have enough.

"We don't know that call was his girlfriend, D. That's merely conjecture."

Dylan didn't say anything for a long spell. When he *did* speak, he reminded me of the story Justice said about Liam treating his last girlfriend so badly, it left her, well...crazy.

He narrowed both eyes. "Sometimes conjecture is fact. And even if it's not, it's something you should investigate before you leave your heart vulnerable. Are you still interested in someone that might be stringing someone else along?"

Honestly? I was just sort of glad someone noticed me.

When I didn't answer, Dylan swallowed more deeply. We faced off chest-to-chest and breath-to-breath. For once, I didn't know what would happen. A part of me wanted to talk more about Liam while the other needed a confessional on the messes I'd gladly jumped into. Still another part needed something I had no words or explanation for.

I shakily exhaled, wondering why I'd been holding my breath. His amber eyes were like a lion assessing its prey. Contemplative. Strategizing. A look that warmed my insides when I should've been running for cover. Dylan's body burned mine everywhere it touched, and let me confess, it was touching in a lot of places. We had some wicked chemistry. So wicked, it literally chipped away at my IQ points.

"D-d-don't look at me like that," I stuttered breathlessly, "I can't think when you do."

His eyes looked ancient and pained. "And yet you're thinking of Liam Woods," he said softly.

"Uh-huh." Well, relatively speaking.

He slightly frowned, the moment zapped to Hades. Dylan took a careful step back, collecting himself—as if touching me would take him to a place he couldn't control. Stuffing his right hand in his pocket, it's almost like he didn't trust it to not betray him in some way. "If he cleans up his personal life, would you still be thinking of him?" he asked. "This is about *you*, not *me*. If *you're* happy, *I* can be happy."

He said that with a ripe conviction, but we both knew that would never be true in a million years. But maybe that was it. Maybe I didn't know how to be happy without him, or maybe I could, and it scared me.

"I wouldn't even know what to do," I mumbled.

———

It was the end of seventh period. Egads, Grumpy was gone. Vinnie didn't even grace Valley with his presence, so that left me...and Bus 150. We hated one another. As I shoved my books into my backpack, Dylan threw a well-muscled arm around my shoulder, walking me outside. Right in front of the Death Mobile, we brushed our cheeks together—our version of a kiss—during our too-long hug.

"I missed you," he whispered into my ear.

Well, I missed him too, and as no surprise "our little disagreement," as he'd termed it, was all but forgotten. My brain, however, was on system failure, red lights blinking, all alarms beeping to exit the building. I was trying to stay alive. The word insurance made me think of that red bandana the last half of the day. How could I ensure it didn't mean something catastrophic in the armpit I called my life? In the spirit of self-preservation, I needed to know its message ASAP.

"Call me later?" I asked him.

"Sooner's preferred," he murmured with a flirty wink.

Taking a step toward the bus, I jolted, or maybe I was instantly frozen because I heard that voice that would forever be in my nightmares, purring my best friend's name.

"Dylan!" Brynn Hathaway yelled, all sticky and sugary sweet.

Well, well, well, guess she couldn't get enough of him either.

I shot a glance over my left shoulder as he gave her his totally undivided attention. The winds were forty miles per hour, and I felt like I was standing in a wind tunnel that was spitting in my face. For Brynn, it merely looked like a light, cool breeze. It kicked up her brown curls, framing her heart-shaped face like she rode horseback in a field of wildflowers.

Hard to compete with a field of wildflowers.

Why was she there? The answer was simple: she was a junior with her driver's license. My guess was she had offered to take him home when I had been doomed to lounge in the urine and stale hamster food smell of Bus 150.

Sooooo unfair.

I read his lips. He reminded her he had baseball practice where she innocently smiled she'd forgotten (the liar) but didn't mind waiting. You see, it wasn't just that she had a crush on my best friend. Brynn literally was the girl-next-door in Dylan's life—her own private mansion beside his in fairyland.

Dylan gave me one last smiling wave, but dang it, I gave him a dirty look—mouth all twisted up into a scowl that'd make Ivy Morrison look like an amateur. His head jerked back startled, and we had one of those heated exchanges with high-powered adjectives and adverbs when all we were doing was staring.

What the heck's up? I said to him.

He narrowed his eyes. *What the heck's up with you? I frigging deserve an explanation pronto.*

Can the cursing. I snorted.

The sentence doesn't pack the same punch, he scoffed sarcastically. *Answer the question, Darcy. What's going on between you and two-timing Woods?*

Before more non-verbal verbiage could be dispensed, the bus driver barked for me to step on or step off. After one last dirty look, I stepped on, realizing once again I wasn't in the driver's seat anywhere in my life. How in the world would I reestablish the upper hand? I could push Dylan to the back burner for the time being, but Northside 12? I wanted to think my fears were one hundred percent bogus, but anyone that had half a brain knew they weren't.

Thirty minutes later, I sat on the floor in my room surrounded by a semi-circle of empty candy wrappers. Candy wasn't my first choice. In fact, Claudia had made a big batch of chocolate chip cookies. I wanted them more than my next breath, but God only knew if they were laced with elephant tranquilizers.

It was full-steam ahead time, and if I would find out anything about the particular idiosyncrasies of Northside 12, or even AVO, I knew who I had to call.

Tapping in my most recent contact, the phone rang six times before he answered.

"Jaws," he said sighing.

"Jester," I said, sighing back.

A deep laugh. "I absolutely love it that you've blocked your number, Jester. There might actually be some brains behind all that stupidity." I thought of a four-lettered word but kept it to myself. "What do you need?" he asked. "Finally, my day might get interesting."

"No more interesting than mine," I said. "I'm teetering on freaked-out, and I don't like to be freaked-out any more than I have to be."

I swear it, the man groaned. "Freaked-out is not a verb, Jester. It's slang vernacular that simple-minded people use who don't have a vast vocabulary."

Not that again. I didn't have the time. "The urban dictionary recognizes it, Jaws, and that's good enough for me."

"We can cover that later. I assume there's a reason you called?"

"Why would Northside 12 tie a red bandana on my locker door?"

He inhaled sharply, muttering what sounded like a prayer. "You've been marked." He then paused, adding quietly, "I'm sorry."

Ah, threats and manipulation. When in doubt, those always

seemed to work. But he acted like whatever was to come was a done deal. Period.

I started to fidget, a prickle working its way up my spine. "How can I undo whatever I've done?"

Another sharp inhale. "It's done, Jester. I suggest you skip town or hire some serious manpower to keep breath in your body. But you're worrying me. I haven't quite grasped your personality yet. You're fifteen. Therefore, you should be terrified and sucking your thumb. What's your family like? Your breeding is either with a high sense of morality or you might be lacking in the brains department."

That took a minute or two for my mind to process. My family wasn't shocked by the occasional threat. That came from being related to two attorneys. When my aunt and uncle put away a drug kingpin last winter, rumor said our family and any close friends were living on borrowed time. Murphy took matters into his own hands along with two of his hillbilly soulmates. They drove downtown armed with a Browning, two sawed-offs, and a Louisville Slugger and busted up a local hangout, Kentucky-style. Murphy said God told him to clean house. I wasn't sure the edict came from God, but Murphy could always walk out of scrapes unscathed when a normal person would be full of bullet holes.

I picked up a Hershey's wrapper and licked off the chocolate residue. "I don't plan on dying tonight, Jaws, so why don't you tell me what you found out about Northside and AVO? Any names other than the ones I know for sure?"

I'd shadowed members all afternoon—of course at a respectable distance—to the bathroom, gym, and lunchroom, but got zilch. I even made eye contact with those in class, and they were either better actors or it wasn't their bandana. Jinx had been all about his homework when he'd practically beat down the door to Belinski's last Thursday night. Furthermore, even though I saw Juan in Spanish (before the bandana was discovered), I had a feeling he'd give me one of those psychotic smiles just to make me sweat. All I got, however, was a big, ole goose egg. I'd even brought up the subject of the dead squirrel and got nothing but "eeeuws" and "grosses." Frankly, I was flummoxed. We'd developed a relationship of firing cannons at one another and then rubbing it in the other's face that we were the one lighting the fuse. Wouldn't they do the same here?

Especially if it were some death calling card?

"If I need to remind you, I'm working with a handicap at the moment," Jaws said, "but my sources cast a very wide net. Be patient, and when I say patient, I mean be straighter than an arrow and try to stay alive." Jaws paused, chuckling darkly. "I must say, I've begun to root for you, Jester. I wouldn't go so far as to say I like you, but dang, it's pretty close." My arms suddenly hurt from digging my grave—shovel after stupid shovel. The one I knew was sure to come. Jaws then said, "If my manners serve me correctly, this is where you're supposed to say thank you."

Well, no kidding, but I felt like I was caught in a stranglehold. Jaws in no way was an idiot. In fact, he appeared sort of dignified with a higher than average intelligence. Then why in the world did he run with people in the circles that he did? My sense of self decided not to answer that question when I realized I was someone trying to get into that group.

———

Jaws promised me on his mother's grave he'd have names by week's end. Somehow, I needed to acquire his given name before he realized I was Darcy Walker. Anonymity—I'd learned the hard way—was the best vehicle by which to work. I wasn't going to rat him out, but I'd like to have something to hold over his head if he ever turned on me.

Regarding Northside, they may have won that round, but I absolutely, unequivocally refused to let them win another. They'd scored with the squirrel and bandana. They weren't going to score again. That was the type of egotistical greed we were playing with—but guess what, my ego was bigger than theirs.

All of that Easter candy bounced around in my gut. I had a sugar hangover and swallowed down two Extra Strength Tylenol with an Alka-Seltzer. Murphy dropped his keys and briefcase on the countertop during the plop-plop, fizz-fizz.

Murphy chuckled deeply. "Too much sugar?" he said.

I rolled my eyes, wishing I had more self-control as I slid onto a stool. "Murphy, can I go out on a date?"

Murphy made some sort of choking sound, losing his smile. He wore a jacket and necktie into work because agents were visiting. Loosening his red tie, he immediately opened the dishwasher. "Your openers suck the marrow from my bones."

Well, I had to get his attention somehow. "You never answered."

Murphy was surprisingly calm. Taking out the top row of glasses and stacking them one-by-one in the cabinet, he eyeballed an orange tumbler and hand-washed it for a second time. After he dried the glass with a hand towel, he said, "It depends on whom the date is with. What's your boy say?"

Dylan actually wasn't saying anything. It was Dylan lecture Darcy, me sorta understand, me cave and do what he wanted—you know, the usual. Plus, I had the added bonus of watching him one-on-one with Brynn-baby. That was a sight I didn't care to repeat.

"In so many words," I explained, "he said Liam was a fastard, and I'd be wasting my time." Murphy understood the term. In fact, he laughed so hard when I told him my definition, he ultimately got ticked off he hadn't invented it himself.

"I have to agree," he said, chuckling and eyes squinting. "It seems your boy's been doing a lot of thinking."

Dylan was always thinking. I couldn't always keep up.

I downed the last of my Alka-Seltzer and shivered as the bubbles traveled up my nose. "Dylan's like a dog, Murphy. Liam even looking at me is like a stray peeing in his yard." Murphy chuckled a coughing-snort. "Whatever," I said shrugging. "I thought the dating process was when you got to know somebody."

"It is, Darcy, but make sure there's at least somewhat of an attraction before you lead someone on. That's not something you want on your conscience. Who is it?"

I spit out, "Liam Woods," immediately wishing I could un-spit it.

The tenor of Murphy's breathing elevated. "That swim team boy you brought home awhile back?"

"Yeah, but he has a girlfriend, or at least he *did*, I think, but she's still sort of in the picture...maybe."

"Uh-huh," he grunted. "That's a major red flag and too many 'I thinks,' 'sort ofs,' and 'maybes.' You have to make sure that some- one's worthy of you, kid. I haven't had time to run a credit check or see if he has any priors. Besides, you're not sixteen yet, and even then we'll have to see. Once a cheat, always a cheat, in my opinion."

The laugh flew out before I could convince it to stay put. That was a case of the pot calling the kettle black. Murphy notoriously cheated on his girlfriends until he met my mother.

Unfortunately, his happily-ever-after didn't last very long.

"Okay," he said with a chuckle. "I retract that statement, but take it from somebody that lived it. If you haven't noticed, I've got a broken nose as an eternal reminder."

I really didn't have time for Liam until Oscar was out of jail and AVO-slash-Northside were out of business anyway. In my fifteen— almost sixteen—years of dysfunction, I'd found I could only handle one obsession at a time. Okay, maybe two at most, but I had a feeling Liam would be a full-time job.

"It's Oscar."

Oscar, I thought. I was sitting in the middle of the bathroom floor with Marjorie, polishing our nails. Putting the lid back on OPI's Don't Know Jacque (loved that name), I stuffed a cinnamon roll in my mouth, halfway glad he'd called, halfway angry he'd left me hanging. The last I'd spoken with him via telephone was the Tuesday after I'd emptied my bank account to listen to his sorry butt. Granted, we spoke again the next day when I masqueraded as a law clerk, but since then he might as well have fallen off the face of the Earth.

"Hey," I said.

I was immediately greeted with, "I apologize I haven't called sooner."

Enter Mother Teresa because right then I felt sorry for him.

I blew out some air, glad that Marjorie excused herself to play with her Barbie dolls. One thing about Marjorie, she idolized me. Not in a million years would she think my actions were illegal. Even if she did, the kid would have my back.

Dropping the used cotton balls into the wastebasket, I stood up and retired to the privacy of my own room. My ego and heart had taken a beating with Oscar, but I had to cover what was on that videotape even if it ultimately alienated us. Why? I didn't want to be defending the wrong guy, now did I.

"What happened?" I asked, sitting down at my desk.

"I got in another fight and lost phone privileges."

My air thinned, and my blood pressure bottomed out. "Why?"

"Someone hit me first, I hit them back."

Such a perfunctory, involuntary reaction—but one that could keep him behind bars indefinitely.

"Makes sense," I muttered.

As we sat in silence, once more I wondered how much money was left on the MoneyGram. Furthermore, it dawned on me his calls could be monitored, but even if they were, Oscar presumably told his attorney whatever it was I planned to pull out of him anyway. I decided to qualify my series of questions first.

"Have you been totally honest with Odell Whitmeyer?"

Not even a pause. "Yes."

Good. That was a good sign. "Then you need to tell me exactly what was on that videotape. There has to be something that makes them believe you not only killed Juarez, but Annie. What was it?"

If he was loose-lipped when he got arrested, talking to him right then was like chasing a schizo coonhound. His conversation was all over the place. He jumped to why he lost phone privileges, telling me he fought because he looked the biggest bully in the eyes. He then made a deal with another bully to have his back, only to find out those two were in cahoots in the first place. He was doing everything I told him not to do. (God help me, how and why did I even know these things?) Oscar next informed me that Frank picked a bicycle worth eight hundred dollars the night before from Heritage Country Club. Before I knew it, an hour had passed, and I still was nowhere.

Taking my lower lip between my teeth, I spit it out. "Oscar, why do they think you would want to hurt Annie?"

"Because I...I *did* hurt her."

My heart flipped over backward, hit my spleen, and settled back somewhere in the middle of my chest.

Question answered: Oscar was the DNA underneath her fingernails.

In my experience, life had three categories: good, bad, and downright sucked. Right then would be the downright sucked category. Oscar's earth-shattering, incredibly too-intense-for-words moment left me wondering if I were the worst judge of character ever. I'd never smelled anything nefarious other than basic deviancy on him—could I have overlooked the worst of the worst?

"Did you do it?" I asked quietly. My voice squeaked like a mouse, worried what his answer was going to be.

"No, Darcy, I was just upset. We fought," he said on a deep exhale. "I shook her by the shoulders when she told me she didn't feel the same way. She scratched me. That was after I gave her all of my money, and I just—I just didn't want her to go."

Ugh, I thought, wincing my eyes shut. *Why?* Why couldn't he have just walked away? That confession shook me to the core. I was going to go out on a limb and say that would convict him quicker than Juarez. The long and short of it—crime of passion. It wouldn't be a hard sell. He'd been playing knight-in-shining-armor to a young woman in a bad marriage. How heartbreaking, and how unbelievably torturous the way it turned out.

"Why aren't you saying anything?" he whispered. The tone of his voice was of deep remorse and sorrow—so deep it was swallowing him in the eddy of the pain.

I tried to talk, but my throat was dry. "I'm trying to think...that's all."

Trouble was, I wasn't getting anywhere. The third body would clear Oscar, but that third body was killed in another city with a different county prosecutor. Did anyone even care they could be related? After a little sleuthing of my own, I narrowed down that John Doe was found off Central Parkway in the parking lot behind George's Menswear, Roe's Restaurant, and Pump & Grind Gym (classy name). Were those clues that tied into Tire Town and Valley High? Possibly...possibly not.

I was confused to the nth degree and didn't know what to do next. There were too many questions and not enough time to find answers.

Chapter Twenty-Four

BAD GIRL

*I*n celebration of the full moon, I loaded Creedence Clearwater Revival on my iPhone—my new ringtone was "Bad Moon Rising." You know how they say a full moon brought out the crazy in people? The night before had brought out the crazy in Dylan and me.

We had an argument. I think I tried to apologize...I think. I tried, but then he'd say something that made me angry, and then *he'd* try to apologize, and I wouldn't let him. It really went downhill faster than an avalanche when I asked if he told Brynn Hathaway any of my secrets. Let's just say we had a cursing-like-a-sailor, domestic violence (not really, but it did get ugly), um, conversation. But there were embarrassing and painful situations about my life only he knew—he wouldn't break those confidences, would he?

Insecurity was an emotion that was all too familiar, and I didn't like it coming back with such full force. Especially with him. Call it a gift or call it a curse, but I was a pro at stuffing things down I didn't want to deal with. I shoved that argument into that compartment of my brain that held all the other scary things I didn't want to deal with and threw away the key.

What I wasn't going to shove down was the fact that, oh, I don't know...I needed to keep air in my body? Top of the to-do list for the day? Liam Woods. I had questions—Liam had answers. How did I find myself in the situation? It all started with the uncontrollable

261

urge to follow Jinx King down that proverbial primrose path. Its root? To get out of class and the fact I'd tanked another test. Who would've thought one uncontrollable urge would've led me to Alfonso Juarez, AVO, Northside, and the eventual framing of one of my friends? The trouble with a personality like mine was I never knew when to stop. That one next step could be the missing puzzle piece I'd been looking for. Looking for that missing clue more than likely would shove me in the ground where worms ultimately had their way with me.

Before I went to bed, I SKYPED Vinnie to see why he wasn't at school. He said he'd hurt himself pulling his shorts on, but hey, who hasn't? When we told one another how sucky our day had been, one thing led to another, and I clued him in on my plans to get close to Liam. Although he didn't like my particular methods of obtaining information (honestly, it did feel sort of skeevy), I knew he'd keep my secrets.

Just to be sure, I got the bright idea to make him a brother. Initiation was simple. Vinnie was injured, and feigning an injury myself, I told him to swear on his hurt leg we'd support one another —no ifs, ands, or buts. Then we performed our secret handshake, which was a modified chicken dance. There were two beaky hands, two flapping of our wings, three hip shakes, and a chest bump— don't knock it, it made sense in Cincinnati.

Evidently, Vinnie took the new brotherhood rules seriously because he soon buckled and gave me advice:

You're too goody-goody, Dolce, he'd said. *You send guys the wrong vibes.*

I wasn't aware I was sending any vibes, I'd told him.

Vinnie's words to me? *Get your bad girl on. I hear Liam likes the bad ones.*

I wasn't sure what that meant but was going to die trying to find my inner-'ho. Evidently, Vinnie felt I'd need help because next thing I knew, he was outside my house bearing gifts. He rolled down his window and threw a red push-up bra at me...I fainted. At least, I think I fainted, but when I looked at my bare feet, I was somehow still vertical. That had to be wrong—had to be. Good boys didn't do that, and God knew, good girls didn't. But it was Vinnie—what did I expect? He had two thoughts: females and moon pies. I was sure the earth would open up and bring us back to our fiery homeland, but I was hit with the realization that maybe Hell didn't want us either.

I must've stood in my closet for fifteen minutes, trying to figure out what look could make me visually compete with Liam's unnamed and unseen ex-girlfriend and Brynn Hathaway. I didn't know anything about Liam's ex, but regarding Brynn, it wasn't even comparing apples to oranges. It was comparing crème brûlée to a pile of shinola. Figurewise, she had me beat. Clothingwise, she *really* had me beat. Other than a few pairs of discounted designer jeans, I didn't own anything from Italy. The most expensive shoes I possessed were two pairs of UGGs, the majority of my wardrobe coming from the consignment store and Target or the clearance racks of Aeropostale's, Abercrombie's, Hollister's, and Kohl's.

Deciding on a pair of super skinny jeans, I shoved my feet into fur-lined flip-flops, topping it off with a lightweight, long-sleeved black sweater that made me look like I had boobs. Underneath were my voodoo cream and a red push-up bra—I'd washed it twice and nuked it for fifteen seconds in the microwave. I blew my hair out straight, but when my freshly cut bangs curled up into a salute, I pulled on a black headband. In general, my makeup routine wasn't fancy. It was lip gloss and mascara. I made it the trifecta by adding blush and lengthened my lashes to twice their size, rolling on two coats of Go Glam! red lipstick in—you guessed it—Hoochie Momma.

That was probably the best I was ever going to get, and when I looked in the mirror, all I saw was a good-girl-trying-too-hard. Blotting my lips, I decided to own the look and hope that Liam appreciated boring.

————

I decided to test drive my outfit. Leaning up against the locker, I swung out a hip and stuck my chest out as far as physics would allow without throwing out my back. Vinnie looked at me oddly, like I was an alien hybrid or something. When I batted my eyelashes, he figured out my MO. His belly bounced up and down like Santa Claus. "That's what you call bad girl, Dolce?" he said chuckling. "I wish you would've told me because I would've dressed you myself."

I looked at my jeans and sweater, ending with a pedicure in Don't Know Jacque that in my opinion was to die for. I thought I looked pretty darn good, but apparently, I was missing the "bad" part. "What's wrong with it?" I said, snoring self-righteously.

"You were supposed to wear something short and tight that will keep a guy up at night."

Vinnie and Finn Lively picked me up in the Bug that morning. Finn was using us as human shields against whatever-her-name-was who was a raging wackjob. Hiding behind my open locker door, he plopped a red Twizzler into his mouth, adding, "Low cut. Lots of skin."

I blushed the color of a raging forest fire. No way in the world would I *ever* wear something low-cut with lots of skin. First, it would probably nauseate the opposite sex, and second...I guess a part of me shockingly was modest.

There were days when I felt like I had it all under control: I had a plan, I fired on all cylinders, and nothing was going to stop me. Those were the days I was sure there was a Divine Plan for my life because all I had to do was think, plan, and execute. Right then was not one of those days. Vinnie told me all I needed were a pair of loafers and reading glasses, and I was middle-aged mom shopping at Talbots, hiding underneath a Spanx girdle. Who would've thought my success would be predicated on the fact whether Vinnie Vecchione felt like I looked like a bad girl? Frankly, that was a blow to my psyche on more than one level.

The hall was bustling with those running to first period when I literally wanted to pile back inside the Bug and head for a slutty girl store. Finn Lively, God love him, was somewhat supportive. He leaned in and said, "Whoever the guy is, be forward, duckie. That'll usually work."

Okay, I was *never* forward...not with boys, at least. I wouldn't recognize forward if it slapped me in the face and kicked my behind. Like an invisible marionette had my head on a string, I glanced to the back hallway and in strutted Liam Woods. Head and shoulders above everyone, he was dark and handsome, slightly tanned, in jeans and a white rugby shirt. If I were a DVR, I'd place him on pause. One word? Gorgeous. Two words? Off-limits.

Work it, Darcy. More teeth. More teeth.

I cupped my hands over my mouth. "Liam!" I yelled. "I see you, I see me, and a lot of foggy windows underneath the midnight-blue sky. I don't know, throw in some baby-making music too."

"Subtle," Finn muttered as he left and went to first period. *Whatever*, I thought. It was a freshman attempt. Maybe I'd get better.

Vinnie gasped like someone just clotheslined him in the wind-pipe. "Dolce! Not everyone's going to know the real you. Don't joke like that and expect things to always go well."

I couldn't help it. I needed his attention and Liam looked good. Like sinfully-delicious-and-bound-for-the-sanitarium good if he didn't notice me. Vinnie chuckled and murmured, "Good luck." He then left me standing, right as it felt like I got harpooned in the backside.

I didn't even turn around. Dylan's anger arrived before he did. "Nice pick-up line, Darcy. It doesn't leave much to the imagination." With an angry palm, he banged his locker door wide, throwing his books in haphazardly. They kerplunked on the bottom, rattling the locker doors adjacent to his. The guy to his right dumbly gave him a look that Dylan silenced in less than one second with a scowl.

The blood drained from my face. With everything that happened, wouldn't you know he'd look cute, all faded jeans and gray T-shirt scrumptious? I sneered, "Yeah, you still angry?" He did nothing but narrow his amber eyes. "Well, good. Me too."

"Good," he repeated even nastier. Heck, I didn't know how to have an argument with him, but it bothered me I was getting the hang of it a little too easily.

He pivoted an angry foot toward me. "Darcy," he started.

"Bye," I said, when out of the blue, a tremor shook me from head to toe. Liam stood to my left, right arm leisurely and posses-sively hanging over my shoulder, his smile on steroids. I must've been smiling something fierce because Dylan looked like I'd just sent him to the gas chamber.

Neither acknowledged the other...shocking. "We're going to be late for class, Darcy," Dylan grumbled. "Let's go."

"The party's just starting," Liam said with a big grin.

There was a weighty silence.

I glanced at Dylan.

I glanced at Liam.

Then I continued the process two more times, considering my options: (A) go with Dylan, preserve my friendship, and be as safe as safe could be; or (B) go with Liam, screw my friendship to heck, and more than likely not live to see my sixteenth birthday. Let's face it, if he had information (which I think he did) I was going to act upon whatever he gave me. The only way to get that information, though, was to be on him like white on rice and (gulp) maybe act like a bad girl.

Be forward, I heard Finn say. I cranked up my smile. "I like parties," I said. Okay, that was corny, but I didn't care.

Dylan took two slow, methodical steps forward, his chest practically bumping Liam's. He wrapped his hand around Liam's arm, removing it from my shoulder, never looking him in the eye once. "You hate parties," he said to me, twining my fingers in his.

Liam tried to mask a frown but wasn't successful. He stopped the scowl and painted on one of those killer grins that were the hallmark of the fastard. "Your best friend has this way of blocking any advances I make," he said smoothly. Translation? Why do you always do as he says? The answer was easy. I heard a lot of noise between my ears and Dylan silenced the noise. It was sort of mandatory for my sanity to keep him around.

"It's going to take medication and extensive psychotherapy to pry me away from Dylan, Liam. Just ignore him," I said.

Something rumbled in Dylan's chest. "Maybe some things aren't meant to be ignored," Dylan snapped. Dylan clenched and unclenched his left fist. I wondered if he thought it was his fist that shouldn't be ignored.

Before I could say anything, Dylan drilled a cold, bored, and emotionless gaze into Liam. A challenge was thrown between them as each negotiated with some emotions best kept private. Perhaps that was the quandary—neither wanted them private. "As much as it may damage your ego, Woods," Dylan said snidely, "it's honestly not been hard to block your advances."

"I haven't really tried yet, Taylor. Just wait until I do," he shot back.

"I don't anticipate breaking a sweat any time soon," Dylan said.

Liam narrowed his eyes. "Cocky, aren't you?"

Dylan gave a small shrug and started speaking slowly. I knew what that meant. He had gone in for the kill and wanted to make sure Liam didn't miss anything—spoken or innuendo. "I prefer the word confident," Dylan finally said. "Believe me. I don't suffer from any identity crisis whatsoever."

Liam didn't like that, coming back with a ready retort. "Is that an implication I might?"

Another small shrug from Dylan. "I don't imply. If you inferred that, then you're obviously insecure."

Liam smirked. "You sound jealous. Maybe it's because I'm the better man."

"Maybe not," Dylan countered.

"No, I'm certain I'm an absolute."

A devilish smile painted on Dylan's lips. "If you're so absolute, then why's Darcy still holding my hand?" Holy crap. I *was* still holding Dylan's hand and straight up looked like the 'ho-bag I was trying to. You had to give Dylan props though. No one could return a barb quicker than he could.

Liam didn't respond. Guess I would have problems finding a response to that too.

Now that Liam was literally within arm's reach, I found myself stalling. Having two strong, virulent males argue over me ought to be a head rush. For some reason, I felt icky and wanted to kick them both between the knees. I'd always heard about those girls that came between males. Murphy told me about them, and I'd never wanted to be someone who found her self-worth in males fighting over her. But they weren't fighting over my love, per se, and their contempt for one another didn't hold me at its core. Both were notoriously competitive, and their fascination with me was merely recognizing and trying to eliminate someone who had wandered into the other's territory.

It was one of those times I knew the universe had a sense of humor. I waited for some sort of cataclysmic event to put the world back on its axis, where things like this didn't happen to someone like me...but it didn't.

Liam's mouth broadened into a grin. "Let me make this easy for you," he purred in my ear. "I'll save you a seat at lunch, and I'll even buy you some cookies."

When I answered with a drooling, "Mmm," I realized I might be a woman of unclean body and lips.

I was too easily bought...not a good sign.

Liam tweaked my nose and left me standing, sauntering off to whatever lair senior fastards hailed from. Jeez, he was cute. If he weren't so cute, I wouldn't have issues with my thinking processes. Thank heavens, he didn't wait for me to accept or even reject. I wasn't sure what would've come from my mouth, and the sanctity of my friendship with Dylan didn't need it spelled out.

Dylan made a gagging sound deep in his throat. "What part of 'stay away from him' didn't you get?"

"The stay away part," I mumbled.

"Obviously."

"You're too bossy."

"Am not."

"Are too," I snapped. "You need to work on your people skills."

He rolled his eyes with a snort, his expression saying, *People need to work on the way they address me.*

"Doesn't that bother you?" I said frowning. "What people think?"

He laughed darkly, finding humor in his own bad reputation. "What are you up to, Darcy?"

I picked some imaginary blonde hairs off my sleeves. *God only knows*, I thought. I'd figure it out along the way. "I need something from Liam."

"You need something from Liam."

"That's what I said."

"That's what you said," he repeated again. I rolled my eyes with massive exaggeration. When Dylan was upset, he had a tendency to go mockingbird and repeat my sentences as though he wasn't even going to dignify them with any follow-up remarks...it would be a waste of time.

Tucking my history book under my arm, I threw my Lucky

bag over my shoulder. My sense of humor was on the verge of extinction, and Dylan had sucked the last bit of manners out of my mouth. "Our conversations sound like a broken record, Dylan."

"Then don't force me to break it."

I gave him a mean look...his was meaner. I finally blurted out, "I don't want to hurt your feelings, but apparently, I need to be blunt. Right now, you're in my way, but everything will go back to normal when you're not."

Wow, that sounded Machiavellian. Maybe I should be scared.

I would've expected an intense anger to ensue. Instead, a grin threatened to show as he took one step forward, his body dangerously invading my personal space. "Good," he murmured. "I intend to stay there. What does he possess that you want?" When I didn't answer, he said, "Is he everlasting?"

At first, I didn't remember why he'd chosen that adjective, but I recalled the conversation where he used that word as a qualification before I had a date. Sure, I wanted a date (I think), but more than that, I merely wanted information. If a date transpired from my bad-girlness, then woohoo for Darcy.

Dear. Lord. Maybe I was fickle.

"I'm not sure," I said, sheepishly shrugging. He just stared. Stared so intently I had to look away. "I could do without the dramatic pause, Dylan."

He captured my chin with his hand, forcing my gaze into his. Dang it, he wasn't going to go away, and it was unusually uncomfortable feeling his chest rise and fall against mine. Tension was inside. Tension that wouldn't abate until it found an outlet. "Infatuation is not your style, Darcy," he said frostily. But then again, maybe it was passionately because the look in his eyes was hard to decode...who the heck knew.

"What *is* my style?" I asked.

His eyes grew dark. "Do you honestly need me to spell that out for you?"

Honestly, I was trying my best not to romanticize the situation with Liam. Taken at face value, he loved me...or really, really liked me. Pragmatically speaking, he was a big, fat, liar. He was Liam. I was Darcy...that was that. Regardless, I needed him, and being a quote-unquote bad girl was the only way I knew to grab his attention.

I blurted out, "I dressed like a bad girl for a reason, D."

Dylan flinched, took one look at my clothes, ran a hand through his thick hair, and did the unspeakable: he burst into laughter. He put his hand over his mouth, trying to choke down the outburst when he realized he'd gut-kicked my pride. "Sweetheart, are you serious? Darc, you're far from a bad girl."

I hated him. And if Liam thought I wanted to be with my best friend, then he was an idiot. Dylan had better hair than me. No girl wanted to be with a guy who had better hair than she did.

I slammed my locker shut, hoping I had that don't-mess-with-me swagger going on. I was done talking, and all he was going to get was a picture of my rear end and the dust it would kick up. With an overly dramatic hair flip, I pivoted on my heels and ran face-first into Brynn Hathaway.

I had the gene for public humiliation.

My plastic tortoiseshell headband twisted with her designer model and snapped in two, tinging on the tile.

Picking up the two SOB pieces, I shoved them in the pocket of my jeans, mortified.

What I didn't need at the moment was a dose of Hathaway-wood, but it seemed like Hathawaywood was on the menu. Why did she worry me? She and Dylan had a history. Murphy never allowed me to attend parties or middle school dances, but evidently, Dylan had a good time without me. Rumor said he and Brynn fell off the grid for an undetermined amount of time, returning all flushed-faced and a little wiser to the ways of the world. I'd asked in the past if the grapevine was true, and his cocky laugh told me his lips could be filming a sequel.

Brynn was Dylan's type, I guess. If he *had* a type. I called it the Five Bs: brunette, beautiful, bedazzled, beguiled, and besotted. A paradigm of perfection when I was a provincial mess.

"Hi, Brynn, how are you this morning?" he asked, placing his palm on the nape of my neck.

She twirled a brown curl around her pale pink fingernail. "I'm great," she gushed. *I just bet you are*, I rolled my eyes to myself. When Dylan talked to girls, it always left them in some mindless la-

la state. It was another fifteen seconds or so before she found her voice. Frankly, her voice was annoying. It was too candy-coated sweet. Almost made me hate candy.

Dressed in head-to-toe pink (someone enlighten me. I don't know where you get pink jeans), she saw Dylan's fingers wrapped around my neck and acted as if she had amputation on her mind.

Suddenly, I felt like the spare tire. I gave him a nudge, whispering, "D, I think you're supposed to let me go now." The way she was looking at him—like he was a hunk of rib eye and she was an unhappy vegan—I figured he'd lost track of me. Next thing I knew, though, he shoved his left hand over my mouth and held on even tighter. Brynn flinched at his aggressiveness, but really, it was status quo for our overly physical relationship anyway. If she didn't like it, she shouldn't have butted in.

"I spoke with Sydney," she finally said sweetly. "So she's having a party this weekend?"

I stopped listening, contemplating my lot in life. I looked like a bad girl—or I had hoped to look like a bad girl—when Brynn oozed good. When forced to look at perfection, no way in the world could I escape comparing someone's excellence to my deficiencies. My push-up bra couldn't hold a candle to hers. Hers was way more than a training bra. Mine was...well?? Borrowed and hopefully disease-free.

As Dylan halfway answered her questions, she grew more and more impatient. I gave her one of those hey-I-tried shrugs and started to step away, but Dylan lunged for my belt loop. Yanking me back toward him, he grabbed me around the waist, his large hands almost spanning the circumference.

I felt like I'd been branded.

He held onto me for the rest of their conversation—and it wasn't pain-free, people. I wanted loose and God knew *she* wanted me loose, but we were dealing with Dylan...the definition of have your cake and eat it too. I started laughing because I hadn't been that amused in a very long time. Brynn shouldn't be jealous of me. That was completely preposterous and defied logic, but maybe in a perfect world, Brynn was dumb. That's it. Down deep she was dumb.

I heard Dylan say, "Sure, I'll do that," when all of a sudden, she marched right up to him and literally (honest to God Himself and any other man, plant, or animal you choose to swear to) no good, lowdown dirty kissed him. There wasn't a second for him to say no. There wasn't a second for him to say yes. Brynn just jumped on him like a virus in cold season. Thing was, she might as well have kissed me too. We were breathing the same air, taking the same space. That was certainly one way to quicken the pulse, and if mine was racing, God only knew what his was doing.

I mean, there was a tongue-licking smack included. It wasn't good when there was a smack, was it?

Cue the sleepless nights. One day soon, she was going to steal him away from me.

Chapter Twenty-Five

PLAYING WITH FIRE

I ignored Dylan all day, and when I say all day, I mean ALL day. Let me amend that...up to lunch, at least, but a girl had to start somewhere. He spoke—I ignored him. He touched my hand—I jerked it away. He put his arm around my shoulder (I'm not kidding), I leaned over and bit it. It wasn't a proud moment, people, but when he laughed out loud, I bit him even harder.

Right. Then. I. Did. Not. Care.

He was behind me in the lunch line, thinking I would sit by him as usual, all dutiful-friend and-good-girl-in-training. Well, guess what? I had a date. A date I intended to keep.

I punched my student ID number into the keypad by the cash register. The little silvery thingy was hooked up to the register and automatically deducted the day's lunch expenses out of my account.

Dylan said, "Darcy, you're killing me. I wish I could be angry with you, but you're too sweet to be mad at for long. Come here and hug me, sweetheart, so I can forget I'm mad at you."

Wrapping my arm around his waist, I gave him some sort of disinterested and passionless half hug, tapping his shoulder like he was a gnat I swatted away.

He pulled back frowning, his buttery eyes boring into mine like a drill bit gone crazy. "Wow, was that as good for you as it was for me?" he asked sarcastically. I gave him a shrug that was even less interested. "Are you sure we're good?" he asked. Ugh. "Listen, last night was bad...and today...I didn't ask for...I know what it looked like...do we need to talk about this more?"

"No, we're—"

"I'm not even sure I understand—"

"—fine, okay?"

"—what the *this* is, but I want to talk about the *this* if we need to, yeah?" He stopped for a breath. "I don't enjoy arguing—"

"Yeah, you do," I said laughing.

"—and I especially don't enjoy arguing with you." The boy had just lied to me. He loved winning arguments—always had—and winning arguments with me was some sort of astronomical aphrodisiac. Especially if it ended with me heeling at his feet.

All I could say was, "We're good." Then I added a confident nod.

Dylan winked as he dug a one hundred-dollar bill out of his back pocket, handing it to the lunch lady. Her eyes bugged out of her head when she pulled the Franklin up to her eyes.

"Are you going to want change?" she asked stupefied.

"It's probably a tip," I mumbled.

Dylan was instantly embarrassed but just as instantaneously came the disarmingly intense charm. "No, ma'am. My mother didn't have anything smaller. If you would, please deposit the rest into my account." That's what happened, folks, when you were richer than God. Heaven only knew the last time they'd touched a bill smaller than a twenty.

When she finished, Dylan ran a hand through his hair. "Maybe we should talk about this some more."

I expelled a worn out sigh. "Pinky swear. We're good."

And that was why I loved Dylan. He suffered from a hyper conscience and couldn't rest until we were back on the same page. But Dylan's problem was he couldn't let bygones be bygones...at least with me. I wanted to ignore what had happened, move on, be done with it. We were speaking, and that meant I didn't have to dive into the reasons I was so short-tempered. The best I could come up with was I was stressed over the situation with Oscar, and maybe the green-eyed monster named Brynn-envy was getting to me. Go figure. His ego didn't need to know that. My word, it was big enough already.

"I owe you an apology, Darc. I've obviously hurt your feelings."

No shizzzz...

So I'd screwed up with my bad-girlness (I would burn my bra as soon as I got home), but I could tell you one thing, it wouldn't happen again. Dylan needed to be turned off, though, before he could fully get turned on. When he was in that mood, it could be an all-day gab session. I talked over my shoulder as we walked. "You owe me nothing, D. I love you, you love me, and we both know it's for always. Just like until the day we die, but I shouldn't have to explain myself. You're a guy. It's all about the shama lama, ding-dong. I may not know a lot, but dang it, I know guys like the shama lama, ding-dong."

My word, was he an idiot? Dylan went still. He cleared his throat once...then again. "The shama lama, ding-dong," he murmured.

"The shama lama, ding-dong," I repeated.

"Am I supposed to know what that means?"

I decided to play the mocking bird, repeating his phrases just to get on his nerves. "You're supposed to know what that means." I smiled in my brain.

"Huh," he said chuckling. "Please enlighten me, oh thee of the creative tongue." My face instantly felt like a five-alarm fire. "Darcy, Darcy, Darcy," he joked. "Are you blushing?"

"You're standing behind me," I said with a snort. "How would you know?"

"I feel you, sweetheart."

I meandered in and out of three tables, making my way toward a waving and grinning Liam. Sweat dripped down my back, causing my shirt to stick to my skin. I didn't know if that was from looking at Liam or being under the gun with Dylan. "You know..." I stalled.

By that time, Dylan was right by my side, leaning into my shoulder. "Uh-huh," he said, chuckling again. "Give me specifics."

I blushed even deeper. "You know, wink-wink."

"What do you mean, wink-wink?"

The best way to shock Dylan into silence was to tell him my limited knowledge of the opposite sex in a thirty-second sound bite. I opened my mouth and unloaded everything I knew from health class, what magazines had warned me about, and what Murphy claimed was a big green light to guys—ergo, don't ever do it. I unveiled everything I knew about the bad girl and how my goal was to be the baddest of the bad—with a reputation that would make the trampy look pure.

Dylan dropped his tray but caught it right before it hit the floor.

I gave him an exactly-what-I-was-going-for smile and marched toward a patiently waiting Liam (shaking my hips), trying to smile like a bad girl on the prowl.

I heard a four-lettered word but kept right on walking.

Lunch was a grilled chicken sandwich and mixed fruit in some sort of red gelatinous mold. I bought a slice of pizza, picked at my salad, and scarfed the three cookies Liam had waiting as an appetizer. Wow, you had to love a man who bought you cookies.

The first ten minutes we talked about TV shows we liked, professional baseball season (he was shocked I could hang), and what plans we had for summer break. I asked him what college he was considering, but Liam gave me a look like nothing was set in stone. Something other than indecisiveness was in that look. It was an unmistakable restlessness as though he couldn't make any decisions until something of greater importance was resolved.

When we neared the fifteen-minute mark, my nerves reminded me lunch was all but over. Indigestion started, and I knew I needed to get to the bottom of what Liam was so desperate to talk to me about. But a part of me didn't want to break the mood. I liked Liam. He laughed easily, really listened when I spoke, and although I'd heard—and probably believed—he was a fastard, there was some genuine goodness in him. But I couldn't let a crush on someone I knew very little about keep me from helping Oscar. Thing was, we were getting along so well there was never a lull in conversation. That left no other recourse than to basically interrupt a male who was telling me the dimple on my chin should be outlawed it was so delicious.

Only my luck. I frowned.

"Liam—" I said.

My iPhone sang "Bad Moon Rising," and when I looked at the screen, I saw Dylan's number and face flashing. For God's sake, he was calling me from two tables over. I rolled my eyes and scratched my head in my mind. I'd never understand him.

I took perverse pleasure in tapping the decline button, sending it straight to voicemail.

I tried again. "Liam, what was it you wanted to speak with me about?"

"You have the most beautiful eyes," he gushed.

Omigosh, I thought. He was really into me. *Dream on, Darcy. Dream on.* For a minute, I tried to picture Liam and me as the school's superstar couple. Crowds parted, and envy followed us everywhere. Then I felt the pressure, the pressure to keep *being* the it-couple. BARF. Who in their right mind would want that kind of life?

I shook my head hard, butting into my own daydream.

"What was the talk you wanted to have with me, Liam? You mentioned it twice, and I could tell both times it was serious in nature." He said nothing, looking like he'd even shut off his breathing. "Could it have something to do with that gang we talked about? You have some details about the Oscar Small case, don't you? Some details that are keeping you up at night."

He clammed up like he was on the bottom of the ocean and someone had gone for his pearl. "I have no answer for that," he said.

"You have no answer or none you're willing to give?" I qualified.

Liam shifted in his chair—half laughing, half thinking he could distract me. He took a drink of milk, unleashing that fastard smile. "Law school?" he murmured.

"Familial hazard. My aunt and uncle are prosecutors." Liam startled, like I'd said something that would wipe out his mood permanently. "What Liam?" I pushed. Still, he said nothing. "Then I'll answer for you," I continued. "You were angry over the red bandana tied to my locker door. I did my own investigating and found out it means I've been marked in some way. Why and by whom?"

Liam looked horrified. "Whatever you're doing, stop it," he warned, lowering his voice.

"I could say the same for you," I said quietly.

Liam stared at me like he was seeing me for the first time. He narrowed his eyes, refocused, and looked over my shoulder as if he were making eye contact with someone else.

I went for broke. "I know the hand signal too, for the gang I now refer to as the Northside 12." Taking a quick glance around, I demonstrated it twice in slow motion.

Liam stiffened, sat up straighter, and developed a tremor in his right hand. He looked at it and fisted his hand around a napkin, trying to get it to stop. "Darcy, you're in over your head," he said coolly. "What have you been doing?"

"I'm afraid it's the same thing *you've* been doing."

I might as well have peeled off a layer of his flesh. He jerked, his brown eyes instantly mistrustful. "What is it you think I've done? You've tried, convicted, and executed me without one word in defense."

"Then defend yourself," I said. Once again, I got nothing but stone-cold silence. "Why don't I trust you, Liam?" Other than being a fastard, of course.

Note to self: if you're looking for information, keep your personal doubts to yourself.

That six-worded sentence cut the conversation short and nuked the mood. All of a sudden, I felt unbelievably stupid. Maybe I should've had a better plan—all I'd succeeded in doing was alienating him, probably permanently.

All Liam said (after I'd basically called him untrustworthy) was, "I don't know what you're talking about." He then picked up his tray and left me sitting. No parting words...no promise to call later... he just left me there.

———

Some of us are born with the tendency to never be satisfied. We were restless. If you find the thing that fills you up, restlessness and desperation won't maim you. If you don't? You're crippled with what-could-have-been thoughts. I hadn't had any long-term thoughts regarding my life—at least ones that I thought were attainable—but my body was hardwired to be a rolling stone. Five minutes into class, I felt like I was in prison waiting to get bail posted—the reason I walked the halls during fifth period on a quote-unquote bathroom break to clear my head. Trouble was, AP Unger was on the same schedule. He found me hanging overtop the second floor balcony, brainlessly staring out into thin air.

My explanation as he folded his arms over his navy blazer was, "A rolling stone gathers no moss," I said in a giggle.

"I see," he said.

"I'm leaving."

"When?"

"Now?"

"Promise?"

"No," I said laughing.

He sighed heavily. "Walker, I'm worn out, and I've barely said three words."

"Actually, it was four words, but maybe you need a vitamin."

He frowned. "What I *need* is for you to go back to class."

"Only if you tell me what you know about Oscar Small. What *do* you know?"

He frowned even deeper, shifting his weight to the other foot. He started jingling the change in his pocket, and I briefly wondered what that meant for him on a psychological level. Maybe he was formulating questions, or maybe he restrained himself from ringing my neck. Heck, maybe it meant nothing, and I simply saw a devil behind every bush. He finally said, "I feel like I'm negotiating with a terrorist, but to answer your question, I know nothing."

I snorted because he wasn't telling the truth. "That's a lie."

"Walker," he warned.

"Humor me, AP Unger. My conversation-slash-date with Liam Woods ended badly. Like vomit-in-your-mouth badly, so unless you want to put me on Ms. Dempsey's normal counseling rotation, then I'd convince your mouth it had a job. Besides, you don't want to put her through the chore of sorting through my particular grey matter. Trust me. No one ever comes out in one piece."

"Ain't that the truth," he shockingly mumbled out loud.

I snorted. He snorted louder, and after a few seconds of sounding like farmyard animals, he raised a brow, thinking. AP Unger was from Kentucky, like Murphy. To him, one date probably meant I was headed down the aisle in a white dress on the weekend. "Liam Woods," he clarified.

"Liam Woods."

"Too old for you."

"So I've been told."

"Well..." he said.

"Well," I mocked, "spit it out."

AP Unger reluctantly looked at his watch and cocked his head to one side, trying—my guess—how to successfully get me back into class without succumbing to my request. I had to hand it to myself. There were days I could throw off the scary and convince those in authority I was one of those really, really smart people they didn't want angry with them.

I shoved my hands into my front pockets, prepared to wait him out.

Finally, after he went through whatever thinking process assistant principals went through, he muttered, "Two minutes, Walker. That's all you get."

I'd take it.

AP Unger took a breath so deep it could've inflated one of those Macy's Thanksgiving Day Parade balloons. He was worn out, or perhaps he felt defeated...perhaps both. It was apparent he'd been thinking about Oscar, and after he decided to unload what he knew, he actually acted like he'd been searching for something to exorcise him of the thoughts anyway. Trouble was, AP Unger's idea of unloading secrets took a skilled litigator to wade through. All he did was spout words, and it was up to me to read between the lines.

"It's not good, Walker."

That could only mean one thing. I left a sufficient amount of time for that statement to jell before responding. "Let me guess. You had to turn over his disciplinary file." No corroboration, but I knew I was right. "Everyone does bad things, AP Unger. Some of us are lucky enough to never feel the ramifications."

He raised a brow with a smirk. Obviously, that was a reference to me, and my luck wasn't that I didn't get caught. It was that I was sharp enough to talk my way out of it. Oscar didn't have that going for him. In fact, when he was backed into a corner, he squealed like a pig and incriminated himself even further.

"Bail was denied," he said.

"Just because you're a flight risk doesn't mean you're guilty. It means the prosecution needs a conviction, and they want to make sure the accused is around for trial."

"What happened to that man and Annie Hughes," he clarified, shivering, "was beyond vile. I could barely read the newspaper articles. And wasn't there a guy downtown too?"

He was losing me, and I was usually pretty good at reading

between the lines. "But there are lots of people at Valley who do bad things," I continued. "People who could've been around for all three crimes when Oscar was only around for two. Don't you find that odd?" I asked. He never commented. In fact, he grew very still like he'd just seen the light at the end of a very dark tunnel. Surely he'd thought about it. I mean, *I'd* thought about it since the report of the second male hit the airwaves. Could he be insinuating that he'd deduced the same things as me? That it couldn't have been Oscar even though evidence pointed to him—because there was someone else who was the killer?

After a few more beats, I laid it all on the line. "I heard through the grapevine that Jinx King, Justin Starsong, and Juan Salas were all hanging in the parking lot that day. Has anyone taken it upon themselves to give them the VIP treatment?" I kid you not...his jaw fell. "I've spoken to Fisher Stanton, and I know he was out there doing whatever people like Fisher do, but what were the others doing? I hope that anyone who saw them had wits enough to tell the authorities." His mouth got even wider.

Was he going to give me anything? Without saying a word, he pretty much admitted what Jubilee Mueller had told me was correct, but I didn't need corroboration of that story from him anyway. My own investigation had given me their names. But what could AP Unger give me that I didn't have?

Something that I didn't even *know* I needed...

I wasn't sure what happened, but his eyes got that faraway look, where he felt he'd said too much when he hadn't given me anything other than a few dropped jaws. "Walker, I can't control what goes on with my students once they go home," he muttered, "and I can only attempt to control them when they're here. Things happen, sometimes right under my nose, but I hear things and I see things. If you've been poking around with those students, my advice to you is simple." He steered me back toward class with only three words. "Watch your back."

I'd like to say that shocked some sense into me, but it didn't.

I honestly felt like I bought a dress and didn't even get to go to the prom. I happened onto AP Unger—or maybe he happened onto me—but we didn't have the time to let the conversation play itself out or dissect it further. Was there more he could give me without jeopardizing what he felt were confidences? I didn't know, but to find out more, I would have to get closer to the fire. Trouble was, that meant I might get burned.

I couldn't stop the wheels that were already set in motion. What I could do, however, was get information to Oscar's attorney of anything that I felt was pertinent. That way he could request a "continuance," which basically was a delay in the trial date. Short of staking out every dumpster in town for fresh bodies, the only way I knew to do that was to keep fishing in the pond where the players were. But they were shrewd, so I needed to get them on my turf and then rattle their cages.

I smiled to myself. I knew exactly how to do that.

———————

I put the vanilla ice cream and root beer back in the refrigerator, taking a long draw on my float. My mug was extra frosty, and it was soothing on what felt like the beginnings of a sore throat.

"Murphy, Dylan wouldn't like a hussy, would he?"

I told Murphy how Brynn Hathaway had her mouth (suction-cupped him, really) all over my best friend when he hadn't even asked for it. He didn't tell her "stop," he didn't tell her "go," and he sure as heck didn't act like it repulsed him in any way whatsoever.

Honestly, I think he might've moaned.

Murphy laughed darkly. "How old is he? Fifteen?"

I frowned. Murphy knew exactly how old Dylan was, and his humor and lack of empathy just could be him offering condolences. I left him and Marjorie eating a balanced meal of pork chops and stuffing, nuked a corn dog, and then SKYPED Mr. Kissy Lips himself.

Our argument had a speedy recovery. I couldn't look at him very long and stay angry. How long that would last, though, was TBD. As long as I chased Liam, Dylan would have an open wound. Thing was, disagreements were new for us, and Dylan acted as if he was still riding the aftershocks. He'd touched the screen half a dozen times, not able to keep his hands from me. I rolled my eyes to myself. Dylan truly was the type that wanted me on a leash. Oh, he could have girls all up in his business, but I couldn't have boys up in mine.

"I love you," he murmured.

"Always," I said, slurping my float.

"And I'll try to not be so overprotective." Big fat zero on the truth meter.

"Don't you mean possessive?" I said, slurping again.

It was Dylan's turn to laugh. "Possessive sounds so unloving. What I do is out of love."

My word. And the Academy Award goes to...

True to my conflict avoider nature, I didn't cover Brynn's extra friendliness when Dylan was probably dying to add it to the agenda. I wasn't sure why I didn't. Maybe I was afraid he'd tell me he really liked it, or maybe I liked having the upper hand. Or maybe I didn't want my life down the toilet any more than it already was, realizing Hathawaywood was somewhere I'd never be. In any case, I felt it was a foreshadowing of the future when the opposite sex wormed its way between us. How was I going to deal?

Spring came out with a roar. Pollen dander was everywhere. Cough. Sneeze. Hiss. Sounds like I have TB. Pray to Die. Pray to Live. Pray to Die. Repeat, repeat, repeat.

Swallowing a Benadryl, I looked in the mirror.

It was Friday night and Sydney Taylor's annual Spring Fling, celebrated in the five-star abode that was her parent's basement. (Ah, the lifestyle of the rich and famous.) Attendees were to come dressed in beachwear, toting a towel and spray-on tan. I didn't particularly want to go, not to mention parading around my megawatt white body. Number one, it meant I had to shave my legs; and number two, Murphy'd insist I wear a one-piece. I'd look like someone's grandma and weirder than a two-dollar bill. But it was the night I'd been waiting for since I'd had the grand scheme to back my enemies into a corner and beat them into submission.

When I'd spoken with AP Unger at the beginning of the week, I realized I needed the major players back on my turf. It hit me instantly how to do that—maybe if I had a conscience, I would've realized the Taylors' turf wasn't technically the Walkers' turf—but inviting them to Sydney's party was believable, and even better, it was public.

My bet was no one's neck would be snapped.

How did I execute my master plan? My entire address book got an invitation...and um, I might've been the town crier. Why did I decide on the entire address book? What if someone was involved unbeknownst to me? I couldn't help but remember there was another individual on that rainy night at the construction site. Mr. Hood in the trenchcoat. The one who took the copper out of the trunk of a car. Frank felt he knew them, and so did I. I figured it was Justin Starsong, but what if I was wrong? I was banking on the fact if they came to the party, they'd cluster together like rattlesnakes in a den.

Thing was, I had hoped to have heard from Jaws. I sent him a voicemail saying, *Spill it, big mouth*, but as of yet, he wasn't spilling anything.

Pulling my hair back in a ponytail, I brushed on some black waterproof mascara and dusted my cheeks with pure pink blush. Rummaging around in my bottom drawer, I snatched a black racing swimsuit from Speedo that crisscrossed between the shoulder blades. Besides a silver suit that had lost its sheen, it was the only one-piece I owned, and even though it hugged my body, it set high on the neck. I mean, throw some lace around the collar, and I might as well be a naughty Pilgrim. Furthermore, it flattened out my chest. My Barely-Bs had become Double-As.

After I tugged it on, I attached Crest White Strips to my teeth, then opened my PJ drawer and slid into a new pair of fluffy pajama bottoms in a zebra print. When I looked down at my toes, I realized only half was still painted. I quickly rolled up my pants and painted them in OPI's Lincoln Park After Dark. Blowing them dry with a hand dryer, I rounded out the look with black rhinestone flip-flops.

Fifteen minutes later, I stood outside Dylan's garage, wondering where in the world they'd acquired a thirty-foot live palm tree that was somehow secured in a bed of mulch. It had pink and turquoise lights strung throughout its leaves. I always felt like I was going to the White House or something equally as grand when we pulled into their private drive. Valley consisted of several country clubs—plus our defunct one—and various private estates. The Taylors owned one on the edge of Valley and the neighboring townships that was ten thousand square feet with a guesthouse. Not too shabby, but then again, I was from the beans and franks crowd. What did I know?

Murphy drove off with three words, "Don't break anything."

For once, we were in agreement.

Not the contemporary feel of their Orlando abode (yep, they had two homes), their mansion had that Old World vibe that made me think there were horses in a stable somewhere. Iron wall grilles, fabric tapestries, and different stains of wood and leather furniture decorated the levels. Although extravagant, it wasn't so opulent I was afraid to sit down. It was warm and inviting, like a favorite blanket or old sweatshirt.

The basement was what most had on the wish list of their upstairs, let alone a lower level. The flooring was a mixture of travertine tile and dark hardwood. Painted in a soothing shade of khaki, as soon as you descended, you entered a fully stocked Sub-Zero kitchen with dark cabinets, marble countertops, and a bar area that could seat twelve. In the middle, were four chocolate leather sofas arranged around three flatscreen televisions with a custom-made entertainment center full of DVDs, CDs, and video games. Pool tables anchored the far two corners in front of a glass wall that housed an indoor swimming pool.

Two inches of sand had been spread on the floor, a shipwrecked rowboat was in a corner, and four red and yellow blow-up rafts floated in the deep end of the twelve-foot pool. I mean, didn't everyone have a pool in the basement? Plus, there were three smaller palm trees.

Those are available at your local florist, right?

Dylan met me at the bottom of the stairs with a hug—a hug so long and suggestive, I frankly got embarrassed. The first to pull away, I stripped off my zip-up hoodie and shoes, stashing them in a closet. Knowing my legs would light up like the aurora borealis, I still peeled off my pajama bottoms, hanging them underneath my coat. While wading in the sand, a few guys who wanted to chat about the Cincinnati Reds stopped Dylan.

I loitered around, feeling like a wallflower. I hated parties, especially if I was supposed to socialize with people I didn't know that well. Those in attendance I did know were full-grown and maxed to efficiency. Me? I was stuck in ugly duckling. I tossed a few mints in my mouth from a nearby table and swished them around, hoping to become...well, minty.

A spring break movie was playing where piranhas ate teenagers. I sat down in front of the TV and watched two feet get gnawed off until a mammoth explosion from the pool stole my attention.

Something was broken, or somebody just died. Maybe both.

Apparently, Dylan was roused too because he grabbed my hand, urgently dragging me into the glass-enclosed room like we alone were the emergency medical technicians. The boy had a hero complex. Someone needed to talk to him about it.

Once inside, it was difficult to not get overcome with the place. The blue pool was totally lit on the bottom. It made the track lighting on the walls and overhead almost a waste of money. A mahogany-finished metal table with four matching chairs anchored every corner. Two basket weave chaise lounges lined the sides.

Eight guys were roughhousing in the shallow end. Red plastic SOLOs had spilled under several chairs. Towels were floating in the pool, and honest to God, orange swimming trunks and a white bikini top were wrapped around the diving board. Hazarding a look up, I saw the bikini bottom hanging from a fake ficus tree.

Frankly, it was impressive.

Dylan scrubbed a hand down his jaw and rotated it around to run through his hair. "Oh, God," he gasped. "Dad's going to kill somebody."

Dylan's father had three rules: he pays, no booze, and clean up after yourself. Those last two were in question. The pool area looked like a tidal wave had a play date with a funnel cloud. Dylan told me on the phone earlier his dad was on a conference call, finalizing some makeup deal with a European conglomerate to invest in Go Glam! Cosmetics—he was an Executive VP there. All I knew was he needed to invest in some body bags once he got a load of his lower level.

Sydney was squatting down in the middle of a group of people, cleaning up broken glass, wearing a red string bikini that had the word "kiss" on her left bum cheek, the word "my" on the right. Right there in big black letters.

Not able to contain the laugh, I hoped to find a suit that said "find" on one boob, the word "my" on the other.

Seriously, we really needed a search party.

She had jet-black hair like Dylan but the refined face of her mother with eyes like coal. Plus, she was teeny-tiny. Two inches shorter than me, she was stacked upstairs with a sway back that tipped her derriere out so far it practically hit her in the back of the head. If the body wasn't enough of a shock to the male population, she had a rich contralto voice. In fact, she sounded hoarse all day long. And when you sounded like you'd just rolled out of bed, I think it gave guys ideas.

Stepping around some of the mess, we snatched the towels out of the pool and hung them on nearby chairs to dry.

Forgoing a greeting, Dylan belted out, "Has Dad seen your suit?"

Sydney dumped the shards into a trashcan, rose up smiling, and said in a gravelly brogue. "Hello, little brother. Hey, Darcy."

I returned the sentiment. Dylan sort of grunted.

She ignored Dylan's question and touched the guy's shoulder next to her. "This is Bronx Allister, Darcy."

Extending my hand, I tried my best to not act shocked, but honestly, there was no other way to react to her new boyfriend.

About my height, Bronx was her newest paramour who by the disinterested hint in her voice was about to become old news. From New York, he and Sydney had dated for three months, but in Sydneyland, three months meant she was bored.

With brown hair and eyes, Bronx was preppy in that Nantucket sort of way. His pants were pink and peach plaid with a yellow oxford underneath a fuchsia velvet jacket, a paisley ascot wrapped around his neck. To top off the bizarre, Bronx was leaning on a mahogany wooden walking stick with a gold-encrusted top.

Dylan looked at him, blinked three times, and shook his head—basically calling him an idiot. "Dude, that's just wrong."

Bronx laughed, not sounding wounded at all. "Sydney likes it."

Dylan muttered, "Sydney's brought all kinds of idiots into the house, but I have to say you bring a whole new level of weird."

He gave a small shrug. "Get used to seeing it, Dylan. I'm going to be around for a while."

Um, good luck with that, I almost said out loud. Sydney liked the chase. She didn't like the prey once it was caught.

Dylan did an exaggerated eye roll. "Well, you're not only weird, you're dumb. Sorry, man, but three months is about the longest relationship she's ever had. My guess is you won't even make it past the weekend."

Bronx's grin grew so big I thought he'd break his face. "Ah, Sydney said you're the possessive type...with every female in your life." Bronx stole a look at me like I'd know what he referred to. Sure, I knew what he referred to. Dylan liked to keep Sydney and me closer than his own shadow. I didn't like anyone busting on Dylan though—especially when I knew the true reason he was over-protective. A part of me wanted to explain away any confusion that existed on the topic. Another part knew if I got really detailed, I'd be revealing parts of my personality and family I'd learned to protect.

For some reason, that comment made Dylan territorial. Pulling me to his side, he grunted, "How did the two of you meet anyway?"

Bronx smoothed down the crease in his slacks. "We have an eight o'clock business class together."

Dylan burst out laughing. "Sydney getting up before noon is tantamount to seeing the yeti. You hear it could happen, but no one's ever around to document the case with a camera. My guess is you're lying, and that's the story you've concocted to impress my father."

Trying not to laugh, I snorted loudly and launched into a coughing fit. I bent over as Dylan pounded on my back in between laughing at his own wit and the way I reacted to it.

As I coughed like a sputtering car, Bronx literally pushed himself between Dylan and me. "Let me help," he said urgently. "I'm premed."

"Premed," Dylan said, snorting with disbelief. "How many classes?"

"One and a half," he told him proudly. "Allergies?" he said to me.

I gave him a coughy and sneezy heck-if-I-know look.

Bronx moaned sympathetically. "'Tis the season."

As Dylan and Bronx debated his credentials, my sneezing subsided, but fate gave me another reason to hyperventilate. When I stood back aright, from the corner of my eye, I saw a string-bikini clad Brynn Hathaway making a beeline through the sand for Dylan.

Oh, God, I prayed, *she's got a cute butt.*

Dylan turned right about the time she wrapped her arms around his waist. She didn't just wrap them. She splayed her fingers and groped in a sight so evocative my jaw dropped wide. His eyes flew open, like they do when life threw something at you that you weren't expecting. Regardless of his reaction, I got a feeling that sort of greeting was a commonplace occurrence. Trouble was, her pink bikini had ruffles on the backside. Honestly, it reminded me of those little bloomers moms put on baby girls just because they were cute. As he awkwardly hugged her back, I tried to console myself with the fact that at least he didn't fluff her ruffles.

Once she was through with the goo-goo eyes, she gave me a tight, "Hello."

Jeez, she didn't even say my name, almost as if it were anathema to her lips.

That meant more than Dylan probably wanted to admit. Bronx seemed to get it. He tapped me with his cane, whispering, "Ooh, watch out for that one."

No kidding. A bad situation just got really worse. She'd added blonde highlights to frame her face, and a look at her toes showed the exact shade of pink as her makeup and suit. It just wasn't fair. It really wasn't. I honed in on the rhythmic wave of the water, gently lapping against the sides of the pool and the nearby bubbling of the hot tub. Relaxing sounds. I tried to distance myself from their conversation—taking in the elements—but no element was bigger in my universe than wondering if I would have to hold hands with Brynn Hathaway at the holiday table.

Watching Dylan interact with her and Sydney's friends made my heart thud irregularly. It wasn't like I was excluded. When I'd try to pull away, he'd gently pull me back in, but the whole deal was overwhelming. I was beginning to understand there were parts of his life we didn't share. They were telling familiar jokes, reminiscing about shared experiences, making me feel like the fifth wheel. Maybe that's what I deserved since he knew nothing about me at that moment. But that was growing up, wasn't it? A person invariably expanded his or her pool of friends.

Successfully stealing away when the crowd grew larger, I meandered through four people shooting pool, said "hey" to three people I'd never met, but then my gaze fall on someone sifting through the CD collection.

Collin Lockhart, Brynn's ex-boyfriend. Yeesh, weren't we just one, big happy family.

He wasn't wearing beachwear—just a nice pair of jeans, a golf shirt, and sneakers. Made me wonder if he crashed the party, or perhaps he was self-conscious he didn't have a tan.

Call me a glutton for punishment, but I stepped right up with the intention of asking what was going on in his personal life. Translation? Was there something between Dylan and Brynn I should know about? The closer I got, the bigger the chicken I became. That's right. Call me Darcy-bock-bock-bock-Walker. Collin was sad. The kind of sad that sucked the good humor out of the people around him. I had a job to do, so the last thing I needed was an emotional distraction.

Right as I'd decided to bolt, he looked up with half a grin, his sky-blue eyes tormented and confused. Jeez, then I felt obligated. "Why aren't you inside with the fun?" I said with a fake smile.

"It's a little crowded," he mumbled, pitching a nod toward Dylan.

Well, it *is* his party.

Dylan's black T-shirt was stretched to capacity, drawing my eyes down to his slim waist, black board shorts, and long and powerful legs. While he casually stood in all his Dylan-ness, he seemed like he was an ocean away on another continent. Closing my eyes, there was no question how it would play itself out: Dylan plus beautiful girls equaled a lonely Darcy.

Swallowing down the dread, I opened my eyes with a sigh, finding Dylan's eyes instantly—like we were tethered together by our subconscious. I swear, it's like he knew because his eyes softened and he winked, his hand touching his heart. He took one step toward me, but Sydney grabbed him by the arm and pulled him back into the dialogue. I waved him off, like I'd be okay by myself for a few (big lie, but oh well). Drawing his hand to his lips, he blew me a tender kiss.

Funny, I felt like the little wife at home.

After five minutes with Collin, I started looking for a cyanide capsule. The clinking and clattering sounds from the outside patio captured my gaze, diverting my interests from the let's-fondle-Sydney's-little-brother thing going on and Collin's list of regrets. I focused on the tiny silhouette of a ponytailed female hunched over the grill. Peeling off her black track jacket, she looked to the sky, grumbling toward it. Like she was praying or asking it to strike her down. Two males with their backs to the french doors were holding platters as she dumped massive amounts of hamburgers onto them.

Dylan's mother. About five foot eight, she had his same amber eyes with delicate features, tawny hair, and an air of class and timeless sophistication.

I headed straight for the coat closet for my jacket and pajama bottoms. They were nowhere to be found. God only knew what that meant. Shrugging it off, as soon as I stepped into the barbecue pit, my nose hairs singed, and my hair blew back in an instant frizz. Coming up behind her, I circled my arms around her waist, giggling. "This is stupid," I said.

That was all it took to light a fire to her mouth.

Slamming the lid shut on the grill, she pivoted around and snapped, "Let me tell you how ridiculous I feel. I'm grilling when there are two inches of sand in my house to keep my daughter happy and the two-dozen people she invited home when it was only supposed to be two. Where am I supposed to have these kids sleep? And why do parents think it's okay for them to spend the night here anyway? Isn't anyone concerned about anyone's virtue anymore?"

Probably not, but then there was Murphy. He had me dressed like an idiot. My virtue was not in question.

She gave her head a quick shake, holding her chin up proudly, finally locating her West Coast debutante breeding. "Excuse me, Darcy," she murmured, motioning to the two boys who spun around. "This is Jinx and Juan. They volunteered to help me."

Shoot, shoot, and sonovagun shoot. Most people walked down dark alleys to find the bogeyman. All I did was go outside to flip burgers and found two. If I was afraid my text would get me nothing, I could rid myself of that thought right then. Both boys, dressed in black shorts with red bandanas hanging out of the back pocket, had gone straight for the lady of the house. She was nothing but smiles when theirs held nothing but secrets, lies, and the promise of more abominations to come. Trouble was brewing. If they wanted to score the first point, let's just say they were dangling me headfirst over the ledge with no intention of pulling me back up.

In silence, we helped Dylan's mother load the next course of food onto a platter while I fleetingly wondered if I was dessert.

My mind flooded with thoughts of Oscar. I'd never been behind prison bars, but I'd lived behind metaphorical bars for a large portion of my life. When I found myself imprisoned like that, I withdrew into myself as protection only to find I'd alienated people and responsibilities because I'd lost blocks of time. In reality, it may have been a matter of weeks or months. For me, it was one continual twenty-four-hour period that was never the end of day or night. When something strips you of your will like that, you either come out a fighter or an eternal victim.

Every day, I reminded myself to not be a victim, but being the hero wasn't exactly a piece of cake either. Some said heroes were born. Others said they were made. Right then, everything in me wanted to cut and run, but that would leave people I loved with one, possibly two murderers. I might be a lot of things—first thought a bona fide fool—but coward in the face of danger wasn't one of them.

That didn't mean I wasn't quaking in my shoes.

After we deposited the food on the countertop, Jinx and Juan followed me to the right side of the basement where a basketball floor/weightroom was located. They'd been partitioned off for the evening—in other words, "stay out"—and when we went inside, I flipped on the lights.

Olympic size barbells, leg machines, a treadmill, and dumbbell weights lined a mirrored wall on top of gray mats. A red punching bag hung from a chain on the ceiling. A bench press sat in the middle. To the left was a fifty-by-fifty foot hardwood basketball court. Four basketballs lay in the middle of the floor. I wasn't sure where to stand. I'd never called an impromptu meeting with my enemies, and that was precisely what the meeting was. If things got out of hand, I figured I could hit them with the dumbbells. It probably wouldn't cause any lasting effects, considering I could throw it with some force, but at least it would buy some time.

Walking next to the rack, I purposely stood beside the ten-pound weights and turned to face them. My blood pressure shot up a few points. I didn't want to be speaking with them in my swimsuit —I felt like they could see clear through me—but somehow I kept my face blank even though I was scared stiff. I wasn't going to give them my fear. I wasn't going to wait for them to address me either. It was *my* show, and I honestly needed to put a period at the end of the sentence...no matter what.

I slowly expelled all of my suspicions, starting from day one. "That's what I think," I told them after I admitted I followed Jinx outside. "I think one of you killed Alfonso Juarez over the copper business, and Oscar just happened to find his body and put his fingerprints all over the place. You then got together with your stories and ratted him out to the authorities. My guess is that was you, Jinx, since your father works for the Valley Police Department. Were you trying to score some points with dear, ole Dad? God knows you need them. And while we're on the subject, what do you know about Annie Hughes and that other guy? Their blood's on your hands too."

*Y*ou'd think Jinx would be the one offended, but it was Juan's face that nearly exploded on his head. It scrunched up and went the color of bright cranberries. "Shut up!" he screamed.

I gave him a shrug. "Why the surprise? You sent Jinx to scare me the other night, didn't you? Couldn't face me yourself? Or was that when you were putting the dead squirrel on my front porch? By the way, you owe my little sister a squirrel, moron, and I intend to collect."

Both looked at me like I was dumber than a box of rocks, their heads jacked to the side like they couldn't quite put their finger on the subject matter. If it wasn't either of them, who was it? Up until that point, both had kept a respectable distance at about eight feet away. When I insulted Juan, however, he closed the distance and was breathing in my face at about one foot. The air around him vibrated with anger. I looked over his shoulder to Jinx...he wasn't moving. His expression was unreadable, his black eyes guarded. Was that regret, or was he simply aware that he and Juan were confronting me in someone else's home? If anything, I would've expected Jinx to provide the knife to off me. Not Juan.

Juan expelled a breath, stepping even closer. His lips twisted into a snarl, and when he opened his mouth, I couldn't tell whether he would speak or bite. Before either happened, Justin Starsong's voice bellowed, "Stand down."

C'mon...I mean, really.

He was here too?

My heart was about to beat right out of my ribcage. Justin came out from the shadows of the basketball court, stalking slowly like a large cat ready to pounce. He'd been listening, and how in the world did I deliver myself up to the person I instantly knew was their leader? Dressed in flowered board shorts and a blue pocket T, he came prepared to blend in. Made me think he was the smart one when the other two were holding onto their identities. Other than the day in UDF, I'd never been face-to-face with Justin—let alone had a conversation—but the way he slowly moved across the hardwood, it was clear he held himself in a high regard. It was obvious when Juan immediately backed away that Justin was the play-caller. My mind reminded me that was what Oscar suspected anyway. He said Jinx wasn't the type. Adam was a "no." Juan was a "maybe," and Justin was a "most definitely."

I was on the verge of hyperventilating when Justin took Juan's spot. His lips were thin and unattractive, his eyes dark and deadly. On a body that was well over two hundred pounds, he certainly was throwing off the crazy.

At first, he did nothing but stare behind me. My OCD kicked in, and I caught myself counting to sixty and then backward to thirty. I then thought, the Pythagorean theorem was $a^2 + b^2 = c^2$, and Descartes said, *I think, therefore I am.* Then it popped into my head, *The shortest distance between two points is a straight line.* My mind fired with random information, although useless at that moment.

When I attempted to recite the presidents backward, Justin finally said coolly, "You know nothing."

Well, well, well, Justin had a voice.

I gave him a mocking, astonished smile. "So it speaks," I said. Jeez, that was confrontational, not to mention degrading. But I had a feeling if I didn't get them mad, they weren't going to say anything.

"And your mouth is bigger than I expected," Justin said sarcastically.

"I am blessed," I said just as cynically.

"You're soon to be dead," Justin added. Mark that in the *Threat File*. If I couldn't get them on anything else, I could get a restraining order and keep myself alive until I had more proof.

"Why Alfonso?" I asked.

Justin did some mental deliberating, wondering if what he'd said was going to incriminate him or perhaps wondering if it even mattered since he'd already decided on my demise. He gave up nothing, so I put words in his mouth. "When you want to send a big message, you send AVO back their biggest game, right?"

Justin looked me square in the eye. It was like reading the spookiest set of tealeaves ever concocted. I saw crimes beyond misdemeanors and years of something that had made him who he was. There was hate, fear, mistrust—and the concept of getting even.

Jinx and Juan were amateurs...Justin? Justin put the psycho in killer.

I tried another angle. "Did you kill the man downtown and stuff him into another dumpster?" Once again, no answer, but I saw a flicker of something in his eyes. More and more I was convinced something had gone wrong with the hit on Alfonso Juarez. In my gut, I felt all three murders were the work of the same individual, but why the extra gift of severing Alfonso's hand?

People like Justin didn't like to be insulted, but for some reason, he wanted or needed to be at the helm of a bunch of losers. I went for broke saying the one thing I knew would goad him into action. "It must be an awful feeling to always fail at something, Justin. The hit with Juarez went south. My guess is with you in the driver's seat that was almost inevitable."

Yup that did it.

Justin went bonkers. "*I* didn't screw it up!" he emphasized, curling his fists. "I had no control over the situation! Things didn't happen the way..." He jerked like he'd just dodged a runaway car. *Aaaah*, I thought to myself. That was all but an admission. I gave him the biggest, face-rubber smile I could muster—an acknowledgment he'd just admitted he was involved, and I finally had him.

Miles and miles of silence stood between us. I wasn't sure what happened first, me screaming or Justin's thick, burly hands encircling my neck. In a matter of seconds, he'd backed me up against the glass, sending breaking and cracking sounds echoing into the air. I wondered if glass was in the back of my head, but the more he squeezed, the harder it was to think. White spots invaded my sight, and the moment my air started thinning, the blur of a body muscled its way between us. I slumped to the floor breathless.

Liam Woods, I thought. *When did he get here?*

Very rarely were fights fair. I wasn't sure why I thought that one would be any different. By the time I was able to stand, no Jinx was in sight, and Juan and Justin were in a war of words with Liam. Liam ripped the red bandana out of Juan's pocket, and when Juan jutted his chin in his face, Liam shoved him up against the mirror with his right hand.

The whole ambiance shifted when Justin jumped into the middle. A rising river of testosterone and mounting threats filled the space. My thoughts were beyond ridiculous. I wanted to make Justin cry. I wanted to hurt him so badly he lost all rational thought and jabbered out Swahili. Inhaling faster and deeper, I fought the urge to help Liam, knowing my best chance was to get backup. When the three mofos amped up the shoving and ultimatums—talking about me like I was nothing less than Lucifer—it became apparent a melee was inevitable. Frightened to my bones, I staggered up and barreled for the door and right into the well-muscled chest of my best friend.

Wrapping his arms around me, it took Dylan half a heartbeat to realize Justin was up to no good.

"Hello, Justin," Dylan said lowly, giving a head jerk to Liam. "I wasn't aware you were on my sister's invite list, but by the way you're currently looking at my best friend, I'm confident you won't be on *any* list if you don't find the exit."

Justin's face went ice-cold, and dumbest of the dumb, he called me a profane name. Dylan flinched, but surprisingly stood still. That wasn't good, folks. That meant he considered something worse than a knee-jerk reaction.

"Shut up with your holier-than-thou statements, Taylor," Justin sneered, suddenly confident. "All of us weren't born with a silver spoon in our mouths like you were."

Justin had an unapologetic arrogance, and I briefly wondered why he was wired the way he was. It wasn't the time to dive into his inner child. I wasn't so sure he didn't come concealing weapons.

Dylan laughed darkly. "Holier-than-thou? This has nothing to *do* with holier-than-thou. You're in *my* home, insulting *my* best friend. That's not holier-than-thou. That's taking care of what's *mine*."

If I had time to think about it, that statement was sort of...*hot*.

Justin dumbly snorted and straightened his back as Dylan slowly and determinedly stalked forward, strategically placing himself between us. When things made me nervous, I found myself hiding behind Dylan's back anyway. I'd place one foot behind him, grab his belt loop, and literally peer around his shoulder. Most of the time, it was my joking that got me into trouble...not something like this.

My word, if he only knew...

As usual, he shoved me further back.

"Darcy invited *me*," Justin said truthfully. I never confirmed, denied, nor did anything other than look stupid. Dylan didn't even turn to catch my eye, assuming Justin was lying.

"Is that right?" Dylan sneered. "Darcy has better taste than to associate with someone as vile and corrupt as you."

"Say it, Taylor," he taunted, laughing. "Say how scared stiff you are of me being here."

Dylan didn't look scared. In fact, he yawned.

Justin dropped an F-bomb, paused two seconds for effect, and then added, "you."

Dylan's words came out with a hiss. "I'm positive you didn't just say that to me in my own home."

Yeah, he did, because he was a foulmouthed letch.

"Go," Dylan warned. "Now."

This is it, I thought. Dylan had paused to think about what was to come next, and that was the last invitation he would offer Justin to exit unscathed. The muscles in his back tensed, power rolling down to his feet. He was itching for action, and he didn't even need to admit it.

Justin had a fake nonchalance going on and was dumb enough to curse at Dylan again.

You know, in a perfect world, males would say, *Sorry, man. No harm, no foul. It was just a misunderstanding.* But with someone as overly inundated with testosterone as Dylan, that just wasn't going to happen. He put on his game-face, rolling his neck and stretching his back, giving that look that said it was just a matter of time before his foot was on Justin's chest as the winner of the round. Sounds came from his throat that were base instinct and animalistic —like something that had been chained too long that was begging to come out and play.

Dylan lunged for Justin first, but Justin came out swinging like he was fighting the devil himself. With an otherworldly speed and unnatural fluidity, Dylan avoided a series of punches, pounding away on Justin's body, but even though Justin was smaller, he kept coming like a wolf seeking blood. Justin landed a few but in no way matched the piercing bite of Dylan's fists on his face. His head bobbed this way and that, and I feared it would roll right off his shoulders.

People did a lot of things when they fought. They cursed, dodged in and out of barbs, probably wondering if it would look too cowardly if they bolted for the door. Then there were those who never looked back and gave into the primordial urge to silence their opponent by any means deemed necessary. Whatever went on between Justin and Dylan's ears, it was clear both were cut from the same cloth.

The moment I swung my gaze to Liam for help, panic overtook me as fighting broke out between him and Juan. In seconds flat, Juan had a cut over his left eye, and Liam had a gash on his cheek. Liam body-slammed Juan onto the mat, and Juan's body shook like it had been hit with fifty thousand volts. A roar broke from his mouth as he headbutted Liam, and then both were a blur of motion as they rolled around on the floor. What was I supposed to do? Jump into the middle? Get in a few punches myself? Raise my hand and say, *Hey, attack me instead?*

I laughed or cried, or some combination of the two. I was having a serious nervous breakdown and came to the conclusion I was one of those people who didn't have the mental wherewithal to save my own sorry rear end, let alone anyone else's. You know, the people in the movies who the audience screamed at because they didn't do anything worthwhile except steal the air of the would-be heroes. It wasn't a proud moment, people, but it was an honest look at myself. I needed to work on my reaction skills, if anything.

I was reminded of when I was ten years old.

My grandfather lived on a farm in Kentucky. Crap happens in Kentucky that neither man nor animal nor preacher could explain, but I'd always categorized those things as one of the mysteries of the South. I fell over a fence into the pasture where Grandpa Winston held his meanest bull. It was quarantined because no matter how many play dates it had, it would always lower its head, charge, and gouge the other animal. When I sailed over into its pasture, I literally was struck dumb. Predictably, it sniffed and charged, but when Winston miraculously appeared—giving it a look that could only come from Hell itself—it literally turned on its hooves and trotted away. Justin looked like that bull. Heck, Dylan looked like a bigger bull. I tried to find my inner-Kentucky, but I was ashamed to say, I might be too much of a city girl.

Note to self: take a trip to Kentucky sometime soon.

Right then, I heard an exasperated and horrified, "Dolce!"

I think I turned to the voice, but frankly I was still scared senseless. By the time I figured out it was Vinnie, he'd thundered to my side, put two-and-two together I was on the job, and attempted to drag Dylan off a bleeding Justin before he left the party—his parting gift a body bag.

Vinnie made no headway with Dylan. No matter how we looked at it, that genie was out, and we couldn't shove him back in the bottle.

Sweating Red Bull and what smelled like barbecued ribs, Vinnie literally dove into the midst and shoved a still-punching Dylan back up against a wall, barked a few garbled words, and peeled a bleeding Justin off the mat. My word, Justin could barely catch a breath while Dylan looked exhilarated.

Once Dylan's eyes bled back into focus, he held his arms wide, and I ran right into them. He crushed me to his body, my arms folded into his chest. "I...can't...breathe," I coughed out.

He laughed darkly, still acting like someone the rest of the world wouldn't recognize. "Breathing is such an overrated concept," he murmured. "I'm more of the hugging type. Are you okay, sweetheart?"

Who me? I thought. I had begun to think I belonged in an insane asylum. *But I was successful*, I reminded myself. Justin had practically given me an admission, so I decided to overlook any indiscretions...like a good, little conflict avoider who buried her conscience.

"Best laid plans of mice and men," Justin said to me, smirking as Vinnie escorted him toward the door. My word, he was pointing out he knew it was my plan to get them there, while rubbing in my face that Dylan foiled my efforts. The glint in his eyes reminded me he came with a plan too. One that got delayed but would happen no matter what kind of perilous state it left me in.

I shivered, crossing my fingers he wasn't successful.

Glancing back to Liam, he was pulling along Juan who pounded himself in the head, as if he was saying, *Stupid, stupid, stupid*. My guess was that wasn't a conscience. It was a competing voice that was angry something went wrong. I think I mumbled, "I'm in trouble," but then Dylan put his arm around me.

"Shh, come on, Darc," he murmured, eyeing the glass mirrors, pleased that no cracks were visible. "Let's go back to the party."

Vinnie and I stole a silent look at one another, assessing the fifteen-year-old before us who literally beat someone to a pulp, stood up, and then wanted to rejoin the fun. He probably wanted a burger when I was about to barf all over the place. Dylan was something the rest of us weren't. How many bodies were there going to be before I figured out what that was?

———

I was floating in that final phase of sleep where I felt like I was awake, but I really wasn't. "Your Cheatin' Heart" was playing two times too loud on the overhead speakers, and maybe that was part of the problem. I liked country music, but it wasn't my go-to genre. I had to be in the mood, but if there was a song written about almost getting knocked off in the weightroom, maybe I'd start wearing cowboy boots.

Of what I did like, Hank Williams was a personal favorite, and according to music history, he wrote and recorded that song from personal experience. Whoever was singing next to me sounded like he'd lived those lyrics but was tone-deaf, depressed, and looking for a bar stool. He either was having relationship problems or pined away for the one that got away.

When the guy belted out about being blue, I finished with, "Your cheatin' heart, will tell on you."

Squinting with one eye, I saw Jon Bradshaw shirtless, wearing a pair of faded navy board shorts. He had a red cup in his hand and a gray ballcap with the bill turned backward.

"You sing worse than me," he said chuckling.

"Shut your pie hole," I mumbled, but it was true. I opened my mouth, and it sounded like I'd swallowed a duck or was a sick cat during mating season on its ninth life.

Last I remember, I was lying on my back in a chaise lounge. Propping myself up by the elbows, I noticed the party was still going strong. A net had been strung across the middle of the pool, and six very aggressive players were playing water polo. Unfortunately, most of the water was outside the pool. Plus, the majority of the sand was wet, and people rolled around in it like dirty pigs. "How long have I been asleep?" I asked, massaging a developing eye twitch.

Grumpy sat down on the edge of my seat, frowning at the blatant disrespect before us. "I've been here about an hour, Walker, and you've snored the entire time. Some party girl you are."

I stuck out my tongue.

Dylan wasn't playing, so I stood up to see if he was shooting pool in the other room. Not there. Casting a glance outside, he wasn't cooking on the grill either. But his mother was bringing in a platter piled high with hot dogs. She stopped in her tracks, her jaw dropping when she stepped onto wet sand. Practically catapulting the food onto the bar, she angrily marched over to Sydney, her mouth running like an oil slick.

Standing up, I mumbled, "This is bad. Where's D?"

Grumpy got a strange look on his face, like panic crossed with a smile. If he ever smiled, and I mean *ever*, it was only seen in his eyes. For a brief moment, they twinkled, and then just as quickly the twinkle vanished. "Umm, he left for a while."

Another eye twitch. "He left for a while," I repeated.

He blurted out, "He walked Brynn home, okay?" He squinted his eyes shut, as if he was preparing for a smack. I forgot how to breathe. Inhale, exhale, inhale, exhale. "Are you all right?" he asked in a chuckle.

My eye twitch grew terminal. "But the party's not over yet."

"I think they went to another party."

A ball whizzed by my head, landing on a glass table in the corner, knocking over a stack of red SOLO cups. "Seriously?" I screeched for clarification.

"Brynn started feeling ill and asked him to walk her home. Sounded fishy to me."

Sounded desperate (or devious) to *me*.

Justice pulled herself out of the pool, presumably to get the ball Finn had almost decapitated me with. Shaking the water out of her auburn hair, she snagged it and pitched it back in the pool, picking up a striped towel and wrapping it around her black swimsuit.

"And Sleeping Beauty finally rises," she said laughing. "Wow, you look horrible." Leave it to Justice to spare no punches.

I groaned. "I've had a rough night." I was pretty sure I would rot in Hell after the stunt I'd just pulled. My guess was the night was only going to get rougher.

Justice sat down and literally dropping from the sky next to her was Liam—a smiling Liam with a tiny bandage on his cheek—like not a darn thing had gone down in the weightroom that probably should send us all to military school or some sort of long-term counseling. He wore blue and white flowered swimming trunks, and his chest was ballooned out so much under his shirt I wanted to touch it. Funny, I hadn't registered what he was wearing before. Guess that happened when a person was trying to stay alive.

I attempted to have one of those silent conversations with him like, *Exactly what do you think happened, Liam? And by the way, were you following me? I thank you because I think you saved my life, but really, how did you know?*

Instead of picking up on my silent request for more information, Liam's eyes locked on my legs like a heat-seeking missile.

Grumpy saw and grunted, "She's taken, and busy, and only fifteen. You're legal, man. That has to be statutory something."

Liam sort of laughed. "I was hoping that little detail wouldn't make a difference." Was that his drawback? Did he just think me too young? Concentrating with a frown, he appeared as if he replayed some past events in his mind. With a shrug that said, "Oh well," he popped up like our little flirtation was all but forgotten. "So do you want to swim?" he asked me.

And that was why you should never lose your heart to a fastard, girls. You were discarded too easily.

Realizing it was probably a slam, I mumbled, "My interests fall more along the culinary. I merely came for the burgers and dogs."

Five minutes later, I stood in the food line with Liam, Grumpy, and Justice. Collin Lockhart was directly across from us, pouring himself another drink. I gave a quick chin-jerk of acknowledgment as he mumbled, "Hey," and ambled away.

"Who invited *him*?" I whispered to Grumpy.

"Sydney said he came on his own—she thinks."

If he came with Brynn, no wonder he lost his party spirit. I picked up a two-liter of Coke and poured it to the rim of a SOLO cup. I took a sip and swallowed down the gloom. Felt like it was catching. While the others neatly constructed hot dogs and hamburgers, I threw a dog on a bun, slathered it with mustard, and pigged out...downing it in three bites.

My hamburger I decided to savor.

Still in her velour tracksuit, Dylan's mother put her arm around my waist with softened eyes. With her hair pulled back in a low ponytail, she looked younger and fresher than anyone at the party. I, however, was sweating like a pig on slaughter day.

"How's your burger, dear?" she asked.

I took a bite, toasting it toward her. "Burgerlicious."

"That's right," Justice said, munching loudly. "So good I'm going to write a poem about it."

Liam inhaled the last of what looked like an extra-loaded, Cincinnati style hot dog, complete with chili, onions, and shredded cheddar cheese. He took a napkin and wiped his mouth. "Thank you for having us over, Mrs. Taylor. I think I've just met my future wife." He tweaked me on the nose.

Coughing up some bun, it dribbled down the front of my suit along with a slice of tomato. My word, I didn't know why they kept me around. It was like I'd been raised by wolves.

Liam cleaned it off with a napkin, tilting my chin toward him. "Isn't she a keeper? She's so sweet and innocent," he murmured.

Mrs. Taylor threw her head back and laughed loudly, caught

herself, and then laughed again. Personally, I wasn't in line when God was passing out the sweet-and-innocent thing. Believe me, I could've used it.

Liam grabbed a black sharpie that was next to the ketchup bottle, removed his white T-shirt and laid it on the countertop, scribbling "Darcy's Boy Toy" in cursive across the front. "Now that's settled. Do you like your new toy?" he asked me.

"*I* like the new toy," Justice whispered in my ear.

I fought to keep my voice from sounding incredulous. "I have self-esteem issues."

I wasn't sure that statement fit into the context of the conversation, but it definitely was what I was feeling at the moment. And why? My best friend was off doing God knew what with Brynn-I-want-to-smack-her-in-the-face-Hathaway.

"You're a dead man," Grumpy said, chuckling behind his cup.

Susan Taylor's amber eyes twinkled with an all-knowing amusement, like she was in on an inside joke. In a dignified and maternal voice, she murmured, "Have you met my son?"

Liam half grinned, half pouted. "He's hard to miss, and I think he growled at me earlier. I'm telling on him to his mommy."

Could a girl die from looking at someone overly cute? Was that possible? If it was, maybe Grumpy should be digging a hole. Wishing I wasn't dressed like a naughty Pilgrim, I opened my mouth to tell him Dylan could kiss my you-know-what, that his *selfish* you-know-what always got what it wanted, and *my* you-know-what wasn't on the list.

He was my hero earlier, I thought. *My*, I emphasized in my brain. *What was he now? Hers?*

Right then, a shift happened in the crowd. I could feel it. Emotions rose as the sound level practically shattered the windows. Someone threw Bronx's walking stick in the air. It ricocheted off the wall and launched into a fifty-two inch LCD television, gold end first.

*I*t was like Hell broke loose, and demons were trashing holy relics. After a few blinks of shock, Justice was the first to mobilize. She flew into motion, roundhouse kicking the thrower. While Liam and Grumpy corralled the flying bodies, Mrs. Taylor bolted upstairs for her husband, and I went to unearth Vinnie. I pulled him out of a closet with a bleached blonde bimbo. Both were messy-haired with red faces and rumpled clothes—the girl apologizing, Vinnie gloating. I didn't want to know, people. I really didn't.

When Vinnie's eyes came back to focus, he jumped into the crowd like a whale frolicking in the ocean. He didn't defuse anything. In fact, he amped it up. Next thing I knew, Liam and Grumpy weren't playing peacemaker anymore. They were in the fray, fighting for their lives.

Liam blocked a shot to his face and flipped someone to his stomach, pinning his hands behind his back. While he fought in an orderly fashion—each fist with an intended outcome—Grumpy was more of a street fighter, using elbows, feet, and profanity that sounded extra dirty. He threw two shots to someone's gut, but when another guy slugged his lip, I didn't want the evening to go down with me as a scaredy cat.

I somehow muscled between them and kneed the offender in

the happies. Suddenly, the dude had an eight-octave vocal range. Girly fighting on my part, but as Murphy claimed, it was definitely effective. The guy dropped to his knees with an "Unh" and curled into a ball.

I wasn't sure why I turned my head. Perhaps it was reflex. Perhaps I'd grown tired of looking at fighting. Whatever the case, I got cocked in the jaw by someone's fist. I saw stars...maybe a few planets. I flailed my arms and legs at some unknown opponent and all of a sudden my air twisted—my breath coming out in hard and painful gasps. Stumbling toward the patio, I circled my hand around the knob, fell into the night, and tumbled into Collin Lockhart—drunker than a monkey.

"What I did was inexcusably dumb," I said to Vinnie and Grumpy, rehashing what happened in the weightroom, "but I beg the both of you to not give Dylan specifics."

Both acted like the weightroom incident was the least of their worries. Grumpy sat down on the bar seat next to me, nursing a can of Coke like he wished it was something harder. He took a long drink and slid his eyes over to Vinnie who looked equally distraught. Colton Taylor, Dylan's father, had just ripped everyone a new pie hole, and anyone that had a smidgeon of a conscience felt guilty.

At one point I thought he was going to chuck a grenade into the crowd. Emotions were bubbling over. Most were civilized, ashamed, and looking at their feet, but a few were dumb enough to mumble under their breaths and look perturbed. Then there was me. I thought the show was so dang entertaining I didn't want it to end.

With an identical face but taller and broader than Dylan, he was dressed in a black golf shirt and black dress slacks, most of his diction in English but peppered with Greek curse words (no kidding, the family was of Greek lineage). I tried not to laugh at his behavior, but when he found his closet door dented in, two sofas overturned, and bleeding appendages from people he didn't know, I guess he should be granted a few choice words.

He'd just wheeled in two SHOP-VACS big enough to clean the

space shuttle, and Grumpy, Vinnie, and I were the ad hoc cleaning crew. Singlehandedly, we sucked every grain of sand off the floor and into the next day's garbage. Taking a break, we watched Liam and Finn pick up shards of plastic from not one, but two demolished large screen televisions.

When I realized neither was paying me any attention, I asked, "What's wrong with you two?"

"Jaws was here," Vinnie grumbled.

I shook my head, wondering if I'd heard him right. "Jaws?" I asked.

"Jaws," they said in unison.

I gasped, a mixture of curiosity and apprehension. Jaws was on house arrest, so how did he manage to get out without being busted? "What did he say?"

"He mumbled something about 'red' and told me to give you this note," Vinnie answered, sliding over a sealed envelope.

I wanted to open it then, but the room was too crowded, and I wasn't exactly sure what either of them would do with the information.

Grumpy added, "He'd removed his ankle bracelet monitor, Walker, but he was desperate for you to have this. When he walked into World War 3, he took out of here like he was outrunning the gravedigger."

Couldn't say I blamed him. "What did he look like?" I said.

Grumpy glanced over to Trudi, shrugging. "A guy," was his moronic answer.

If Grumpy had on his girl-vision, I might as well have a convo with the wall. He was watching Trudi—in a purple bikini that barely qualified as a Band-Aid—hang all over some guy none of us had ever laid eyes on before. The 'ho.

Vinnie mumbled, "I've got indigestion," but when a door slammed upstairs, the three of us shot a look amongst ourselves that said indigestion was the least of our worries. All of us knew it was Dylan. He was one of those people who you could feel from yards away. Trouble was, he'd missed the fight and most of the cleanup. His father was...well? Let's just say, he contemplated how to legally rearrange his son's face.

Savagely tromping across the floor, Colton yanked the walking stick out of the television as tiny shards of black plastic and circuitry tumbled to the floor. They fell in slow motion, like gravity was making a point. He pitched it in Dylan's direction as he took the stairs two at a time, yelling my name again and again.

Amaaaazing. Simply amazing.

What made him think I'd want to answer?

Catching the stick with his left hand, Dylan was right in the middle of another "Darc—" when his eyes landed on the multi-thousand dollar catastrophe, lying at his father's feet. He looked to the right, the left, his jaw dropped once, and then he stopped to scratch his head.

"Where in God's name were you, son?" Colton bellowed to him. "You know I told you to look after the place. I not only paid for the beach. Evidently, I got the bums."

Dressed in jeans and zipped in a black leather jacket, I let my eyes linger over the stretch of muscle across his chest, the way his jeans gripped every well-framed curve. He looked irresistible.

I was a naughty Pilgrim.

Craning his neck to find me, I gave him a circled wave as his eyes bounced from his father, to me, to the "Darcy's Boy Toy" shirt Liam was still proudly wearing. I didn't know what it was with some guys. They liked to goad another male they considered equally as strong. Liam gave him a look like I've-done-your-job, and I'm-taking-your-girl-too.

I could feel the freeze between them. It was colder than the polar icecaps.

Emptying his dustpan into a trashcan, Liam sauntered to my side and draped his arm over my shoulder with a chuckle—like we were the happy little couple. My arm wrapped around his waist even though I told it not to.

Dylan and I had another one of our nonverbal exchanges.

Where were you? I screamed.

You have the audacity to wonder where I was? he said with a frown. *What in the,* bleep profanity, *were you doing with Woods in my weightroom?*

Quit cursing at me, I said snorting.

Answer the freaking question, Darcy.

You answer the freaking question. I grinned evilly.

Yank. Yank. Yank Dylan's chain.

His jaw ticced, and you could feel the steam rolling off him. Dylan took one step forward and stopped, giving me that face like he expected me to meet him half way. When I didn't budge, he finally prayed a one-worded, "Jesus."

His father gave an exaggerated eye roll, regarding him cynically. "There are a lot of people who need to be praying tonight."

Funny thing was, my gut told me I should be one of them.

———

Whatever was to come unfolded beneath stormy, charcoal-shadowed skies. In the distance, thunder rumbled and the weather sirens roared. Mother Nature wasn't happy. A storm was in its infancy, and I had a feeling it was going to come out screaming.

I walked outside with Vinnie but got into the car with Liam. What Murphy didn't know wouldn't hurt him, and while Dylan was enduring an accessory-after-the-fact lecture from his father, I scribbled a note claiming Vinnie was taking me home and then ditched him.

What's good for the goose, I thought, *is good for the gander.*

Still clasped tightly in my hand was the note from Jaws. There had been no chance to read it, and driving with Liam wasn't exactly the most opportune time either. At first, I thought Liam would let the whole thing slide, but his easy-go attitude suddenly shifted to a dark mania when we were behind closed doors.

"We need to have a talk," he said stiffly. "We need to talk now. *No*," he amended, "*I'm* going to talk, and *you're* going to listen."

"I assumed this was coming," I mumbled.

"There are a lot of things coming, Darcy, if you don't stop what you're doing. And by the way, why *are* you doing it anyway?"

That wasn't the Liam Woods I knew. He was dictatorial, abrasive, unstable, and a part of me was getting scared. "Maybe we should define what I'm doing, Liam," I said quietly.

"Where do I start?" he said, laughing with no humor. "You're provoking three of the most volatile individuals I've ever run across. That's not only stupid. It borders suicide mission."

"I'm worried about Oscar," was the phrase I offered as explanation.

Liam idled his black Ford Explorer at a red light, angrily reaching over and squeezing my left hand between his. His hand was so large it nearly folded around mine twice. He was squeezing hard, hard enough to hurt, and I was totally taken aback with his blatant show of force. "You're hurting me," I tried not to gasp.

Liam actually squeezed harder. "Good. I honest to God don't have time for your games right now, Darcy. I'm trying my best to..."

Good ole "Bad Moon Rising" broke the mood. I wasn't sure I wanted the mood broken, but I knew my hand did. A glance at the number showed Fisher Stanton. Liam angrily released his grasp as I fished my phone out of my purse. I gave Liam one of those gimme-a-sec looks he didn't appreciate. When the light changed to green, he hit the gas pedal so fast he laid down some rubber.

On instinct, I moved a little closer to the door. "Hey," Fisher said when I answered. "What in the heck happened at the Taylors' house tonight? Facebook's blowing up, and I've had over a dozen texts about the destruction."

I mumbled, "What you read is probably true. I've got to go, Fisher. Let me call you—"

"Wait!" he practically screamed. "I just wanted you to know I figured out who that guy was I saw next to the dumpster that day. It's that swimmer dude. It's Liam Woods." My vision blurred, my sense of survival telling me to open the door and drop and roll. Liam had never admitted that to me, and there was more than one opportunity for him to do so...but why? When my eyes cleared, I heard Fisher say, "He's the one you need to talk to...or stay away from," he added worriedly. "He knows something."

And I was riding in the car with him...

"Are you sure?" I shakily whispered.

Fisher snorted. "Yeah, I'm sure. He was right next to that dumpster wearing the same red shirt I'd just bought, which really made me mad. I paid good money for that shirt and was hoping it was a one-of-a-kind at school. But au contraire. Big Boy had to..."

I might've briefly passed out, but when I felt my pulse pound in my neck, I realized I was still sucking in air. I was under the erroneous assumption Liam was one of the good guys. The knight-in-shining armor type every girl dreamt about. Could I have been wrong? Why did I feel like everyone I'd spoken to was hiding something?

To make the conversation appear benign, I launched into a recap of Sydney's party, sparing no gory detail of the unbelievable destruction, reliving each moment from the color of the bright orange streamers all the way down to the bamboo rings around the napkins. When I threw in the demise of Bronx's walking stick, Fisher feigned rapt concern, sounding appropriately aghast. *Suck up.* I knew and he knew he was campaigning for an invitation to next year's shindig.

I hung up, figuring my best defense was a good offense. Liam knew what I'd been up to. I might as well admit it and play the thing out. As soon as I hung up, Liam belted out, "Answer me."

I thought about what Fisher said: Liam was across the road too. That meant I needed to get closer to him—wouldn't be hard—but what exactly did he consider close? And could that "close" cost me my life? It dawned on me if he was involved in killing Alfonso Juarez, I was locked up tight with an accomplice, or worse yet, a murderer.

Note to self: never get in an automobile with someone until you're sure he or she's a good person.

Again, I looked to the side of the road, telling myself I could jump out if worse came to worse. *Keep your voice cool, Darcy*, I told myself.

I started talking...

"Obviously, I'm trying to prove that Justin, Juan, and Jinx had something to do with Alfonso Juarez's murder. Not something," I amended. "*All* of it. I know they're involved in an underground copper business, and AVO was there first. My guess is AVO wasn't in favor of any sort of profit sharing."

His voice dripped with sarcasm. "Aren't you little Miss Nancy Drew?"

I rested my right hand on the handle of the door, fudging on the truth. "Let's shoot straight here, Liam. I know you were out there. I saw you," I lied. "Do you know anything that could possibly help Oscar? And before you answer no, why would you *not* want to help him?"

Liam didn't act guilty. He didn't act innocent. In fact, he was almost nothing at all, and that was even scarier. He quietly said, "Have you ever wanted something you couldn't explain, Darcy, even if you knew it was wrong and probably impossible to get it? Possibly dangerous?"

The one thing I wanted more than anything wasn't ever going to be possible, and if it was wrong to want it, then I'd already committed the unpardonable. That was life, though, wasn't it? Wanting what you couldn't have? But sometimes the reasons for that wanting took on a life and breath all its own. I couldn't outrun what was in the room with me. So yes, I understood the longing. One single incident left me with compulsion issues, for God's sake.

Compulsions that I had to let take over, or I'd lose my mind.

Was that dangerous? It depended on whether I valued my sanity.

When I didn't answer, all he gave me was some bone-chilling silence. Next thing I knew, we were in my driveway, and when I opened my door, he literally skidded off with me falling out into the bushes. Liam was guilty of something, of what I didn't know, but I could smell it all over him like stinky cheese. I gave myself forty-eight hours. Forty-eight hours to piece things together, and if I couldn't, I was contacting the authorities. I'd made that promise to myself before, but I had no choice but to heed to the deadline. I was sure I'd obstructed justice ten ways from Sunday, but I'd take my punishment, whatever that would be.

———

It was a little past midnight when I wandered through the door, cigar smoke nearly blasting my eyebrows away. Thankfully, Murphy was in a carcinogen-induced stupor and didn't ask many questions. After he was convinced I was still in the good girl league—seriously, it was never in question—he snuffed out his cigar and stumbled up the stairs.

I nuked myself a cup of hot chocolate, grabbed a handful of Lucky Charms, and went to my room. After I did my thing in the bathroom, I jumped into some leopard print pajamas and crawled under the covers. My heart was palpitating, the letter from Jaws practically burning a hole in my hand. I clicked on my iPhone flashlight and pulled out the folded white sheet of paper.

Drawing them both to my eyes, I nearly vomited on the spot, my mouth expelling language best kept private in my brain. It wasn't a list of names. It was a threat.

Did you really think I'd let you have that list? Jaws might be smart, but he's not as smart as me. One day soon you're going to pay the piper.

Chapter Twenty-Nine
GAME CHANGER

I mean, seriously? It was one of those things that left my jaw unhinged, dragging across my chest. Who could have written it, and what could I have missed? The obvious was Jinx since he'd skipped out on the fighting, but I literally didn't know whether to call him on it or act as if I didn't care.

I phoned Jaws too many times to count, texted him until my fingers went numb, and did everything but send up a gosh-danged smoke signal. If Jaws was still alive, it was safe to say he was ignoring me or the ensuing chaos.

It was Sunday night. The storm passed but didn't break, and I'd just come home from The Double-B. Dylan was sitting at the kitchen table, sneakers and discarded socks underneath him, a US history book open on the table. Dang, guess we had a test. In between reading paragraphs, he was eating pot roast, potatoes, and carrots, looking up with a roguish smile that would tempt a saint. Murphy never mentioned our dinner guest on the ride home—made me feel like I was ensnared in a trap.

We ate in silence. Well, Dylan ate in silence and didn't resist my barbs when I made veiled and not so veiled references to his what-ever-it-was with Brynn Hathaway. He murmured a soul searching, "We should talk."

I growled back a manic, "Later."

True to Dylan fashion, he didn't take no for an answer. He whispered even sweeter, "I can promise that whatever it is you think I've done exists only in the throes of your imagination. I love you, Darcy, and I always will."

A pure sweetness consumed his angular face, which almost made me cry. Did that salve my wounded heart?

Make that a big, fat, freaking no.

I wasn't feeling very conciliatory, and down deep I didn't think he'd actually agree to the conversation amidst my barbs. Once he had, however, the last thing I wanted to hear was that he'd had a wonderful time and ditched me in the process. And that's what he'd done, right? I mean, he never even asked why I was alone in a room with three other guys. Sure, there was a nonverbal communiqué but not his usual hold-me-down-until-I-talk thing. Was he metaphorically waiting to gut me *now*? Or was he going to confess Brynn was the love of his life and our own love affair was over? Bottom line was, if Dylan wanted to play huggy-kissy with Brynn Hathaway, there wasn't a whole lot I could do about it. Besides, it was a question of pride—that small smidgeon I was trying to preserve. Where was the rest? It was pummeled somewhere in between Brynn and the countless others wanting to jump on his boom boom, hoo-hah, that's where.

I stuffed the last morsel into my mouth, biting the side of my cheek to keep from sobbing.

Regardless of my state of mind, I had to give kudos to Murphy. I considered myself more of a sugar freak than someone that favored the savory, but Murphy's pot roast made me want to shack up with a cow. Savoring the last bite, I washed it down with an ice-cold can of Coke, thirty-seven degrees preferred. For some reason, my hand forgot how to work, and I spilled the last quarter of the can down my shirt, soaking me to the bone.

"Mother of pearl," I mumbled. And the day kept getting brighter and brighter.

My eyes slid over to Dylan who was stuck somewhere in the middle of a laugh. I pointed a finger at his neck mouthing, "Colombian necktie. In your sleep."

He threw his head back laughing, trying to pull me onto his lap, but I juked out of the way and angrily tromped up the stairs.

It was chilly in the house. We could probably use a night of heat since springtime temperatures were like a yo-yo, but as soon as the calendar indicated it was springtime, that meant no more heat, by the Murphy Walker Rule, even if it dipped to freezing.

I'm surrounded by control freaks. I groaned.

Grabbing a white turtleneck from my closet, I tugged it over my head, layering it with my favorite green T-shirt. A Christmas gift from Dylan, it said "Game Changer" on it.

Obviously, he thought more highly of me than I did.

Our house was transitional in style, or open, so to say. Consequently, when I stood on the second floor balcony, I could see in almost every room. When I hit the top of the stairs, I took an appraising look at my best friend. Voyeuristically speaking, he was splendidly masculine. I repeatedly pored over every rippled inch of his body, looking for evidence to whether he was real or dropped onto Earth from a planet far, far away. Wearing a simple gray T-shirt and his favorite worn-out jeans, he'd just cleared away the table and was falling into the recliner. Effortless. Sensual. Freaking poetry in motion. Heck, I think I joined the club and developed my own personal crush.

Just thinking it gave me an eye twitch.

With one deep breath and involuntary body shake, I held my chin high and traipsed down the stairs, sitting on the end of the brown leather couch. I'd removed my contacts and wore my glasses, a spider web of bloodshot eyes the culprit.

Dylan must've noticed because first thing he did was lean over and caress my hand with his thumb. "Talk to me," he murmured.

And that's all she wrote.

I burst into tears, covering my face with my hands.

Dylan was my confidante, but I couldn't tell him what I was up to...not all of it...not yet, at least, if ever. "Whoa," he said taken aback. "Sweetheart, whatever's going on between us, it's out of hand. The last thing I ever want is to be the cause of your tears, but if you'd just let me talk to you, I think you'd be surprised and hopefully happy by what I'm going to say."

Um, not as surprised as he was going to be.

I felt his gaze right above mine and didn't know whether to open my eyes or blink him away. Peering between two fingers, I cracked open a lid and wasn't sure who—or what—I was looking at. He was different—more dark and mysterious, his eyes hazed over to the point of looking sleepy. Normally, I could predict his moods and sentences before they left his mouth. Right then, I didn't even know where to begin. Something dark and primitive bled like rivers into the whites of his eyes, and I didn't know if that was fascinating or run-for-the-hills scary. Whatever Dylan felt, he felt it deeply, and it was almost like he was willing me to feel it too.

Dylan slowly pulled my hands from my face and leaned in even closer, his breath and lips lightly brushing against mine. "Darcy," he spoke softly into them, "we need to talk."

What I needed was a cold shower—that's what *I* was thinking.

I backed away and out of his gaze. Whenever he looked at me like that, I forgot how to spell my own name.

Here were my options: I could beg him to kiss me—like really, really kiss me—or I could concoct some sort of lie to get him off my back. Or I could tell him the cold, hard facts and see how he wore the truth. Not many people could handle the truth when it was placed before them. I wasn't sure where Dylan fell within that equation.

The mental tug of war was taking its toll. Trouble was, I wanted all three of those things to happen—especially the first—but I didn't have the time to dissect what that meant or the possible ramifications.

I bit my bottom lip and put my pinky nail in my mouth, ripping off its tip.

When he pushed with another, "Darcy," I finally blurted out, "It's Oscar. I'm sort of in a mess, and when I say mess, I mean a big, freaking mess that might mean I'll be headless by morning."

Whoo, that felt better. Guess I was going with option three.

Dylan looked like someone just skinned him alive and then force-fed him the scraps. Getting up from his chair, he squatted down in front of me and grabbed both my hands, rolling them over and over like he tried to dissect my very soul. "Define trouble," he murmured softly.

"Maybe something illegal," I said with a sniffle.

He cleared his throat. "How illegal?"

"Illegal enough."

Nothing for a while. Just us staring at one another. Finally, he murmured, "Tell me everything, Darcy. Tell me, so I can help."

Dylan stood up twice during the telling. Then he sat down, got back up, paced around some more, ran his hands through his hair, and ultimately did some deep-knee bends. I spared nothing. Not the threat from the bandana. My AVO suspicions. The dead squirrel. Not the questions of Annie Hughes, No-Name Man, or Adam Neeley. Not even Liam, Darth Vader, or the threats of Justin Starsong. The only thing I omitted was Jaws. I asked Jaws to keep Jester quiet, and I felt I needed to return the favor—especially since he'd removed his ankle bracelet, willingly placing himself in danger. Besides, I didn't get a list of names, so it wasn't like I would do something stupid like directly confront them.

My word, that was the first thing I'd do if I had names, but right then, that point was moot.

"Shiii—" was his final, profane assessment.

I sniffed again. "Don't curse," I told him. "I need Heaven to help me."

He looked to the ceiling in agreement. "I'm sorry, but there's nothing around for me to hit. We need to tell Murphy, Darcy."

"Not yet," I gasped.

"Okay, tomorrow," he said, frowning deeply, "but let's begin when all of this started. Ms. Dempsey and AP Unger."

"You want to hit *them*?" I gasped again.

He let out a sound of exasperation. "No," he said. "We should tell them everything you know."

"They won't get it." I wasn't sure *I* got it. Why ask sane people to? Murphy always said, *Take care of your name. It arrives before you do.* Maybe that was what bothered me. I wasn't sure I had a good name. My good reputation, if I ever had one, was pretty much shot.

I cried. And cried. *Annnnnd cried.*

When I removed my glasses, Dylan spied Murphy's bottle of TUMS on the countertop and popped a handful of rainbow colored tablets in his mouth. He bent his back over, stretched it around, and slid onto the couch next to me. I was hiding under a mass of sticky, blonde hair that had fallen in my face.

He tilted toward me, tenderly pushing it off my cheeks. "AP Unger and Ms. Dempsey think I'm a loser," I whispered.

"They don't think you're a loser," he murmured. "You're arguably the smartest person that's ever walked the halls. They just don't know how to motivate you."

That statement stung. "I'm motivated."

He ran a hand through his hair again. "True, but not with the things—"

A crying jag struck again before he could finish the sentence. I wasn't the type of student every educator dreamt of. I, honest to God, wasn't the type *anyone* dreamt of—especially guys. That hadn't really bothered me. I'd been happily single. Sure, I thought about the opposite sex, but had it ever truly bothered me that I was alone? Probably not until the moment. And it sure as heck didn't help that it was my time of the month for my ovaries and uterus to do their thing. I took my hand and patted my chest, negotiating with my breathing.

I started, "It's just that I..." Dylan narrowed his eyes, inching closer for what he innately knew was extremely confidential. "I just, um...oh shoot," I said, sniffling frustrated. "D, it doesn't help that I just started," I said with a shrug, "my monthly—*you know*." Dylan coughed so loudly I feared his tongue fell off and was permanently detached. "I'm over sharing," I whispered.

I cried even harder.

Dylan grabbed my hand and sheltered it between both of his. When I looked in his face, his amber eyes were wide and frightened with worry. I didn't see that often. In fact, I wasn't sure I'd ever seen that until then.

"We're on the same side, honey," he finally murmured. He took a deep breath and carefully chose his words. "Darcy, you mentioned that another body was found. Another body that appeared to have been murdered in the same way as Alfonso Juarez and Annie Hughes. For the sake of argument, did you ever think it might be Frank? They're twins. Could Frank have done the same thing?"

Murphy entered the kitchen before the conversation could take another direction. I was glad for the intrusion, but a part of me wanted to explore the idea of Frank and Oscar being co-murderers a little bit further. My mother was a twin, and I knew there were strange connections no one could ever explain, but to take it to the felony level? Was I willing to believe that or even think it? That would, however, be one explanation for the murders being similar. What if they had some twin pact of homicidal crime going on in their bloodline? What if they were copycat murderers, and I was defending the wrong guy? The other explanation—the one I was sure to be true—was that the killer or killers were still at large. I knew who was involved. I just didn't know who pulled the trigger.

———

All the lights were off in my room, and I was settled under my comforter with the television on mute. It was nine o'clock when Oscar called, and I'd just filled him in on what'd gone down since we'd last chatted—the only thing substantial was Justin basically admitting guilt. Justin had yelled, *I didn't screw up...I had no control over the situation...things didn't happen the way.*

You know, blah, blah, blah, and foot-in-your-mouth blah.

After Oscar celebrated for a while, he then dissolved back into the doldrums, realizing—once again—the answers weren't spelled out enough for our liking. Ergo, charges weren't exactly going to be dropped yet, but it was definitely enough to speak with the powers-that-be.

Trying to brainstorm, we went over the specific sites where the bodies were found and what the significance of those could be. Murphy suspiciously walked back and forth in the hallway, wearing bare a strip of carpet that would need to be replaced if he didn't can the pacing. I gave him a big, innocent smile (I tried, at least) and acted as if it were Dylan. We'd dropped Dylan back at his home earlier, and it wasn't unusual for us to find something else to talk about...although Murphy didn't seem quite convinced.

"Any ideas?" I whispered.

"No," Oscar said. "All I know is site five always has great stuff in its dumpster."

I sucked down the last of a Coke, mentally crossing my fingers it would relax me as usual. I had a feeling I needed something one-hundred-proof instead. "Okay," I said with an exhale, "has anything strange gone on at those places, other than you seeing Annie at Tire Town?"

"No," he said, growing agitated. "Nothing that—" He stopped, gasped like he was dying for air, and started praying, "Oh, God," over and over.

I sat up so fast I banged the back of my head on the headboard. "What?" I asked excitedly.

"Darcy," he whispered, "I think I know who—"

I had only a second's warning before a dial tone lambasted my ear. I closed my eyes and nearly cried again for the umpteenth time that day.

My MoneyGram expired.

———

There was an old Yiddish saying: *Man plans; God laughs.* I feared God was having a rip-roaring time at the moment, possibly at my expense. I had grandiose plans of solving everything and being the quiet victor from afar. That wasn't going to happen, and I couldn't shake the feeling God was waving a finger at me from Heaven, saying, *My world...not yours.*

Oscar had figured out something substantial—possibly the person guilty—and I was left with a dead phone in my hand. Made me think solving things wasn't meant to be.

Dylan and I'd just left Ms. Dempsey's office. She took a copious amount of notes and pulled AP Unger in for the last fifteen minutes of my confessional or whatever it was you called the admission of all the crap I'd been doing. I gave them names, dates, and suspicions that were corroborated with cold, hard fact. The only thing I couldn't guarantee was the get-out-of-jail-free-card for Oscar. I still didn't have the shooter or the definitive names of all gang members because it was obvious there were more. They both...well, they both frankly looked afraid of me. I'd said everything with the conviction of a deathbed confession. There wasn't a lot you could do with someone like that. You either jumped on their crazy train or figured out how to derail them.

We had about ten minutes left of our lunch period. I was huddled between Dylan and Rudi (who was picking at a salad) while I convinced my tastebuds the mystery meat inside the tacos was actually ground beef. All in all, it was another NCIP day until Justice opened her mouth.

She leaned forward, elbows resting on the table. "I swear it, guys, and I don't like to swear, Eddie got bit by a *bleeping* rat last night. She had to get *bleeping* stitches and a *bleeping* rabies shot in her *bleeping* stomach." Justice claimed she didn't like to curse but had four instances that she might want to check on the cursing chart. "It was the best news of my life," she said laughing. "She then dumbly came to the, *bleeping* dojo, so I kicked her in the *bleeping* abs when she was distracted." Make that six instances. But hey, who's counting?

Rudi and I cringed, thinking that was slightly high on the mean-o-meter. The guys at the lunch table shrugged, thinking anything less would be spitting in the universe's face that had so kindly served her up to Justice.

My Spanish book was open next to me, and in between listening to nothing in particular, I translated a few paragraphs to English so I wouldn't have to do it that evening. That was the new and improved me. Multitasking, on the ball, in charge, and in control. Someone asked how landing Liam was going (seriously, I thought I'd been subtle), and a bite of taco got caught sideways in my throat.

Rudi read whoever-said-it's lips and pounded on my back like a jackhammer. I coughed into my napkin, stuttering out, "*Whh-aat?*"

Grumpy chuckled, grumbling, "You blew that, didn't you?"

I felt Dylan's gaze like hot, molten lava. I looked at him and had one run-on thought: *Whatdidyoudotome?* He smiled that bloody enigmatic grin, his face showing nothing but best-friend-ever rolled up into the all-American boyish smile. For all that boy-next-door stuff, there was a part that was dark and forbidden. That was Dylan though. One moment he was the consummate gentleman. The other, he liked dangling a carrot in front of me, just to yank it away —sadistic, if you asked me. He winked and took a bite of his third taco like nothing odd had happened at all. Maybe talking into someone's lips wasn't odd for him. Maybe that was the problem.

I frowned. The fact of the matter, my dating life was a barren wasteland. My reserve of past experiences was from trashy magazines and romance novels I hid under my mattress. And even then, I didn't understand everything that was printed.

"Whatever it is you're thinking about, I'm your answer, babe," someone said.

I wasn't sure what my face was doing, but I was pretty sure Jagger Cane wasn't the answer to its confusion. Dressed in his usual studliness, he stood overtop me with a dark grin that shouted things so indecent I said, "Forgive me, God," for him.

Anger sliced the air, and Dylan jostled in his seat. I didn't move. No one moved. It was like being around a venomous snake I feared would strike if I breathed the wrong way.

Dylan's voice was low and tight. "Hit the road, Cane. Everyone was fine here until your stench killed our appetites."

Jagger ignored him, stooping down at my feet. Reaching out with his hand, he rubbed his thumb along my jaw. "What's wrong, babe? You seem tense."

I looked in Jagger's inky-black eyes and wasn't sure what I saw. Lothario, con artist, mixed with a little bit of genuine concern? That was too many competing questions to take even a friendship further. Before I could lie, blow him off, or even tell the truth, Jagger cupped my face in his hand and pulled me within inches of his lips. "Come on, babe. Talk to Jagger. We've gotten really close lately," he said with a wink, insinuating something immoral.

I slapped him in my mind.

Dylan was out of his seat so fast you'd think his butt was on fire. I heard a gasp, a grunt, and the beginnings of an apology. Jagger's arm was drawn up between his scapulas, straining to the point of needing an MRI to check for permanent damage.

There was jawing on both parts, and when I looked at Grumpy, he was shooting daggers at Jagger, his mouth painted into an angry scowl. I got the distinct feeling the situation with Dylan and Jagger was a continuation of something that happened earlier. I might not know a lot about the opposite sex in general, but when it came to Dylan, I could see someone crystal clear. Jagger hated him—so much so that it gave me a feeling of disquiet.

And it should...

Why? Whatever Jagger felt for me was eclipsed by his desire to be a permanent burr in Dylan's derrière. It'd been that way since junior high, and my guess was it would never change.

The attention embarrassed me. I slumped over my tray, ignoring whatever conversation anyone tried to have with me afterward. When I finished what I could choke down, I lost myself in the crowd and stole off to the library. I was in desperate need of some me-time and wound up on the second floor of the media center. Completely worn out, I struggled to keep my pupils from going all fixed and dilated. Folding my arms on the desk, I lay my head on top of them, crossing my fingers the bell would wake me for next period. I'd only shut my eyes for a few seconds when I awoke with a jump.

I knew who was running Northside 12 and how I was going to stop him.

Chapter Thirty

SORE LOSER

*M*aybe it was right. Maybe it was wrong. Whatever the case, I did it anyway.

I left a message for Rainn Webster, the roving reporter who came to my home to telecast the miracle of the Jesus cookie. Rainn complained the town was too clean, that there wasn't enough suburban news to keep him happy. Well, I had news for him—some news that might spur Oscar's situation along if there was a nosy reporter asking all the right questions.

Since he was a reporter—and supposedly of sharp mind—I decided to phone him on Jubilee's cell phone. I'd left mine last period in the gym in my backpack. Don't ask me how that was even possible. Fifth period was English for me—not gym—yet, I found myself walking through the gym just to—confession time—watch the guys in short pants. It worked out well because I didn't want to chance Rainn figuring out I was Darcy Walker, and as smart as Jubilee was, it was too far off the chart of normal behavior for her to fathom. If he ever called her back, thankfully, she was a genius that operated on a lot of dumb.

I heard what sounded like mice in the radiator, squeaking and cheeping and doing whatever it was that furry, little vermin did. I shook it off, counting my blessings they were behind the cinderblock walls and not marching out in the open.

Time was growing short. The teachers had an impromptu

meeting in the media center, and I had to confess when nature called, I went to the restroom of my own volition. I desperately needed to get back to class but had one more phone call to make that was more important than Rainn's.

I huddled in the bathroom stall, whispering into Harold King's voicemail. I couldn't leave well enough alone. The reason? It was simple. I felt like I'd lost the challenge, and I was a sore loser...so sue me.

"Mister King, I know you don't know me, but please know I'm coming from a pure place. Something's going on at Valley and your son, Jinx, is involved. Jinx is mixed up with Juan Salas and Justin Starsong...maybe Adam Neeley. They admitted to me they had information on the murder of Alfonso Juarez. They were competing with AVO in the copper business and obviously something went south...like way south. I'm a nobody, Mister King. I have nothing to gain from this other than seeing an innocent boy go free." I paused taking a breath, telling myself again this was the right thing to do. "I'll call you back in a few hours, and I'll testify to anything, but I want anonymity. I know how they did it, and my name is...Jester."

I hung up and repeated the exact same message to Odell Whit-meyer, Oscar's attorney.

The commode in the adjacent stall flushed, the water swirling fast and loud as the sound of frantic footfalls hit the tile. The bath-room door slammed open then shut, the jolt echoing inside my over stimulated brain and traveling all the way down to the tips of my toes. In my heart, I knew someone had heard, and that I'd said too much—why did I think that would come back to haunt me?

———

Drawing and painting was shaping up to be a period of me-time. Our teacher hadn't showed, and twenty minutes into class I'd polished my toenails neon green and sneak-texted Dylan. It appeared we'd been graced by the gods, but then Mr. Rafferty—my Spanish teacher, for God's sake—slouched in to sub for the student teacher we'd had all year.

If only there was a dart gun around...

Chewing on a red apple, he looked me square in the face and

rolled his eyes with a groan. "No, I don't know anything about drawing and painting, and no, I don't want to be here. This is my planning period, but evidently, the-powers-that-be think it's a good idea for me to fill in."

Sitting right in front of the teacher's desk, I bust out laughing while those behind me groaned even deeper. Mr. Rafferty wasn't Teacher of the Year by a long shot. We did, however, speak the same language. It was called: *get me out of here.*

"Here's what we're going to do," he said, munching his apple while sliding behind the wooden desk and bending over it. Rummaging around, he flipped open the lesson plan, ran a stubby finger down the page, and ultimately looked outside. "Seems we're going to take a little field trip. Get out your sketch books and pencils because you're going to do a drawing of the human anatomy."

Ah, the human anatomy. I'd forgotten. A permission slip went home before spring break to be signed by a parent it was okay for their child to see a shirtless male. Murphy might've had the ink pen in his hand, but I was pretty sure I was the one that actually moved it.

Opening my backpack, I removed my sketchpad and quickly sharpened three pencils. Like a brownnose, I enthusiastically skipped to the front of the line. Mr. Rafferty chucked his apple core into the garbage and pushed his way to the door.

"Número trece," he said in my ear, "you've got to help me out. I have no clue what I'm doing. AP Unger was supposed to cover, but he's obsessed with why the phones have been down all day. Holy cow," he groaned, "it's sixth period. Give it up and try again tomorrow. At least, I've got two models waiting in the field out back. What you don't finish today, you can tomorrow."

Two models, I reminded myself. That's right. A female was joining us in what I knew, without asking, would be some sort of sports bra or tankini top. No way in the world would she be shirtless. It was Ohio, for Pete's sake.

We traveled down the stairs to the first floor, took a right, and headed for the rear entrance. About twenty feet from the door, Frank came out of the cafeteria doors, and when I gave him a big smile, he gave me a bristling half a "Hey," irritated I'd even addressed him. My face fell. I wasn't sure what that meant. I felt like we were friends, and I'd just spent the last fourteen days or so trying to free his brother. Something about him was out-of-kilter. His eyes were bloodshot, his nostrils flared, and his normally hairy self had crossed over into woolly mammoth. He wasn't a boy that was worrying. He was a boy trying to talk himself out of doing something. Shoving both hands in his pockets, he angrily brushed past me, but when I turned to inquire, I received a disgruntled noise from Mr. Rafferty.

Interpretation? Keep moving.

Mystified, one way or another I would make a point of speaking with Frank before the day ended.

Once outside, we passed the football stadium and baseball fields, balls whizzing over the plate where sixth period gym was in session. A group of guys and disinterested girls were huddled in the cinderblock dugout. We headed for a field on the edge of the property about four hundred meters away, next to a creek. It held promise of a beautiful future watercolor, but at the moment, the pastel buds were intermingled amidst last season's hay-like grass.

I'd worn red flip-flops to match my Adidas shorts and shirt. As we pushed our way through waist high foliage, my skin screamed that had been a behemoth mistake. I itched all over. When we finally made it to a small clearing where the grass had worn bare, I sat down in the dirt and crossed my legs in the Lotus position, immediately looking at the only subject present...the shirtless guy.

Cue the drooling lips.

I grinned at Mr. Rafferty and mouthed the words, "Thank you."

He rolled his eyes.

Seated on what looked like a wooden apple crate, I studied him the way a coroner would a corpse. He was magnificently built with a physique that was either a gift from Heaven or came from working out while everyone else was munching fries. Arrogance was in the expanse of his shoulders, and a raw sensuality was in the curve of his spine. Power rolled down his arms that were resting on his knees, and sleek muscle trailed to his trim abs, stopping at the waistband of his worn-out Levi's.

I caught myself nibbling my lower lip—sitting up straighter, shoulders back, chest out—trying to impress him even though I was at his back. I couldn't take the daydream further because Mr. Rafferty took a glance at his watch and grumbled, "Seems we've been stood up, kids. We've got about fifteen minutes, so do your drawing of the young man here, and we'll call it a day." He crossed his arms over his white short-sleeved shirt, snorting to himself, "Figures. When I read that girl's name on the lesson plan, I wouldn't have picked her to model if my life depended on it."

Whoever the she was, I was glad she'd ditched us. No way in the world would I have been able to peel my eyes off of Mr. Broad-Shoulders. "Who *is* he?" I heard a girl nervously say.

Mr. Rafferty scratched his bald head and shoved his drooping black glasses up onto his nose. "Where are my manners? Say hello to Liam Woods."

I had a moment of incomprehension and then the ripple effect took over.

I coughed, snorted, and giggled all at the same time. Then I blushed—my face feeling like it had a third-degree sunburn. A look to my right showed the girl who'd asked literally fanning her sweaty face with her sketchpad. Two guys behind her rolled their eyes, sticking their chests out as if to say, *He ain't all that*.

But he *was* all that. That was the problem.

Liam didn't turn around. In fact, he was almost motionless, and when I glanced at his ribs, they weren't rising and falling with respirations.

Unease settled among the crowd. Mr. Rafferty narrowed his eyes and took one cautious step forward, like he was sidestepping smoldering coals. "Liam? Son, are you all right?"

When Liam didn't answer, a distant voice in my brain put its hand on the panic button. Something was wrong. Before Mr. Rafferty made another move, I anxiously dropped my things and rushed to Liam's side. When I touched his shoulder with a soft, "Liam," he slumped over to the side and sprawled into a lifeless mass onto the ground.

My God, was he dead?!

It was instant chaos: prayers, gasps, and "oh my Gods" filling the air. In a matter of seconds, Mr. Rafferty reined in the ensuing panic and dropped into a crouch beside me. As though he was breakable, we carefully turned Liam over, limb-by-limb. I'll never forget what I saw. His mouth was moving, but no words came out. Blood bubbled in the corners of his lips as his eyes glazed over, empty. He couldn't breathe, he couldn't speak, or do anything except battle some form of catatonia.

Mr. Rafferty examined Liam, his fingers on his neck and wrist, putting his ear to his chest and nose for breaths. "Call the office and 911!" he yelled to anyone that had a phone.

Frantically patting myself down, I checked and rechecked my shorts until I finally accepted the fact I had no pockets and no phone. Four other cell phones were immediately dialed, but after several tries, we realized we were so far down in a valley we'd reached a dead zone.

"Nothing," someone muttered.

"I've tried three times," a guy desperately groaned.

"Didn't you say the phones were down?" a girl asked anxiously.

"Maybe I'll just run back to the office," still another added.

Mr. Rafferty didn't have the chance to respond or even consider the requests because whizzing past our ears was what I immediately knew to be a bullet through a silencer. It sounded like a *Pffft*—a very loud release of steam coming from the west.

Mr. Rafferty and I gaped at one another and yelled, "Down!" at the same time.

Tackling me to the ground, we both tried to shield Liam underneath us.

I was in shock.

If I wanted to strike "getting shot at" from my Bucket List, I could check that off right then. A part of my brain wanted to think it was just Frank and Oscar doing Frank-and-Oscar stuff—Oscar once brought a BB gun to school and shot up some road signs—but then I reminded myself Oscar was in a six-by-nine foot cell surrounded by metal bars. And Frank was, *well?*

Frank wasn't speaking to me.

When we heard another *Pffft*, everyone went deadly quiet. It was another gunshot...that time from the north. My heart jumped around uncontrollably. Honestly, I felt like I was having a heart attack. What were the signs? Chest pain, nausea, shortness of breath? I wasn't sure what to do, where to go, whom to run to, and by the mortified look on Mr. Rafferty's face, he didn't have the answers.

I stopped the sob threatening to erupt by biting my wrist, trying to will away the panic. Murphy always said nothing was accomplished with panic. It robbed you of valuable seconds that could change a situation. *What would you do, Murphy?* I muttered several times. He'd say, *Harness your fear into something useful.*

I needed to get a grip if I was going to survive or help others survive.

Mr. Rafferty must've seen the horror on my face. He latched onto my hand, whispering, "Número trece, stay with me." With a deep breath, I refused to grant my fear an audience. Somehow I squeezed his hand back and both of us quickly checked Liam's torso, running our hands up and down his jeans for a bloody wound of some kind. Thankfully, there was nothing. Liam started to moan guttural sounds coming deep from his soul, like he was having a hard time shaking whatever atrocity had been done.

I bent down in his ear and whispered, "Shhh, I won't let anyone else hurt you, but you need to keep quiet."

Even though his gaze was fixed on mine, there was no acknowledgment he understood, but I hoped the message seeped in somewhere. Suddenly, I was jolted with the enormity of what I'd promised...had I just lied to him?

He gasped out, "Darcy."

I looked in his brown eyes. "Who did this?" I whispered.

"I didn't...think...it was..." Dang it, he zoned out again. I lightly shook him, and he sucked in a big gasp of air, sliding back into semi-consciousness.

"You okay?" I asked him warily. I didn't expect an answer, but he managed a weak nod anyway. His eyes said, *What now?* Heck if I knew, but my guess was he was relying on me to get a burst of creativity.

I rubbed Liam's hands, trying to warm him because he felt ice-cold. Amidst a wheezy voice, he moaned. "T-ttell her I'm—*sorry*." No one had to tell me whom he referred to—the ex-girlfriend—but to think of her when he was moments from whatever was to come? That signaled regret...or unresolved feelings.

I nodded, overcome with the fact I wouldn't tell anyone anything if I didn't get to safety. It was best to keep moving—some place far away and fast—but I wasn't about to leave him behind. He closed his eyes again, and a white-knuckled panic overtook me. *He's dead*, I thought, until Mr. Rafferty whispered, "No, número trece, he's passed out again."

I fought the urge to shake him awake, to ask again who'd done it, but I didn't know if I was risking injuring him more. Plus, when he was awake, he'd moaned. Moaning would give up our position if it hadn't already.

Once Mr. Rafferty ensured no one else had been hurt, we all lay facedown as he decided what would be the best course of action. Policemen came to our school at the beginning of the year, helping each room come up with a plan should anything heinous happen, like a gunman ever enter the school. Someone was supposed to break out a window so students could jump. Someone was then to remind students of their next course, which was to run for their lives and meet later at an agreed-upon place. In the past, students were advised to stay inside, hunker down, and hide—but after a few disasters where that theory proved fatal—we were told to get out as soon as possible. But what were we supposed to do when the enemy was outdoors? When we wanted to get back inside?

Mr. Rafferty's mind, I was sure, ran through the same scenarios as mine. Before us, we had one injured, a teacher near retirement, eight girls, and two guys with the combined testosterone of a dozen prepubescent boys. No one was looking especially heroic in the group, and I knew he was thinking the same thing as me...we were going to have to rely on our brains because brawn wasn't going to cut it.

I tried not to think that whoever was shooting would run into Dylan in a few minutes when seventh period started. Time was a blur. How long had we been outside? The emotions were choking me, but I willed away the sounds of terror trying to hear if baseballs were being hit. The only echo I heard was of my own beating heart. Had the shooter already killed the sixth period class?

...then I saw him.

Someone was ducked low about two hundred meters to my left, slowly creeping toward the creek behind us. The person wore a ski mask and was shouldering a semiautomatic rifle, wearing a black jacket and white pants so roomy they were whipping around in the wind. I nearly threw up in my mouth.

I jerked my head in that direction as Mr. Rafferty's eyes lit up with an instant acknowledgment. We didn't have a chance to do anything, say anything, plan anything because next thing I knew, I heard a man scream, "Stop! Juan, is that you? Stop!"

Juan, I gasped. I should've known.

When I woke from my brief nap in the media center, I'd all but convinced myself Adam Neeley—the guy I'd witnessed get jumped-into Northside 12—was the murderer. *Perhaps Northside*, I thought, *has the same initiation as AVO*—which was murdering someone to enter the fold. Even if I couldn't prove it, that seemed to be the way things happened in the movies. The real mastermind and/or killer was always the one who appeared halfway involved, a minor charac-ter. Then at the last moment—most usually a moment that cost the protagonist something dearly—it was revealed the person had more going on underneath the surface than originally expected. Even if he wasn't the mastermind (at the moment, that initial thought sounded dumb), I'd decided to show up on his doorstep, feel him out, and appeal to his sense of mind that real friends didn't beat the crap out of one another. Right then, it looked like Juan was who I'd always thought he was: homicidal and certifiably deranged.

I thought back on the day Alfonso was discovered. I could place Jinx, Juan, and Justin at the scene. But those shots came from two different directions? West and north.

If it was Juan, then who was the other??

Unable to talk myself out of it, I got up on all fours and gazed in the direction of the voice. It was like slow motion in an action-hero-movie-gone-bad. AP Unger came from the direction of the school, running an Olympic pace straight at who he thought was Juan Salas.

I jumped up and down, waving my arms over my head, shouting, "No! No! They're real bullets," but it was too late. AP Unger took a shot to the chest, going ashen and gasping for breath, as he took three more running steps trying to apprehend Juan. Before Juan could squeeze off another shot, AP Unger fell to his knees then face-planted with a horrifyingly, loud thud.

I flinched. I flinched so hard I felt the tendons in my neck snap. Trouble was, as I yelled, "No!" I gave up my location. In doing so, I gave up the location of everyone else. Juan took one glance in my direction, but instead of blowing me to kingdom come, he slung the rifle around his back and kept walking a straight line toward the creek. That didn't make sense. I'd provoked him—he should want my head on a stick—but I took that as opportunity to break for AP Unger.

Mr. Rafferty felt my plans, latching hard onto my leg. "Número trece," he pleaded desperately. "Stay down."

It wasn't in me to stay down. "There are two shooters," I told him. "Look for the other. If he follows Juan, then go back to school where it's safe. But he's out there. Whoever he is, he's coming."

Logic said I was dead. Faith said I should give it a try. Amidst his protests, I twisted away, kicked off my shoes, and gave a hunched-over run toward AP Unger. With each step, my feet were painfully scraped and scratched, possibly down to the bone.

Sneakers would've been a plus...Chuck Taylors preferred.

When I made it to his side, blood was pooling around him, close to a foot from his body. I didn't know how many pints he'd lost, but the anemic color of his skin said it was already too much. Dropping down beside him, relief enwrapped me when his brown eyes fluttered open.

He was lying in a prone position on his stomach. He was wheezy with a sucking chest wound, and there was a good possibility one of his lungs had collapsed. There was no exit wound on his back, and when he moved his arms and legs a little, I knew he probably didn't have any spinal cord injuries. The bleeding was like a broken dam, though, and I had nothing plastic to plug the hole. My options were to watch him bleed out or try something else. Even if wrong, I made the quick decision to attempt to keep his airways open—if he couldn't breathe, he was a goner.

I asked which side of his chest hurt, and when he mumbled, "Right," I tucked his right arm under his body and propped him up a few inches to keep the stronger, left lung unimpeded. He sucked air through gritted teeth, trying his best to not make any unnecessary noise. When I moved him just a fraction, my eyes fixed on a gunshot wound to his left femur. Juan must've squeezed off another round. I was out of my league, but that leg would be the death of him if it nicked his femoral artery.

Loosening his tie, I pulled it from his neck, placing a tourniquet high on his groin. "Run, Walker," he begged. "It's...too late—"

"Shhh," I comforted him, securing the tie. "I need your phone."

He understood my request, responding, "Belt loop." Unclipping his cell phone, I glanced to his hand and saw the gold wedding band on his ring finger. As stupid and unproductive as it was, I pointed out the doughnut stain on his tie as I secured it even further.

"Your wife must love you for your personality because it's not for your stellar manners or sense of style. Jelly on your tie—major turn-off."

Just the mention of her made his chin tremble and quake. "My wife. T-tell her—"

I cut him off, not wanting to get lost in the grief. His dying thoughts were as Liam's, and I didn't want to think they'd both placed their hearts in my hands. I had to stay alive, if only to carry out their last wishes.

I needed to laugh, or I wasn't going to make it through things. I choked out, "I'll tell her your dying words were of your mistress, Bambi, and how she made you feel eighteen years old again."

He gargled a laugh, blood oozing through his chest. "God...help us," he mumbled. No dispute from me there, especially when he whispered what I recognized as the Lord's Prayer. I think I prayed with him. I wasn't sure, but seeing him like that reminded me of my father—and what my father stood for. Murphy was a Christian. He prayed at every meal, before bedtime, and daily mumbled to the sky. It wasn't that I didn't believe in it. It's just that I prayed a few prayers so fervently as a child only for them to be answered in the negative. That hurt me so deeply that if I took the time to think about it, I always wound up in tears. No one wanted to be ignored by the Big Guy Upstairs. It made me feel second-rate and maybe even third. But for some reason, I didn't care about Heaven's pecking order, if it even had one. Murphy swore there was none— that you were accepted warts and all—*even the wartiest of people*, he'd said with a laugh. So maybe, just maybe, it would for once be on my side.

I wasn't sure what I was doing or if I was even doing it right, but I closed my eyes until he drifted off after an, "Amen."

Dialing 911, I wiped my nose and willed my breathing to slow. I heard, "Hello? Hello? Talk to me," the person said frantically. "Hello? Are you at Valley High?"

I was so transfixed I'd forgotten I'd dialed. "Y-yes," I said. "I'm surprised I got a signal."

"What's going on?" the woman asked. "We're getting dropped calls and can't get through to the school switchboard."

"The phones have been down all day, and we're in a dead zone," I explained. "I'm in the sixth period drawing and painting class, and we're in a field behind the school. There are ten students—er, eleven, one wounded—and Mr. Rafferty. We were shot at twice. Once from the west, once from the north. A third and fourth shot took down our assistant principal, who's not looking so good at the moment. He can't talk, so I don't know if he merely happened upon us, or if anyone else is aware we're even out here."

"What's your name, honey?"

I didn't know what to do. If I told her I was Darcy Walker, even the dumbest of detectives would deduce I was Jester once they spoke with Harold King. I surprised myself when I mumbled, "I'm Jester. Just Jester." She started to speak, but I cut her off. "I might not have much time, but I want you to know the shooter who hit AP Unger is a member of the Northside 12 gang. His face was behind a black ski mask, but AP Unger called him Juan Salas. The other shooter has to be either Justin Starsong, Jinx King, or Adam Neeley."

"You're sure?"

"A strong conviction."

I looked up to the sky, and it struck me funny how beautiful the day was—seventy-six degrees, bright blue sky, very few clouds with the promise of a warm day come sunup. But tomorrow wouldn't be warm, would it? Who wouldn't wake up, whose dreams would be shattered, and whose funerals would we be planning?

It wasn't in my nature to stay put. Maybe that was stupid. Maybe that would be on my tombstone, but I figured someone had to try to stop whatever it was Juan had planned even if it meant I would die trying. I wasn't sure what I was going to do next until I heard someone Darth Vadering me.

Chapter Thirty-One

MANHUNT

*I*f that didn't send a chill up my spine, then I needed to have my pulse checked. "Come and get me, Darcy," the person taunted.

Biiiiig problem.

Darth Vader was here...and it was all about *me*.

Some sort of morbid fascination compelled me to run after him. It was stupid, reckless, and unbelievably illogical. Still, I couldn't fight the urge to follow and find the answers I'd so desperately been after. I took a deep breath, realizing what I'd planned could be the end of me. I could stay put, but if I got killed in the process, who would make sure Oscar was set free? I told myself repeatedly I was Darcy Walker, and Darcy Walker had had worse things happen to her than a gunman at school. Plus, if I made myself the target, then everyone else had a chance at going free.

The dispatcher must've heard me sprinting. "What are you doing?"

Good question. Probably being scarred for life.

"I'm following...Juan Salas," I told her, feet hitting the dirt. "He wants me to play...and I guess," I huffed out, "I am."

"No, no, no," she warned, but it fell on deaf ears.

Most girls wanted to play dress-up. I wanted to play Manhunt with the guys. You know, go outside and pretend you're soldiers then drag whoever you catch back to your camp. Who would've thought I'd be playing the real life version?

Running was difficult. I tried to ignore my aching feet and the beating they were taking. I should've worn my Chuck Taylors. Heck, I should've done a lot of things. In a few more steps, it wouldn't matter. I'd be back at the clearing and could put my head together with Mr. Rafferty, get everyone to safety, and then...well, I guess I'd follow Juan.

When I passed the clearing, though, no one was there! There were absolutely no signs of life. No movement, no grass rustling, nothing. My breath caught in my throat. Had something just happened? If so, where had they gone? Did they drag Liam with them? The only answer that made sense was when I triaged AP Unger, Juan double-backed around and took them to the creek.

I looked in all four directions and jumped up and down but got nothing but weed after weed. "They're not here!" I told her hysterically.

"The others have gotten to safety?"

One could hope, but I feared the worst. When I told her what I suspected, once again she begged me to run to the school. But how could I? Under ideal circumstances, Juan and whoever-else-this-was would've taken me and been done with it, but why take a teacher and ten other students as hostage/witnesses? They were scot-free! For that matter, why come for me at school? Shouldn't they have nabbed me at work? Half the time, it was Rudi and me and an inebriated boss. Why would they willingly place themselves in a situation where they could possibly be identified and overpowered?

My legs felt like lead as I pumped them faster. I made it to the edge of the property, slid down a muddy bank, and skidded to a stop at the edge of the water, hiding behind a cluster of trees. Standing in the middle of the creek with a gun to his temple was Mr. Rafferty. My heart seized in my chest. He'd taken some sort of beating because his nose had dribbled blood onto his white shirt. The other students were facedown on the opposite bank with their fingers laced behind their heads. Another gunman was corralling them, babbling incoherently, pacing around like a dog on rabies watch. Without warning, he pounded himself in the head as though he were punishing himself. My God, it was definitely Juan. He'd done the same thing when he was caught in Dylan's home. If it were Juan, then who in the heck had the gun at Mr. Rafferty's temple? My guess was Justin. Jinx was short. Adam was shorter. That person was taller than Mr. Rafferty who was around the same size as me.

I took a moment to center myself, to remember why I'd even found myself in the situation. The goal? Set Oscar free. If I didn't make it out alive, I needed to fill in the rest of the blanks. I whispered, "We're at the creek behind the school. There are two shooters. Justin Starsong, I think, has a gun on Mister Rafferty and Juan Salas is holding the students on the other side of the creek. They're guilty of killing Alfonso Juarez over the copper business in town. All of Northside 12 is. They framed Oscar Small, but I think someone is going to have to torture them into fingering the exact one. Annie Hughes?" I added. "I'm not sure how she's connected. Just tell the prosecutor she has the wrong person and that Annie, and maybe even the man killed downtown, are on their list of offenses."

My foot hit a twig, snapping it in two.

All eyes shot up the hill where I'd just stripped my covert status. An icy chill ran over my whole body. "Busted," I mumbled into the phone, but then I promptly dropped it, and watched it tumble down the bank, splashing into the creek.

Grade A stupid.

My heart sank. Suddenly my actions felt like a royally stupid idea because I had no plan that didn't include begging for my life. They weren't the begging-for-your-life type. My only line of defense was to do what I did best...talk and bargain. I counted back from ten, heard the director yell, *Lights, camera, action*...and it was game-ON.

Straightening my spine, I directed my questions to the one I definitely knew was Juan. "What is it you want, Juan?"

First to speak was Mr. Rafferty. "Número trece," he muttered, shaking his head. "Honey, it's—" Before he could finish, he was struck on his temple with the butt of the handgun. Mr. Rafferty's head jerked like he'd been punched by a heavyweight. He fell forward but caught himself by bracing his hands on his knees. I wanted to close my eyes, will myself to some place other than where I was. Some place peaceful and tropical with guys in painted on swimming trunks. But I was afraid to even blink—afraid what giving

Juan and Justin one split second of not being on my toes could mean.

I didn't know what to do, but it wasn't the time to shrink away. Plus, I didn't know if they were going to start firing at will. I then directed my questions to the one holding Mr. Rafferty, assuming he was Justin. I knew nothing about Justin personally, only that he had a chip on his shoulders the size of a two-by-four. I could only hope my next statement rattled him.

"What's your endgame, Justin? I don't see anything here but some hostages you intend on doing something with. Frankly, that makes no sense to me. I know you've got an attitude, so what's wrong? Copper business going south? Or did killing Alfonso not get you the notoriety you wanted? Is Northside 12 just a little too small time for you, and you wanted the rest of the world and city to know it?"

He stood in silence, ruminating the words I immediately hoped weren't a mistake. Imagine my surprise when both he and Juan simultaneously ripped their masks from their heads, exposing themselves to not one, but everyone else as the culprits.

Could things get any more bizarre?

In the creek, Justin was the one who finally opened his mouth. "I didn't kill Alfonso. I was cleanup."

I fought the urge to scratch my head in confusion. Did that mean it was Juan? When I looked at Juan he didn't say, "Huh-uh, wasn't me either." He just stood there...almost like it was understood. Something instantly didn't feel right. Once again, I looked at Justin still subduing Mr. Rafferty. He was wearing old jeans with a hole in the knee. Juan was wearing almost a duplicate outfit when the person who shot AP Unger was wearing white cotton pants. If I had two of the major psychos in front of me, then who did that leave? Jinx?

Mr. Rafferty slowly righted himself and gazed at me like we were all as good as dead. His shoulders sagged—he'd given up. I was hit with the magnitude of the situation. I realized he was human, just like the rest of us. A man longing for retirement, fishing at dawn, sleeping 'til noon, long walks with his wife on a weeknight—things he feared he might never get.

When he opened his mouth, I would've sworn on a stack of

Bibles it was going to be his Last Will and Testament. Instead, he threw his gaze behind me and gasped, "Número nueve," and started praying out loud.

Número nueve, I thought. *Número nueve*. Nah, it couldn't be.

I didn't even have time for panic to knock me down because right behind me I heard Darth Vader whispering, "Boo."

I froze, my heart deliberating whether to pump again or send me to the Great Beyond. So this was it. I was going to die. When most kids had the occasional question about death, I'd learned from an early age none of us were invincible. Superheroes weren't real. No one stopped the bridge from breaking or the bullet from hitting your chest or even called on the phone to say, "Get your house in order." If those people existed, death could be avoided or, at the least, made easier. Things had happened in my life that made me try to grasp the hereafter, but I'd always assumed I'd live a long life and have more adventure-packed days to just keep grasping. But I swear to God Himself if He would help me outrun the psychopathic rat killer named Eddie Lopez—dubbed número nueve in Spanish class —I'd do something worthwhile with the rest of my days.

I briefly wondered what kind of gun was at my back and whether it was real. All I knew was there was a good chance it was the kind that went bang. AP Unger could attest to that. Call me stupid, but I'd rather have a bullet in the chest than my back. I inhaled and turned around, willing my voice not to shake. "How's the rat business, Eddie?"

Eddie was unfazed, her black-eyed stare implacable and ready for more carnage. I should've known. She was wearing her karate pants and a facemask that had some sort of voice distortion unit under-neath. In her right hand, she cupped a nickel-plated 9mm gun. Somewhere along the way, she'd ditched the rifle but came prepared with an extra firearm.

She removed her mask, threw it to the ground, and pulled a piece of paper to her eyes and read a few sentences.

The person always wears red, Jester. Be careful. My source is petrified of this person, and her name is Eddie Lopez.

Now would be a good time for a meteor to fall from the sky.

Eddie must've been at Sydney's party and had somehow intercepted the note from Jaws during the brawl. Maybe a better description would've been a cranberry colored hoodie. I closed my eyes in my mind. Vinnie mumbled the word red when he relayed Jaws's conversation, but it meant nothing at the time so I let it go. My God, why couldn't Justice be here? Justice could take care of things with her eyes closed. I wasn't even somebody who fought like a girl...I fought like a moron with a death wish.

A scuffle broke out in the line of students Juan was holding hostage. Eddie glanced past me—hearing their cries and mewls—and if she was hungry, her mouth was dripping drool with the prospect of more victims. When she raised her gun to silence them, I pivoted toward them on instinct, but something told me to stop. The only hope they had was for Eddie to find me bigger game. With the force of fear and years of disappointment and scary-movie training, I threw my whole body into her, hoping to rattle her long enough so I could get a quick start. My nose bumped her chest, my teeth rattled, and all she did was stagger an inch and laugh in my face.

Yup, it was dying time.

I ran. I ran faster than I'd ever run before. Fearing she wasn't behind me, I took a quick glance over my shoulder in a purposeful taunt—somehow mustering an even sicker smile than she was wearing.

She fired off two shots just to remind me that she was.

I tripped in a rabbit hole, split the bottom of my foot wide open, but staggered up and ran some more. When she expelled another bullet, I ducked down in the weeds, trying to hide as I sprinted. But next thing I knew, I was hurtled through the air, landing flat on my back with Eddie's 9mm in my face, her laughing like a goon. Instinct barely had time to take over when someone came out of nowhere, diving on her, slamming her to the ground. Eddie let out a pained, "Ugh," trying to gather herself.

Dylan, I gasped in my brain.

In the blink of an eye, he jerked me up, pulling me toward the school and away from Eddie whose head had just cracked so loudly it sounded like a melon busting. We fell overtop one another, sprinting past the ratmobile parked in the middle of the field. It looked like she'd gone four wheeling in it. Brown streaks covered the sides and part of the windshield. The mud flaps were caked with clods of dirt that had hardened into clay. My guess was more ammunition was inside and hopefully something concrete that would tie her and the others to the murders of Alfonso, Annie, and the man who still was nameless. Eddie worked for Saxon Brothers' Exterminators. Theoretically, it was reasonable to believe she would have access to firearms—especially if she had to take down an animal that wouldn't go willingly. But Eddie Lopez? I shook my head in my mind. How in the heck did I miss *that*?

Then my mind put that puzzle piece in its place. Eddie was the one at the construction site who I referred to as Mr. Hood—who pulled a bundle of copper pipes from the trunk of a car. She fit the physical build, and maybe the trench coat didn't even have a hood. Perhaps it was her normal hoodie with a coat over top. Thing was, when each of them gave her the hand signal, she didn't return it. What did that mean? Was she some unknown variable that screwed up whatever the day's plans had been? She'd already shot AP Unger, I could attest to that, and even though Juan and Justin were holding hostages, they hadn't shot anyone. But all three were at school with guns...that meant something was planned...but *what*?

We didn't make it anywhere except in what felt like circles.

We were crouched low, breathing heavily. Dylan looked me in the face. The glint in his eyes was murderous, but underneath was a tender edge I'd come to expect from the best friend I'd ever had. "Tell me you're okay, sweetheart."

All I could manage was a nod, but when I opened my mouth—to unravel the tangled feelings his presence always gave me—Dylan suddenly engulfed my hands in his and simply promised, "You're not going to die."

Tears stung with the sting of a beehive.

I geared up to do some quality sobbing, but the instant I almost laid my soul bare—to ask, *What's been going on between us?* I know, bad timing—I could feel Eddie closing in. She wasn't quiet. She wanted us to know she was coming, and right then I knew why some people only watched horror movies with the sound turned low. It was the noise—that crazy music of what was to come—that was worse than knowing someone was after you. Eddie had begun to sing. Singing some psychotic song that I thought she might've made up until I realized she said...

"Don't fear the reaper."

Loved that song...unfortunately, Eddie was taking it literally.

In half a second, Dylan forcibly yanked me up again, and we raced back toward the school. When Eddie fired off a round that nearly grazed our heads, he drove us to the ground, covering me with his body. We willed our breathing to still, but when I gazed into his face, I saw it in his eyes. If we stayed put, we were sitting ducks. If we ran, we gave her a target to shoot at. He looked tired, worn out, and aged beyond his years—all because of me. When a single tear rolled down his cheek, it was like a fist to the stomach.

Tears blinded me as I mouthed out the words, "Always," then did the unspeakable...

I stood up and ran.

"Darcy, no!" he screamed, his arms lunging for me. But I took off in Eddie's line of vision anyway. I hightailed it across the field like a gazelle outrunning a lion, dipping low into the wild grass that had only begun to bloom. I dropped down and crawled for a while, ignoring Dylan's cries and his rising desperation that he couldn't locate me. Finally, I made it to some storage units at the property's edge—the right side of my body behind an air conditioning unit, the left side hanging out for target practice.

"Don't fear the reaper..."

My mouth went slack, and I began to tremble all over. My grip on my sanity was slipping. I couldn't continue to run. I was only a human, a girl to boot, and I wasn't even sure Heaven was on my side. I listened for that little angel on my shoulder and got nothing.

I fell to the earth on all fours, wrenching the grass between my hands, speaking into the ground. "I just wanted to help," I whimpered, "but I'm tired."

Then I heard that voice again. It was too close. I felt her heat, all trigger-friendly happy, and knew for sure when she kicked me in the ribs. I winced, swallowed down a yell, and met her eyes. As I shakily stood, I zeroed in on her right hand, holding the silver 9mm. It was stamped with the initials AVO.

Aw, c'mon, surely not.

Eddie gave me a carnivorous gaze, her empty black eyes locking on mine as if she'd read my mind. "I wanted in AVO. They told me what I had to do to get in. Alfonso was a snitch. They don't like snitches."

"Annie?"

She frowned as if she'd forgotten about Annie altogether. "The girl always with Oscar?" she said, cocking her head to the side. I only stared. "I saw them fighting," she explained. "I was getting tires put on the ratmobile. After he left, I made fun of him, and she went loco. It really wasn't a big deal."

She added a sociopathic shrug.

Oh, wow, I marveled at the coldblooded attitude. I wasn't sure how she'd killed Annie without being caught on camera, but my guess was there was evidence of her in that parking lot somewhere. My thoughts went back to two weeks earlier when I saw Eddie kicking the tires on the ratmobile in the school parking lot—the day Oscar was arrested. Was she trying them out then? If so, she'd just killed Annie the night before.

Well, hallelujah. Can I get an amen?? I got a confession. Two confessions that would free Oscar. A part of me was ecstatic. Another part wanted to keep a bullet from hitting its mark. As much as I tried, I didn't seem to have the sense to shut up. "Well, murder's easy for you, isn't it, Eddie? Did you get the man downtown too?"

She gave me another shrug as though it meant nothing to her. "I didn't want him in the gym," she said. Right then, it all made sense. He was discovered in a dumpster behind Pump & Grind Gym.

So that other man wasn't AVO? I thought.

"Was he AVO?" I asked.

"No, I was bored...and mad."

"Maybe you should talk to your shrink about that."

Another head cock. "And why would I do that?"

"My guess is you're under-medicated."

Taunting Eddie made a bad situation even worse. She spouted off a foul litany of words, and instead of buying me time, I'd just signed my death certificate. But I felt like I needed to make a deposit in the karma bank, and what better way to do that than guarantee that Dylan, at least, walked away unharmed. Eddie wanted *me*, especially after what came out of my mouth next.

"You probably screwed that up somehow too, didn't you? Just like you did with Alfonso. You cut off his hand, Eddie. That was dumb. You should've taken his tongue too. You're just as dumb as Justice said you were."

Eddie looked like she'd swallowed a bowling ball.

Her Adam's apple almost tripled.

I waited for her to shoot, charge me like a bull, take bites out of me, or go for my neck like everyone else. But two earsplitting shots rang through the air, sending us both to our knees. The first sounded like it struck something metal. The second? I wasn't sure. It missed me—at least, I thought it missed me. I was so deaf from the blast I didn't know if it hit me and I didn't feel it or if the shooter truly was a bad shot. Was that Juan or Justin? Or had the cavalry finally arrived? Eddie didn't care that shots were being fired —she kept smiling like a loony person—but I sure as heck cared. I had the answers, but what good did it do if I wasn't alive to tell?

Clouds rolled in, and the sky darkened almost on cue—like the heavens were upset at what it was seeing. A big branch was right by my feet. When Eddie looked back toward the shooter, I picked it up and swung like I was going for a grand slam, cracking her square in the neck. Her feet went out from underneath her, and she crashed to the ground with a startled, "Umpf."

As I ran, all I kept thinking was, *Someone will come. Someone will come.* I should've known it would be my best friend. Dylan charged through the field, not one ounce of hesitation in his gait, yelling my name at the top of his lungs. "Darcy, run!" he roared, frantically demanding I go faster. "Run!"

Pushing my legs until they burned, I met his eyes. They held a volatile combination of fury, revenge, and fear. He didn't like to be afraid and usually annihilated the thing he felt made him weak. But mere feet from me, he abruptly stopped, going immediately still, like the blood had completely drained from his body.

It was too late.

Here we were within arm's reach, and the only thing separating us was Eddie's gun I felt at my back. Dylan and I had one of those moments—a moment that was just the two of us—and I saw dread seep into his eyes. He was promising that I would live, and he would go down making sure that happened. But there was a glimmer of, *I may not make it in the process...but remember I love you.* "I love you," he then murmured out loud. "I love you more than anything in my life, and I always will."

My tongue twisted, and I wanted to speak. I wanted to tell him he was my world, that I loved him, and that I thought he had a great butt—but Eddie fisted a handful of my hair, twisting it to my scalp. Dylan went white as a ghost as the hairs painfully popped one by one, but as excruciating as it was, I tilted my head toward her and calmly said, "Eddie."

A thwack broke the silence as Dylan attacked like a pit bull tasting blood.

With his left elbow, he knocked me out of the way, circling both hands around the gun, the rest of his body going straight for Eddie's knees. Somehow I wound up underneath, coughing and crawling out to the side like I was on my last breath. Dylan's movements were a blur of violence and animal wildness, kneeing her in the stomach, headbutting her in the nose, all with the intended outcome of Eddie never speaking again. Eddie pulled every trick she had in the book. She returned the headbutt, doing something to his ribs, and then swiped him at the ankles, laughing sadistically in the process. Dylan went down hard on his back but dragged Eddie along with him in the grass. A few slugs were squeezed off in the process as Eddie's hands wrapped around his, trying to jar the gun free.

That shouldn't be happening. Dylan should've already overpowered her, and I was struck with the realization of the strength psychotic people must possess. I grabbed Eddie by the hair, yanking her neck so far back it almost gave her a permanent flip-top head. When another round was released, I got so afraid she'd shoot Dylan I dropped my hands and froze.

When Dylan maneuvered his body into a better position, he attacked with the force of a charging bull, thrusting his hands upward, cracking Eddie's jaw. She staggered backward and spit out blood, cursing, and then dropped both hands, cradling her throbbing head. As a result, the gun launched high, and while Dylan lunged for it, Eddie hurled her entire body into the air, caging him to the ground.

Dylan's face was a ball of fury, ripped and contorted with anger, literally dodging Eddie's gnashing teeth. Seconds counted here. I needed to do something. I needed to go for the gun. The moment I took one step toward it, Frank Small dove into the pile like some dimwitted caveman, and if he was looking to pass the baton, he "franked it up" on the last lap.

The sound of knuckles popping filled the air. No one knew who to grab, who was on what team, who had the gun, nothing. Desperately, I tried to find the gun to no avail. Somehow making my body function, I jumped up and down in desperation, screaming and waving my arms, trying to alert anyone in the field the real fight was by me. The feeling of despair and defeat was eclipsed only when I saw a sea of blue charge toward us, guns pointed and aimed at Eddie.

In a perfect world, Eddie would've surrendered. Instead, she crawled out of the pile and located the gun, pivoted toward the police, raised her right hand, and opened fire. *They had no choice*, I told myself.

I closed my eyes as the three officers squeezed off a shot.

EPILOGUE: THE ROAD TO REDEMPTION

*O*ne critical, seven injured, thirteen students all with future insurance claims to the psych ward. Not bad for a day that could be compared to front row seats in a hellish nightmare featuring the criminally insane.

Things had died down, perpetrators were in handcuffs, parents were trying desperately to get to their children, and the highway was finally moving from a citywide deadlock. I'd just finished being questioned by a group of detectives and had watered down my activities as much as possible without watering down the incriminating facts of those involved. All in all, the day's events were the master plan of resident rat killer, Eddie Lopez, which was quote-unquote "stumbled upon" by Justin Starsong and Juan Salas.

You couldn't escape the irony...

Finding rodents was the end-all, be-all to Eddie. Who would've thought it was Justin who turned out to be a rat himself? Evidently, as soon as his butt hit the squad car, he sang like a canary. My guess was he was cutting his losses and going for a deal. Apparently, he and Juan knew Eddie had recently jumped ship to AVO, and when they found out what she was doing, they'd jumped aboard because they had no other idea how to take her down. He said they were playing her, waiting for the right opportunity to set everyone free, and that Juan was the shooter from the north trying to stop her before it got worse. And I had some gold bullion stashed under my bed—*insert sarcasm*. They could've called the authorities, and I sure as heck hoped a jury saw through their line of bull.

All I knew was secrets could die with Eddie. Secrets and crimes that could be pinned solely on her, and the dead couldn't talk...and wouldn't that be convenient for everyone else? Last I saw, she was being whisked away in an ambulance, traveling the speed of light. It didn't seem fair if she'd survive, and I guess it was a good thing I had no power over her fate.

The squirrel remains on my front porch more than likely were by her hands. Maybe even the shoe. The chemicals on Juarez's body? Since I knew she was the murderer, they were probably rodent killers.

Adam Neeley? Strangely, Justin claimed he wasn't in on the escapade, opting according to school records to be absent for the day. I found it odd that Justin so openly threw Juan under the bus—admitting he was the shooter from the north—but why protect Adam? My guess was there was a jail cell waiting for him anyway.

Then there was Jinx King. Maybe he wasn't as soulless as I'd thought. Somewhere after my call, his father tracked him down, and Jinx got a burst of conscience. I knew that would go in his favor when he stood before the judge, but how far was yet to be seen. Jinx confessed Eddie murdered all three, and Justin told them to cover it up. Thankfully, the police were en route to arrest Eddie, but from my call as Jester, they thought the activity was at the edge of the property by the creek. When they got there, the others told them I was still at large.

How did Dylan find me? Listen, Dylan was a great accessory to have. Seventh period had started when he heard a gunshot and got an uneasy feeling. By the time the second fired (that had to have been when Eddie had me in her sights), he alerted his coach who replied, *Son, it's just the wind,* to which Dylan countered, *Respectfully, sir, that sounds like sniper shot in every language.* By the third, his hero complex kicked into high gear, and he saw me running like a buffoon. Dylan was Dylan. Taking no prisoners, believing he alone could stop a speeding bullet. And Frank? He was Frank...he sort of fell on top of everybody, "franking" the whole thing up. Why was Frank out there though? Oscar somehow got word to him that

Eddie would be coming for me. Jeez, shouldn't he have told me *before* I went outside?

I was correct in assuming Eddie doubled back around to the students. When she took them hostage, Mr. Rafferty led her to believe Liam was dead. Thankfully, Liam crawled his way back to school where I found him in the back of an ambulance. He was surprisingly coherent after what Eddie unloaded on him. Evidently, while they were waiting for the drawing and painting class to arrive, all hell broke loose when he confronted her about her new tattoo. I could only assume that was when Eddie's wheels started rolling, she went dojo on him, and then decided to take me out of the equation too.

Liam disclosed he'd been suspicious of them for a while and challenged their odd behavior the day Alfonso Juarez was discovered. Apparently, Justin was calling the shots then, and when Liam strode over to check out the dumpster, he honestly didn't see anything. When he headed back to class, he ran into Oscar who could barely breathe but looked him straight in the eyes and said, *I didn't do it.* Liam was clueless to his meaning until everything fell into place.

Harold King was walking around like a crazy man looking for Jester, and it remained to be seen whether I could keep my alter ego under wraps. I telephoned on AP Unger's phone, which luckily for me, I then lost in the creek. AP Unger? He was "hanging on," I was told. I pushed that thought to the back of my mind, telling myself I'd cry sufficiently later.

And good, ole Rainn Webster. He was filming live, and suffice it to say, he didn't have the decency to say he was operating on a tip. He claimed he'd been after Northside 12 for a while and had been writing an exposé/tell-all. The nerve. I'd just given him a story that would go national. He owed me, and when the time was right, I would expose myself and call in that marker.

While Dylan was getting patched up, I briefly spoke with Murphy and was all alone, standing next to Vinnie's Bug. I allowed myself a moment to be proud of myself—reveling in what I'd accomplished—but the cockiness barely had a chance to settle because next thing I knew, tires screeched and an angry hand was flat on my back, shoving me face-first into the trunk of a car.

Huh-uh, I thought.

This isn't happening.

Not again.

Someone would have to convince me I wasn't screaming like a banshee, but no one was around to ask. I couldn't breathe. I couldn't think. Then I was thinking too much—the biggest voice in my brain telling me I was headed for a permanent nap in the county morgue. The sudden shifting and grinding of gears jarred me from the panic, placing me in what I'd quickly concluded was the trunk of a yellow Dodge Charger. I'd forgotten about that man...and how foolish to do so. It didn't take a genius to deduce he'd had something to do with Alfonso Juarez all along. But what did he want from *me*? Especially when Eddie had confessed?

I saw a television show once where a victim in the trunk of a car knew exactly where she was once the engine died. She'd memorized stops and turns and listened for distinctive sounds. Let me assure you that was a bunch of hogwash if you were someone who battled motion sickness. The only thing I knew for sure was we traveled at a higher speed than normal, we'd idled four times, and my tacos had come up twice.

We drove for miles on end, the sudden bumping making me think we'd taken an unpaved side road. I felt around the floor of the trunk. No chainsaw, no blowtorch, no guns, knives, or explosives— the best I could tell. The only thing I found was a small rag. That gave me an idea. Wrapping the rag around my foot, I attempted to kick out a taillight and wave my arm, hoping a passing motorist would see and call the authorities. After three vigorous kicks, nothing happened. I kicked one last time even harder. When that got me nowhere, I wrapped it around my fist, and after two tries was able to clear a path for my hand. I waved and waved, praying someone would see.

I tried to piece things together. Who was he? The only thing I could come up with was he was AVO. Who in the heck else would even care? My stomach was in my mouth when he finally slammed on the brakes, shut down the engine, and shoved his key in the trunk.

I cut short the shiver that shook my bones. I didn't have time for fear. When he popped open the trunk, the sunlight's red and orange rays blinded me, clutching my throat with a pressurized heat that didn't come from the sun.

I literally was in the hot seat...and I didn't know why.

Meeting his cold, black eyes, I had one run-on thought: *omigosh-heisgoingtokillme*. The man was a tank, a walking space station of three-hundred-plus pounds in size seventeen shoes. Wearing a black shirt, cargo pants, and combat boots, he was mission-ready, but I had a feeling he could morph into anything else just as easily. Something glowed around him that was not only dangerous, but unyielding nobility. A faded black ballcap was shoved down over coal black hair, hiding a face that was chiseled and Romanesque.

"Out," was his only command.

Well, guess what...I got out.

Looking around, I honest to goodness couldn't tell where we were. It was an old dirt road in the middle of nowhere. Old dirt roads in the middle of nowhere weren't good. I'd watched too many scary movies and knew the outcome. As best I could tell, we weren't close to the highway. Interstate 75 ran next to the school, and I heard nothing but birds singing, bugs buzzing, the lull of a nearby creek, and nothing but more nothing.

My bare feet stumbled out onto the gravelly surface, and if I needed to burst into a run, it wouldn't be anything short of sprinting on broken glass. My feet had been bandaged but were beginning to throb like a toothache.

So here we were. Just me, the gravel, and a man whose name I didn't even know.

I started with an introduction, extending my hand, hoping he didn't chop it off in the process. "I'm Darcy Walker."

He didn't shake it...shocking. Before he uttered a word, he narrowed his eyes, cocking his head to the side as though I reminded him of someone. He stared for a long time, taking in every line of my face, my height and build, and then rubbed a hand down his week-old beard that was as black and cunning as his all-knowing eyes. Who in the heck was the man? In any other situation—where odds were he wasn't going to kill me—I might find him attractive. In fact, he was a far cry from Darwin's Missing Link I'd compared him to the first time we'd met. His nose looked broken then or swollen. It had completely healed. He'd also appeared frumpy that day. But I realized that quadruple-X hoodie he had been wearing wasn't hiding flab. It was disguising a brawn that could take down an elephant.

His next statement blew me out of the water. It oozed from a voice so deep it stripped me of my will, reminding me of a cobra trance where all of a sudden the victim was dead.

"She was in your backyard to kill you that night, but I stopped her."

I considered myself a fast thinker, but I have to say, that shook me for a minute. What was the night in question? Was he speaking of Eddie? "You stopped Eddie Lopez?" I asked incredulously.

"I stopped Eddie Lopez. You stepped outside to look at the stars, I suppose, and she was waiting for you."

Ah, the night Murphy won the lottery. "But you didn't take her to jail?" I guffawed.

He gave me a look, and suddenly, I knew why. If he took her to jail, then he couldn't pin the murder on her that he needed to. Was he a fed? If he were a fed, then he would've taken over the operation as soon as he hit Valley Township. He considered his next statement carefully, as though he didn't want to give away too much about what he'd been doing or who he actually was. "I don't normally make it a practice to come back and make sure people are okay," he murmured. "Call this my Road to Redemption."

I snorted at his method of communication. "Couldn't you have just sent an email?"

He threw his head back, laughter rolling darkly. I couldn't decide if the sound was simple humor or from realizing his methods were skewed a little toward the bizarre.

He glanced down to my feet, frowning. "I returned your shoe. Did you forget to wear it?"

Whoa..."I figured that was Jinx. Then I figured it was Eddie," I said.

"I wanted you to keep figuring," was his explanation, as he casually leaned up against the car. "So what's next for you?"

Jeez, I felt like I was taking a college entrance exam. I lived in Darcyville, which meant no plan for tomorrow, no topic for my term paper, and fighting a case of boredom that was slowly enveloping my body. When I sheepishly shrugged as an answer, he folded his arms over his chest and appraised me as though I were some sort of lab experiment. There it was again. His black eyes went darker—with that all-knowing stare—as though I reminded him of someone—someone I was surprised to say—he liked.

I asked, "Do I *know* you?"

Combat Boots looked at the digital watch on his right wrist, checking the time. "First of all, I know *you*, and at this point, that's all that matters. Secondly, you need to foster your relationship with Jaws if you're going to survive doing what you're doing. You may get dirty in the process because God knows the man is up to his eyeballs in shit even I don't understand, but if you want to live, you need to stick close to him. He has a knack for outthinking the Devil."

Well, sure. No problem. Whatever you say. And furthermore, I knew it was useless to ask how he even knew Jaws and I had a relationship.

"Is there a third?" I said.

He raised a mocking brow. "I have a feeling all you can handle are two things at a time. Good luck, Darcy," he paused, "you're going to need it."

———

I knocked on the front door of the first house I encountered, requested a telephone, and dialed 911, calling off the manhunt I was sure was underway. Whoever the man was, he might've out-crazied me. He didn't grace me with a return ride home. In fact, he simply piled back into the Charger and drove off into more nothingness. I came up with my own story. I told the 911 operator he was an associate of Alfonso Juarez and merely wanted to know what I knew. I then said he got spooked by some passing motorists and dumped me at the side of the road. That wasn't much unlike what actually happened, so it wasn't like I had to pull out an award-winning performance. Still, it was an odd meeting, with an even odder ending. I wasn't sure what his *Road to Redemption* was about and why he felt I was included. All I knew was if someone needed redeemed, then they'd committed a lot of sins. I assume he thought he was in good company, or maybe he thought his redemption was redeeming *me*.

As soon as I was reunited with the crowd, I passed out. Like lights-out-bit-the-pavement-passed-out. Holy bejeezus, how embarrassing. Once I regained consciousness, to hear Vinnie tell it, if I were a baby pig, I thought Dylan was my momma. I rolled all over him, nothing short of a girls-gone-wild video in the making. I'm glad it was fuzzy on the recall. Otherwise I'd be obsessing over whether it was reciprocated or if my body was captured at the right angle (okay, don't judge. I'm joking). He also added when Liam found me, we were like snakes mating, the weird spectacle where they slither all over one another and forget their surroundings. I literally put my hands over my ears, singing out a la-la-la, immortally embarrassed. Vinnie was a cad. I didn't want to believe him but feared it could be marginally true.

In the privacy of my own thoughts, I realized Liam might not be for me. When we were basically looking down a barrel, Liam didn't pledge his undying love. He didn't even pledge his undying like. He thought of someone else...and so did I.

By the time the evening wound down, I was fighting exhaustion, shakes, nausea, and epic weeping. But if I had to describe the awesomeness that was this day, it would be simple...*please do again*. I shuddered at my own actions. I was to disarm...I provoked. I was to defuse...I poured gasoline on the fire. My idea of a forced confession luckily ended well.

Textbook speaking, it was a train wreck.

It was that thought which took me out of bed and into the darkness of my closet. Standing on an old, tattered suitcase, I looked at the antique jewelry box on the top shelf I swore to never open again. I reached out to touch it and drew my hand back as though it'd been singed by a flame. Nothing I endured would ever be as scary as opening its lid. I took one measured breath after another and willed myself not to cry. *I will not cry. I will not cry*, I told myself. With a resigned and heavy sigh, I got down and slid back under the covers.

I couldn't help but think of Eddie. Eddie, who probably never uttered a nice word to anyone (at least in my presence), was barely alive. Maybe never to breathe air again. Had she opened "her box?" Had someone opened it for her? Regardless, Eddie was someone's little girl, and even though I wasn't mourning her personally as a friend, her parents were as a daughter...well, mourning who they thought she was. Life was hard to fathom, but all I could come back to was Eddie had a choice, and she chose wrong.

At ten o'clock, my iPhone predictably pinged with an invitation to SKYPE. Reaching over to my nightstand, I switched on the light and answered the call for the one person who never made me feel less than perfect. Dylan was my default setting. One sound of his voice and my emotions tumbled out.

"Thanks for having my back, D," I said in a wispy breath.

That was a sight I'd never forget—Dylan taking off through the field with the determination and bravery of a knight. All that was missing was a lance and white horse. I expected vintage Dylan—überlicious and heavy on the flirt—instead a breath caught in his throat, and silent tears slid down his cheeks.

A weakened Dylan wasn't something I was used to. Burying his head in his hand, I was hit with the immediate understanding something was different about him. He'd lost something, or maybe a better description was something had changed—or evolved. Like me, he was lying in bed, trying to unscramble a day we'd never forget. Dylan didn't even try to mask his feelings, and the sound of my voice was the force that broke the dam.

After several struggled seconds, he wiped his face with his wrist. "I was so afraid for you," he whispered.

With good reason, I thought, because for a second there I wasn't on my A-game. Heck it wasn't even my B-game. "I froze," I whispered back.

Dylan's voice was as smooth as silk, wrapping itself around the wounded part of my soul. "You didn't freeze, sweetheart. You saved AP Unger and two times drew the fire away from other people. Crazy," he said, laughing hollowly, "but it's what I've come to expect from Darcy."

"Why couldn't I have done that when it counted?" I asked, referring to the darkest part of my life.

Dylan knew I referred to the day that changed my life forever. He opened his mouth and closed it, procrastinating on an answer.

"You were nine," he finally said softly. "You didn't freeze, and it was already..."

He didn't complete the thought, suddenly as overwhelmed with emotion as I was. "Too late, right?" I finished for him.

"Darc, don't do this to yourself. You're a wonderful person, the person I love more than anything. Please," he pleaded, briefly wincing, "don't beat yourself up over something you had no control over. Be proud of yourself...I am."

Talking to Dylan was so satisfying it was borderline erotic.

He was the eternal optimist: good conquered evil, bad guys went to jail, sunrises brought joy, all wrapped up in a big, red bow. There were a bajillion reasons I could think of that were wrong with that theory—the biggest being I was Darcy Walker. Life with me was tantamount to being Sisyphus, condemned to rolling that boulder up the hill only for it to tumble back down once it reached the top. But Dylan's words and personality were addictive, and I was a codependent mess. Whoever wound up with him would be the luckiest girl alive. I hated her already.

After his delusional rants and ravings about how awesome I was, he'd all but convinced me I was the first female president, one summit away from achieving world peace. I was feeling good again. I had purpose, by God, and I did the best I could in an im-freaking-possible situation.

Maybe I wouldn't change a thing about the day after all...well, except the shoes I was wearing.

NOTE FROM THE AUTHOR

Thank you so much for reading Grade A Stupid! If you read this book and enjoyed it, I'd be honored if you'd recommend it to other friends or readers' groups and leave a star rating at the retailer in which you purchased the book. Your words mean so much to authors and help other readers discover new worlds.

ABOUT THE AUTHOR

A.J. lives in Cincinnati with her husband, two daughters, an ADD dog, and a spoiled hamster burial site in her backyard. When she's not writing, she's reading, binge-watching the heck out of some show or eavesdropping-slash-creeping on those around her. And maybe searching the skies for aliens whenever the mood hits.

For more books and updates, connect with her on social media and at:
https://www.ajlape.com

ALSO BY A. J. LAPE

DARCY WALKER
TEENAGE SLEUTH THRILLERS

Grade A Stupid

No Brainer

100 Proof Stud

DEFCON Darcy

Foolproof

DARCY WALKER INVESTIGATIONS

Side Hustle

Gut Check

Ride or Die

Medusa Effect

5 Pounds of Pressure

Heist & Seek

White Noise

Nuclear Blonde

Righteous Shot

RIVERA & GUTIERREZ SERIES

Vice

Vice Versa

Of Vice & Men

Vice or Consequences

ACKNOWLEDGMENTS

A special thank you to my husband, Dean, and my daughters, Zoe and Mackie, for your unending enthusiasm and nightly prayers that Darcy's world would come to life. Thank you for smiling in spite of my mood swings; my parents, Gene and Dodie Miracle, and my sister, Jeri Conner, for a lifetime of love, loyalty, and conversations where you remind me anything is possible; my amazing beta readers —Joyce Stevens, Sandra Ruiter, Mary-Nancy Smith, and Mom & Dad; Lavinia Urban and Melanie Osmond for just being you; Julie Cassar and Jen Logan for pulling me out of rabbit holes; Jessica Barnard for the medical advice; Dana Barnard, Debbie Brooks, Chris Cunningham, and Susan Trammel for proofreading; and to my girlfriends and Facebook friends who read a chapter here and there, I am forever indebted that you gave this stay-at-home mom the courage to take the jump.

www.ingramcontent.com/pod-product-compliance
Lightning Source LLC
Chambersburg PA
CBHW011430240626
47153CB00011B/2922